Mary Higgins Clark is the author of twenty-four worldwide bestselling works of fiction and a memoir. She lives with her husband in Saddle River, New Jersey.

Praise for Mary Higgins Clark

'There's something special about Clark's thrillers, and it's not just the gentleness with which the bestselling writer approaches her often lurid subject matter . . . special above all is the compassion she extends to her characters. Grace, charm and solid storytelling' PUBLISHERS WEEKLY

'Clark plays out her story like the pro that she is . . . flawless' DAILY MIRROR

'The 'Queen of Suspense' is renowned for her fast-moving prose and dazzling plot twists' GOOD BOOK GUIDE

'Clark keeps you reading . . . very engaging' ASIAN AGE

MARY HIGGINS CLARK

Moonlight Becomes You

POCKET
BOOKS

LONDON • SYDNEY • NEW YORK • TORONTO

First published in Great Britain by Simon and Schuster UK Ltd, 1996
First published in paperback by Pocket Books, 1997
This edition published by Pocket Books, 2007
An imprint of Simon & Schuster UK Ltd
A CBS COMPANY

1 3 5 7 9 10 8 6 4 2

Simon & Schuster UK Ltd
Africa House
64–78 Kingsway
London WC2B 6AH

www.simonsays.co.uk

Simon & Schuster Australia
Sydney

A CIP catalogue record for this book is available from the British Library

ISBN 978-1-8473-9295-4

Printed and bound in Denmark by
Nørhaven Paperback A/S, Viborg

ACKNOWLEDGMENTS

How can I thank thee? . . . Let me count the ways.

No words are sufficient to express my gratitude to my longtime editor, Michael Korda, and his associate, senior editor Chuck Adams. A story, like a child, thrives best when it is encouraged, helped, and guided in a wise and caring atmosphere. Again and always . . . sine qua non . . . I love you guys.

Gypsy da Silva, who has been copy supervisor for many of my manuscripts, remains a candidate for sainthood with her eagle eye and cheerful patience. Bless you, Gypsy.

Kudos to my pal, author Judith Kelman, who has repeatedly gone on the Internet, the mystery of which I have not fathomed, to procure information I needed immediately.

A thousand thanks to Catherine L. Forment, Vice President of Merrill Lynch, for willingly and knowledgeably answering my many questions about stock investment and confirmation procedures.

A grateful tip of the hat to R. Patrick Thompson, President of the New York Mercantile Exchange, who interrupted a meeting to answer my inquiries about temporary restraining orders.

When I decided that it would be interesting if funeral customs became part of this story, I read fascinating books on the subject. In particular, they were *Consolatory Rhetoric*

Acknowledgments

by Donovan J. Octs, *Down to Earth* by Marian Barnes, and *Celebrations of Death* by Metcalf Huntington.

The Newport Police Department has responded to all my phone calls with great courtesy. I'm grateful to everyone who has been so kind and hope that the police procedure contained in these pages passes inspection.

And finally, loving thanks to my daughter Carol Higgins Clark for her infallible ability to pick up my unconscious idiosyncrasies. *Do you know how often you used the word* decent? . . . *No thirty-two-year-old would say it like that . . . You used that same name for a different character ten books ago . . .*

And now I can happily quote the words written on a monastery wall in the Middle Ages: "The book is finished. Let the writer play."

For Lisl Cade
and
Eugene H. Winick
—my publicist and my literary agent—
and both my very dear friends.

Tuesday, October 8th

Maggie tried to open her eyes, but the effort was too great. Her head hurt so much. Where was she? What had happened? She raised her hand, but it was stopped inches above her body, unable to move any farther.

Instinctively she pushed at the overhead barrier, but it did not move. What was it? It felt soft, like satin, and it was cold.

She slid her fingers to the side and down; the surface changed. Now it felt ruffled. A quilt? Was she in some kind of bed?

She pushed out her other hand to the side and recoiled as that palm immediately encountered the same chill ruffles. They were on both sides of this narrow enclosure.

What was tugging at her ring when she moved her left hand? She ran her thumb over her ring finger, felt it touch string or cord. But why?

Then memory came rushing back.

Her eyes opened and stared in terror into absolute darkness.

Frantically her mind raced as she tried to piece together what had happened. She had heard him in time to whirl around just as something crashed down on her head.

She remembered him bending over her, whispering, "Maggie, think of the bell ringers." After that, she remembered nothing.

Still disoriented and terrified, she struggled to understand. Then suddenly it came flooding back. The bell ringers! Victorians had been so afraid of being buried alive that it became a tradition to tie a string to their fingers before interment. A string threaded through a hole in the casket, stretching to the surface of the burial plot. A string with a bell attached to it.

For seven days a guard would patrol the grave and listen for the sound of the bell ringing, the signal that the interred wasn't dead after all . . .

But Maggie knew that no guard was listening for her. She was truly alone. She tried to scream, but no sound came. Frantically she tugged at the string, straining, listening, hoping to hear above her a faint, pealing sound. But there was only silence. Darkness and silence.

She had to keep calm. She had to focus. How had she gotten here? She couldn't let panic overwhelm her. But how? . . . How? . . .

Then she remembered. The funeral museum. She'd gone back there alone. Then she'd taken up the search, the search that Nuala had begun. Then he'd come, and . . .

Oh, God! She was buried alive! She pounded her fists on the lid of the casket, but even inside, the thick satin muffled the sound. Finally she screamed. Screamed until she was hoarse, until she couldn't scream anymore. And still she was alone.

The bell. She yanked on the string ... again ... and again. Surely it was sending out sounds. She couldn't hear them, but someone would. They must!

Overhead a mound of fresh, raw earth shimmered in the light of the full moon. The only movement came from the bronze bell attached to a pipe emerging from the mound: The bell moved back and forth in an arrhythmic dance of death. Round about it, all was silent. Its clapper had been removed.

☽ 1

I HATE COCKTAIL PARTIES, MAGGIE THOUGHT WRYLY, WON-dering why she always felt like an alien when she attended one. Actually I'm being too harsh, she thought. The truth is I hate cocktail parties where the only person I know is my supposed date, and he abandons me the minute we come in the door.

She looked around the large room, then sighed. When Liam Moore Payne had invited her to this reunion of the Moore clan, she should have guessed he would be more interested in visiting with his cousins-by-the-dozens than worrying about *her*. Liam, an occasional but normally thoughtful date when he was in town from Boston, was tonight displaying a boundless faith in her ability to fend for herself. Well, she reasoned, it was a large gathering; surely she could find someone to talk to.

It was what Liam had told her about the Moores that had been the factor that made her decide to accompany him to this affair, she remembered, as she sipped from her glass of white wine and maneuvered her way through the crowded Grill Room of the Four Seasons restaurant on Manhattan's East Fifty-second Street. The family's founding father—or at least the founder of the family's original wealth—had been the late Squire Desmond Moore, at one time a fixture of Newport society. The occasion of tonight's party/reunion was to celebrate the great man's one hundred fifteenth birthday. For convenience's sake, it had been decided to have the gathering in New York rather than Newport.

Going into amusing detail about many members of the clan, Liam had explained that over one hundred descendants, direct and collateral, as well as some favored ex-in-laws, would be present. He had regaled her with anecdotes about the fifteen-year-old immigrant from Dingle who had considered himself to be not one of the huddled masses yearning to be free but, rather, one of the impoverished masses yearning to be rich. Legend claimed that as his ship passed the Statue of Liberty, Squire had announced to his fellow steerage-class passengers, "In no time a-tall I'll be wealthy enough to buy the old girl, should the government ever decide to sell her, of course." Liam had delivered his forebear's declaration in a wonderfully broad Irish brogue.

The Moores certainly did come in all sizes and shapes, Maggie reflected as she looked about the room. She watched two octogenarians in animated conversation, and narrowed her eyes, mentally framing them through the lens of the camera she now wished she had brought. The snow white hair of the man, the coquettish smile on the woman's face, the pleasure they were obviously taking in each other's company—it would have made a wonderful picture.

"The Four Seasons will never be the same after the Moores are finished with it," Liam said as he appeared suddenly beside her. "Having a good time?" he asked, but then without waiting for an answer, introduced her to yet another cousin, Earl Bateman, who, Maggie was amused to note, studied her with obvious and unhurried interest.

She judged the newcomer to be, like Liam, in his late thirties. He was half a head shorter than his cousin, which made him just under six feet. She decided there was something of a scholarly bent reflected in his lean face and thoughtful expression, although his pale blue eyes had a vaguely disconcerting cast to them. Sandy haired with a sallow complexion, he did not have Liam's rugged good looks. Liam's eyes were more green than blue, his dark hair attractively flecked with gray.

She waited while he continued to look her over. Then, after a long moment, with a raised eyebrow, she asked, "Will I pass inspection?"

He looked embarrassed. "I'm sorry. I'm not good at remembering names and I was trying to place you. You *are* one of the clan, aren't you?"

"No. I have Irish roots going back three or four generations, but I'm no relation to this clan, I'm afraid. It doesn't look as though you need any more cousins anyhow."

"You couldn't be more right about that. Too bad, though, most of them aren't nearly so attractive as you. Your wonderful blue eyes, ivory skin and small bones make you a Celt. The near-black hair places you among the 'Black Irish' segment of the family, those members who owe some of their genetic makeup to the brief but significant visit from survivors of the defeat of the Spanish Armada."

"*Liam! Earl!* Oh, for the love of God, I guess I'm glad I came after all."

Forgetting Maggie, both men turned to enthusiastically greet the florid-faced man who came up behind them.

Maggie shrugged. So much for that, she thought, mentally retreating into a corner. Then she remembered an article she had recently read that urged people who felt isolated in social situations to look for someone else who seemed to be even more desperate and start a conversation.

Chuckling to herself, she decided to give that tactic a try, then if she ended up still talking to herself she would slip away and go home. At that moment, the prospect of her pleasant apartment on Fifty-sixth Street near the East River was very attractive. She knew she should have stayed in tonight. She'd only been back a few days from a photo shoot in Milan and longed for a quiet evening with her feet up.

She glanced around. There didn't seem to be a single Squire Moore descendant or in-law who wasn't fighting to be heard.

Countdown to exit, she decided. Then she heard a voice nearby—a melodic, familiar voice, one that spurred sudden, pleasant memories. She spun around. The voice belonged to a woman who was ascending the short staircase to the restaurant's balcony area and had stopped to call to someone below her. Maggie stared, then gasped. Was she crazy? Could it possibly be Nuala? It had been so long ago, yet she sounded just like the woman who once had been her stepmother, from the time she was five until she was ten. After the divorce, her father had forbidden Maggie to even mention Nuala's name.

Maggie noticed Liam passing on his way to hail another relative and grabbed his arm. "Liam, that woman on the stairs. Do you know her?"

He squinted. "Oh, that's Nuala. She was married to my uncle. I mean I *guess* she's my aunt, but she was his second wife, so I never thought of her that way. She's a bit of a character but a lot of fun. Why?"

Maggie did not wait to answer but began to thread her

way through the clusters of Moores. By the time she reached the stairs, the woman she sought was chatting with a group of people on the balcony level. Maggie started up the stairs but near the top paused to study her.

When Nuala had left, so abruptly, Maggie had prayed that she would write. She never did, though, and Maggie had found her silence especially painful. She had come to feel so close to her during the five years the marriage had lasted. Her own mother had died in an automobile accident when she was an infant. It was only after her father's death that Maggie learned from a family friend that her father had destroyed all the letters and returned the gifts that Nuala had sent to her.

Maggie stared now at the tiny figure with lively blue eyes and soft honey-blond hair. She could see the fine skein of wrinkles that detracted not a bit from her lovely complexion. And as she stared, the memories flooded her heart. Childhood memories, perhaps her happiest.

Nuala, who always took *her* part in arguments, protesting to Maggie's father, "Owen, for the love of heaven, she's just a child. Stop correcting her every minute." Nuala, who was always saying, "Owen, all the kids her age wear jeans and tee shirts. . . . Owen, so what if she used up three rolls of film? She loves to take pictures, and she's good. . . . Owen, she's not just playing in mud. Can't you see she's trying to make something out of the clay. For heaven's sake, recognize your daughter's creativity even if you don't like my paintings."

Nuala—always so pretty, always such fun, always so patient with Maggie's questions. It had been from Nuala that Maggie had learned to love and understand art.

Typically, Nuala was dressed tonight in a pale blue satin cocktail suit and matching high heels. Maggie's memories of her were always pastel tinted.

9

Nuala had been in her late forties when she married Dad, Maggie thought, trying to calculate her age now. She made it through five years with him. She left twenty-two years ago.

It was a shock to realize that Nuala must now be in her mid-seventies. She certainly didn't look it.

Their eyes met. Nuala frowned, then looked puzzled.

Nuala had told her that her name was actually Finnuala, after the legendary Celt, Finn MacCool, who brought about the downfall of a giant. Maggie remembered how as a little girl she had delighted in trying to pronounce *Finn-u-ala.*

"Finn-u-ala?" she said now, her voice tentative.

A look of total astonishment crossed the older woman's face. Then she emitted a whoop of delight that stopped the buzz of conversations around them, and Maggie found herself once again enfolded in loving arms. Nuala was wearing the faint scent that all these years had lingered in Maggie's memory. When she was eighteen she had discovered the scent was Joy. How appropriate for tonight, Maggie thought.

"Let me look at you," Nuala exclaimed, releasing her and stepping back but still holding Maggie's arms with both hands as though afraid she would get away.

Her eyes searched Maggie's face. "I never thought I'd see you again! Oh, Maggie! How is that dreadful man, your father?"

"He died three years ago."

"Oh, I'm sorry, darling. But he was totally impossible to the end, I'm sure."

"Never too easy," Maggie admitted.

"Darling, I was *married* to him. Remember? I know what he was like! Always sanctimonious, dour, sour, petulant, crabby. Well, no use going on about it. The poor man is dead, may he rest in peace. But he was so old-fashioned and so stiff, why, he could have posed for a medieval stained-glass window . . ."

Aware suddenly that others were openly listening, Nuala slid her arm around Maggie's waist and announced, "This is my child! I didn't give birth to her, of course, but that's totally unimportant."

Maggie realized that Nuala was also blinking back tears.

Anxious both to talk and to escape the crush of the crowded restaurant, they slipped out together. Maggie could not find Liam to say good-bye but was fairly sure she would not be missed.

Arm in arm, Maggie and Nuala walked up Park Avenue through the deepening September twilight, turned west at Fifty-sixth Street and settled in at Il Tinello. Over Chianti and delicate strips of fried zucchini, they caught up on each other's lives.

For Maggie, it was simple. "Boarding school; I was shipped there after you left. Then Carnegie-Mellon, and finally a master's in visual arts from NYU. I'm making a good living now as a photographer."

"That's wonderful. I always thought it would be either that or sculpting."

Maggie smiled. "You've got a good memory. I love to sculpt, but I do it only as a hobby. Being a photographer is a lot more practical, and in all honesty I guess I'm pretty good. I've got some excellent clients. Now what about you, Nuala?"

"No. Let's finish with you," the older woman interrupted. "You live in New York. You've got a job you like. You've stuck to developing what is a natural talent. You're just as pretty as I knew you'd be. You were thirty-two your last birthday. What about a love interest or significant other or whatever you young people call it these days?"

Maggie felt the familiar wrench as she said flatly, "I was married for three years. His name was Paul, and he graduated from the Air Force Academy. He had just been selected for the NASA program when he was killed on a training flight. That was five years ago. It's a shock I guess I may never get over. Anyway, it's still hard to talk about him."

"Oh, Maggie."

There was a world of understanding in Nuala's voice. Maggie remembered that her stepmother had been a widow when she married her father.

Shaking her head, Nuala murmured, "Why do things like that have to happen?" Then her tone brightened. "Shall we order?"

Over dinner they caught up on twenty-two years. After the divorce from Maggie's father, Nuala had moved to New York, then visited Newport, where she met Timothy Moore —someone she actually had dated when she was still a teenager—and married him. "My third and last husband," she said, "and absolutely wonderful. Tim died last year, and do I ever miss him! He wasn't one of the wealthy Moores, but I have a sweet house in a wonderful section of Newport, and an adequate income, and of course I'm still dabbling at painting. So I'm all right."

But Maggie saw a brief flicker of uncertainty cross Nuala's face and realized in that moment that without the brisk, cheerful expression, Nuala looked every day of her age.

"Really all right, Nuala?" she asked quietly. "You seem . . . worried."

"Oh, yes, I'm fine. It's just . . . Well, you see, I turned seventy-five last month. Years ago, someone told me that when you get into your sixties, you start to say good-bye to your friends, or they say good-bye to you, but that when you hit your seventies, it happens all the time. Believe me, it's true. I've lost a number of good friends lately, and each loss hurts a little more than the last. It's getting to be a bit lonely in Newport, but there's a wonderful residence—I *hate* the word nursing home—and I'm thinking of going to live there soon. The kind of apartment I want there has just become available."

Then, as the waiter poured espresso, she said urgently, "Maggie, come visit me, *please*. It's only a three-hour drive from New York."

"I'd love to," Maggie responded.

"You mean it?"

"Absolutely. Now that I've found you, I'm not going to let you get away again. Besides, it's always been in the back of my mind to go to Newport. I understand it's a photographer's paradise. As a matter of fact—"

She was about to tell Nuala that as of next week she had cleared her calendar to allow time to take a much-needed vacation when she heard someone say, "I thought I'd find you here."

Startled, Maggie looked up. Standing over them were Liam and his cousin Earl Bateman. "You ran out on me," Liam said reprovingly.

Earl bent down to kiss Nuala. "You're in hot water for spiriting away his date. How do you two know each other?"

"It's a long story." Nuala smiled. "Earl lives in Newport, too," she explained to Maggie. "He teaches anthropology at Hutchinson College in Providence."

I was right about the scholarly look, Maggie thought.

Liam pulled a chair from a nearby table and sat down. "You've got to let us have an after-dinner drink with you." He smiled at Earl. "And don't worry about Earl. He's strange, but he's harmless. His branch of the family has been in the funeral business for more than a hundred years.

They bury people. *He* digs them up! He's a ghoul. He even makes money talking about it."

Maggie raised her eyebrows as the others laughed.

"I lecture on funeral customs through the ages," Earl Bateman explained with a slight smile. "Some may find it macabre, but I love it."

) 2

HE STRODE BRISKLY ALONG THE CLIFF WALK, HIS HAIR blown by the stiff ocean breeze that had sprung up during the late afternoon. The sun had been wonderfully warm at the height of the day, but now its slanting rays were ineffectual against the cool wind. It seemed to him that the shift in the air reflected the changing quality of his own mood.

Till now he had been successful in his plan of action, but with Nuala's dinner party only two hours away, a premonition was coming over him. Nuala had become suspicious and would confide in her stepdaughter. Everything could start to unravel.

The tourists had not yet abandoned Newport. In fact there was an abundance of them, postseason day-trippers, anxious to stalk the mansions managed by the Preservation Society, to gape at the relics of a bygone age before most of them were closed until next spring.

Deep in thought he paused as he came to The Breakers, that most marvelously ostentatious jewel, that American palace, that breathtaking example of what money, and imagination, and driving ambition could achieve. Built in the early 1890s for Cornelius Vanderbilt II and his wife, Alice, it was enjoyed only briefly by Vanderbilt himself. Paralyzed by a stroke in 1895, he died in 1899.

Lingering for a moment longer in front of The Breakers, he smiled. It was Vanderbilt's story that had given him the idea.

But now he had to act quickly. Picking up his pace, he passed Salve Regina University, formerly known as Ochre Court, a hundred-room extravagance that stood splendid against the skyline, its limestone walls and mansard roof beautifully preserved. Five minutes later he came upon it, Latham Manor, the magnificent edifice that had been a worthy, more tasteful competitor to the vulgarity of The Breakers. Originally the proud property of the eccentric Latham family, it had fallen into disrepair in the lifetime of the last Latham. Rescued from ruin and restored to reflect much of its earlier grandeur, it was now the residence of wealthy retirees, living out their last years in opulence.

He stopped, feasting his eyes on Latham Manor's majestic white marble exterior. He reached into the deep pocket of his windbreaker and pulled out a cellular phone. He dialed quickly, then smiled slightly as the voice he had hoped to hear answered. It meant one thing less he had to worry about later.

He said two words, "Not tonight."

"Then, when?" a calm, noncommittal voice asked after a slight pause.

"I'm not sure yet. I have to take care of something else."

His voice was sharp. He did not permit questions about his decisions.

"Of course. Sorry."

Breaking the connection without further comment, he turned and began to walk swiftly.

It was time to get ready for Nuala's dinner party.

) 3

NUALA MOORE HUMMED AS SHE SLICED TOMATOES ON THE cutting board of her cheerfully untidy kitchen, her movements quick and confident. The late afternoon sun was about to set, and a stiff breeze was rattling the window over the sink. She could already feel a slight chill seeping through the poorly insulated back wall.

Even so, she knew her kitchen was warm and inviting with its red-and-white colonial paper, worn red-brick linoleum, and pine shelves and cabinets. When she finished slicing the tomatoes, she reached for the onions. A tomato-and-onion salad marinated in oil and vinegar and generously sprinkled with oregano was a perfect accompaniment to a roast leg of lamb. Her fingers were crossed that Maggie still loved lamb. When she was little it had been one of her favorites. Maybe I should have asked her, Nuala thought, but I want to surprise her. At least she knew Maggie wasn't a vegetarian—she had ordered veal the night they were together in Manhattan.

The potatoes were already bouncing in the big pot. When they had finished boiling, she would drain them but not mash them until the last minute. A tray of biscuits was ready to pop in the oven. The green beans and carrots were all prepared, ready to be steamed minutes before she seated her guests.

Nuala peered into the dining room, double-checking. The table was set. She had done that first thing this morning. Maggie would sit opposite her in the other host chair. A symbolic gesture, she knew. Cohostesses this evening, like mother and daughter.

She leaned against the door frame for a moment, reflecting. It would be wonderful to have someone with whom she could at last share this terrible worry. She would wait a day or two, then she would say, "Maggie, I have to talk with you about something important. You're right, I am worried about something. Maybe I'm crazy or just an old, suspicious fool, but . . ."

It would be so good to lay her suspicions before Maggie. Even when she was little she had had a clear, analytical mind. "Finn-u-ala," she would begin when she wanted to share a confidence, her way of letting me know that this was going to be a very serious discussion, Nuala remembered.

I should have waited until tomorrow night to have this party, she thought. I should have given Maggie a chance to at least catch her breath. Oh well, typical of me—I always act first and think afterwards.

But she had wanted to show Maggie off to her friends after talking about her so much. And also, when she asked them to dinner, she had thought that Maggie was arriving a day earlier.

But Maggie had phoned yesterday to say there was a problem with one of the jobs, that it was going to take a day more than expected to complete. "The art director is a nervous Nelly and is agonizing over the shots," she had explained, "so I can't start up until around noon tomorrow. But I still should be there by four or four-thirty."

At four, Maggie had phoned. "Nuala, I tried to call a couple of times earlier, but your line was busy. I'm just now finishing up and heading out to my car."

"No difference as long as you're on your way."

"I just hope I arrive before your guests so I'll have time to change."

"Oh, it doesn't matter. Just drive carefully and I'll ply them with cocktails till you get here."

"It's a deal. I'm on my way."

Thinking about the conversation, Nuala smiled. It would have been awful if Maggie had been delayed yet another day. By now she should be around Bridgeport, she thought. She'll probably get caught in some commuter traffic, but at least she's on her way. Dear God, Maggie's on her way to me.

Since there was nothing more she could do for the moment, Nuala decided to sit down and watch the early evening news. That would still leave her time for a nice hot, relaxing bath before people started to arrive.

She was about to leave the kitchen when there was a rap at the back door. Before she could look through the window to see who it was, the handle turned. For the moment she was startled, but as the door opened and her visitor stepped in, she smiled warmly.

"Hello there," she said. "Good to see you, but you're not due for a couple of hours, so you can't stay long."

"I don't plan to stay long," her visitor said quietly.

) 4

AFTER HIS MOTHER MOVED TO FLORIDA, SELLING THE house that had been old Squire's wedding present to Liam's grandmother, Liam Moore Payne had bought a condominium on Willow Street. He used it regularly during the summer, but even after his sailboat was put into storage at the end of the season, he frequently would come down from Boston on weekends to escape the hectic world of international finance.

The condo, a spacious four-room unit with high ceilings and a terrace overlooking Narragansett Bay, was furnished with the choice contents of the family home. When she had moved, his mother had said, "These things don't work in Florida, and anyhow I never cared for any of it. You take them. You're like your father. You love this heavy old stuff."

As Liam stepped from the shower and reached for a bath towel, he thought of his father. *Was* he really so much like him? he wondered. Upon arriving home after a day of trading on the ever-mercurial market, his father always had gone straight to the bar in the study and prepared himself a very dry, very cold martini. He would sip it slowly, then, visibly relaxed, he would go upstairs to bathe and dress for the evening.

Liam toweled vigorously, half smiling at the thought that he and his father were very much alike, although they differed on the details. His father's almost ritualistic soaks would have driven Liam crazy; he preferred a bracing shower. Also, he preferred his martini *after* he had bathed, not before.

Ten minutes later, Liam stood at the bar in his study, carefully pouring Finlandia vodka into a chilled and ice-filled silver goblet and stirring. Then, straining the drink into a delicate stemmed glass, he drizzled a drop or two of olive juice over the surface, hesitated, and with an apprecia-tive sigh, took the first sip. "Amen," he said aloud.

It was ten of eight. He was due at Nuala's in ten minutes, and while it would take at least nine minutes to drive there, he wasn't worried about being precisely on time. Anyone who knew Nuala was aware that her cocktail hour was apt to last at least until nine and sometimes later.

Liam decided to allow himself a little downtime. He sank onto the handsome couch covered in dark brown Moroccan leather and carefully placed his feet on an antique coffee table that was shaped to resemble a stack of ancient ledgers.

He closed his eyes. It had been a long and stressful week, but the weekend promised to be interesting.

Maggie's face floated into his mind. It was a remarkable coincidence that she happened to have a tie to Newport, a very strong tie, as it turned out. He had been astonished when he had learned of her connection to Nuala.

He remembered how upset he had been when he realized that Maggie had left the party at the Four Seasons without telling him. Angry at himself for so thoroughly neglecting her, he had been anxious to find her and straighten out the situation. When his inquiries revealed that Maggie had been seen leaving with Nuala before dinner, he had had a hunch that they might be at Il Tinello. For a young woman, Maggie was pretty much set in her ways.

Maggie. He pictured her for a moment, her beautiful face, the intelligence and energy that she radiated.

Liam sipped the last of the martini and, with a sigh, hoisted himself out of his comfortable spot. Time to go, he thought. He checked his appearance at the foyer mirror, noting that the red-and-blue Hermès tie his mother had sent for his birthday went well enough with his navy blazer, although a traditional stripe might be better. With a shrug he decided not to worry about it; it really was time to go.

He picked up his key ring, and, locking the door behind him, set off for Nuala's dinner party.

》 5

EARL BATEMAN WAS STRETCHED OUT ON THE COUCH, A glass of wine in his hand, the book he'd just finished on the table beside him. He knew it was time to change for Nuala's dinner party, but he was enjoying a sense of leisure, using the moment to contemplate the events of the past week.

Before coming down from Providence, he had finished grading the papers turned in by his Anthropology 101 class and was pleased to note that all but a few of the students had performed at the A or B level. It would be an interesting —and perhaps challenging—semester with them, he decided.

And now he could look forward to Newport weekends mercifully free of the crowds jamming restaurants and traffic tie-ups so typical of the summer season.

Earl lived in the guest wing of the family home, Squire Hall, the house Squire Moore had built for his youngest daughter on the occasion of her marriage to Gordon Bateman, "the ghoul" as Squire called him because the Batemans had been funeral directors for four generations.

Of all the residences he had presented his seven children, it was by far the smallest, a reflection of the fact that he had been opposed to the marriage. Nothing personal, but Squire had a horror of dying and even forbade the word "death" to be mentioned in his presence. To take into the family bosom the man who undoubtedly would attend to the rituals surrounding his own demise was a continual reminder of the forbidden word.

Gordon Bateman's reaction had been to convince his wife to name their home Squire Hall, a mocking tribute to his father-in-law and a subtle reminder that none of his other children had thought to so honor him.

Earl had always believed that his own given name was another jab at Squire, since the old man had always tried to convey the impression that he'd been named for generations of Moores who in the county of Dingle had had the courtesy title of squire. A squire in Dingle tugged his forelock in homage to an earl.

After Earl finally convinced his father that he had no intention of becoming the next Bateman funeral director, his parents sold the mortuary to a private corporation that retained the family name and hired a manager to run it.

His parents now spent nine months of the year in South Carolina, near his married sisters, and had urged Earl to take over the entire house during those months, an offer he declined. The wing was arranged to his liking, with his books and artifacts locked away in glass-fronted cabinets against the possibility of careless dusting. He also had a sweeping view of the Atlantic; Earl found the sea infinitely calming.

Calm. That was perhaps the word he valued most.

At the noisy New York reunion of Squire Moore's descendants, as much as possible he had stayed on the sidelines where he could simply observe the lot of them. He tried not to be too judgmental, but he did not join in their "can you top this?" tales. His cousins all seemed to be given to bragging about how well they were doing, and like Liam, they all loved to regale each other with far-fetched stories about their eccentric—and occasionally ruthless—ancestor.

Earl also knew how gleefully some of them seized on his father's background as a fourth-generation funeral director. At the reunion, he had overheard two of them belittling him and making snide jokes about undertakers and their profession.

A pox on the lot of them, he thought now as he swung his feet to the floor and sat up. It was ten of eight, time to get a move on. He wasn't looking forward to going to Nuala's dinner party tonight, but on the other hand, Maggie Holloway would be there. She was extremely attractive . . .

Yes, her presence would ensure that the evening would not be dull.

) 6

DR. WILLIAM LANE, DIRECTOR OF THE LATHAM MANOR Residence, looked at his watch for the third time in five minutes. He and his wife were due at Nuala Moore's place at eight o'clock; it was ten of eight now. A large, balding man in his fifties, Dr. Lane had a soothing bedside manner with his patients—an attitude of forbearance that did not extend to his thirty-nine-year-old wife.

"Odile," he called, "for God's sake, get a move on."

"Right with you." Her voice, breathy and musical, floated down the stairs of their home, a structure that once had been the carriage house of Latham Manor. A moment later she rushed into the living room, still fastening an earring.

"I was reading to Mrs. Patterson," she said. "You know how it is, William. She's not used to the residence yet, and she resents the fact that her son sold her house out from under her."

"She'll settle in," Lane said dismissively. "Everyone else seems to have managed to end up being quite happy here."

"I know, but it sometimes takes a while. I still say a little TLC while a new guest is adjusting is important." Odile walked to the mirror over the carved marble fireplace. "How do I look?" She smiled at her wide-eyed, blond-haired reflection.

"You look lovely. You always do," Lane said shortly. "What do you know about this stepdaughter of Nuala's?"

"Nuala told me all about her when she visited Greta Shipley last Monday. Her name is Maggie, and Nuala was married to her father years ago. She's going to stay for two weeks. Nuala seems very happy about it. Don't you think that's sweet, that they met each other again?"

Without answering, Dr. Lane opened the front door, then stood aside. *You're* in a great mood, Odile thought, as she walked past him and down the steps to the car. For a moment she paused and looked at Latham Manor, its marble façade glistening in the moonlight.

Hesitantly she suggested, "I meant to tell you that when I looked in on Mrs. Hammond, she was a bit out of breath and rather pale. I wonder if you should check her before we go."

"We're late already," Dr. Lane replied impatiently as he opened the car door. "If I'm needed I can be back in ten minutes, but I can *assure* you that Mrs. Hammond will be all right tonight."

) 7

MALCOLM NORTON WAS NOT LOOKING FORWARD TO THE evening. A silver-haired man with an erect, military posture, he made an imposing appearance. It was an appearance, however, that concealed a troubled mind.

Nuala's call three days ago, asking him to come to dinner tonight and meet her stepdaughter, had been a shock—not the invitation to dinner itself, but the unexpected news that Nuala had a stepdaughter.

A lawyer with a general practice, working alone, Norton had seen his client list reduced drastically in the past few years, partly through attrition—he had become almost expert at handling estates of the deceased—but also due, he was certain, to the arrival of several young, aggressive lawyers in the area.

Nuala Moore was one of his few remaining clients, and he thought he knew her affairs inside out. Never once had she mentioned this stepdaughter.

For some time Malcolm Norton had been quietly urging Nuala to sell her home and become a resident of Latham Manor. Until recently she had shown signs of agreeing that it would be a good move. She admitted that since her husband, Tim, had died, the house was lonely, and it was beginning to cost more and more in repairs. "I know it needs a new roof, that the heating system is antiquated, and anyone who bought it would want to put in central air-conditioning," she had told him. "Do you think I could get two hundred thousand for it?"

He had reacted carefully, responding, "Nuala, the real estate market here falls apart after Labor Day. Maybe next summer we'd get that much. But I want to see you settled. If you're ready to move to Latham now, I'll take the house off your hands for that price and do some basic fixing up. I'll get my money back eventually, and you won't have any more expenditures on it. With Tim's insurance money and the house sale, you could have the best accommodation at Latham, maybe even turn one room of a suite into a studio for yourself."

"I'd like that. I'll put in my application," Nuala had said at the time; then she had kissed his cheek. "You've been a good friend, Malcolm."

"I'll draw up the papers. You're making a good decision."

What Malcolm had not told Nuala was something a friend in Washington had passed along. A proposed change in environmental protection legislation was sure to go through, which meant that some property now protected by the Wetlands Preservation Act would be freed from development restrictions. The entire right end of Nuala's property would be included in that change. Drain the pond, cut down a few trees, and the view of the ocean would be spectacular, Malcolm reasoned. Moneyed people wanted that view. They would pay plenty for the property, would probably even tear down the old house and build one three times the size, facing the ocean. By his calculations, the property alone would be worth a million dollars. If it all went as planned, he should turn over an eight-hundred-thousand-dollar profit within the next year or two.

Then he would be able to get on with his life. With the profit he would make from the sale of the property, he would have enough cash to settle with his wife, Janice, retire, and move to Florida with Barbara.

How his life had changed since Barbara started working for him as a legal secretary! Seven years younger than he, she was a very pretty widow of fifty-six. Her children were grown and scattered, so she had taken the job in his office just to keep busy. It wasn't long, however, before the mutual attraction between them was palpable. She had all the warmth Janice had never offered him.

But she wasn't the kind who would get involved in an office affair—that much she had made clear. If he wanted her, he would have to come to her as a single man. And all it would take to make that happen was money, he told himself. Then . . .

"Well, are you ready?"

Malcolm looked up. His wife of thirty-five years was standing before him, her arms folded.

"If *you* are," he said.

He had been late getting home and had gone directly to his bedroom. This was the first time he had seen Janice since this morning. "What kind of day did you have?" he asked politely.

"What kind of day do I always have?" she snapped, "keeping books in a nursing home? But at least one of us is bringing home a regular paycheck."

) *8*

AT 7:50 P.M., NEIL STEPHENS, MANAGING DIRECTOR OF Carson & Parker Investment Corporation, stood up and stretched. He was the only one left in the office at 2 World Trade Center, except for the cleaning crew, whom he could hear vacuuming somewhere down the hall.

As the firm's senior executive, he had a large corner office that afforded him a sweeping view of Manhattan, a view which, unfortunately, he had little time to savor. That had been the case today, especially.

The market had been extremely volatile the last few days, and some of the stocks on the C&P "highly recommended" list had reported disappointing earnings. The stocks were all solid, most of them blue chips, and a dip in price now wasn't really a problem. What *was* a problem was that too many smaller investors then became anxious to sell, so it was up to him and his staff to convince them to be patient.

Well, enough for today, Neil thought. It's time to get out of here. He looked around for his jacket and spotted it on one of the chairs in the "conversation area," a grouping of comfortable furniture that gave the room what the interior designer had called "a client-friendly atmosphere."

Grimacing as he saw how wrinkled his jacket had become, he shook it and thrust his arms into the sleeves. Neil was a big man who, at thirty-seven, managed to keep his body muscle from sliding into fat by a program of disciplined exercise, including racquetball sessions two nights a week. The results of his efforts were apparent, and he was a compellingly attractive man with penetrating brown eyes that bespoke intelligence and an easy smile that inspired confidence. And, in fact, that confidence was well placed, for as his associates and friends knew, Neil Stephens missed very little.

He smoothed down the sleeves of his jacket, remembering that his assistant, Trish, had hung it up this morning but pointedly ignored it when he had once again tossed it down after lunch.

"The other assistants get mad at me if I wait on you too much," she had told him. "Besides, I do enough picking up after my husband. How much can a woman take?"

Neil smiled at the memory, but then the smile faded as he realized that he had forgotten to call Maggie to get her phone number in Newport. Just this morning he had decided to go to Portsmouth next weekend for his mother's birthday; that would put him just minutes away from Newport. Maggie had told him she would be staying there for a couple of weeks, with her stepmother. He had thought they would get together there.

He and Maggie had been dating casually since early spring, when they met in a bagel shop on Second Avenue, around the corner from their East Fifty-sixth Street apartment buildings. They had begun chatting there whenever their paths crossed; they then bumped into each other one evening at the movies. They sat together and later walked over to Neary's Pub for dinner.

Initially, Neil liked the fact that Maggie apparently took the dates as casually as he did. There was no indication on her part that she viewed the two of them as anything more than friends with a shared interest in movies. She seemed as wrapped up in her job as he was in his.

However, after six months of these occasional dates, the

fact that Maggie continued to act uninterested in him as anything other than a pleasant film and dinner companion was beginning to annoy Neil. Without realizing it was happening, he had found himself becoming more and more intent on seeing her, on learning all he could about her. He knew that she had been widowed five years ago, something that she mentioned matter-of-factly, her tone suggesting that emotionally she had put that behind her. But now he had started wondering whether she had a serious boyfriend. Wondering and being worried about it.

After puzzling for a minute, Neil decided to see if maybe Maggie had left her Newport number on her answering machine. Back at his desk, he listened to her recorded message: "Hi, this is Maggie Holloway. Thanks for calling. I'm out of town until October 13th." The machine clicked off. Obviously she wasn't interested in getting messages.

Great, he thought glumly as he replaced the receiver and walked over to the window. Manhattan stretched before him, ablaze with lights. He looked at the East River bridges and remembered that when he had told Maggie his office was on the forty-second floor of the World Trade Center, she had told him about the first time she had gone for a cocktail at Windows on the World atop the center. "It was just becoming dusk. The lights of the bridges went on, and then all the buildings and streetlights started glowing. It was like watching a highborn Victorian lady put on her jewelry— necklace, bracelets, rings, even a tiara."

The vivid image had stayed with Neil.

He had another image of Maggie as well, but this one troubled him. Three weeks ago, on Saturday, he had dropped in to Cinema I to see the thirty-year-old French classic *A Man and a Woman*. The theater wasn't crowded, and halfway through the film, he had noticed that Maggie was sitting alone a few rows ahead of him, four seats over. He had been about to join her when he realized that she was crying. Silent tears coursed down her cheeks, and she held her hand to her mouth to prevent sobs, as she watched the story of a young widow who could not accept her husband's death.

He had hurried out while the credits rolled, not wanting her to see him, thinking that she would be embarrassed to be caught so emotionally vulnerable.

Later that evening, he had been in Neary's having dinner with friends when she came in. She had stopped by his table to say hello, then had joined a group at the big corner table. There had been nothing in her face or manner to indicate that earlier she had been watching a film and identifying with a heartbroken young widow.

Damn! Neil thought, she's gone for at least two weeks, and I have no way to reach her. I don't even have the faintest idea of her stepmother's name.

) **9**

EXCEPT FOR THAT UPTIGHT ART DIRECTOR, IT HAD BEEN A good week, Maggie reflected as she turned off Route 138 in Newport. Both photo shoots this week had turned out exceptionally well, especially the one for *Vogue*.

But after the meticulous attention she had to give to noting how the camera was capturing every fold of the astronomically priced gowns she was photographing, it was a distinct joy to put on jeans and a plaid shirt. In fact, with the exception of a blue silk print blouse and matching long skirt she planned to wear tonight for Nuala's dinner party, everything she had brought to wear on this vacation was quite casual.

We're going to have such fun, she thought. Two uninterrupted weeks in Newport. Nuala and I really will have a chance to catch up with each other! She smiled at the prospect.

It had been a surprise when Liam called to say that *he* would be at Nuala's tonight, as well, although she should have realized he spent a fair amount of time in Newport. "It's an easy drive from Boston," he had pointed out. "I go there fairly regularly for weekends, especially off-season."

"I didn't know that," she had said.

"There's a lot you don't know about me, Maggie. Maybe if you weren't out of town so much . . ."

"And maybe if you didn't live in Boston and use your New York apartment so little . . ."

Maggie smiled again. Liam *is* fun, she thought, even though he does take himself too seriously much of the time. Stopping at a red light, she glanced down and rechecked her directions. Nuala lived just off the fabled Ocean Drive, on Garrison Avenue. "I even have a view of the ocean from the third floor," she had explained. "Wait till you see it and my studio."

She had called three times this week to be sure there were no changes of plan. "You *are* coming, Maggie? You won't disappoint?"

"Of course not," she had assured her. Still, Maggie had wondered if it was only her imagination or was there something in Nuala's voice, an uneasiness that perhaps she had detected in her face the night they had dinner in Manhattan. At the time, she had rationalized that Nuala's husband had died only last year, and she was starting to lose her friends as well, one of the nonjoys of living long enough to get old. Naturally a sense of mortality has to be setting in, she reasoned.

She had seen the same look on the faces of nursing home residents she had photographed for *Life* magazine last year. One woman had said wistfully, "Sometimes it bothers me a lot that there's no one left who remembers me when I was young."

Maggie shivered, then realized the temperature in the car had dropped rapidly. Turning off the air-conditioning, she opened the window a few inches and sniffed the tangy scent of the sea that permeated the air. When you've been raised in the Midwest, she thought, you can't ever get enough of the ocean.

Checking her watch, she realized it was ten of eight. She would barely have time to freshen up and change before the other guests began to arrive. At least she had phoned Nuala to let her know she was getting off to a late start. She had told her she should be arriving just about now.

She turned onto Garrison Avenue and saw the ocean in front of her. She slowed the car, then stopped in front of a charming clapboard house with weathered shingles and a wraparound porch. This had to be Nuala's home, she thought, but it seemed so dark. There were no outside lights turned on at all, and she could detect only a faint light coming from the front windows.

She pulled into the driveway, got out, and, without bothering to open the trunk for her suitcase, ran up the steps. Expectantly she rang the bell. From inside she could hear the faint sound of chimes.

As she waited, she sniffed. The windows facing the street were open, and she thought she detected a harsh, burning smell coming from inside. She pressed the doorbell again, and again the chimes reverberated through the house.

There was still no answer, no sound of footsteps. Something has to be wrong, she thought anxiously. Where was Nuala? Maggie walked over to the nearest window and crouched down, straining to see past the lacy fringe on the partly drawn shade, into the darkness inside.

Then her mouth went dry. The little she could see of the shadowy room suggested it was in wild disorder. The contents of a drawer were strewn on the hooked carpet, and the drawer itself was leaning haphazardly against the ottoman. The fireplace was opposite the windows and flanked by cabinets. All of them were open.

What faint light there was came from a pair of sconces over the mantel. As her eyes adjusted to the dim light, Maggie was able to pick out a single high-heeled shoe, turned on its side in front of the fireplace.

What was that? She squinted and leaned forward, then realized she was seeing a small stockinged foot, extending from behind a love seat near where the shoe had fallen. She lunged back to the door and twisted the handle, but it was locked.

Blindly, she rushed to the car, grabbed the car phone and punched in 911. Then she stopped, remembering: Her phone was attached to a New York area code. This was Rhode Island; Nuala's number began with a 401 area code. With trembling fingers she punched in 401–911.

When the call was answered, she managed to say "I'm at 1 Garrison Avenue in Newport. I can't get in. I can see someone lying on the floor. I think it's Nuala."

I'm babbling, she told herself. Stop it. But as the calm, unhurried questions came from the dispatcher, with absolute certainty Maggie's mind was shouting three words: *Nuala is dead.*

❱ *10*

NEWPORT CHIEF OF POLICE CHET BROWER STOOD ASIDE AS the police photographer snapped pictures of the crime scene. Aside from the wrenching fact that someone in his jurisdiction had been savagely murdered—Nuala Moore had suffered multiple blows to her head—there was something about the entire picture that bothered him.

There had been no reported incidents of housebreaking in this area for several months. That kind of thing started when many houses were closed for the winter and so became favorite targets for looters looking for television sets and such. Amazing how many people still didn't have an alarm system, Brower thought. Amazing, too, how many people were careless about locking their doors.

The chief had been in the first squad car to answer the 911 call. When they had arrived at the house, and the young woman who identified herself as Mrs. Moore's stepdaughter pointed to the front window, he had looked in and seen just what she had reported. Before forcing the front door, he and Detective Jim Haggerty had gone to the back of the house. Careful to barely touch the doorknob to avoid smudging existing fingerprints, he had found the door unlocked and they had gone in.

A flame was still flickering under a pot, now burned black. The acrid smell of charred potatoes overwhelmed the other, more pleasant scent. Roasting lamb, his mind had registered. Automatically he had turned off the stove's burners before going through the dining room into the living room.

He hadn't realized that the stepdaughter had followed them until they reached the body and he heard her moan. "Oh, Nuala, Finn-u-ala," she had said as she sank to her knees. She reached out her hand toward the body, but he grabbed it.

"Don't touch her!"

At that moment the front doorbell chimed, and he remembered noticing that the table in the dining room was set for company. Approaching sirens announced that more squad cars were on the scene, and in the next few minutes the officers had managed to get the stepdaughter and other arriving guests into a neighbor's house. Everyone was told not to leave until the chief had a chance to talk to them.

"Chief."

Brower looked up. Eddie Sousa, a rookie cop, was beside him.

"Some of the folks waiting to talk to you are getting kind of restless."

Brower's lifelong habit of frowning, whether in deep thought or annoyance, furrowed the skin of his forehead. The cause this time was annoyance. "Tell them I'll be over in ten minutes," he said testily.

Before leaving, he walked through the house once more. The place was a mess. Even the third-floor studio had been ransacked. Art supplies were thrown on the floor, as though hastily examined and discarded; drawers and cabinets had been emptied. Not too many intruders who had just committed murder would have taken the time for so thorough a search, he reasoned. Also, it would seem obvious from the overall appearance of the house that no money had been spent on it in a long time. So what was there to steal? he wondered.

The three second-floor bedrooms had been subjected to

the same search. One of them was tidy, except for the open closet door and yanked-out dresser drawers. The bedding had been turned back, and it was obvious the linen was fresh. It was Brower's guess that this room had been prepared for the stepdaughter.

The contents of the largest bedroom were scattered everywhere. A pink leather jewelry chest, the same kind he once gave his wife for Christmas, was open. What was obviously costume jewelry was scattered on the surface of the maple lowboy.

Brower made a note to ask Nuala Moore's friends about any valuable jewelry she might have had.

He spent a long moment studying the bedroom of the deceased in its disarray. Whoever did this wasn't a vicious, common thief, or a drug-addicted burglar, he decided. He had been *looking* for something. Or *she* had been looking for something, he amended. Nuala Moore had apparently realized her life was in danger. From the look of things, his guess was that she had been running in an attempt to escape when she was struck down from behind. Anyone could have done that—man or woman. It didn't require great strength.

And there was something else Brower noticed. Moore had obviously been preparing dinner, which suggested she was in the kitchen when the intruder arrived. She had tried to escape her attacker by running through the dining room, which meant the intruder must have been blocking the kitchen door. He or she probably came in that way, and since there was no sign of forced entry, the door must have been unlocked. Unless, of course, Mrs. Moore had let the intruder in herself. Brower made a note to check later whether the lock was the kind that stayed open once it was released.

But now he was ready to talk to the dinner guests. He left Detective Haggerty to wait for the coroner.

) *11*

"NO, THANK YOU," MAGGIE SAID AS SHE PRESSED HER index fingers to her temples. She vaguely realized that she hadn't eaten since noon, ten hours ago, but the thought of food made her throat close.

"Not even a cup of tea, Maggie?"

She looked up. The kind, solicitous face of Irma Woods, Nuala's next-door neighbor, hovered over her. It was easier to nod assent than to continue to refuse the offer. And to her surprise the mug warmed her chilled fingers, and the near-scalding tea felt good going down.

They were in the family room of the Woodses' home, a house much bigger than Nuala's. Family pictures were scattered on tabletops as well as on the mantel—children and grandchildren, she supposed. The Woodses appeared to be contemporaries of Nuala.

Despite all the stress and confusion, Maggie thought she had the others straight, the ones who were to have been the dinner guests. There was Dr. William Lane, the director of Latham Manor, which she gathered was a senior citizens' residence. A large, balding man somewhere in his fifties, Dr. Lane had a soothing quality about him as he expressed his condolences. He had tried to give her a mild sedative, but Maggie had refused. She found that even the mildest of sedatives could make her sleepy for days.

Maggie observed that whenever Dr. Lane's very pretty wife, Odile, said anything, her hands began to move. "Nuala came to visit her friend Greta Shipley at the home almost every day," she had explained, her fingers gesturing in a come-hither movement as though inviting someone to come closer. Then she shook her head and clasped her fingers together as though in prayer. "Greta will be heartbroken. *Heartbroken,*" she repeated decisively.

Odile had already made the same remark several times, and Maggie found herself wishing she wouldn't say it again. But this time Odile amended it with an additional remark: "And everyone in her art class will miss her so much. The guests who attended it were having so much fun. Oh dear, I didn't even think of that until this moment."

That would be like Nuala, Maggie thought, to share her talent with others. A vivid memory of Nuala giving her her own palette for her sixth birthday flooded her mind. "And I'm going to teach you how to paint lovely pictures," Nuala had said. Only it didn't happen that way, because I was never any good, Maggie thought. It wasn't until she put clay in my hands that art became real to me.

Malcolm Norton, who had introduced himself to Maggie as Nuala's lawyer, was standing at the fireplace. He was a handsome man, but it seemed to her that he was striking a pose. There was something superficial—almost artificial—about him, she thought. Somehow his expression of grief, and his statement, "I was her friend and confidant as well as her lawyer," suggested that he felt *he* was the one who deserved sympathy.

But then why should anyone think I'm the one to receive condolences? she asked herself. They all know that I've only just met Nuala again after over twenty years.

Norton's wife, Janice, spent most of the time talking quietly to the doctor. An athletic type, she might have been attractive except for the downward lines at the corners of her mouth that gave her a harsh, even bitter, expression.

Thinking about that, Maggie wondered at the way her mind was dealing with the shock of Nuala's death. On the one hand, she hurt so much; on the other, she was observing these people as though through a camera's eye.

Liam and his cousin Earl sat near each other in matching fireside chairs. When Liam came in, he had put his arm around her and said, "Maggie, how horrible for you," but then he seemed to understand that she needed physical and mental space to absorb this by herself, and he did not take the place next to her on the love seat.

Love seat, Maggie thought. It was behind the love seat that they had found Nuala's body.

Earl Bateman leaned forward, his hands clasped in front of him, as though in deep thought. Maggie had met him only on the night of the Moore reunion, but she remembered that he was an anthropologist who lectured on funeral customs.

Had Nuala indicated to anyone what kind of funeral she would want? Maggie wondered. Maybe Malcolm Norton, the lawyer, would know.

The sound of the doorbell made everyone look up. The police chief Maggie had followed into Nuala's house now came into the room. "I'm sorry to have detained you," he said. "Several of my men will take your individual statements, so we will have you out of here as soon as possible. First, though, I have some questions I want to ask you as a group. Mr. and Mrs. Woods, I wish you'd stay, too."

The chief's questions were general, things like, "Was Mrs. Moore in the habit of leaving her back door unlocked?"

The Woodses told him that she always left it unlocked, that she even joked about forever mislaying the key to the front door, but she knew she could always sneak in the back.

He asked if she had seemed troubled recently. Unanimously they reported that Nuala had been happy and excited and looking forward to Maggie's visit.

Maggie felt tears sting the back of her eyes. And then the realization came: But she *was* troubled.

It was only when Chief Brower said, "Now if you'll just bear with us a few minutes more while my men ask you each a few questions, I promise you we'll have you home soon," that Irma Woods timidly interrupted.

"There is just one thing that maybe we ought to explain. Yesterday, Nuala came over. She had handwritten a new will and wanted us to witness her signature. She also had us call Mr. Martin, a notary public, so that he could make it official. She seemed a bit upset because she said that she knew Mr. Norton might be disappointed that she was canceling the sale of her house to him."

Irma Woods looked at Maggie. "Nuala's will asks that you visit or phone her friend Greta Shipley, at Latham Manor, as often as you can possibly manage it. Except for a few charitable bequests, she left her house and everything else she owned to you."

) *12*

IT WAS OBVIOUS THAT MAGGIE HOLLOWAY WAS NOT SATIS-
fied with the theory that an intruder had murdered Nuala.
He had seen that at the funeral parlor. Now at the Requiem
Mass, he watched with narrowed eyes when she shook her
head in disbelief as the priest spoke about the random vio-
lence that today claims so many innocent lives.

Maggie was much too smart, too observant. She could
easily become a threat.

But as they filed out of St. Mary's Church, he comforted
himself with the thought that undoubtedly she would now
go back to New York and put Nuala's house up for sale.
And we know who's going to step in there with an offer
before she leaves, he thought.

He was glad to note that Greta Shipley had been accompanied by a nurse when she arrived at the Mass, and then
had had to leave almost immediately afterwards. Maggie
would probably pay her a courtesy call at the residence
before she took off.

He stirred restlessly. At least the Mass was nearly over. The soloist was singing "Here I am, Lord," and the casket was being wheeled slowly down the aisle.

He didn't really want to go to the cemetery now, although he knew there was no way out of it. Later. He would go there later . . . and alone. As with the others, his special gift would be a private memorial to her.

He filed out of the church with the thirty or so others who accompanied Nuala to her final resting place. It was the cemetery in which many of Newport's more prominent longtime Catholic residents were buried. Nuala's grave was beside that of her last husband. The legend on the marble would soon be complete. Next to Timothy James Moore's name and birth and death dates, her name and birth date were already inscribed. Soon, Friday's date would be added. "Rest in peace" was already there.

He forced himself to look solemn as the final prayers were read . . . rather too rapidly, he thought. On the other hand, it was obvious that the dark clouds above were about to release a heavy torrent of rain.

When the service ended, Irma Woods invited everyone back to her house for refreshments.

He reasoned that it would be awkward to refuse, and besides, it would be a good time to learn exactly when Maggie Holloway planned to leave. Go away, Maggie, he thought. You'll only get in trouble here.

An hour later, as the guests mingled and chatted, drinks and sandwiches in their hands, he was stunned to hear Irma Woods tell Maggie that the cleaning service had completed straightening the house and removing the mess created by the police when they had dusted for fingerprints.

"So the house is ready for you, Maggie," Mrs. Woods

told her. "But are you sure you won't be nervous there? You know you're welcome to continue staying here."

Trying to seem casual, he moved closer, straining to hear. His back was turned toward them as Maggie said, "No, I won't be nervous in Nuala's home. I'd intended to stay two weeks, and so I shall. I'll use the time to sort out everything, and, of course, to visit Greta Shipley at Latham Manor as Nuala requested."

He stiffened as she added, "Mrs. Woods, you've been so kind. I can't thank you enough. There's just one thing. When Nuala came to see you Friday morning with that handwritten will, didn't you question her? I mean, weren't you surprised that she was so anxious to have it witnessed and notarized, so intent on having it done at once?"

It seemed to him that an eternity passed before Mrs. Woods answered, her response measured. "Well, yes, I did wonder. At first I just thought it was impulsive. Nuala had been very lonely since Tim died and was absolutely ecstatic that she'd found you. But since her death, I've been thinking that there was more to it than that. It was almost as if Nuala knew something terrible might happen to her."

He drifted toward the fireplace, joining a group gathered there. He responded to their remarks, but his mind was racing. Maggie would be visiting Greta Shipley. How much did Greta know? How much did she suspect? Something had to be done. It could not be risked.

Greta. Obviously she was not well. Everyone had seen her helped out of church today. Everyone would believe that the shock of her friend's death had contributed to a fatal heart attack. Unexpected, of course, but not really a surprise.

Sorry, Greta, he thought.

) *13*

WHEN SHE WAS STILL A RELATIVELY YOUNG AGE SIXTY-
eight, Greta Shipley had been invited to a reception at the
newly renovated Latham House, just rechristened the Latham Manor Residence. The new home for retirees was open
and was accepting applications.

She liked everything she saw there. The house's magnificent first floor included the grand salon and marble and
crystal dining room, where the enormous banquet table she
remembered from her youth had been replaced by smaller
tables. The handsome library, with its deep leather chairs
and cheerful fireplace, was inviting, and the smaller salon,
which would serve as a television room, suggested shared
evenings of companionable viewing.

Greta also approved of the regulations: The social hour
would begin at 5:00 P.M. in the grand salon, followed by
dinner at six. She was pleased that guests would be required
to dress for the evening, as though they were dining in a
country club. Greta had been raised by a stern grandmother
who could wither with a glance the luckless individual
garbed in inappropriate attire. Any residents not up to dressing appropriately would be served in their own quarters.

There also was a section set aside for long-term nursing
care, should that be required.

The admission fee was steep, of course. It began at two
hundred thousand dollars for a large private room and bath,
and climbed to five hundred thousand for a two-bedroom

suite, of which there were four in the mansion. And while the resident got full and exclusive use of the apartment during his or her lifetime, at the time of death, ownership reverted to the residence, which would make the rooms available for sale to the next applicant. Guests would also pay a maintenance fee of two thousand dollars a month, which, of course, was partially covered by Social Security payments.

Guests were invited to furnish their own quarters, but only with staff approval of what they chose to bring. The model studios and apartments were exquisitely comfortable and impeccably tasteful.

Recently widowed and nervous about living alone, Greta had gladly sold her home on Ochre Point, moved to Latham Manor, and felt she had made a good decision. As one of the first occupants, she had a select studio. Large, with a living area alcove, it accommodated all her most treasured furnishings. And best of all, when she closed her door, it was with the secure sense of not being alone in the night. There always was a guard on the premises, a nurse on duty, and a bell to summon help if necessary.

Greta enjoyed the companionship of most of the other residents and easily avoided the ones who got on her nerves. She also kept up her long friendship with Nuala Moore; they often went out to lunch together, and at Greta's request Nuala agreed to give art classes twice a week at the residence.

After Timothy Moore died, Greta had begun a campaign to get Nuala to move to the residence. When Nuala demurred, saying she would be fine alone and insisting further that she couldn't do without her art studio, Greta urged her to at least put in her application so that when one of the two-bedroom suites became available, she would be in a position to change her mind. Nuala had finally agreed, admitting that her lawyer was encouraging her to do the same thing.

But now that would never happen, Greta thought sadly, as she sat in her easy chair, the virtually untouched dinner tray in front of her.

She was still upset that she had experienced that weak spell at Nuala's funeral earlier in the day. She had been feeling perfectly fine until this morning. Perhaps if she had taken time to eat a proper breakfast it wouldn't have happened, she reasoned.

She simply could not allow herself to become ill now. Especially now she wanted to keep as active as possible. Being busy was the only way to work out grief; life had taught her that. She also knew it wasn't going to be easy, for she would miss Nuala's cheerful presence very much.

It was reassuring to know that Nuala's stepdaughter, Maggie Holloway, would be visiting her. At the funeral parlor yesterday, before the service, Maggie had introduced herself and said, "Mrs. Shipley, I hope you're going to let me spend time with you. I know you were Nuala's closest friend. I want to make you my friend, too."

There was a tap at the door.

Greta liked the fact that unless they had reason to suspect a problem, the staff was instructed to enter a guest's room only when invited. Nurse Markey, however, didn't seem to understand: Just because the door isn't locked doesn't mean that she is free to barge in at any time. Some appeared to like the intrusive nurses. Greta did not.

Predictably, before Greta could respond to the knock, Nurse Markey strode in, a professional smile wreathing her strong features. "How are we doing tonight, Mrs. Shipley?" she asked loudly as she came over and perched on the hassock, her face uncomfortably close to Greta's.

"*I'm* quite fine, thank you, Miss Markey. I hope you are."

The solicitous "we" always irritated Greta. She had mentioned that fact several times, but this woman clearly did not intend to change anything, so why bother? Greta asked herself. Suddenly she realized that her heartbeat was beginning to accelerate.

"I hear we had a weak spell in church . . ."

Greta put her hand on her chest as though by that act she could stop the wild pounding.

"Mrs. Shipley, what's the matter? Are you all right?"

Greta felt her wrist being seized.

As suddenly as it had begun, the pounding slackened. She managed to say, "Just give me a moment. I'll be fine. I just felt a little breathless, that's all."

"I want you to lean back and close your eyes. I'm going to call Dr. Lane." Nurse Markey's face was barely inches from hers now. Instinctively Greta turned away.

Ten minutes later, propped up on pillows in bed, Greta tried to reassure the doctor that the little spell she had had was completely past. But later, as she drifted off to sleep with the help of a mild sedative, she could not escape the chilling memory of how just two weeks ago, Constance Rhinelander, who had been here so briefly, had died of heart failure, so unexpectedly.

First Constance, she thought, then Nuala. Grandmother's housekeeper used to say that deaths come in threes. Please don't let me be the third, she thought as she drifted off.

) *14*

No, IT HAD NOT BEEN A NIGHTMARE; IT REALLY HAD HAP-
pened. The full reality of events of the past few days settled
firmly in Maggie's mind as she stood in Nuala's kitchen, in
the house that now, incredibly, was hers.

At three o'clock, Liam had helped carry her bags here
from the Woodses' guest room. He had left them at the top
of the stairs. "Do you know which bedroom you're going
to use?" he had asked.

"No."

"Maggie, you look ready to collapse. Are you *sure* you
want to stay here? I don't think it's such a hot idea."

"Yes," she had replied after a thoughtful pause, "I do
want to stay."

Now as she put the kettle on, Maggie reflected with gratitude that one of Liam's nicest qualities was that he didn't
argue.

Instead of objecting further, he had said simply, "Then
I'll leave you alone. But I do hope you'll rest for a while.
Don't start unpacking or trying to sort out Nuala's things."

"Certainly not tonight."

"I'll call you tomorrow."

At the door, he had put an arm around her and given her
a friendly hug. Then he was gone.

Feeling suddenly exhausted, moving as though it was an
effort to put one foot in front of the other, Maggie had
locked the front and back doors, then climbed the stairs.

Glancing through the bedrooms, she saw immediately that the one Nuala had meant her to have was the second largest. It was simply furnished—a maple double bed, a dresser with mirror, a night table and rocking chair—and there were no personal effects around. The dresser top held only an old-fashioned enamel toiletry set: comb, brush, mirror, buttonhook and nail file.

After dragging her bags into that room, Maggie had peeled off her skirt and sweater, slipped into her favorite robe, and climbed under the covers.

Now, after a nearly three-hour nap, and aided by a cup of tea, she was finally beginning to feel clearheaded. She even sensed that she was over the shock of Nuala's death.

The sadness, though, that's another story, she thought. That won't go away.

She realized suddenly that for the first time in four days she was hungry. She opened the refrigerator and saw that it had been stocked: eggs, milk, juice, a small roasted chicken, a loaf of bread, and a container of homemade chicken soup. Obviously Mrs. Woods, she thought.

She settled on making herself a chicken sandwich, slicing and skinning the chicken and using only a trace of mayonnaise.

She had just gotten comfortable at the table when she was startled by a rap at the back door. She spun around and was on her feet even as the handle turned, her body tense, poised to react.

She gasped with relief as Earl Bateman's face appeared in the oval window that comprised most of the top half of the door.

Chief Brower theorized that Nuala had been surprised by an intruder in this kitchen, an intruder who had come in the back door. That thought, and the mental image it conjured up, ran through her mind as she quickly crossed the room.

Part of her worried if she was doing the right thing to even open the door, but now more annoyed than worried for her safety, she unlocked it and let him in.

The absentminded professor look that she associated with Bateman was more in evidence at that moment than at any time in the last three days.

"Maggie, forgive me," he said. "I'm heading back to Providence until Friday, and as I got in the car, it occurred to me that you might not have locked this door. I know that Nuala was in the habit of leaving it unlocked. I spoke to Liam, and he mentioned that he had left you here earlier and thought you were going to go to bed. I didn't mean to intrude; I thought I'd just drive by and check, and slip the lock myself if it wasn't set. I'm sorry, but from the front of the house there was no sign that you were still up."

"You could have phoned."

"I'm one of those holdouts who doesn't have a phone in the car. Sorry. I never was much good at playing the Boy Scout. And I've interrupted your dinner."

"It's okay. It was just a sandwich. Would you like something?"

"No, thanks. I'm on my way. Maggie, knowing how Nuala felt about you, I think I have a sense of how special your relationship with her was."

"Yes, it was special."

"If I may give you one bit of advice, it's to heed the words of the great researcher Durkheim, on the subject of death. He wrote, 'Sorrow like joy becomes exalted and amplified when leaping from mind to mind.' "

"What are you trying to tell me?" Maggie asked quietly.

"I'm distressing you and that's the last thing I want to do. What I mean is that I suspect you have the habit of hugging grief to yourself. It's easier if you are more open at a time like this. I guess what I'm attempting to say is that I'd like to be your friend."

He opened the door. "I'll be back Friday afternoon. Double lock the door, please."

He was gone. Maggie snapped the lock and sank into a chair. The kitchen was suddenly frighteningly still, and she realized she was trembling. How could Earl Bateman have thought she would be grateful to him for appearing unannounced and surreptitiously trying the lock?

She rose and with quick, silent steps ran through the dining room into the dark front room and knelt at the window to look out under the fringe of the shade.

She saw Bateman walking down the path to the street.

At his car, he opened the door, then turned and stood for a long moment, staring back at the house. Maggie had the feeling that even though she was surely hidden by the dark interior of the house, Earl Bateman knew, or at least sensed, that she was watching him.

The torchlight at the end of the driveway shone a pool of light near him, and as she watched, Bateman stepped into the light and gave a broad wave of his hand, a farewell gesture clearly directed at her. He can't see me, she thought, but he knows I'm here.

) *15*

WHEN THE PHONE RANG AT 8:00 A.M., ROBERT STEPHENS reached with his left hand to answer it, while his right maintained a firm hold on his coffee cup.

His "good morning" was a trifle curt, his wife of forty-three years noted with amusement. Dolores Stephens knew that her husband did not appreciate early morning phone calls.

"Anything that can be said at eight can wait until nine," was his axiom.

Usually these calls were from one of the senior-citizen clients whose taxes he handled. He and Dolores had come to Portsmouth three years ago, looking to retire, but Robert decided to keep his hand in, as he put it, by taking on a few selected clients. Within six months he had all he could handle.

The hint of annoyance disappeared quickly from his voice as he said, "Neil, how are you?"

"Neil!" Dolores exclaimed, her tone immediately apprehensive. "Oh, I hope he's not going to say he can't make it this weekend," she murmured.

Her husband waved her into silence. "The weather? Great. Couldn't be better. I'm not taking the boat out of the water yet. You can get up Thursday? Wonderful. Your mother will be delighted. She's grabbing the receiver. You know how impatient she is. Fine. I'll call the club for a two o'clock tee-off."

Dolores got on the line and heard the amused voice of her only child. "Aren't you impatient this morning," he said.

"I know. It's just that it will be so good to see you. I'm so glad you're able to come. And you will stay till Sunday, won't you, Neil?"

"Of course. Looking forward to it. Okay, gotta run. Tell Dad his 'good morning' sounded more like 'go to hell.' He still hasn't finished that first cup of coffee, huh?"

"You got it. Bye, dear."

The parents of Neil Stephens looked at each other. Dolores sighed. "The one thing I miss about leaving New York is having Neil just drop by anytime," she said.

Her husband got up, went over to the stove, and refilled his cup. "Did Neil say I sounded grouchy when I answered?"

"Something like that."

Robert Stephens smiled reluctantly. "Well, I know I'm not all sunshine early in the morning, but just now I was afraid the call was from Laura Arlington. She's all upset. Keeps calling me."

Dolores waited.

"She made some serious investments that haven't worked out, and she thinks now that she's getting a big run-around."

"Is she right?"

"I think she is. It was one of those supposedly hot tips. The broker persuaded her to invest in a small high-tech company that was supposed to be bought out by Microsoft. She bought one hundred thousand shares of stock at five dollars a share, convinced she'd end up with a big profit."

"Five hundred thousand dollars! What's it worth now?"

"The stock was just suspended from trading. As of yesterday, if you could sell it, you'd get eighty cents a share. Laura can't afford to lose that kind of money. I wish to God she'd talked to me before she got into that one."

"Isn't she thinking of going into the Latham Manor Residence?"

"Yes, and that was the money that was going to pay for it. It was just about all she had. Her children wanted her to get settled there, but this broker convinced her that with this investment she'd not only be able to live at Latham but have money to leave her kids as well."

"Was what he did illegal?"

"I don't think so, unfortunately. Unethical perhaps, but probably not illegal. Anyway, I'm going to talk it over with Neil. That's why I'm especially glad he's coming up."

Robert Stephens walked to the large window that overlooked Narragansett Bay. Like his son, he was a broad, athletic-looking man. At sixty-eight, his once-sandy hair was now white.

The water in the bay was quiet, almost as still as a lake. The grass behind the house, sloping down to the water, was starting to lose its velvety green. The maples were already displaying clusters of orange, copper, and burgundy leaves.

"Beautiful, peaceful," he said, shaking his head. "Hard to believe that six miles from here, a woman was murdered in her own home."

He turned and looked at his wife, effortlessly pretty, her silver hair knotted at the top of her head, her features still delicate and soft. "Dolores," he said, his tone suddenly stern, "when I'm out, I want you to keep the alarm system on at all times."

"Fine," she agreed amiably. In fact, she had not wanted her husband to realize just how deeply that murder had shaken her, or that when she had read the paper's graphic account, she had checked both her front and back doors, and, as usual, found them unlocked.

❭ *16*

DR. WILLIAM LANE WAS NOT ESPECIALLY PLEASED BY Maggie Holloway's request for an appointment. Already irritated by his wife's aimless, nonstop chatter over the lunch table, and behind in completing the ever-increasing load of forms the government required of him as director of Latham Manor, he found the thought of another lost half-hour galling. He regretted now having agreed to it. He couldn't imagine what she needed to talk to him about.

Particularly since Nuala Moore had never signed the final papers committing her to move to the residence. She had completed all the forms for entrance, had taken her physical, and, when she started to seem hesitant, he had taken it upon himself to have the second bedroom of the available suite stripped of the carpeting and furniture to show her how easily it would accommodate her easels and art supplies and cabinets. But then she called and simply said she had decided to keep her house instead.

He wondered why she had changed her mind so suddenly.

She had seemed the perfect candidate. Surely it wasn't because she fantasized that the stepdaughter would come live with her and wanted to have a place for her to stay?

Ridiculous! Lane muttered to himself. How likely was it that an attractive young woman with a successful career would come rushing up to Newport to play house with a woman she hadn't seen in years? Lane figured that now that she had been left the place, Maggie Holloway would take a good look at all the work and expense involved to fix it up and would decide to sell it. But in the meantime she was coming here to take up his time, time that he needed to spend getting that suite put back in order to make it suitable for viewing. The management of Prestige Residence Corporation had made it clear that they would not tolerate empty living space.

Still, an uneasy thought would not go away: *Was there any other reason Nuala had backed out of the arrangement?* And if there was, had she confided it to her stepdaughter? What could it be? he wondered. Maybe it was all to the good that she was coming to see him after all.

He looked up from his work as the door to his office opened. Odile wandered in, as usual without knocking, a habit that drove him crazy. And one that she unfortunately shared with Nurse Zelda Markey. In fact, he would have to do something about that. Mrs. Shipley had complained about Nurse Markey's habit of opening doors without waiting to be invited.

As he expected, Odile ignored his look of annoyance and began speaking. "William, I don't think Mrs. Shipley is that well. As you saw, she had a little episode after the funeral Mass yesterday and a dizzy spell last evening. I wonder if she shouldn't go into the nursing section for a few days of observation?"

"I intend to keep a close eye on Mrs. Shipley," Dr. Lane

said brusquely. "Try to remember, my dear, that in our family, I'm the one with the medical degree. You never finished nursing school."

He knew it was a stupid thing to say and regretted it immediately, knowing what was coming next.

"Oh, William, that's so unfair," she cried. "Nursing is a vocation, and I realized it wasn't for me. Perhaps it would have been better for you—and others—if you had made the same choice." Her lip quivered. "And I think you should keep in mind that it was only because of me that Prestige Residences considered you for this job."

They stared at each other in silence for a moment; then, as usual, Odile became contrite. "Oh, William, that was unkind of me. I know how devoted you are to all our guests. It's just that I want to help you, and I worry that another episode could ruin you."

She came over to the desk and leaned over him. She reached for his hand, lifting it to her face, moving it so that it caressed her cheek and chin.

Lane sighed. She was a lightweight—"a ninny," his grandmother would have snapped—but she *was* pretty. He had felt himself most fortunate eighteen years ago, to have convinced an attractive—younger—woman to marry him. Plus, she *did* care about him, and he knew her frequent, sugary-warm visits to the residents delighted most of them. She might seem cloying at times, but she was nonetheless sincere, and that counted for a lot. A few residents, like Greta Shipley, found her vacuous and irritating, which to Lane only proved Mrs. Shipley's intelligence, but there was no question that here at Latham Manor, Odile was an asset to him.

Lane knew what was expected of him. With virtually no show of the resignation he felt, he stood up, put his arms around his wife and murmured, "What would I do without you?"

It was a relief when his secretary buzzed him on the intercom. "Miss Holloway is here," she announced.

"You'd better go, Odile," Lane whispered, forestalling her inevitable suggestion that she stay and be part of the meeting.

For once she didn't argue but slipped out the unmarked door of his suite that led to the main corridor.

) 17

THE NIGHT BEFORE, BLAMING THE THREE-HOUR NAP SHE had taken earlier, Maggie had been still wide awake at midnight. Giving up on going to sleep anytime soon, she had gone downstairs again and, in the small study, found books, several of them fully illustrated, on the "cottages" of Newport.

Carrying them up to bed, she had propped pillows behind her back and read for nearly two hours. As a result, when she was admitted to Latham Manor by a uniformed maid who then called Dr. Lane to announce her arrival, she was able to take in her surroundings with some degree of knowledge.

The mansion had been built by Ernest Latham in 1900, as a deliberate rebuke to what he considered the vulgar ostentation of the Vanderbilt mansion, The Breakers. The layout for the two houses was almost the same, but the Latham house had livable proportions. The entrance hall was still overwhelmingly large, but was, in fact, only a third of the size of The Breakers' "Great Hall of Entry." Satinwood—rather than Caen limestone—covered the walls, and the staircase of richly carved mahogany, carpeted in cardinal red, stood in place of the marble staircase The Breakers boasted.

The doors on the left were closed, but Maggie knew the dining room would be there.

To the right, what originally must have been the music room looked most inviting, with comfortable chairs and matching hassocks, all richly upholstered in moss green and floral patterns. The magnificent Louis Quinze mantel was even more breathtaking in reality than it had appeared in the pictures she had seen. The ornately carved space above the fireplace stretched to the ceiling, filled with Grecian figures, tiny angels, and pineapples and grapes, except for the smooth center, where a Rembrandt-school oil painting had been hung.

It really *is* beautiful, she thought, mentally comparing it with the unspeakably squalid condition of a nursing home interior she had surreptitiously photographed for *Newsmaker* magazine.

She realized suddenly that the maid had spoken to her. "Oh, I'm sorry," she apologized, "I was just trying to take it all in."

The maid was an attractive young woman with dark eyes and olive skin. "It is lovely, isn't it?" she said. "Even working here is a pleasure. I'll take you to Dr. Lane now."

His office was the largest in a suite of offices along the back of the house. A mahogany door separated the area from the rest of the first floor. As Maggie followed the maid down the carpeted corridor, she glanced through an open office door and noticed a familiar face—Janice Norton, the wife of Nuala's lawyer, sat behind a desk.

I didn't know she worked here, Maggie thought. But then I really don't know much at all about any of these people, do I?

Their eyes met, and Maggie could not help feeling uncomfortable. She had not missed the bitter disappointment on Malcolm Norton's face when Mrs. Woods revealed that Nuala had canceled the sale of her house. But he had been cordial at the wake and funeral yesterday and had suggested that he would like to have a chat with her about her plans for the house.

She paused just long enough to greet Mrs. Norton, then followed the maid down the corridor to the corner office.

The maid knocked, waited, and at the invitation to enter, opened the door for Maggie and stepped back, closing it once Maggie was inside.

Dr. Lane stood up and came around his desk to greet her. His smile was cordial, but it seemed to Maggie that his eyes were appraising her professionally. His greeting confirmed that impression.

"Ms. Holloway, or Maggie, if I may, I'm glad to see that you look a bit more rested. Yesterday was a very difficult day for you, I know."

"I'm sure it was difficult for everyone who loved Nuala," Maggie said quietly. "But I'm really concerned about Mrs. Shipley. How is she this morning?"

"She had another weak spell last evening, but I looked in on her just a while ago, and she seems quite fit. She's looking forward to your visit."

"When I spoke to her this morning, she particularly asked if I would drive her out to the cemetery. Do you think that's a good idea?"

Lane indicated the leather chair in front of his desk. "Sit down, please." He returned to his own chair. "I wish she'd wait a few days, but when Mrs. Shipley makes up her mind to do something . . . well, nothing changes it. I do think that both of her little spells yesterday were caused by her deep emotion over Nuala's death. The two of them were really very close. They'd gotten into the habit of going up to Mrs. Shipley's studio after Nuala's art class, and they would gossip and have a glass or two of wine. I told them they were like a pair of schoolgirls. Frankly, though, it probably was good for both of them, and I know Mrs. Shipley will miss those visits."

He smiled, reminiscing. "Nuala once told me that if she were hit over the head and then asked her age when she came to, she'd say twenty-two and mean it. Inside, she said, she really was twenty-two."

Then as he realized what he had said, he looked shocked. "I'm so sorry. How careless of me."

Hit over the head, Maggie thought. But feeling sorry for the man's acute embarrassment, she said, "Please don't apologize. You're right. In spirit Nuala never *was* older than twenty-two." She hesitated, then decided to plunge in. "Doctor, there's one thing I must ask you. Did Nuala ever confide to you that something was troubling her? I mean, did she have a physical problem she may have mentioned?"

He shook his head. "No, not physical. I think Nuala was having a great deal of difficulty with what she perceived to be giving up her independence. I really think that if she had lived she eventually would have made up her mind to come here. She was always concerned about the relatively high cost of the large apartment with the extra bedroom, but as she said, she had to have a studio where she could both work and close the door when she was finished." He paused. "Nuala told me that she knew she was a bit untidy by nature but that her studio was always the scene of organized chaos."

"Then you believe that canceling the sale of her house

and the hasty will she left were simply a last-minute panic attack of sorts?"

"Yes, I do." He stood up. "I'll ask Angela to bring you up to Mrs. Shipley. And if you do go to the cemetery, observe her carefully, please. If she seems in any way distraught, return immediately. After all, the families of our guests have entrusted their lives to our care, and we take that responsibility very seriously."

) *18*

MALCOLM NORTON SAT IN HIS OFFICE ON THAMES STREET, staring at his appointment calendar for the remainder of the day. It was now *entirely* empty, thanks to the cancellation of his two o'clock appointment. It wouldn't have been much of a case—just a young housewife suing her neighbor over a nasty dog bite. But the dog had a previous complaint against it—another neighbor had fought off an attack with a broom—so it was a foregone conclusion that the insurance company would be anxious to settle, particularly since the gate had been carelessly left open, and the dog allowed to run loose.

The trouble was, it was *too* easy a case. The woman had phoned to say the insurance company had settled to her satisfaction. Meaning I'm out three or four thousand dollars, Norton thought glumly.

He still could not get over the sickening realization that less than twenty-four hours before she died, Nuala Moore had secretly canceled the sale of her house to him. Now he was stuck with the two-hundred-thousand-dollar mortgage he had raised on his own house.

It had been hell getting Janice to agree to co-sign for the mortgage. Finally he had told her about the impending change in the Wetlands Act, and about the profits he hoped to reap in reselling Nuala Moore's property.

"Look," he had said, trying to reason with her, "you're tired of working in the nursing home. God knows I hear that every day. It's an absolutely legitimate sale. The house needs everything done to it. The worst possible scenario is that the new wetlands legislation doesn't go through, which won't happen. In that case, we take a renovating mortgage on Nuala's place, fix it up, and sell it for three-fifty."

"A second mortgage," she had said sarcastically. "My, my, you're quite the entrepreneur. So I quit my job. And what will you do with your new-found wealth, after the change in the Wetlands Act goes through?"

It was, of course, a question he was not prepared to answer. Not until after the sales had been completed. And that, of course, was not going to happen now. Not unless things changed. He could still hear Janice's furious words after they got home Friday night. "So now we have a two-hundred-thousand-dollar mortgage and the expense we went through to get it. You march yourself right down to the bank and pay it off. I don't intend to lose my home."

"You're not going to lose it," he had said, pleading for time to work everything out. "I already told Maggie Holloway that I wanted to see her. She knows it's about the house. Do you think she'll want to stay in a place where her stepmother was murdered? Ms. Holloway will get out of Newport as fast as possible, and I'm going to point out that over the years I've been a big help to Nuala and Tim Moore without charging them my usual fee. By next week she'll have agreed to sell the house."

She *had* to agree to sell the house, he told himself morosely. It was his only way out of this mess.

The intercom buzzed. He picked it up. "Yes, Barbara," he said, his voice formal. He was careful never to let an intimate quality intrude into their exchanges when she was in the outer office. He could never be certain that someone else had not come in.

From her tone of voice today, it was obvious to him that she was alone. "Malcolm, may I talk to you for a few minutes?" was all she said, but immediately he sensed that something was wrong.

A moment later she was sitting opposite him, her hands folded in her lap, her lovely hazel eyes averted. "Malcolm, I don't know how to say this, so I'd better just plunge in. I can't stay here. I feel rotten about myself these days." She hesitated, then added, "Even loving you as much as I do, I can't get away from the fact that you're married to someone else."

"You've seen me with Janice. You know our relationship."

"But she's still your wife. It's better this way, believe me. I'm going to visit my daughter in Vail for a couple of months. Then, when I come back, I'll find a different job."

"Barbara, you can't just walk out like this," he pleaded, suddenly panicked.

She smiled sadly. "Not this minute. I wouldn't do that. I'm giving you a week's notice."

"By that time, Janice and I will be separated, I *promise* you. *Please* stay! I *can't* let you go."

Not after all I've done to keep you! he thought desperately.

☽ *19*

AFTER MAGGIE PICKED UP GRETA SHIPLEY, THEY MADE A stop at the florist's to buy flowers. As they were driving to the cemetery, Greta reminisced to Maggie about her friendship with Nuala.

"Her parents rented a cottage here for several years when we both were about sixteen. She was such a pretty girl, and so much fun. She and I were inseparable during that time, and she had many admirers. Why, Tim Moore was always hanging around her. Then her father was transferred to London, and she moved there and went to school there, as well. Later, I heard she was married. Eventually we just lost track of each other, something I always regretted."

Maggie steered the car through the quiet streets that led to St. Mary's cemetery in Newport. "How did you happen to get together again?" she asked.

"It was just twenty-one years ago. My phone rang one day. Someone asked to speak to the former Greta Carlyle. I knew the voice was familiar but for the moment couldn't place it. I responded that *I* was Greta Carlyle Shipley, and Nuala whooped, 'Good for you, Gret. You landed Carter Shipley!' "

It seemed to Maggie that she was hearing Nuala's voice coming from everyone's lips. She heard it when Mrs. Woods talked about the will, when Doctor Lane reminisced about her feeling of being twenty-two, and now in Mrs. Shipley's memories about the same kind of warm reunion Maggie herself had experienced less than two weeks ago.

Despite the warmth in the car, Maggie shivered. Thoughts of Nuala always came back to the same question: Was the kitchen door unlocked, allowing an intruder to come in, or did Nuala unlock the door herself to let someone she knew —someone she trusted—enter her home?

Sanctuary, Maggie thought. Our homes ought to offer us sanctuary. Had Nuala pleaded for her life? How long did she feel the blows that rained on her head? Chief Brower had said that he thought whoever had killed Nuala had been looking for something, and, from the look of things, might not have found it.

". . . and so we picked up immediately where we left off, went right back to being best friends," Greta continued. "Nuala told me she'd been widowed young and then remarried, and that the second marriage had been a terrible mistake, except for you. She was so soured on marriage that she said hell would freeze over before she'd try it again, but by then Tim was a widower, and they started going out. One morning she phoned and said, 'Gret, want to go ice-skating? Hell just froze over.' She and Tim were engaged. I don't think I ever saw her happier."

They arrived at the gate of the cemetery. A carved limestone angel with outstretched arms greeted them.

"The grave is to the left and up the hill," Mrs. Shipley said, "but of course you know that. You were here yesterday."

Yesterday, Maggie thought. Had it really been only yesterday?

They parked at the top of the hill, and with Maggie's hand tucked firmly under Greta Shipley's arm, they walked along the path that led to Nuala's grave. Already the ground had been smoothed over and resodded. The thick green grass gave the plot an air of soothing timelessness. The only sound was the rustle of the wind through the fall-colored leaves of a nearby maple.

Mrs. Shipley managed a smile as she placed flowers on the grave. "Nuala loved that big tree. She said when her time came she wanted plenty of shade so that her complexion wouldn't be ruined by too much sun."

They laughed softly as they turned to go. Then Greta hesitated. "Would I be imposing terribly if I asked you to stop for just a moment at the graves of some of my other friends? I saved a few flowers for them, too. Two are here in St. Mary's. The others are in Trinity. This road goes directly there. The cemeteries are side by side, and the north gate between them is always open during the day."

It didn't take long to make the five other stops. The headstone on the last grave was inscribed, "Constance Van Sickle Rhinelander." Maggie noted that the date of death was only two weeks ago.

"Was she a close friend?" Maggie asked.

"Not nearly as close as Nuala, but she lived in Latham Manor, and I had gotten to know her very well." She paused. "It's sudden, it's all so sudden," she said, then turned to Maggie and smiled. "I'd better get back. I'm afraid I'm a bit tired. It's so hard to lose so many people you care about."

"I know." Maggie put her arm around the older woman and realized just how frail she seemed.

On the twenty-minute drive back to the residence, Greta Shipley dozed off. When they reached Latham Manor, she opened her eyes and said apologetically, "I used to have so much energy. All my family did. My grandmother was still going strong at ninety. I'm beginning to think I'm being waited on too much."

As Maggie escorted her inside, Greta said hesitantly,

"Maggie, I hope you'll come to see me again before you leave. When are you going back to New York?"

Maggie surprised herself by answering firmly, "I was planning to stay two weeks and that's exactly what I'm going to do. I'll call you before the weekend and we'll make a date."

It was not until she got back to Nuala's house and put the kettle on that she realized something was troubling her. There was a kind of unease about Greta Shipley, and about their visit to the cemeteries. Something wasn't right. But what *was* it?

) 20

LIAM MOORE PAYNE'S OFFICE OVERLOOKED BOSTON COMmon. Since leaving his former brokerage house and opening his own investment firm, he had been overwhelmingly busy. The prestigious clients he had brought with him demanded and received his meticulous personal attention, earning him their complete confidence.

He had not wanted to phone Maggie too early, but when he did call, at 11:00 A.M., he was disappointed not to reach her. After that he had his secretary try her every hour, but it was nearly four o'clock when he finally heard the welcome news that Ms. Holloway was on the phone.

"Maggie, at last," he began, then stopped. "Is that a kettle I hear whistling?"

"Yes, hold on a minute, Liam. I was just fixing a cup of tea."

When she picked up the receiver again, he said, "I was afraid you might have made up your mind to go home. I wouldn't blame you for being nervous in that house."

"I'm careful about locking up," Maggie told him, then added almost without pause, "Liam, I'm glad you called. I've got to ask you something. Yesterday, after you brought my bags here, did you have a discussion with Earl about me?"

Liam's eyebrows raised. "As a matter of fact, I didn't. What makes you think I did?"

She told him about Earl's sudden appearance at the kitchen door.

"You mean he was just going to check the lock without even letting you know? You're kidding."

"No, I'm not. And I don't mind saying that he really frightened me. I was shaky enough as it was about being alone here, and then to have him just show up that way . . . Plus, he started quoting something about sorrow like joy leaping from mind to mind. It was weird."

"That's one of his favorite quotes. I don't think I've ever heard him give a lecture when he hasn't included it. It always gives me the creeps, too." Liam paused, then sighed. "Maggie, Earl is my cousin and I'm fond of him, but he *is* somewhat odd, and there's no question that he's obsessed with the subject of death. Do you want me to speak to him about that little visit to you?"

"No. I don't think so. But I'm going to have a locksmith put dead bolts on the doors."

"I'm selfish enough to hope that means you'll be staying in Newport for a while."

"At least the two weeks I had initially planned."

"I'll be down on Friday. Will you have dinner with me?"

"I'd like that."

"Maggie, get that locksmith in today, will you?"

72

"First thing in the morning."

"All right. I'll call you tomorrow."

Liam replaced the receiver slowly. How much should he tell Maggie about Earl, he wondered. He didn't want to overdo warning her, but still . . .

Clearly it was something he would have to think over.

☽ *21*

AT QUARTER OF FIVE, JANICE NORTON LOCKED THE DESK in her office at Latham Manor Residence. Out of habit, she tugged at the handle of each one of the drawers and confirmed that they were indeed secured. It was a safeguard that William Lane would have been wise to adopt, she thought sarcastically.

Lane's assistant, Eileen Burns, worked only until two each day, and after that Janice doubled as both bookkeeper and assistant. She smiled to herself, reflecting that her unquestioned access to Lane's office had been extremely useful over the years. Just now when she'd copied the information she wanted from two more files, she'd had a sense that she should hold off. Call it a premonition.

She shrugged. Well, she'd done it, and the copies were in her briefcase and the originals where they belonged in Lane's desk. It was ridiculous to get jumpy about it now.

Her eyes narrowed with secret satisfaction as she thought of the undisguisable shock on her husband's face when Irma Woods had told them about Nuala Moore's last-minute will.

What pleasure she had had since then, berating him about repaying the mortgage on their own house.

She knew, of course, that he wouldn't do any such thing. Malcolm was destined to wander forever through a field of broken dreams. It had taken her far too long to figure out that one, but working at Latham had been an eye-opener. Some of the guests there may not have had fancy backgrounds, but they had been born sucking on the proverbial silver spoon; they had never known a day's worry about money. Others were like Malcolm, blue bloods with lineage they could trace back past the Mayflower to the aristocracy, even to the crowned heads of Europe, passionately proud that they were the great-great-nephews or whatever, nine times removed, of the prince regent of some idiotic duchy.

However, the blue bloods at Latham differed from Malcolm in one very important way. They hadn't rested on their genealogical charts. They had gone out and made their own fortunes. Or married them.

But not Malcolm, she thought. Oh, no, not handsome, debonair, courtly, so-well-bred Malcolm! At her wedding, she had been the envy of her girlfriends—except for Anne Everett. On that day, in the yacht club powder room, she had overheard Anne refer to Malcolm disparagingly as the "ultimate Ken doll."

It was a remark that had burned into her mind, because even then, on what was supposed to be the happiest day of her life, dressed as she was, like a princess, in billowing yards of satin, she had realized it was true. To put it another way, *she had married the frog.* And then spent thirty-plus years trying to give reality the lie. What a waste!

Years of giving intimate dinners for clients and potential clients, only to see them take their lucrative accounts to other attorneys, leaving Malcolm with token bones to pick over. Now even most of *those* were gone.

And then the ultimate insult. Despite the way she had stuck by him all these years, knowing she would have done better to strike out on her own, yet clinging stubbornly to what little dignity she had left, she had realized that he was mooning over his secretary and planning to get rid of *her!*

If only he'd been the man I thought I married, Janice mused as she pushed back the chair and stood, flexing her stiff shoulders. Even better, if only he'd been the man *he* thinks he is! Then I really *would* have had a prince.

She smoothed the sides of her skirt, taking a modicum of pleasure from the feel of her slim waistline and narrow hips. In the early days, Malcolm had compared her to a thoroughbred, slender, with long neck, lean legs, and shapely ankles. A beautiful thoroughbred, he had added.

She *had* been beautiful when she was young. Well, look what that had gotten her, she thought ruefully.

At least her body was still in excellent shape. And not because of regular visits to spas and pleasant days at the golf course with her well-heeled friends. No, she had spent her adult life working, and working hard—first as a real estate agent, then for the last five years as bookkeeper in this place.

She remembered how, as a real estate agent, she used to salivate over properties that went for a song because people needed ready cash. How many times she had thought, "If only I had the money . . ."

Well, now she had it. Now she could call the shots. And Malcolm didn't even have a clue.

Not ever to have to set foot in this place again! she thought exultantly. Never mind the Stark carpet and brocaded draperies, even in the office area. It might be pretty, but it was still a nursing home—God's waiting room—and at fifty-four, she was hurtling rapidly toward the age when she would be a candidate for admittance herself. Well, she would get out of here long before that ever happened.

The phone rang. Before she picked up the receiver, Janice glanced around the room, checking lest someone might have tiptoed in behind her back.

"Janice Norton," she said sternly, holding the receiver close to her mouth.

It was the call she had hoped to receive. He didn't bother with a greeting. "Well, for once dear Malcolm got something straight," he said. "That Wetlands Act amendment absolutely will go through. That property will be worth a fortune."

She laughed. "Then isn't it time to make a counteroffer to Maggie Holloway?"

) 22

AFTER LIAM'S CALL, MAGGIE SAT AT THE KITCHEN TABLE, sipping tea and nibbling on some cookies she had found in the cupboard.

The box was almost full and looked as though it had been opened recently. She wondered if only a few nights ago Nuala had been sitting here sipping tea, eating cookies, planning her menu for the dinner party. She had found a shopping list next to the telephone: leg of lamb, green beans, carrots, apples, grapes, new potatoes, biscuit mix. And then there was a scribbled, typical Nuala note to herself: "Forgetting something. Look around store." And Nuala obviously forgot to bring the list.

It's funny, Maggie thought, but in an odd and certainly unexpected way, being here in Nuala's house is giving her back to me. I feel almost as though I've lived here with her all these years.

Earlier she had glanced through a photograph album she found in the living room, and realized that the pictures of Nuala with Timothy Moore began the year after Nuala and her father divorced.

She also found a smaller album filled with pictures of herself taken during the five years Nuala had been part of her life. On the back pages were taped all the notes she had written to Nuala in those years.

The unmounted picture at the very end was of Nuala and her father and herself on their wedding day. She had been beaming with joy to have a mother. The expression on Nuala's face had been just as happy. The smile on her father's lips, however, was reserved, questioning, just like him.

He wouldn't let her inside his heart, Maggie thought. I've always heard he was crazy about my mother, but she was dead, and wonderful Nuala was there. He was the big loser when she finally left because she couldn't stand his carping.

And I was the loser, too, she reflected as she put the cup and saucer in the dishwasher. The simple act brought back another memory, that of her father's annoyed voice: "Nuala, why is it so impossible to transfer dishes directly from the table to the dishwasher without first piling them in the sink?"

For a while, Nuala had cheerfully laughed about being genetically messy, but later she would say, "Dear God, Owen, this is the first time I've done that in three days."

And sometimes, she'd burst into tears and I'd run after her and put my arms around her, Maggie thought sadly.

It was four-thirty. The window over the sink framed the handsome oak tree that stood to the side of the house. It should be trimmed, Maggie thought. In a bad storm, those dead branches could break and land on the house. She dried her hands and turned away. But why worry about that? She wasn't going to stay here. She would sort out everything and earmark usable clothes and furniture for charity. If she started now, she could be done by the time she had to leave. Of course she would keep a few mementos for herself, but most things she would just get rid of. She supposed that after the will was probated, she would sell the house "as is," but she preferred that it be as empty as possible. She didn't want strangers going through Nuala's home and perhaps making sarcastic comments.

She began in Nuala's studio.

Three hours later, grimy from the dust of cabinets and countertops that had been cluttered and jammed with stiffened paint brushes, dried-up tubes of oils, paint rags, and small easels, Maggie had an impressive number of tagged trash bags lined up in a corner of the room.

And even though she had only made a start, just that much clearing up changed the appearance of the room for the better. Loyally, she reminded herself that Police Chief Brower had told her this space had been thoroughly ransacked. It was obvious that the cleaning service had not bothered to do more than shove as many items as possible back into the cabinets, and the spillover had been left on the countertops. The result was a sense of chaos that Maggie found disconcerting.

But the room itself was quite impressive. The floor-to-ceiling windows that seemed to be the only major alteration made in the house must let in wonderful northern light, Maggie thought. When Nuala had urged her to bring her sculpting materials with her, she had promised that she would find the long refectory table a perfect work area. Even though she was sure she wouldn't use them, to please

Nuala she had brought along a fifty-pound tub of wet clay, several armatures, the frameworks on which the figures would be constructed, and her modeling tools.

Maggie paused for a minute, wondering. On that table she could make a portrait head of Nuala. There were plenty of recent pictures of her around to use as models. As though I need them, Maggie thought. It seemed to her that Nuala's face would be forever imprinted in her mind. Except for visiting Greta and clearing out the house, she had no real plans. As long as I know I'm staying until a week from Sunday, it would be nice to have a project, she told herself, and what better subject than Nuala?

The visit to Latham Manor and the time she had spent with Greta Shipley had served to convince her that the uneasiness she thought she had perceived in Nuala was simply the result of her concern over the effects of radically changing her life by selling the house and moving to the residence. There doesn't seem to have been anything else weighing on her, she thought. At least, not that I can see.

She sighed. I guess there's no way I can be sure. But if it *was* a random break-in, wasn't it risky to kill Nuala, then take time to search the house? Whoever was here could smell the food cooking and see that the table was set for company. It would make sense that the killer would be terrified that someone might arrive while he was ransacking the house, she told herself. Unless that someone already knew dinner was scheduled for eight o'clock, and that I wouldn't be arriving until nearly that time.

A window of opportunity, she reasoned. There certainly had been one for a person who knew the plans for the evening—perhaps was even part of them.

"Nuala *wasn't* killed by a random thief," Maggie said aloud. Mentally she reviewed the people who had been expected at the dinner. What did she know about any of them? Nothing, really.

Except for Liam; he was the only one she really knew. It was only because of him that she had run into Nuala again, and for that she always would be grateful. I'm also glad he felt the way I did about his cousin Earl, she thought. His showing up here really gave me the creeps.

The next time she and Liam talked, she wanted to ask him about Malcolm and Janice Norton. Even in that quick moment this morning, when she had greeted Janice at Latham Manor, she could detect something amiss in the woman's expression. It looked like anger. Because of the canceled sale? Maggie wondered. But surely there were plenty of other houses like this one available in Newport. It couldn't be that.

Maggie walked over to the trestle table and sat down. She looked at her folded hands and realized they were itching for the feel of clay. Whenever she was trying to think something through, she found working in clay helped her to find the answer, or at least come to some kind of conclusion.

Something had bothered her today, something she had noticed subconsciously. It had registered mentally but had not made an impression at the moment. What could it have been? she asked herself. Moment by moment, she retraced her day from the time she got up, to the cursory inspection of the downstairs floor at Latham Manor and her appointment with Dr. Lane, to the drive with Greta Shipley to the cemeteries.

The cemeteries! Maggie sat up. That was it! she thought. That last grave they went to, of the Rhinelander woman, who died two weeks ago—I noticed something.

But what? Try as she might, she could not conceive of what had troubled her there.

In the morning, I'll go back to the cemeteries and look

around, she decided. I'll take my camera, and if I don't see exactly what it is, I'll take pictures. Maybe whatever it is that's nagging at me will show up when I develop them.

It had been a long day. She decided to bathe, scramble an egg, then go to bed and read more of the books about Newport.

On the way downstairs, she realized that the phone in Nuala's bedroom was ringing. She hurried to answer it but was rewarded by a decisive click at the other end.

Whoever it was probably didn't hear me, she thought, but it doesn't matter. There was no one with whom she wanted to talk right now.

The closet door in the bedroom was open, and the light from the hallway revealed the blue cocktail suit Nuala had worn to the reunion party at the Four Seasons. It was haphazardly draped over a hanger, as though carelessly put away.

The suit was expensive. A sense that it might be damaged if left that way made Maggie go over to the closet to rehang it properly.

In the course of straightening the fabric, she thought she heard a soft thud, as though something had dropped on the floor. She looked down into the cluttered array of boots and shoes in the closet bottom and decided that if something *had* fallen, it would just have to wait.

She closed the closet door and left the room, headed for her bath. The solitude she enjoyed on many evenings in her New York apartment was not appealing in this house with flimsy locks and dark corners, in this house where a murder had been committed—perhaps by someone whom Nuala had counted as a friend.

) *23*

EARL BATEMAN HAD NOT INTENDED TO DRIVE TO NEWPORT on Tuesday evening. It was while preparing for a lecture he would be delivering the following Friday that he realized that for illustrative purposes he needed some of the slides he kept in the museum on the grounds of the Bateman Funeral Home. The home of his great-great-grandfather, the narrow Victorian house and the acre it stood on had been separated from the main house and property ten years earlier.

Technically the museum was private and not open to the public. It could only be visited by written request, and Earl personally escorted the few visitors through it. In response to the derisive humor heaped on him by his cousins whenever they discussed "Death Valley"—as they called his little museum—his icy and knowingly humorless retort was that, historically, people of all cultures and breeding attached great importance to the rituals surrounding death.

Over the years, he had gathered an impressive array of materials, all having to do with death: slides and films; recorded funeral dirges; Greek epic poems; paintings and prints, such as the apotheosis picture of Lincoln being received into heaven; scale reproductions of the Taj Mahal and the pyramids; native mausoleums of brass-trimmed hardwood; Indian funeral pyres; present-day caskets; replicas of drums; conch shells, umbrellas, and swords; statues of riderless horses with reversed stirrups; and examples of mourning attire throughout the ages.

"Mourning Attire" was the subject of the lecture he was to deliver to members of a reading group that had just finished discussing an assortment of books on death rituals. For the occasion, he wanted to show them slides of the costumes in the museum.

Visuals always help make for a lively lecture, he decided, as he drove along Route 138, over the Newport Bridge. Until last year, the final slide used when he lectured on attire was an excerpt from the 1952 *Amy Vanderbilt's Etiquette Guide,* in which she instructed that patent-leather shoes were never appropriate at a funeral. Accompanying the text he had placed pictures of patent-leather shoes, from children's Mary Janes to ladies' pumps and men's bowed evening slippers, all, he felt, to whimsical effect.

But now he had thought of a new twist for ending the lecture. "I wonder what generations in the future will say of us when they see illustrations of widows in red miniskirts and family mourners in jeans and leather jackets. Will they perhaps read social and cultural custom of deep significance into these costumes, as we ourselves try to read it into the clothing of the past? And if so, wouldn't you like to have an opportunity to eavesdrop on their discussions?"

He liked that. It would lessen the uneasy reaction he always received when he discussed the fact that the Beerawan community dressed the widow or widower in rags, because of their belief that the soul of the dead person begins wandering immediately after cessation of breath and might reflect hostility to the living, even to those people the deceased had loved. Presumably the rags reflect grief and appropriately deep mourning.

At the museum, that thought had stayed with him as he collected the slides he wanted. He sensed a tension between the dead Nuala and the living Maggie. There was hostility to Maggie. She must be warned.

He knew Nuala's phone number from memory, and in the dim light of his museum office, he dialed it. He had just started to hang up when he heard Maggie's breathless greeting. Even so, he replaced the receiver.

She might think the warning odd, and he didn't want her to think he was crazy.

"I am *not* crazy," he said aloud. Then he laughed. "I'm not even odd."

) **24**

NEIL STEPHENS WAS NORMALLY ABLE TO GIVE HIS TOTAL, undivided attention to the shifting tides of the stock market. His clients, both corporate and private, swore by the accuracy of his predictions and his strong eye in discerning trends. But in the five days since he had been unable to reach Maggie, he had found himself distracted when he needed to be attentive, and as a result, needlessly sharp with his assistant, Trish.

Finally allowing her irritation to show, she put him in his place by raising her hand in a gesture that clearly said *stop*, and saying, "There's only one reason for a guy like you to be so grouchy. You're finally interested in someone, and she isn't buying it. Well, I guess I should say 'welcome to the real world,' but the fact is, I am sorry and so I'll try to be patient with your unnecessary carping."

After a feeble and unanswered "Who runs this place anyhow?" Neil retreated to his own office and renewed his memory search for the name of Maggie's stepmother.

The frustration from a nagging sense that something was wrong made him uncharacteristically impatient with two of his longtime clients, Lawrence and Frances Van Hilleary, who visited his office that morning.

Wearing a Chanel suit that Neil recognized as one of her favorites, Frances sat elegantly straight on the edge of a leather club chair in the "client-friendly conversation area" and told him of a hot tip on an oil-well stock they had received at a dinner party. Her eyes sparkled as she gave him the details.

"The company is based in Texas," she explained enthusiastically. "But ever since China opened to the West, they've been sending top engineers there."

China! Neil thought, dismayed, but leaned back, trying to give the appearance of listening with courteous attention while first Frances and then Lawrence talked excitedly of coming political stability in China, of pollution concerns there, of oil gushers waiting to be tapped, and of course, of fortunes to be made.

Doing rapid mental calculations, Neil realized with dismay that they were talking about investing roughly three quarters of their available assets.

"Here's the prospectus," Lawrence Van Hilleary concluded, pushing it at him.

Neil took the glossy folder and found the contents to be exactly what he had expected. At the bottom of the page, in print almost too small to read, were cautionary words to the effect that only those with at least half a million dollars in assets, excluding their residences, would be allowed to participate.

He cleared his throat. "Okay, Frances and Lawrence, you pay me for my advice. You are two of the most generous people I've ever dealt with. You've already given away a tremendous amount of money to your children and grandchildren and charities in the family limited partnership, real estate trust, generation-skipping trusts, and charitable IRAs. I firmly believe that what you have left for yourselves should not be wasted on this kind of pie-in-the-sky investment. It's much too high risk, and I'd venture to say that there is more oil dripping from the car in your garage than you'll ever see spurting from one of these so-called gushers. I couldn't with any conscience handle a transaction like this, and I beg you not to waste your money on it."

There was a moment of silence, broken by Frances who turned to her husband and said, "Dear, remind me to get the car checked."

Lawrence Van Hilleary shook his head, then sighed with resignation. "Thanks, Neil. There's no fool like an old fool, I guess."

There was a soft knock, and Trish came in carrying a tray with coffee. "Is he still trying to sell you that Edsel stock, Mr. Van Hilleary?"

"No, he just cut me off at the pass when I was about to buy it, Trish. That coffee smells good."

After discussing a few items in their investment portfolio, the subject changed to a decision the Van Hillearys were pondering.

"We're both seventy-eight," Lawrence said, glancing fondly at his wife. "I know we look pretty good, but there's no question that we can't do things we used to do even a few years ago . . . None of the kids live in the area. The house in Greenwich is expensive to maintain, and to top it off, our old housekeeper has just retired. We're seriously considering looking for a retirement community somewhere in New England. We'd still go down to Florida in the winter, but it might be nice to get rid of all the responsibilities of a house and grounds."

"Where in New England?" Neil asked.

"Perhaps the Cape. Or maybe Newport. We'd like to stay near the water."

"In that case, I might be able to do some scouting for you over the weekend." Briefly he told them how several of the women whose income tax his father handled had moved to Latham Manor Residence in Newport and were very happy there.

When they got up to go, Frances Van Hilleary kissed Neil's cheek. "No oil for the lamps of China, I promise. And let us know what you find out about the place in Newport."

"Of course." Tomorrow, Neil thought, tomorrow I'll be in Newport and maybe I'll bump into Maggie.

Fat chance! said a niggling voice in the back of his mind.

Then the brainstorm hit him. One night, when they had had dinner at Neary's, Jimmy Neary and Maggie had talked about her pending visit to Newport. She told Jimmy her stepmother's name, and he said something about it being one of the grandest of old Celtic names. Jimmy would remember, surely, he told himself.

A much happier Neil settled down to finish up the day's business. Tonight he would have dinner at Neary's, he decided, then go home and pack. Tomorrow he would head north.

At eight o'clock that evening, as Neil was contentedly finishing sautéed scallops and mashed potatoes, Jimmy Neary joined him. Mentally keeping his fingers crossed, Neil asked whether Jimmy could remember the name of Maggie's stepmother.

"Ah-hah," Jimmy said. "Give me a minute. It's a grand name. Let's see." Jimmy's cherubic face puckered in concentration. "Nieve ... Siobhan ... Maeve ... Cloissa ... no, none of those. It's—it's—by God, I've *got* it! Finnuala!

It means 'the fair one,' in Gaelic. And Maggie said the old girl's known as Nuala.''

"At least that's a start. I could kiss you, Jimmy," Neil said fervently.

A look of alarm crossed Jimmy's face. "Don't you dare!" he said.

☾ 25

MAGGIE HAD NOT EXPECTED TO SLEEP WELL, BUT WRAPPED as she was in the soft eiderdown quilt, her head burrowed in the goose-down pillows, she did not wake up until the phone rang at nine-thirty in the master bedroom.

Feeling clearheaded and refreshed for the first time in several days, she hurried to answer it, even taking note of the bright sunbeams that spilled into the room around the edges of the window shades.

It was Greta Shipley calling. Almost apologetically, she began, "Maggie, I wanted to thank you for yesterday. It meant so much to me. And please don't agree to this unless it's something you really want to do, but you mentioned that you wanted to collect the art supplies Nuala left here and, well . . . You see, we're allowed to invite a guest for dinner on a rotating basis. I thought that if you don't have any plans, you might consider joining me this evening."

"I don't have any plans at all, and I'd enjoy it very much," Maggie said sincerely. Then a sudden thought flashed through her mind, a kind of mental picture. The cemetery. Mrs. Rhinelander's grave. Or was it? Something had caught her attention there yesterday. But what? She'd have to go back. She thought it had been at Mrs. Rhinelander's grave, but if she were wrong, she would have to revisit all the other ones they had gone to.

"Mrs. Shipley," she said, "while I'm up here, I'm going to be taking some pictures around Newport for a project I'm working on. It may sound macabre, but St. Mary's and Trinity have such a tranquil, old-world feeling about them, they're perfect for my purposes. I know that some of the graves we left flowers on yesterday had beautiful vistas behind them. I'd like to go back there. Can you tell me which ones we visited?"

She hoped the hastily assembled excuse didn't sound too lame. But I *am* working on a project, she thought.

Greta Shipley, however, did not seem to find Maggie's request peculiar. "Oh, they are beautifully situated, aren't they?" she agreed. "Certainly, I can tell you where we went. Have you got a pen and paper handy?"

"Right here." Nuala had left a small writing pad and a pen next to the phone.

Three minutes later, Maggie had jotted down not only the names but specific directions to each plot. She knew she could locate the grave sites; now if she only knew what it was she hoped to find.

After hanging up, Maggie got out of bed, stretched, and decided on a quick shower to complete the wake-up process. A warm bath at night to put you to sleep, she thought, a cool shower to wake you up. I'm glad I wasn't born four hundred years ago. She thought of the line she had read in a book about Queen Elizabeth I: "The Queen takes a bath once a month whether she needs it or no."

The showerhead, obviously an addition to the beautiful claw-footed tub, provided a spray that was needle sharp and thoroughly satisfying. Wrapped in a chenille robe, her still-damp hair in a towel turban, Maggie went downstairs and fixed herself a light breakfast, which she carried back to her room to enjoy as she dressed.

Ruefully she realized that the casual clothes she had packed for the vacation with Nuala would not get her through her two-week stay here. This afternoon she would have to find a boutique or whatever and get herself an extra skirt or two and a couple of blouses or sweaters. She knew that dress at Latham Manor was a bit on the formal side, plus she had agreed to have dinner with Liam on Friday night, and that probably meant dressing up. Whenever she and Liam had been out to dinner in New York, he invariably chose fairly pricey restaurants.

Raising the shade, she opened the front window and felt the warm, gentle breeze that confirmed that after yesterday's chilly dampness, Newport was experiencing picture-perfect early fall weather. There would be no need for a heavy jacket today, she decided. A white tee shirt, jeans, a pullover blue sweater and sneakers were what she picked to wear.

When she was dressed, Maggie stood for a moment in front of the mirror that hung over the bureau, studying herself. Her eyes no longer held traces of the tears she had wept for Nuala. They were clear again. Blue. Sapphire blue. That's how Paul had described her eyes the night they met. It seemed a lifetime ago. She had been a bridesmaid at Kay Koehler's wedding; he had been a groomsman.

The rehearsal dinner was at the Chevy Chase Country Club, in Maryland, near Washington. He had sat next to her. We talked to each other all night, Maggie thought, remembering. Then, after the wedding, we danced practically every dance. When he put his arms around me, I felt as though I had suddenly come home.

They were both only twenty-three at the time. He was attending the Air Force Academy, she, just finishing the master's program at NYU.

Everyone said what a handsome couple we were, Maggie reminisced. A study in contrasts. Paul was so fair, with straight blond hair and ice-blue eyes, the Nordic look he said he had inherited from his Finnish grandmother. Me, the dark-haired Celt.

For five years after his death, she had kept her hair the way Paul liked it. Finally, last year, she had chopped off three inches; now it barely skimmed the collar line, but as a bonus the shorter length emphasized the bouncing natural curl. It also required a lot less fussing, and for Maggie that was paramount.

Paul also had liked the fact that she wore only mascara and almost-natural lipstick. Now, at least for festive occasions, she had a more sophisticated supply of makeup.

Why am I thinking about all this now? Maggie asked herself, as she prepared to leave for the morning. It was almost as though she were telling Nuala all about this, she realized. These were all the things that had happened in the years since they had seen each other, things she wanted to talk about with her. Nuala was widowed young. She would have understood.

Now, with a final silent prayer that Nuala would use her influence with her favorite saints so that Maggie might understand just *why* she was being compelled to go to the cemeteries, she picked up her breakfast tray and carried it back downstairs to the kitchen.

Three minutes later, after checking the contents of her shoulder bag, double locking the door, and getting her Nikon and camera equipment out of the car trunk, she was on her way to the cemeteries.

) 26

MRS. ELEANOR ROBINSON CHANDLER ARRIVED AT LATHAM
Manor Residence promptly at ten-thirty, the appointed time
for her meeting with Dr. William Lane.

Lane received his aristocratic guest with the charm and
courtesy that made him the perfect director and attending
physician for the residence. He knew Mrs. Chandler's history by heart. The family name was well known throughout
Rhode Island. Mrs. Chandler's grandmother had been one
of Newport's social grandes dames during the city's social
zenith in the 1890s. She would make an excellent addition
to the residence and very possibly attract future guests from
among her friends.

Her financial records, while impressive, were a shade
disappointing. It was obvious that she had managed to give
away a great deal of her money to her large family. Seventy-
six years old, she had clearly done her share to help populate
the earth: four children, fourteen grandchildren, seven great-
grandchildren, and no doubt more to come.

However, given her name and background, she might
well be persuaded to take the top apartment that had been
intended for Nuala Moore, he decided. It was clear that she
was used to the best.

Mrs. Chandler was dressed in a beige knit suit and low-
heeled pumps. A single strand of matched pearls, small pearl
earrings, a gold wedding band, and a narrow gold watch
were her only jewelry, but each item was superb. Her classic

features, framed by pure white hair, were set in a gracious, reserved expression. Lane understood full well that *he* was the one being interviewed.

"You *do* understand that this is only a preliminary meeting," Mrs. Chandler was saying. "I am not at all sure that I'm prepared to enter *any* residence, however attractive. I *will* say that from what I've seen so far, the restoration of this old place is in excellent taste."

Approbation from Sir Hubert is praise indeed, Lane thought sarcastically. He smiled appreciatively, however. "Thank you," he said. If Odile were here she would be gushing that, coming from Mrs. Chandler, such praise meant so much to them, and on and on.

"My eldest daughter lives in Santa Fe and very much wants me to make my home there," Mrs. Chandler continued.

But you don't want to go there, do you? Lane thought, and suddenly he felt much better. "Of course, having lived in this area so many years, it's a little hard to make such a complete change, I would think," he said sympathetically. "So many of our guests visit their families for a week or two, then are very glad to come back to the quiet and comfort of Latham Manor."

"Yes; I'm sure." Mrs. Chandler's tone was noncommittal. "I understand you have several units available?"

"As a matter of fact one of our most *desirable* units just became available."

"Who most recently occupied it?"

"Mrs. Constance Van Sickle Rhinelander."

"Oh, of course. Connie had been quite ill, I understand."

"I'm afraid so." Lane did not mention Nuala Moore. He would explain away the room that he had emptied for her art studio by saying that the suite was being totally redecorated.

They went up in the elevator to the third floor. For long

minutes, Mrs. Chandler stood on the terrace overlooking the ocean. "This *is* lovely," she conceded. "However, I believe this unit is five hundred thousand dollars?"

"That's correct."

"Well, I don't intend to spend that much. Now that I've seen this one, I would like to see your other available units."

She's going to try to bargain me down, Dr. Lane thought, and had to resist the urge to tell her that such a ploy was of absolutely no use. The cardinal rule of all Prestige Residences was absolutely no discounts. Otherwise, fury resulted, because the word of special deals always got around to those who hadn't gotten them.

Mrs. Chandler rejected out of hand the smallest, the medium-size, and then the largest single bedroom apartments. "None of these will do. I'm afraid we're wasting each other's time."

They were on the second floor. Dr. Lane turned to see Odile walking toward them, arm in arm with Mrs. Pritchard, who was recovering from foot surgery. She smiled at them, but to Lane's relief did not stop. Even Odile occasionally knew when not to barge in, he thought.

Nurse Markey was seated at the second-floor desk. She looked up at them with a bright, professional smile. Lane was itching to get to her. This morning Mrs. Shipley had told him she intended to have a dead bolt put on her door to insure privacy. "That woman regards a closed door as a challenge," she had snapped.

They passed Mrs. Shipley's studio apartment. A maid had just finished cleaning it, and the wide door was open. Mrs. Chandler glanced in and stopped. "Oh, this is lovely," she said sincerely, as she absorbed the large alcove seating area with the Renaissance fireplace.

"Step in," Dr. Lane urged. "I know Mrs. Shipley won't mind. She's at the hairdresser's."

"Just this far. I feel like an intruder." Mrs. Chandler took in the bedroom section and the magnificent ocean views on three sides of the unit. "I think this is preferable to the largest suite," she told him. "How much is a unit like this?"

"Three hundred and fifty thousand dollars."

"Now *that* I would pay. Is there another like it available? For that price, of course?"

"Not at the moment," he said, then added, "But why don't you fill out an application?" He smiled at her. "We'd very much like to have you as a guest someday."

) 27

DOUGLAS HANSEN SMILED INGRATIATINGLY ACROSS THE table at Cora Gebhart, a peppery septuagenarian who was clearly enjoying the scallops over braised endive she had ordered for lunch.

She was a talker, he thought, not like some of the others that he'd had to shower with attention before he could elicit any information from them. Mrs. Gebhart was opening up to him like a sunflower to the sun, and he knew that by the time the espresso was served, he would have a good chance of winning her confidence.

"Everyone's favorite nephew," one of these women had called him, and it was just the way he wanted to be perceived: the fondly solicitous thirty-year-old, who extended to them all the little courtesies they hadn't enjoyed for years.

Intimate, gossipy luncheons at a restaurant that was either upscale gourmet like this one, Bouchard's, or a place like the Chart House, where great views could be enjoyed over excellent lobster. The lunches were followed up with a box of candy for the ones who ordered sweet desserts, flowers for those who confided stories of their long-ago courtships, and even an arm-in-arm stroll on Ocean Drive for a more recent widow who wistfully confided how she and her late husband used to take long walks every day. He knew just how to do it.

Hansen had great respect for the fact that all of these women were intelligent, and some of them were even shrewd. The stock offerings he touted to them were the kind that even a moderate investor would have to admit had possibilities. In fact, one of them had actually worked out, which in a way had been disastrous for him, but in the end turned out to be a plus. Because now, in order to cap his pitch, he would suggest that a would-be client call Mrs. Alberta Downing in Providence, that she could confirm Hansen's expertise.

"Mrs. Downing invested one hundred thousand dollars and made a three-hundred-thousand-dollar profit in one week," he was able to tell prospective clients. It was an honest claim. The fact that the stock had been artificially inflated at the last minute, and that Mrs. Downing had ordered him to sell, going against his own advice, had seemed like a disaster at the time. They had had to raise the money to pay her her profits, but now at least they had a genuine blue-blood reference.

Cora Gebhart daintily finished the last of her meal. "Excellent," she announced as she sipped at the chardonnay in her glass. Hansen had wanted to order a full bottle, but she had informed him adamantly that one glass at luncheon was her limit.

Douglas laid his knife on the plate and carefully placed the fork beside it with prongs turned down, European style.

Cora Gebhart sighed. "That's the way my husband always left the silver on his plate. Were you educated in Europe as well?"

"I spent my junior year at the Sorbonne," Hansen responded with studied nonchalance.

"How delightful!" Mrs. Gebhart exclaimed, and immediately slipped into flawless French, which Douglas desperately tried to follow.

After a few moments, he held up his hand, smiling. "I can read and write French fluently, but it has been eleven years since I was there, and I'm afraid I'm a bit rusty. *En anglais, s'il vous plaît.*"

They laughed together, but Hansen's antenna went up. Had Mrs. Gebhart been testing him? he wondered. She had commented on his handsome tweed jacket and his overall distinguished appearance, saying it was unusual in a time when so many young men, her grandson included, looked as though they had just returned from a camping trip. Was she telling him in a subtle way that she could see right through him? That she could sense that he wasn't really a graduate of Williams and the Wharton School of Business, as he claimed?

He knew that his lean, blond, aristocratic appearance was impressive. It had gotten him entry-level jobs with both Merrill Lynch and Salomon Brothers, but he hadn't lasted six months at either place.

Mrs. Gebhart's next words reassured him, however. "I think I've been too conservative," she complained. "I've tied up too much of my money in trusts so my grandchildren can buy more faded jeans. Because of that, I don't have a lot left for myself. I've thought about moving into one of the retirement residences—I even recently toured Latham Manor with that in mind—but I would have to move into one of the smaller units, and I'm just used to more space."

She paused, then looked Hansen squarely in the face. "I'm thinking favorably about putting three hundred thousand dollars in the stock you recommended."

He tried not to let his emotions register on his face, but it was a struggle. The amount she mentioned was considerably more than he had hoped for.

"My accountant is opposed to it, of course, but I'm beginning to think he's a fuddy-duddy. Do you know him? His name is Robert Stephens. He lives in Portsmouth."

Hansen did know the name. Robert Stephens took care of the taxes for Mrs. Arlington, and she had lost a bundle investing in a high-tech company he had recommended.

"But I pay him to do my taxes, not to run my life," Mrs. Gebhart continued, "so without discussing it with him, I'm going to cash in my bonds and let you make me a killing, too. Now that the decision is made, maybe I *will* have that second glass of wine."

As the midafternoon sun bathed the restaurant in golden warmth, they toasted each other.

) 28

MAGGIE SPENT ALMOST TWO HOURS AT ST. MARY'S AND Trinity cemeteries. Funerals were taking place in some of the areas she wanted to photograph, so in each case she waited until the mourners had departed before taking out her camera.

The beautiful warm day ran counter to her chilling quest, but she persevered, revisiting all the graves she had been to with Greta Shipley, and taking pictures from every angle.

Her initial hunch had been that she had detected something odd at Mrs. Rhinelander's grave, which had been the last they had visited. For that reason she reversed the order she and Mrs. Shipley had followed yesterday, starting with the Rhinelander plot and ending at Nuala's grave.

It was at this final stop that a young girl of about eight or nine appeared and stayed nearby, watching her intently.

When Maggie finished shooting a roll of film, she turned to the little girl. "Hi, I'm Maggie," she said. "What's your name?"

"Marianne. What do you want to take pictures here for?"

"Well, I'm a photographer and I do some special projects, and this is one I'm working on."

"Do you want to take a picture of my grandfather's grave? It's right over there." She pointed off to the left, where Maggie could see several women standing by a tall headstone.

"No, I don't think so. I'm actually done for the day. But thank you. And I'm sorry about your grandfather."

"Today's his third anniversary. He got married again when he was eighty-two. Mom says that woman wore him out."

Maggie tried not to smile. "That happens sometimes, I guess."

"My dad said that after fifty years with Grandma, at least he had some fun for two years. The lady he was married to has a new boyfriend now. Dad says *he's* probably got only a couple years left."

Maggie laughed. "I think your dad must be fun."

"He is. Okay, I gotta go. Mom's waving to me. See you."

It was a conversation Nuala would have enjoyed, Maggie

reflected. What *am* I looking for? she asked herself as she stared down at the grave. The flowers Greta Shipley had left were starting to wilt, but otherwise, this plot looked exactly like the others. Even so, she shot one more roll of film, just to be safe.

The afternoon passed quickly. Consulting the map on the passenger seat, Maggie drove into the center of Newport. Because as a professional photographer she always preferred to do her own developing, it was with real reluctance she dropped off her rolls of film at a drugstore. But realistically there was no other way. She hadn't brought any of her darkroom equipment with her; it would have been just too complicated for so brief a trip. After securing a promise that her pictures would be ready the next day, she had a burger and a Coke at the Brick Alley Pub, then found a boutique on Thames Street where she was able to find two cowl-necked sweaters—one white, one black—two long skirts and a cream-colored tapered jacket with matching slacks. Used in combination with what she had, these additions to her wardrobe would take care of anything that might come up in Newport for the next ten days. And besides, she really liked them.

Newport is special, she thought as she drove along Ocean Drive, back to Nuala's house.

My house, she amended, still surprised at the realization. Malcolm Norton had had an agreement with Nuala to buy the house, that Maggie knew. He said he wanted to talk with me, she reflected. Of course it has to be about the house. Do I *want* to sell it? she asked herself. Last night I'd have said, "Probably." But now, at this moment, with that glorious ocean and this lovely, quaint town on this special island, I'm not so sure.

No. If I had to make up my mind right now, she thought, I *wouldn't* sell it.

) 29

AT FOUR-THIRTY, NURSE ZELDA MARKEY WAS RELIEVED from duty and reported as directed to the office of Dr. William Lane. She knew she was going to be called on the carpet, and she knew why: Greta Shipley had complained about her. Well, Nurse Markey was ready for Dr. Lane.

Look at him, she thought contemptuously, as he frowned across the desk at her. I bet he can't tell the difference between measles and chicken pox. Or palpitations and congestive heart failure.

He was frowning, but the telltale beads of perspiration on his forehead told Nurse Markey exactly how uncomfortable he was with this session. She decided to make it easier for him because she was well aware that the best defense was always a good offense.

"Doctor," she began, "I know exactly what you're going to say: Mrs. Shipley has complained that I walk in on her without knocking. The fact is, Mrs. Shipley is doing a great deal of sleeping, much more than she did even a few weeks ago, and I've been a little concerned. It's probably just the emotional response to the death of her friends, but I assure you that I open that door without invitation *only* when there is no response to repeated knocking."

She saw the flicker of uncertainty in Lane's eyes before he spoke. "Then I would suggest, Miss Markey, that if Mrs. Shipley does not respond after a reasonable period, you open the door slightly and call in to her. The fact is she's becoming quite agitated about this, and I want to head it off before it becomes a real problem."

"But, Dr. Lane, if I had not been in her room two nights ago when she had that spell, something terrible might have happened."

"The spell passed quickly, and it turned out to be nothing. I do appreciate your concern, but I can't have these complaints. Do we understand each other, Miss Markey?"

"Of course, Doctor."

"Is Mrs. Shipley planning to be at dinner this evening?"

"Oh, yes, she'll not only be there, but she's having a guest, Miss Holloway, the stepdaughter of Mrs. Moore. Mrs. Lane was told about that. She said that Miss Holloway is going to collect Mrs. Moore's art supplies while she is here."

"I see. Thank you, Miss Markey."

As soon as she had left, Lane picked up the phone to call his wife at home. When she answered, he snapped, "Why didn't you tell me Maggie Holloway would be having dinner here tonight?"

"What difference could that possibly make?" Odile asked in a puzzled tone.

"The difference is—" Lane closed his lips and took a deep breath. Certain things were better left unsaid. "I want to know about any guests who are at dinner," he said. "For one thing, I want to be there to greet them."

"I know that, dear. I arranged for us to dine in the residence tonight. Mrs. Shipley declined rather ungraciously when I suggested that she and her guest join us at our table. But at least you'll be able to chat with Maggie Holloway at the social hour."

"All right." He paused, as though there was more he wanted to say but had changed his mind. "I'll be home in ten minutes."

"Well, you had better be if you want to freshen up." Odile's trilling laugh set Lane's teeth on edge.

"After all, darling," she continued, "if the rules insist that the guests be dressed for dinner, I think the director and his wife should at least set a good example. Don't you?"

) *30*

EARL BATEMAN KEPT A TINY APARTMENT ON THE HUTCH-inson campus. He found the small liberal arts college, situated in a quiet section of Providence, an ideal spot from which to do research for his lectures. Overshadowed by the other institutions of higher learning in the area, Hutchinson nonetheless had excellent standards, and Earl's class in anthropology was considered a major attraction there.

"Anthropology: The science that deals with the origins, physical and cultural development, racial characteristics, and social customs and beliefs of mankind." Earl began any new term by having his students memorize those words. As he was fond of repeating, the difference between many of his colleagues and himself was that he felt true knowledge of any people or culture began with the study of their rituals of death.

It was a subject that never failed to fascinate him. Or his listeners, as demonstrated by the fact that he was increasingly in demand as a speaker. In fact several national speakers bureaus had written to offer him substantial fees to be the luncheon or dinner speaker at events as far as a year and a half away.

He found their correspondence most gratifying: "From what we understand, Professor, you really make even the subject of death very entertaining," was typical of the letters he received regularly. He also found their response rewarding. His fee for such engagements was now three thousand dollars, plus expenses, and there were more offers than he could accept.

On Wednesdays, Earl's last class was at 2:00 P.M., which today gave him the rest of the afternoon to polish his speech for a women's club, and to answer his mail. One letter he had received recently intrigued him to the point that he could not get it off his mind.

A cable station had written to ask whether he felt he had sufficient material to do a series of half-hour, illustrated television programs on the cultural aspects of death. The remuneration would not be significant perhaps, but they had pointed out that similar exposure had proven beneficial to a number of their other hosts.

Sufficient material? Earl thought sarcastically, as he propped his feet on the coffee table. Of *course* I have sufficient material. Death masks, for example, he thought. I've never spoken on that topic. The Egyptians and Romans had them. The Florentines began to make them in the late fourteenth century. Few people realize that a death mask exists of George Washington, his calm and even noble face in permanent repose, with no hint of his ill-fitting wooden teeth that in life marred his appearance.

The trick was always to inject an element of human interest so that the people discussed were not perceived as objects of macabre interest but as sympathetic fellow humans.

The subject of tonight's lecture had led Earl to thinking

of many other possibilities for lectures. Tonight, of course, he would talk about mourning attire through the ages. But his research had made him realize that etiquette books were a rich source of other material.

Some Amy Vanderbilt dictums he included were her half-century-ago advice on muffling the clapper on the doorbell for the protection of the bereaved, and avoiding the use of words such as "died," "death," or "killed" in notes of sympathy.

The clapper! The Victorians had a horror of being buried alive and wanted a bell hung over the grave, with a string or wire threaded through an air vent into the coffin so that the person inside could ring in case he or she wasn't really dead. But he wouldn't, *couldn't,* touch *that* subject again.

Earl knew he had or could find enough material for any number of programs. He was about to become famous, he mused. He, Earl, the family joke, would show them all—those sprawling, raucous cousins, those misbegotten descendants of a crazed, avaricious thief who had cheated and schemed his way to wealth.

He felt his heart begin to pound. Don't think about them! he warned himself. Concentrate on the lecture, and on developing subjects for the cable program. There was another topic he had been pondering, one that he knew would be extremely well received.

But first . . . he would have a drink. Just *one,* he promised himself, as he prepared a very dry martini in his combination kitchen-dinette. As he took the first sip, he reflected on the fact that often before death someone close to the soon-to-be-deceased experienced a premonition, a kind of uneasiness or warning of what was to come.

When he sat down again, he removed his glasses, rubbed his eyes, and leaned his head back on the convertible couch that also served as his bed.

Someone close . . . "Like *me*," he said aloud. "I'm not really that close to Maggie Holloway, but I sense that she isn't close to *anyone*. Maybe that's why I'm the one who has been given the premonition. I know that Maggie is going to die very soon, just as I was sure last week that Nuala had only hours to live."

Three hours later, to the enthusiastic applause of the audience, he began his lecture with a beaming and somewhat incongruous smile. "We don't want to talk about it, but we're all going to die. Occasionally the date is deferred. We've all heard of people who were clinically dead, then returned to life. But other times the gods have spoken and the biblical prophecy, *'Ashes to ashes, dust to dust,'* is fulfilled."

He paused, while the audience hung on his words. Maggie's face filled his mind—that cloud of dark hair surrounding the small, exquisite features, dominated by those beautiful, pain-filled blue eyes . . .

At least, he consoled himself, soon she won't experience any more pain.

) *31*

ANGELA, THE SOFT-SPOKEN MAID WHO HAD ADMITTED HER yesterday, showed Maggie the supply closet where Nuala's art materials were kept. Typical of Nuala, she thought affectionately. They had been piled on the shelves haphazardly, but with Angela's help, it didn't take long to get them into boxes and, with the assistance of a kitchen helper, stowed in Maggie's car.

"Mrs. Shipley is waiting for you in her apartment," the maid told her. "I'll take you to her now."

"Thank you."

The young woman hesitated for a moment, looking around the large activity room. "When Mrs. Moore had her classes here, everyone had such a good time. It didn't matter that most of them couldn't draw a straight line. Just a couple of weeks ago, she began by asking everyone to remember a slogan from World War II, the kind that were on posters hanging everywhere. Even Mrs. Shipley joined in, despite the fact that she had been so upset earlier that day."

"Why was she upset?"

"Mrs. Rhinelander died that Monday. They were good friends. Anyhow, I was helping to pass out materials, and they came up with different slogans like, 'Keep 'em Flying,' which Mrs. Moore sketched—a flag flying behind an airplane—and everyone copied it. And then someone suggested 'Don't Talk, Chum. Chew Topps Gum.' "

"*That* was a slogan?" Maggie exclaimed.

"Yes. Everybody laughed, but as Mrs. Moore explained, it was meant as a serious warning to people who worked in defense industries not to say anything that a spy might overhear. It was such a lively session." Angela smiled reminiscently. "It was the last class Mrs. Moore taught. We all miss her. Well, I'd better take you up to Mrs. Shipley," she said.

Greta Shipley's warm smile when she saw Maggie did not disguise the fact that there was a grayish pallor under her eyes and around her lips. Maggie noticed too that when she stood up, she had to rest her hand on the arm of the chair for support. She seemed tired, and distinctly weaker than she had just yesterday.

"Maggie, how *lovely* you look. And how kind of you to come on such short notice," Mrs. Shipley said. "But we have a very pleasant group at the table, and I do think you'll enjoy them. I thought we'd have an aperitif here before we join the others."

"That would be nice," Maggie agreed.

"I hope you like sherry, I'm afraid that's all I have."

"I do like sherry."

Unbidden, Angela went to the sideboard, poured the amber liquid from a decanter into antique crystal glasses, and served them both. Then she quietly left the room.

"That girl is a *treasure*," Mrs. Shipley said. "So many little courtesies that would never occur to most of the others. Not that they're not well trained," she added quickly, "but Angela is special. Did you collect Nuala's art supplies?"

"Yes, I did," Maggie told her. "Angela helped me, and she was telling me about one of Nuala's classes that she sat in on, the one where you all drew posters."

Greta Shipley smiled. "Nuala was positively *wicked!* When she and I came up here after the class, she took my drawing—which, of course, was pretty bad—and added her own touches to it. You must see it. It's in that second drawer," she said, pointing to the table next to the sofa.

Maggie opened the drawer indicated and removed the heavy sheet of sketching paper. Looking at it, she felt a sudden chill. Mrs. Shipley's original sketch vaguely resembled one defense worker with a hard hat talking to another on a train or bus. Behind them a long-faced figure in a black cape and hat was obviously eavesdropping.

Nuala had drawn what was clearly her face and Greta Shipley's over those of the defense workers. The image of a nurse with narrowed eyes and an outsized ear floated above the spy.

"Does this represent anyone here?" Maggie asked.

Mrs. Shipley laughed. "Oh, yes. That dreadful sneak, Nurse Markey. Although that day I thought it *was* just a joke, all her snooping around. But now I'm not so sure."

"Why is that?" Maggie asked quickly.

"I don't know," she said. "Maybe I'm just getting to be a bit fanciful. Old ladies do that sometimes, you know. Now I think we really should go downstairs."

Maggie found the grand salon to be a wonderfully attractive room, rich in both design and furnishings. The air was filled with the buzzing of well-bred voices that emanated from handsome senior citizens who were seated about the room. From what Maggie could see, they ranged in age from late sixties to late eighties, although Greta whispered that an attractive woman in a black velvet suit, with a ramrod straight back and lively eyes, had just turned ninety-four.

"That's Letitia Bainbridge," she whispered. "People told her she was crazy to pay four hundred thousand dollars for an apartment when she came here six years ago, but she said that with the genes in her family, the money would be well spent. And, of course, time has proven her right. She'll be at our table, and you'll enjoy her, I promise.

"You'll notice that the staff serves the guests without asking what they want," Mrs. Shipley continued. "Most guests are allowed by the doctor to have a glass of wine or a cocktail. Those who aren't are served Perrier or a soft drink."

A lot of careful planning created this place, Maggie thought. I can see why Nuala thought seriously of living here. She remembered that Dr. Lane had said he was sure Nuala would have reinstated her application if she had lived.

Glancing around, Maggie noticed that Dr. Lane and his wife were approaching. Odile Lane was wearing an aqua silk shirt and matching long skirt, an outfit Maggie had seen in the boutique where she herself had shopped. On the other occasions when she had seen Mrs. Lane—the night Nuala died and at the funeral—she hadn't really focused on her. Now she realized that Odile was actually a beautiful woman.

Then she acknowledged to herself that even though he was balding and somewhat portly, Dr. Lane was attractive as well. His demeanor was both welcoming and courtly. When he reached her, he took Maggie's hand and raised it to his lips, stopping just before they touched it, in the European fashion.

"What a *great* pleasure," he said, his tone resonating with sincerity. "And may I say that even in one day you look considerably more rested. You're obviously a very strong young woman."

"Oh, darling, must you always be so clinical?" Odile Lane interrupted. "Maggie, it's a pleasure. What do you think of all this?" She waved her hand in an all-encompassing gesture, obviously indicating the elegant room.

"I think that compared to some of the nursing homes I've photographed, it's heaven."

"Why did you choose to photograph nursing homes?" Dr. Lane asked.

"It was an assignment for a magazine."

"If you ever wanted to do a 'shoot' here—that *is* the expression, isn't it?—I'm sure it could be arranged," he offered.

"I'll certainly keep that in mind," Maggie replied.

"When we learned you were coming, we so hoped to have you sit at our table," Odile Lane said and then sighed, "but Mrs. Shipley wasn't having any of it. She said she wanted you with *her* friends, at her *usual* table." She wagged her finger at Greta Shipley. "Naughty, naughty," she trilled.

Maggie saw Mrs. Shipley's lips tighten. "Maggie," she said abruptly, "I want you to meet some of my other friends."

A few minutes later soft chimes announced that dinner was being served.

Greta Shipley took Maggie's arm as they walked down the corridor to the dining room, and Maggie couldn't help but notice a distinct quiver in her movement.

"Mrs. Shipley, are you sure you don't feel ill?" Maggie asked.

"No, not a bit. It's just that it's such a pleasure to have you here. I can see why Nuala was so happy and excited when you came back into her life again."

There were ten tables in the dining room, each with place settings for eight people. "Oh, tonight they're using the Limoges china and the white linen," Mrs. Shipley said with satisfaction. "Some of the other settings are a little too elaborate for my taste."

Another beautiful room, Maggie thought. From what she had read of this mansion, the original banquet table for this room had seated sixty people.

"When the house was renovated and refurbished, the draperies were copied from the ones in the state dining room of the White House," Mrs. Shipley told her as they took their seats. "Now, Maggie, you must meet your dinner companions."

Maggie was seated at Greta Shipley's right. The woman next to her was Letitia Bainbridge, who opened the conversation by saying, "You're so pretty. I understand from Greta that you're not married. Is there anyone special in your life?"

"No," Maggie said with a smile, as the familiar ache stabbed at her.

"Excellent," Mrs. Bainbridge said decisively. "I have a grandson I'd like to introduce to you. When he was a teenager I used to think he was a bit dim. Long hair and a guitar, all that. Dear God! But now, at thirty-five, he's everything anyone could hope for. He's president of his own company, doing something important with computers."

"Letitia the matchmaker," one of the others said, laughing.

"I've met the grandson. Forget it," Greta Shipley whispered to Maggie, then in a normal tone introduced her to the others—three women and two men. "I managed to snare the Buckleys and the Crenshaws for our table," she said. "One problem in any of these places is that they tend to become a pavilion of women, so that getting any male conversation becomes a struggle."

It proved to be an interesting, lively group at the table, and Maggie kept asking herself why Nuala had changed her mind so abruptly about living here. Surely she wouldn't have done it because she thought I needed the house, she reasoned. She knew Dad left me a little money, and I can take care of myself. Then why?

Letitia Bainbridge was particularly amusing as she told stories of Newport when she was young. "There was so much Anglomania then," she said, sighing. "All the mothers were anxious to marry their daughters off to English nobility. Poor Consuelo Vanderbilt—her mother threatened to commit suicide if she didn't marry the Duke of Marlborough. She finally did, and stuck it out for twenty years. Then she divorced him and married a French intellectual, Jacques Balsan, and was finally happy.

"And there was that dreadful Squire Moore. Everyone knew he came from nothing, but to hear him talk he was a direct descendant of Brian Boru. But he *did* have a bit of charm, and at least the pretense of a title, so of course he married well. And I suppose there isn't much difference between impoverished nobility marrying an American heiress and an impoverished Mayflower descendant marrying a self-made millionaire. The difference is that Squire's god *was* money and he'd do anything to accumulate it. And unfortunately, that characteristic has shown up in a number of his descendants."

It was over dessert that Anna Pritchard, who was recovering from a hip operation, joked, "Greta, when I was walking with Mrs. Lane this morning, guess who I saw? Eleanor Chandler. She was with Dr. Lane. Of course, I know she didn't recognize me, so I didn't say anything to her. But she was admiring your apartment. The maid had just cleaned it, and the door was open."

"Eleanor Chandler," Letitia Bainbridge mused. "She went to school with my daughter. A rather forceful person, if I'm not mistaken. Is she thinking of coming here?"

"I don't know," Mrs. Pritchard said, "but I can't imagine any other reason she'd be looking around. Greta, you'd better change your locks. If Eleanor wants your apartment, she'd think nothing of having you dispossessed."

"Let her try," Greta Shipley said with a hearty laugh.

When Maggie left, Mrs. Shipley insisted on walking her to the door.

"I wish you wouldn't," Maggie urged. "I know you're rather tired."

"Never mind. I'll have my meals sent up tomorrow and give myself a lazy day."

"Then I'm going to call you tomorrow, and I'd better find you doing just that."

Maggie kissed the soft, almost translucent cheek of the older woman. "Till tomorrow," she said.

) 32

IN THE SIX DAYS SINCE NUALA MOORE HAD BEEN FOUND murdered in her home, Chief of Police Chet Brower's initial instinct had become a certainty, at least in his own mind. No random thief had committed that crime, of that he was now sure. It *had* to be someone who knew Mrs. Moore, probably someone she trusted. But who? And what was the motive? he asked himself.

It was Brower's habit to think through such questions out loud with Detective Jim Haggerty. On Thursday morning, he called Haggerty into his office to review the situation.

"Mrs. Moore may have left her door unlocked, and in that case *anyone* could have walked in. On the other hand, she might very well have opened it for someone she knew. Either way, there was no sign of forced entry."

Jim Haggerty had worked with Brower for fifteen years. He knew he was being used as a sounding board, so while he had his own opinions, he would wait to share them. He had never forgotten overhearing a neighbor describe him once, saying, "Jim may look more like a grocery clerk than a cop, but he *thinks* like a cop."

He knew that the remark was meant as a compliment of sorts. He also knew that it wasn't totally unjustified—his mild, bespectacled appearance was not exactly a Hollywood casting director's image of a supercop. But that disparity sometimes worked to his advantage. His benign demeanor tended to make people more comfortable around him, so they relaxed and talked freely.

"Let's proceed on the premise that it *was* someone she knew," Brower continued, his brow creased with thought. "That opens the suspect list to nearly everyone in Newport. Mrs. Moore was well liked and active in the community. Her latest project was to give art lessons at that Latham Manor place."

Haggerty knew that his boss did not approve of Latham Manor or of places like it. He was bothered by the idea of senior citizens investing that much nonrefundable money in a kind of gamble that they would live long enough to make the investment worthwhile. His own opinion was that since Brower's mother-in-law had been living with him for almost twenty years now, the chief was just plain envious of anyone whose parent could afford to live out her declining years in a luxurious residence instead of her child's guest bedroom.

"But I think we can eliminate most of Newport by considering the fact that whoever killed Mrs. Moore, and then ransacked her house, could hardly help seeing the preparations she'd been making for a dinner party," Brower mused.

"The table was set—" Haggerty began, then quickly closed his lips. He had interrupted his boss.

Brower's frown deepened. "I was getting to that. So that means that whoever was in the house wasn't worried that somebody might arrive on the scene any minute. Which means that it is a good chance the killer will turn out to be one of the dinner guests we talked to in the neighbor's house Friday night. Or less likely, someone who knew when the guests were expected."

He paused. "It's time to take a serious look at all of them. Wipe the slate clean. Forget what we know about them. Start from scratch." He leaned back. "What do you think, Jim?"

Haggerty proceeded carefully. "Chief, I had a hunch you might be thinking along those lines, and you know how I like to pass the time of day with people, so I did a little looking in that direction already. And I think I've turned up a few things that might be interesting."

Brower eyed him speculatively. "Go on."

"Well, I'm sure you saw the expression on the face of that pompous windbag, Malcolm Norton, when Mrs. Woods told us about the will change and the canceled sale."

"I saw it. What I'd call shock and dismay, heavily tinged with anger."

"You know it's common knowledge that Norton's law practice is down to dog bites and the kind of divorces that involve splitting the pickup truck and the secondhand car. So it interested me to find out where he'd get the kind of money he'd need to buy Mrs. Moore's house. I also unearthed a little gossip about him and his secretary, a woman named Barbara Hoffman."

"Interesting. So where *did* he get the money?" Brower asked.

"By mortgaging his own house, which is probably his biggest asset. Maybe his *only* asset. Even talked his wife into co-signing."

"Does she know he has a girlfriend?"

"From what I gather, that woman misses nothing."

"Then why would she jeopardize their one mutual asset?"

"That's what *I'd* like to know. I talked to someone at Hopkins Realtors—and got their opinion on the transaction. Frankly they were surprised that Norton was willing to pay two hundred thousand for the Moore place. According to them, the house needs a total overhaul."

"Does Norton's girlfriend have money?"

"No. Everything I could find out indicated that Barbara Hoffman's a nice woman, a widow who raised and educated her kids alone, and who has a modest bank balance." Haggerty forestalled the next question. "My wife's cousin is a teller at the bank. Hoffman deposits fifty dollars in her savings account twice a month."

"The question then is why did Norton want that house? Is there oil on the property?"

"If there is, he can't touch it. The section of the property on the water side is designated wetland. The buildable part of the lot is small, which restricts even enlarging the house much, and unless you're on the top floor, you don't have a view."

"I think I'd better have a talk with Norton," Brower said.

"I'd suggest having a talk with his wife, too, Chief. Everything I learned indicates she's too shrewd to be talked into mortgaging her house without a very good reason, and it would have to be one that will benefit *her*."

"Okay, it's as good a place as any to start." Brower stood up. "By the way, I don't know if you've seen the background check we did on Maggie Holloway. It would appear she's clean. Her father apparently left her a little money, and she seems to be very successful as a photographer, bringing down fairly big bucks, so there's no money motive on her part that I can see. And there's no question that she's telling the truth about what time she left New York. The doorman at her apartment building verified it."

"I'd like to have a chat with her," Haggerty offered. "Mrs. Moore's phone bill shows that she talked to Maggie Holloway a half-dozen times in the week before the murder. Maybe something Moore told her about the people she was inviting to the dinner would come out, something that might give us a lead."

He paused, then added, "But, Chief, you know the thing that's driving me nuts is not having any idea what Nuala Moore's murderer was looking for when he or she ransacked that house. I'll bet my bottom dollar that's the key to this crime."

) 33

MAGGIE AWOKE EARLY BUT WAITED UNTIL ELEVEN BEFORE she phoned Greta Shipley. She had been deeply concerned about how frail Greta had seemed last evening, and hoped that she had gotten a good night's sleep. There was no answer in the room. Maybe Mrs. Shipley is feeling much better and went downstairs, she told herself.

The telephone rang fifteen minutes later. It was Dr. Lane. "Maggie, I have very sad news," he said. "Mrs. Shipley had asked not to be disturbed this morning, but an hour ago Nurse Markey thought it best to check on her anyway. Sometime last night, she died peacefully in her sleep."

* * *

Maggie sat for a long time after the phone call, numb with sadness, but also angry at herself for not being more insistent that Mrs. Shipley get a medical opinion—an *outside* medical opinion—to determine what was wrong. Dr. Lane said that all indicators pointed to heart failure. Clearly she had not felt well all evening.

First Nuala; now Greta Shipley. Two women, best friends, now both dead in one week, Maggie thought. She had been so excited, so happy to have Nuala back in her life. And now this . . .

Maggie thought of the time when Nuala had first given her a jar of wet clay. Although she was only six, Nuala recognized the fact that if Maggie had any particular artistic talent, it was not as a painter. "You're no Rembrandt," Nuala had said, laughing. "But just seeing you play with that crazy plastic clay, I have a hunch . . ."

She had propped up a picture of Maggie's miniature poodle, Porgie, in front of her. "Try to copy him," she had instructed. That had been the beginning. Ever since, Maggie had enjoyed a love affair with sculpting. Early on, however, she had realized that as satisfying as it was artistically, for her it could only be a hobby. Fortunately she also had an interest in photography—in which she proved to be genuinely talented—and so she had made that her career. But her passion for sculpting had never left her.

I still remember how wonderful it felt to put my hands in that clay, Maggie thought as, dry-eyed, she climbed the stairs to the third floor. I was clumsy with it, but I recognized something was happening, that with clay there was a connection from my brain to my fingers.

Now with the news of Greta Shipley's death, something that still hadn't really sunk in, Maggie knew she had to get her hands into wet clay. It would be therapeutic, and it would also give her a chance to think, to try to work out what she should do next.

She began work on a bust of Nuala but soon realized that it was Greta Shipley's face that now filled her mind.

She had looked so pale last night, Maggie remembered. She rested her hand on the chair when she got up, and then took my arm when we walked from the grand salon in to dinner; I could feel how weak she was. Today she had intended to stay in bed. She wouldn't admit it, but she was feeling ill. And the day we went to the cemeteries, she talked about feeling as if she was being waited on too much, as if she had no energy.

That's the way it happened to Dad, Maggie remembered. His friends told her that, pleading fatigue, he had skipped a scheduled dinner with them and had gone to bed early. He never woke up. Heart failure. Exactly what Dr. Lane said happened to Greta.

Empty, she thought. I feel so empty. It was no use trying to work now. She felt no inspiration. Even the clay was failing her.

Dear God, she thought, another funeral. Greta Shipley had never had children, so probably there would be mostly friends in attendance.

Funeral. The word jogged her memory. She thought of the pictures she had taken at the cemeteries. Certainly they would be developed by now. She should pick them up and study them. But study them for what? She shook her head. She didn't have the answer yet, but she was sure there was one.

She had left the rolls of film at a drugstore on Thames Street. As she parked the car, she reflected how only yesterday, just down the block, she had bought an outfit to wear to last night's dinner with Greta. How less than a week ago, she had driven up to Newport, so excited about her visit with Nuala. Now both women were dead. Was there some connection? she asked herself.

The thick packet of prints was waiting for her at the photography counter at the back of the drugstore.

The clerk raised his eyes when he looked at the bill. "You *did* want all of these enlarged, Ms. Holloway?"

"Yes, that's right."

She resisted the urge to open the packet immediately. When she got home she would go right upstairs to the studio and study the photos carefully.

When she arrived at the house, however, she found a late-model BMW backing out of her driveway. The driver, a man who appeared to be about thirty, hastily pulled out to make room for her. He then parked on the street, got out of his car, and was already walking up the driveway as Maggie opened her car door.

What does he want? she wondered. He was well dressed, good looking in an upscale sort of way, so she felt no sense of insecurity. Still, his aggressive presence bothered her.

"Miss Holloway," he said, "I hope I didn't startle you. I'm Douglas Hansen. I wanted to reach you, but your phone number isn't listed. So, since I had an appointment in Newport today, I thought I'd swing by and leave you a note. It's on the door."

He reached in his pocket and handed her his card: Douglas Hansen, Investment Advisor. The address was in Providence.

"One of my clients told me about Mrs. Moore's passing. I didn't really know her, but I'd met her on several occasions. I wanted to tell you how sorry I was, but also to ask you if you're planning to sell this house."

"Thank you, Mr. Hansen, but I haven't made any decision," Maggie said quietly.

"The reason I wanted to speak to you directly is that before you list the place with a realtor, if indeed you do decide to sell, I have a client who would be interested in acquiring it through me. Her daughter is planning a divorce and wants to have a place to move to when she breaks the news to her husband. I know there's a lot of work to be done here, but the mother can afford that. Her name is one you would recognize."

"Probably not. I don't know many Newport people," Maggie said.

"Then let's say that many people would recognize the name. That's why they have asked me to act as intermediary. Discretion is very important."

"How do you even know that the house is mine to sell?" Maggie asked.

Hansen smiled. "Miss Holloway, Newport is a small town. Mrs. Moore had many friends. Some of them are my clients."

He's expecting me to ask him in to discuss this whole thing, Maggie thought, but I'm not going to do it. Instead she said, noncommittally, "As I told you, I have made no decision as yet. But thank you for your interest. I'll keep your card." She turned and started walking toward the house.

"Let me add that my client is willing to pay two hundred and fifty thousand dollars. I believe that that amount is significantly higher than the offer Mrs. Moore was prepared to accept."

"You seem to know a great deal, Mr. Hansen," Maggie said. "Newport must be a *very* small town. Thank you again. I will call if I decide to sell." Again she turned toward the house.

"Just one more thing, Miss Holloway. I have to ask you not to mention this offer to anyone. Too many people would guess the identity of my client, and it could become a significant problem for her daughter.''

''You needn't worry. I'm not in the habit of discussing my business with anyone. Good-bye, Mr. Hansen.'' This time she moved briskly up the walk. But obviously he was intent on slowing her down. ''That's quite a stack of photographs,'' he said, indicating the package under her arm as she looked back once more. ''I understand you're a commercial photographer. This area must be a wonderland for you.''

This time Maggie did not answer, but with a dismissive nod, she turned and crossed the porch to the door.

The note Hansen had mentioned had been wedged in next to the door handle. Maggie took it without reading it, then slipped the key into the lock. When she looked out the living room window, she saw Douglas Hansen driving away. Suddenly she felt terribly foolish.

Am I starting to jump at my own shadow? she asked herself. That man must have thought I was a fool, the way I scurried in here. And I certainly can't ignore his offer. If I *do* decide to sell, that's fifty thousand dollars more than Malcolm Norton offered Nuala. No wonder he looked so upset when Mrs. Woods told us about the will—he knew he was getting a bargain.

Maggie went directly upstairs to the study and opened the envelope containing the photographs. It didn't help her state of mind that the first one her eye fell on was of Nuala's grave, and on it the now fading flowers Greta Shipley had left lying at the base of the tombstone.

) 34

AS NEIL STEPHENS TURNED HIS CAR IN TO THE DRIVEWAY that led to his parents' home, he took in the trees that lined the property, their leaves now ablaze with the gold and amber, the burgundy and cardinal red colors of fall.

Coming to a stop, he admired as well the fall plantings around the house. His father's new hobby was gardening, and each season he displayed a new array of flowers.

Before Neil could get out of the car, his mother had flung open the side door of the house and rushed out. As he stepped out, she hugged him, then reached up to smooth his hair, a familiar gesture he remembered from childhood.

"Oh, Neil, it's *so* good to see you!" she exclaimed.

His father appeared behind her, his smile an indication of his pleasure at seeing his son, although his greeting was somewhat less effusive. "You're running late, pal. We tee up in half an hour. Your mother has a sandwich ready."

"I forgot my clubs," Neil said, then relented when he saw his father's horrified expression. "Sorry, Dad, that was a joke."

"And not funny. I had to talk Harry Scott into switching starting times with us. If we want to play eighteen holes, we've got to be there by two. We're having dinner at the club." He clasped Neil's shoulder. "Glad you're here, son."

It was not until they were on the back nine of the golf course that his father opened the subject he had mentioned on the phone. "One of the old girls whose income tax I handle is on the verge of a nervous breakdown," he said. "Some young fellow in Providence talked her into investing in some fly-by-night stock, and now she's lost the money that was supposed to take care of her later. She had hoped to move into that fancy retirement residence I told you about."

Neil eyed his shot and selected a club from the bag the caddie was holding. Carefully he tapped the ball, swung, then nodded with satisfaction as it rose in the air, soaring over the pond and landing on the green of the next hole.

"You're better than you used to be," his father said approvingly. "But you'll notice I went farther on the green using an iron."

They talked as they walked to the next hole. "Dad, what you just told me about that woman is something I hear all the time," Neil said. "Just the other day a couple whose investments I've been handling for ten years came in all fired up and wanting to pour most of their retirement income into one of the craziest harebrained schemes I've ever come across. Fortunately I was able to dissuade them. Apparently this woman didn't consult with anyone, right?"

"Certainly not with me."

"And the stock was on one of the exchanges, or was it over the counter?"

"It was listed."

"And it had a brief, fast run-up, and then dropped like a stone. And now it isn't worth the paper it was written on."

"That's about it."

"You've heard the expression, 'There's a sucker born every minute.' For some reason that goes double in the market; otherwise fairly bright people go brain dead when someone gives them a hot tip."

"In this instance I think there was some kind of extraordinary pressure applied. Anyhow, I wish you'd talk to her.

Her name is Laura Arlington. Maybe you can go over the rest of her portfolio with her and see what she can do to enhance her remaining income. I told her about you, and she said she'd like to talk to you."

"I'd be glad to, Dad. I just hope it's not too late."

At six-thirty, dressed for dinner, they sat on the back porch, sipping cocktails and looking out at Narragansett Bay.

"You look great, Mom," Neil said with affection.

"Your mother's always been a pretty woman, and all the tender loving care she's received from me over the last forty-three years has only enhanced her beauty," his father said. Noticing the bemused expression on their faces, he added, "What are you two smiling at?"

"You know full well I've also waited on you hand and foot, dear," Dolores Stephens replied.

"Neil, are you still seeing that girl you brought up here in August?" his father asked.

"Who was that?" Neil wondered momentarily. "Oh, Gina. No, as a matter of fact I'm not." It seemed the right time to ask about Maggie. "There is someone I've been seeing who's visiting her stepmother in Newport for a couple of weeks. Her name is Maggie Holloway; unfortunately she left New York before I got her phone number here."

"What's the stepmother's name?" his mother asked.

"I don't know her last name, but her first name is unusual. Finnuala. It's Celtic, I believe."

"That sounds familiar," Dolores Stephens said slowly, searching her memory. "Does it to you, Robert?"

"I don't think so. No, that's a new one on me," he told her.

"Isn't it funny. I feel as though I've heard that name

recently," Dolores mused. "Oh well, maybe it will come to me."

The phone rang. Dolores got up to answer it.

"Now no long conversations," Robert Stephens warned his wife. "We've got to leave in ten minutes."

The call, however, was for him. "It's Laura Arlington," Dolores Stephens said as she handed the portable phone to her husband. "She sounds terribly upset."

Robert Stephens listened for a minute before speaking, his voice consoling. "Laura, you're going to get yourself sick over this. My son, Neil, is in town. I've spoken to him about you, and he will go over everything with you in the morning. Now promise me you'll calm yourself down."

) 35

EARL BATEMAN'S LAST CLASS BEFORE THE WEEKEND HAD been at 1:00 that afternoon. He had stayed in his campus apartment for several hours, grading papers. Then, just as he was about to leave for Newport, the phone rang.

It was his cousin Liam, calling from Boston. He was surprised to hear from Liam. They had never had much in common. What's this all about? he asked himself.

He responded to Liam's hearty attempts at general conversation with monosyllabic answers. It was on the tip of his tongue to tell him about the cable series, but he knew it would only become yet another family joke. Maybe he should invite Liam over for a drink and leave the latest three-thousand-dollar check from the speakers bureau where he couldn't miss seeing it. Good idea, he decided.

But then he felt anger build as Liam gradually got to the point of the call, the gist of which was that if Earl was going to Newport for the weekend, he shouldn't just drop in on Maggie Holloway. His visit the other day had upset her.

"Why?" Earl spat out the word, his irritation growing.

"Look, Earl, you think you can analyze people. Well, I've known Maggie for a year. She's a terrific girl—in fact, I hope I can soon make her realize just how special she is to me. But I promise you she's not the kind who's going to cry on someone's shoulder. She's *contained*. She's not one of your prehistoric cretins, mutilating herself because she's unhappy."

"I lecture about tribal customs, not prehistoric cretins," Earl said stiffly. "And I stopped in to see her because of genuine concern that she, like Nuala, might carelessly leave the door unlocked."

Liam's voice became soothing. "Earl, I'm not saying this right. What I'm trying to tell you is that Maggie isn't *fey*, the way poor old Nuala was. It isn't necessary to warn her, especially when it comes out more like a threat. Look, why don't we have a drink over the weekend."

"Fine." He'd shove the check under Liam's nose. "Come over to my place tomorrow night around six," Earl said.

"Not good. I'm having dinner with Maggie. How about Saturday?"

"All right, I guess. See you then."

So he's interested in Maggie Holloway after all, Earl thought as he hung up the phone. One would never have guessed it from the way he left her by herself at the Four Seasons party. But that was typical of Liam the glad-hander, he reasoned. He did know one thing for certain, though: If *he'd* been seeing Maggie for a year, he would have paid much more attention to her.

Once again a strange feeling came over him, a premonition that something was about to go wrong, that Maggie Holloway was in danger, the same sensation he'd had last week regarding Nuala.

The first time Earl had had such a premonition was when he was sixteen. He had been in the hospital at the time, recovering from an appendix operation. His best friend, Ted, stopped in to see him on his way to an afternoon of sailing.

Something had made Earl want to ask Ted not to go out on the boat, but that would have sounded stupid. He remembered how all afternoon he had felt as though he were waiting for an ax to fall.

They found Ted's boat two days later, adrift. There were a number of theories as to what had gone wrong, but there were never any answers.

Earl, of course, never talked about the incident, nor about his failure to give his friend a warning. And now Earl didn't ever let himself think about the other times the presentiment had come.

Five minutes later, he set off on the thirty-six-mile drive to Newport. At four-thirty he stopped at a small store in town to pick up some groceries, and it was there that he heard about the death of Greta Shipley.

"Before she went to live in Latham Manor, she used to do her shopping here," the store's elderly owner, Ernest Winter, said regretfully. "A real nice lady."

"My mother and father were friends of hers," Earl said. "Had she been ill?"

"From what I hear, she wasn't feeling well the last couple of weeks. Two of her closest friends died recently, one at Latham Manor, and then Mrs. Moore was murdered. I guess that really got to her. That can happen, you know. Funny I should remember it, but I recall years ago Mrs. Shipley told me that there was a saying, 'Death comes in threes.' Looks like she was right. Kind of gives you the chills, though."

Earl picked up his packages. Another interesting lecture topic, he thought. *Is it possible that there is a psychological basis for that expression as there is for so many others? Her close friends were gone. Did something in Greta Shipley's spirit cry out to them, "Wait! I'm coming too!"*

That made two new topics he had come up with just today for his lecture series. Earlier, he had come across a newspaper item about a new supermarket about to open in England where the bereaved could select all the necessary trappings for a funeral—casket, lining, clothing for the deceased, flowers, guest book, even the grave site, if necessary —and thereby eliminate the middleman, the funeral director.

It's a good thing the family got out of the business when they did, Earl decided as he said good-bye to Mr. Winter. On the other hand, the new owners of the Bateman Funeral Home had handled Mrs. Rhinelander's funeral, Nuala's funeral, and would undoubtedly handle Greta Shipley's funeral, too. It was only appropriate, since his father had taken care of her husband's final arrangements.

Business is booming, he thought ruefully.

☽ 36

AS THEY FOLLOWED JOHN, THE *MAÎTRE D'*, INTO THE YACHT club dining room, Robert Stephens stopped and turned to his wife. "Look, Dolores, there's Cora Gebhart. Let's go by her table and say hello. Last time we talked, I'm afraid I was a little harsh with her. She was going on about cashing in some bonds for one of those crazy venture schemes, and I got so irritated I didn't even ask her what it was, just told her to forget it."

Ever the diplomat, Neil thought, as he dutifully trailed in his parents' footsteps as they crossed the restaurant, although he also noted that his father did not signal their detour to the *maître d'*, who was blithely heading for a window table, unaware that he had lost the Stephens family.

"Cora, I owe you an apology," Robert Stephens began expansively, "but first I don't think you've ever met my son, Neil."

"Hello, Robert. Dolores, how are you?" Cora Gebhart looked up at Neil, her lively eyes warm and interested. "Your father brags about you all the time. You're the head of the New York office of Carson & Parker, I understand. Well, it's a pleasure to meet you."

"Yes, I am, and thank you, it's nice to meet you, too. I'm glad to hear my father brags about me. Most of my life he's been second-guessing me."

"I can understand that. He's always second-guessing me,

too. But Robert, you don't owe me an apology. I asked for your opinion and you gave it."

"Well, that's fine. I'd hate to hear that another one of my clients lost her shirt investing in high-risk flings."

"Don't worry about this one," Cora Gebhart responded.

"Robert, poor John is waiting with the menus at our table," Neil's mother urged.

As they threaded their way through the room, Neil wondered whether his father had missed the tone Mrs. Gebhart used when she said not to worry about her. Dollars to donuts, she didn't take his advice, Neil thought.

They had finished their meal and were lingering over coffee when the Scotts stopped by their table to say hello.

"Neil, you owe Harry a word of thanks," Robert Stephens said by way of introduction. "He switched tee-off times with us today."

"Didn't matter," Harry Scott responded. "Lynn was in Boston for the day, so we planned on a late dinner anyway."

His wife, stocky and pleasant faced, asked, "Dolores, do you remember meeting Greta Shipley at a luncheon here for the Preservation Society? It was three or four years ago, I think. She sat at our table."

"Yes, I liked her very much. Why?"

"She died last night, in her sleep, apparently."

"I'm so sorry."

"What upsets me," Lynn Scott continued contritely, "is that I'd heard that she had lost two close friends recently, and I'd been meaning to call her. One of the friends was that poor woman who was murdered in her home last Friday. You must have read about that. Her stepdaughter from New York discovered the body."

"Stepdaughter from New York!" Neil exclaimed.

Excitedly, his mother interrupted him. *"That's* where I

read that name. It was in the newspaper. *Finnuala*. Neil, she was the woman who was murdered!"

When they got back home, Robert Stephens showed Neil the neatly bound newspapers in the garage, waiting for re-cycling. "It was in Saturday's paper, the 28th," his father told him. "I'm sure it's in that pile."

"The reason I didn't remember the name right away was that in the article they called her Nuala Moore," his mother said. "It was only somewhere toward the end of the article that her complete first name was mentioned."

Two minutes later, with increasing dismay, Neil was read-ing the account of Nuala Moore's death. As he did, his mind kept replaying the happiness in Maggie's eyes when she told him about finding her stepmother again, and the plans she had made to visit her.

"She gave me the five happiest years of my childhood," she had said. *Maggie, Maggie,* Neil thought. Where was she now? Had she gone back to New York? He quickly called her apartment, but her phone message was unchanged—she would be gone until the 13th.

The address of Nuala Moore's home was in the newspa-per account of the murder, but when he called information, he was told that the phone there was unlisted.

"Damn!" he exclaimed as he snapped the receiver back on the cradle.

"Neil," his mother said softly. "It's quarter of eleven. If this young woman is still in Newport, whether at that house or somewhere else, it's no time to go looking for her. Drive over there in the morning, and if you don't find her there, then try the police station. There's a criminal investigation taking place, and since she discovered the body, the police will certainly know where to reach her."

"Listen to your mother, son," his father said. "Now, you've had a long day. I suggest you pack it in."

"I guess so. Thanks, both of you." Neil kissed his mother, touched his father's arm and walked dejectedly into the hallway that led to the bedrooms.

Dolores Stephens waited until her son was out of earshot, then quietly said to her husband, "I have a feeling Neil has finally met a girl he really cares about."

) 37

EVEN A PAINSTAKING EXAMINATION OF EACH OF THE ENlarged photographs did not reveal to Maggie anything on those graves that should have troubled her subconscious so greatly.

They all looked the same, showed the same things: headstones with varying degrees of plantings around them; grass still velvety green in this early fall season, except Nuala's, which had sod that showed some patchy spots.

Sod. For some reason that word struck a note with her. Mrs. Rhinelander's grave must have been freshly sodded as well. She had died only two weeks earlier.

Once more, Maggie studied all the photographs of Constance Rhinelander's grave, using a magnifying glass to pore over every inch of them. The only thing that attracted her attention was a small hole showing in the plantings around the headstone. It looked as though a rock or something might have been removed from there. Whoever had taken it had not bothered to smooth over the earth.

She looked again at the best close-ups she had of the tombstone at Nuala's grave. The sod there was smooth to the point where the plantings began, but in one of the shots she thought she could detect something—a stone?—just behind the flowers Greta Shipley had left yesterday. Was whatever it was there simply because the earth had been carelessly sifted for clods and stones after the interment, or was it perhaps a cemetery marker of some sort? There was an odd glint . . .

She studied the pictures of the other four graves but could see nothing on any of them that should have attracted her attention.

Finally she laid the prints down on a corner of the refectory table and reached for an armature and the pot of wet clay.

Using recent pictures of Nuala she'd found around the house, Maggie began to sculpt. For the next several hours, her fingers became one with clay and knife as she began to shape Nuala's small, lovely face, suggesting the wide, round eyes and full eyelashes. She insinuated the signs of age in the lines around the eyes, and around the mouth and neck, and in the shoulders that curved forward.

She could tell that when she was done, she would have succeeded in catching those traits she had so loved in Nuala's face—the indomitable and merry spirit behind a face that on someone else might have been merely pretty.

Like Odile Lane, she thought, and then winced at the memory of how the woman had wagged her finger at Greta Shipley barely twenty-four hours ago. "Naughty, naughty," she had said.

As she cleaned up, Maggie thought about the people she had dined with last evening. How distressed they must be, she thought. It was obvious how much they enjoyed Greta, and now she is gone. So suddenly.

Maggie looked at her watch as she went downstairs. Nine o'clock: not really too late to phone Mrs. Bainbridge, she decided.

Letitia Bainbridge answered on the first ring. "Oh, Maggie, we're all heartsick. Greta hadn't been feeling well for a few weeks, but till then she was perfectly fine. I knew she was on blood pressure and heart medicine, but she'd been on them for years and never had any problems."

"I came to like her so much in such a short time," Maggie said sincerely. "I can imagine how all of you must feel. Do you know what the arrangements are?"

"Yes. Bateman Funeral is handling them. I guess we'll all end up there. The Requiem is Saturday morning at eleven at Trinity Episcopal Church, and interment is at Trinity Cemetery. Greta had left instructions that the only viewing was to be at Bateman's between nine and ten-thirty."

"I'll be there," Maggie promised. "Did she have any family?"

"Some cousins. I gather they're coming. I know that she left her securities and the contents of her apartment to them, so they certainly should show that much respect for her." Letitia Bainbridge paused, then added, "Maggie, do you know what has haunted me? Practically the last thing I said to Greta last night was that if Eleanor Chandler had been seen eyeing her apartment, then she should change her locks."

"But she was amused by the remark," Maggie protested. "Please, you mustn't let that upset you."

"Oh, that's not what upsets me. It's the fact that I'd bet anything, no matter who else may be on the list, Eleanor Chandler gets that place now."

I'm specializing in late dinners, Maggie thought, as she put on the kettle, scrambled some eggs and dropped bread into the toaster—and not particularly exciting ones, she added. At least tomorrow night I can count on Liam to buy me a good meal.

It would be good to see him, she reflected. He was always fun in an outrageous kind of way. She wondered if he had talked to Earl Bateman about his unexpected visit Monday night. She hoped so.

Not wanting to spend any more time in the kitchen, she prepared a tray and carried it into the living room. Even though Nuala had met her death in this room less than a week ago, Maggie had come to realize that for Nuala this had been a happy, warm room.

The back and sides of the fireplace were blackened with soot. The bellows and tongs on the hearth showed signs of frequent use. Maggie could imagine having roaring fires here on cold New England evenings.

The bookcases were overflowing with books, interesting titles all of them, many familiar, others she would love to explore. She had already gone through the photo albums— the dozens of snapshots of Nuala with Tim Moore showed two people who obviously enjoyed each other's company.

Larger, framed pictures of Tim and Nuala—boating with friends, picnicking, at formal dinners, on vacations—were scattered on the walls.

The deep, old club chair with the hassock probably had been his, Maggie decided. She remembered that whether engrossed in a book, chatting, or watching television, Nuala had always liked to curl up, kitten-like, on the couch, propped in a corner between the back and armrest.

No wonder the prospect of moving to Latham Manor had proven daunting, Maggie thought. It would be quite a wrench for Nuala to leave this home where obviously she had been happy for so many years.

But clearly she had considered moving there. That first

evening, when they had had dinner after they met at the Moore reunion, Nuala had mentioned that the kind of apartment she wanted in the residence home had just become available.

What apartment *was* it? Maggie wondered. They had never discussed that.

Maggie realized suddenly that her hands were trembling. She carefully replaced the teacup on the saucer. *Could the apartment that had become available to Nuala possibly be the one that had belonged to Greta Shipley's friend Constance Rhinelander?*

) 38

ALL HE ASKED FOR WAS A LITTLE QUIET, BUT DR. WILLIAM Lane knew he was not going to be granted that wish. Odile was as wound up as a top about to spin. He lay in bed with his eyes closed, wishing to God that at least she would turn off the damn light. But instead she sat at her dressing table, brushing her hair as a torrent of words poured from her lips.

"These days are so trying, aren't they? Everyone just loved Greta Shipley, and she *was* one of our charter members. You know, that's two of our sweetest ladies in as many weeks. Of course, Mrs. Rhinelander was eighty-three, but she'd been doing so well—and then, all of a sudden, you could see her start to fail. That's the way it happens at a certain age, isn't it? Closure? The body just closes down."

Odile did not seem to notice that her husband did not respond. It didn't matter; she continued anyway. "Of course,

Nurse Markey was concerned about that little spell Mrs. Shipley had Monday night. This morning she told me she spoke to you about it again yesterday."

"I examined Mrs. Shipley right after she had that spell," Dr. Lane said wearily. "There was no reason for alarm. Nurse Markey brought up that episode only because she was trying to justify the fact that she'd been barging into Mrs. Shipley's apartment without knocking."

"Well, of course, you're the doctor, dear."

Dr. Lane's eyes flew open with sudden realization. "Odile, I don't want you discussing my patients with Nurse Markey," he said sharply.

Ignoring the tone of his voice, Odile continued, "That new medical examiner is quite young, isn't she? What was her name, Lara Horgan? I didn't know that Dr. Johnson had retired."

"He retired as of the first. That was Tuesday."

"I wonder why anyone would choose to be a medical examiner, especially such an attractive young woman? But she does seem to know her business."

"I doubt if she'd have been appointed if she didn't know her business," he responded tartly. "She stopped in with the police only because she was in the neighborhood and wanted to see our layout. She asked very competent questions about Mrs. Shipley's medical history. Now, Odile, if you don't mind, I really must get some sleep."

"Oh, darling, I'm sorry. I know how tired you are, and how upsetting this day has been." Odile put down the brush and took off her robe.

Ever the glamour girl, William Lane thought as he watched his wife's preparations for bed. In eighteen years of marriage, he had never seen her wear a nightgown that wasn't frilly. At one time she had charmed him. No longer, though—not for years.

She got into bed, and at last the light went out. But now William Lane was no longer sleepy. As usual, Odile had managed to say something that would gnaw at him.

That young medical examiner *was* a different cut from good old Dr. Johnson. He had always approved death certificates with a casual wave of his pen. *Be careful,* Lane warned himself. In the future, you've got to be more careful.

) *39*

WHEN MAGGIE FIRST AWOKE ON FRIDAY MORNING, SHE squinted at the clock and saw that it was only six. She knew she probably had had enough sleep, but she wasn't yet willing to get up, so she closed her eyes again. About half an hour later she fell into an uneasy sleep in which vague, troublesome dreams came and went, then faded altogether when she woke up again at seven-thirty.

She arose feeling groggy and headachy and decided that a brisk, after-breakfast walk along Ocean Drive would probably help clear her head. I need that, she thought, especially since I've got to go to the cemeteries again this morning.

And tomorrow you'll be at Trinity Cemetery for Mrs. Shipley's funeral, an interior voice reminded her. For the first time, Maggie realized that Mrs. Bainbridge had said that Greta Shipley was being buried there. Not that that made a difference. She would have gone to both cemeteries today no matter what. After spending so much time going over those photographs last night, she was anxious to see what was causing the odd glint she detected on Nuala's grave.

She showered, dressed in jeans and a sweater, and had a quick juice and coffee before she went out. Maggie was immediately glad she had made the decision to take the walk. The early fall day was magnificent. The sun was brilliant as it rose in the sky, though there was a cool ocean breeze that made her thankful she had reached for her jacket. There was also the glorious sound of the crashing waves, and the unique, wonderful scent of salt and sea life that filled the air.

I could fall in love with this place, she thought. Nuala spent her summers here when she was a girl. How she must have missed this when she moved away from it.

After a mile, Maggie turned and retraced her steps. Looking up, she realized that only a glimpse of the third floor of Nuala's house—*my* house, she thought—showed from the road. There are too many trees around it, she told herself. They should come down or at least be trimmed. And I wonder why the end of the property that would afford a drop-dead view of the ocean has never been built on. Could there be restrictions against building there?

The question nagged at her as she finished her walk. I really should look into that, she thought. From what Nuala told me, Tim Moore bought this property at least fifty years ago. Haven't there been any changes in building restrictions since then? she wondered.

Back at the house, she paused only long enough to have another quick cup of coffee before she left promptly at nine. She wanted to get the cemetery visits over with.

❯ *40*

AT QUARTER PAST NINE, NEIL STEPHENS STOPPED HIS CAR in front of the mailbox with the name MOORE painted on it. He got out, walked up the path and onto the porch, and rang the bell. There was no answer. Feeling like a voyeur, he went over to the window. The shade was only half drawn, and he had a clear view into what seemed to be the living room.

Not knowing what he was looking for, other than for some tangible sign that Maggie Holloway might be there, he walked around to the back and peered through the window in the kitchen door. He could see a coffeepot on the stove, and next to the sink a cup and saucer and juice glass were upturned, suggesting that they had been rinsed and left to dry. But had they been there for days or only minutes?

Finally he decided he had nothing to lose by ringing a neighbor's bell and inquiring whether anyone had seen Maggie. He received no response at the first two houses he tried. At the third house, the doorbell was answered by an attractive couple who appeared to be in their mid-sixties. As he quickly told them why he was there, he realized he had lucked out.

The couple, who introduced themselves as Irma and John Woods, told him of Nuala Moore's death and funeral, and of Maggie's presence in the house. "We were supposed to visit our daughter last Saturday but didn't go until after Nuala's funeral," Mrs. Woods explained. "Just got back late last night. I know Maggie is here. I haven't spoken to her since we got back, but I saw her go for a walk this morning."

"And I saw her drive past about fifteen minutes ago," John Woods volunteered.

They invited him in for coffee and told him about the night of the murder.

"What a sweet girl Maggie is," Irma Woods sighed. "I could tell how heartbroken she was about losing Nuala, but she isn't one to carry on. The hurt was all in her eyes."

Maggie, Neil thought. I wish I could have been here for you.

The Woodses had no idea where Maggie might have gone this morning, or how long she would be out.

I'll leave her a note to call me, Neil decided. There's nothing else I can do. But then he had an inspiration. When he drove away five minutes later, he had left a note for Maggie on the door, and he also had her phone number tucked securely in his pocket.

) *41*

REMEMBERING THE CURIOUS QUESTIONS ASKED BY THE child who had wanted to know why she was taking pictures at Nuala's grave, Maggie stopped at a florist's and bought an assortment of fall flowers to place on the graves she intended to inspect.

As before, once she passed the entrance to St. Mary's, the welcoming statue of the angel and the meticulously kept plots seemed to impart a sense of peace and immortality. Veering to the left, she drove up the winding incline that led to Nuala's grave.

As she stepped from the car, she sensed that a workman weeding the gravel path nearby was watching her. She had heard of people being mugged in cemeteries, but the thought passed quickly. There were other workmen in the area as well.

But given the fact there was someone so close by, she was glad she had thought to pick up the flowers; she would rather not seem to be examining the grave. Squatting down next to the plot, she selected a half dozen of the flowers and laid them one by one at the base of the tombstone.

The flowers Greta Shipley had placed there on Tuesday had been removed, and Maggie quickly consulted the snapshot she was holding to see exactly where she had detected the glint of some metal-like object.

It was fortunate she had brought the picture, she realized, because the object she was looking for had sunk more deeply into the moist earth and easily could have been missed. But it *was* there.

She looked swiftly to the side and realized she had the workman's undivided attention. Kneeling forward, she bowed her head and crossed herself, then let her folded hands drop to the ground. Still in the posture of prayer, her fingers touching the sod, she dug around the object and freed it.

She waited for a moment. When she glanced around again, the workman had his back turned to her. With one motion, she yanked the object up and hastily concealed it between her joined palms. As she did this, she heard a muffled ringing sound.

A bell? she thought. Why in God's name would anyone bury a bell on Nuala's grave? Certain that the workman had heard the sound as well, she got up and walked quickly back to her car.

She laid the bell down on top of the remaining flowers. Not wanting to stay another minute under the scrutiny of the watchful maintenance worker, she drove slowly in the direction of the second grave she wanted to visit. She parked in the nearby cul-de-sac, then looked around. There was no one nearby.

Opening the car window, she carefully picked up the bell and held it outside. After brushing off the loose earth that clung to it, she turned it around in her hand, examining it, her fingers holding the clapper to keep it from pealing.

The bell was about three inches high, and surprisingly heavy, not unlike an old-fashioned miniature school bell, except for the decorative garland of flowers bordering the base. The clapper was heavy too, she noticed. When allowed to hang freely, it no doubt could make quite a sound.

Maggie closed the car window, held the bell near the floor of the car and swung it. A melancholy but nevertheless clear ringing sound resounded through the car.

A Stone for Danny Fisher, she thought. That was the title of one of the books that had been in her father's library. She remembered that as a child she had asked him what the title meant, and he had explained that it was a tradition in the Jewish faith that anyone stopping by the grave of a friend or relative would place a stone there as a sign of the visit.

Could this bell signify something like that? Maggie wondered. Feeling vaguely as though she were doing something amiss in taking the bell, she slid it out of sight under the seat of the car. Then she selected another half-dozen flowers, and with the appropriate photograph in hand, went to revisit the grave of another of Greta Shipley's friends.

*   *   *

Her last stop was at Mrs. Rhinelander's grave; it had been the photograph of this grave that most clearly seemed to show a gap in the sod near the base of the tombstone. As Maggie arranged the remaining flowers on the damp grass, her fingers sought and found the indented area.

Maggie needed to think, and she was not ready to go back to the house where there might be interruptions. Instead she drove into the center of town and found a luncheonette, where she ordered a toasted blueberry muffin and coffee.

I *was* hungry, she admitted to herself as the crusty muffin and strong coffee helped to dissipate the all-encompassing uneasiness she had experienced in the cemeteries.

Another memory of Nuala flashed into her mind. When Maggie was ten, Porgie, her roguish miniature poodle, had jumped on Nuala as she lay dozing on the couch. She had let out a shriek, and when Maggie went running in, Nuala had laughed and said, "Sorry, honey. I don't know why I'm so jumpy. Someone must be walking on my grave."

Then, because Maggie had been at an age when she wanted to know everything, Nuala had had to explain that the expression was an old Irish saying meaning that someone was walking over the spot where you would someday be buried.

There *had* to be a simple explanation for what she had found today, Maggie reasoned. Of the six burial plots she had visited, four, including Nuala's, had bells at the base of the tombstone, each exactly like the others in weight and size. It appeared as well that one had been removed from the ground near Mrs. Rhinelander's tombstone. So that meant only one of Greta Shipley's friends had not received this odd tribute—if, indeed, that was what it was.

As she drained the last of the coffee and shook her head,

refusing the waitress's smiling offer of a refill, a name popped into Maggie's mind: Mrs. Bainbridge!

Like Greta Shipley, she had been at Latham Manor since it opened. She must have known all those women too, Maggie realized.

Back in her car, Maggie called Letitia Bainbridge on the cellular phone. She was in her apartment.

"Come right over," she told Maggie. "I'd love to see you. I've been a bit blue this morning."

"I'm on my way," Maggie replied.

When she replaced the phone in its cradle, she reached under the seat for the bell she had taken from Nuala's grave. Then she put it in her shoulder bag.

She shuddered involuntarily as she pulled away from the curb. The metal had felt cold and clammy to her touch.

) 42

IT HAD BEEN ONE OF THE LONGEST WEEKS OF MALCOLM Norton's life. The shock of having Nuala Moore cancel the sale of her house, followed by Barbara's announcement that she was going to visit for an extended period with her daughter in Vail, had left him numbed and frightened.

He *had* to get his hands on that house! Telling Janice about the impending change in the Wetlands Act had been a terrible mistake. He should have taken a chance and forged her name on the mortgage papers. He was *that* desperate.

Which was why, when Barbara put through the call from Chief Brower on this Friday morning, Malcolm felt perspiration spring out on his forehead. It took him a few moments to compose himself enough to be satisfied that his tone of voice would radiate good cheer.

"Good morning, Chief. How are you?" he said, trying to put a smile in his voice.

Chet Brower clearly was not in the mood for chitchat. "I'm fine. I'd like to drop over and talk with you for a few minutes today."

What about? Malcolm thought, momentarily panicked, but said in a hearty voice, "That would be great, but I warn you, I already bought my tickets to the Policemen's Ball." Even in his own ears, his stab at humor fell flat.

"When are you free?" Brower snapped.

Norton had no intention of telling Brower exactly how free he was. "I had a closing at eleven that's been postponed till one, so I do have an opening."

"I'll see you at eleven."

Well after hearing the dismissive click, Malcolm stared nervously at the receiver he held in his hand. Finally he set it down.

There was a gentle tap on the door, and Barbara poked her head in the office. "Malcolm, is there anything wrong?"

"What could be wrong? He just wants to talk to me. The only thing I can imagine is that it has to do with last Friday night."

"Oh, of course. The murder. The usual procedure is for the police to keep asking close friends if they might have remembered anything that didn't seem important at the time. And, of course, you and Janice did go to Mrs. Moore's for the dinner party."

You and Janice. Malcolm frowned. Was that reference intended to remind him that he still had taken no action to legally separate from Janice? No, unlike his wife, Barbara didn't play word games filled with hidden meanings. Her son-in-law was an assistant district attorney in New York; she had probably heard him talk about his cases, Malcolm reasoned. And, of course, television and movies were filled with details of police procedure.

She started to close the door again. "Barbara," he said, his voice pleading, "just give me a little more time. Don't leave me now."

Her only answer was to close the door with a firm click.

Brower arrived promptly at eleven. He sat bolt upright in the armchair opposite Norton's desk and got right to the point.

"Mr. Norton, you were due at Nuala Moore's home at eight o'clock the night of the murder?"

"Yes, my wife and I arrived at perhaps ten after eight. From what I understand, you had just arrived on the scene. As you know, we were instructed to wait in the home of Nuala's neighbors, the Woodses."

"What time did you leave your office that evening?" Brower asked.

Norton's eyebrows raised. He thought for a moment. "At the usual time . . . no, actually a bit later. About quarter of six. I had a closing outside the office and brought the file back here and checked on messages."

"Did you go directly home from here?"

"Not quite. Barbara . . . Mrs. Hoffman, my secretary, had been out that day with a cold. The day before, she had taken home a file I needed to study over the weekend, so I stopped at her house to pick it up."

"How long did that take?"

Norton thought for a moment. "She lives in Middletown. There was tourist traffic, so I'd say about twenty minutes each way."

"So you were home around six-thirty."

"Actually, it was probably a bit after that. Closer to seven, I should think."

In fact, he had gotten home at seven-fifteen. He remembered the time distinctly. Silently, Malcolm cursed himself. Janice had told him that his face could have been read like an open book when Irma Woods had delivered the news about Nuala's will. "You looked as if you wanted to kill someone," she had said, a smirk on her face. "You can't even plan to cheat someone without something going wrong."

So this morning he quickly had prepared answers to questions that he anticipated Brower would ask about his reaction to the canceled sale. He would not let his emotions show again. And he was glad he had thought the situation through thoroughly, because, in fact, the officer asked a number of questions, probing for details of the proposed sale.

"Must have been a bit of a letdown," Brower mused, "but on the other hand, every realtor in town has a house like Nuala Moore's, just begging to be bought."

Meaning, why did I want this one? Norton thought.

"Sometimes people can really want a house just because it grabs them. It says 'Buy me, I'm yours,' " the chief continued.

Norton waited.

"You and Mrs. Norton must have really fallen in love with it," Brower conjectured. "Word is, you mortgaged your own house to pay for it."

Now Brower was leaning back, his eyes half closed, his fingers locked together.

"Anybody who wants a house that badly would hate to know that a relative of sorts was about to arrive on the scene and maybe mess things up. Only one way to prevent that. Stop the relative, or at least find a way to keep the relative from influencing the owner of the house."

Brower stood up. "It's been a pleasure talking to you, Mr. Norton," he said. "Now, before I go, do you mind if I have a word with your secretary, Mrs. Hoffman?"

Barbara Hoffman did not enjoy dissembling. She had stayed home last Friday, pleading a cold, but actually what she had wanted was a quiet day to think things through. To placate her conscience, she had brought home a stack of files from the office, which she intended to clean up; she wanted them to be in good order if she decided to tell Malcolm she was leaving.

Oddly enough, he had inadvertently helped her to make her decision. He almost never came to her house, but then unexpectedly he had dropped by on Friday evening to see how she was feeling. He, of course, did not realize that her neighbor Dora Holt had stopped in. When Barbara had opened the door, he had bent to kiss her, then at her negative look, had stepped back.

"Oh, Mr. Norton," she had said quickly, "I have that file on the Moore closing that you wanted to pick up."

She had introduced him to Dora Holt and then made a show of going through the files and picking out one to hand him. But she hadn't missed the knowing smirk and the lively curiosity in the eyes of the other woman. And that was the moment when she knew the situation was intolerable.

Now, as she sat facing Chief Brower, Barbara Hoffman felt sneaky and very uncomfortable telling him the lame story about why her employer had come to her home.

"Then Mr. Norton only stayed a moment?"

She relaxed a bit; at least here she could be entirely truthful. "Yes, he took the file and left immediately."

"What file was it, Mrs. Hoffman?"

Another lie she had to tell. "I . . . I'm . . . actually, it was the file on the Moore closing." She cringed inwardly at the stammered apology in her voice.

"Just one more thing. What time did Mr. Norton get to your house?"

"A little after six, I believe," she replied honestly.

Brower got up and nodded at the intercom on her desk. "Would you tell Mr. Norton that I'd like another moment with him, please."

When Chief Brower returned to the lawyer's office, he didn't waste words. "Mr. Norton, I understand the file you picked up from Mrs. Hoffman last Friday evening was one concerning Mrs. Moore's closing. When exactly was the closing scheduled?"

"On Monday morning, at eleven," Norton told him. "I wanted to be sure everything was in order."

"You were the purchaser, but Mrs. Moore didn't have a separate lawyer representing her? Isn't that rather unusual?"

"Not really. But actually it was her idea. Nuala felt it was absolutely unnecessary to involve another attorney. I was paying a fair price and was handing the money over to her in the form of a certified check. She also had the right to stay there until the first of the year if she desired."

Chief Brower stared silently at Malcolm Norton for a few moments. Finally he stood to leave. "Just one more thing, Mr. Norton," he said. "The drive from Mrs. Hoffman's house to your home shouldn't have taken more than twenty minutes. That would have gotten you home by a few minutes past six-thirty. Yet you say it was nearly seven. Did you go anywhere else?"

"No. Perhaps I was mistaken about the time I arrived home."

Why is he asking all these questions? Norton wondered. *What does he suspect?*

) 43

WHEN NEIL STEPHENS GOT BACK TO PORTSMOUTH, HIS mother knew immediately from the look on his face that he had not been successful in locating the young woman from New York.

"You only had a piece of toast earlier," she reminded him. "Let me fix you breakfast. After all," she added, "I don't get much chance to fuss over you anymore."

Neil sank into a chair at the kitchen table. "I should think fussing over Dad is a full-time job."

"It is. But I like it."

"Where *is* Dad?"

"In his office. Cora Gebhart, the lady whose table we stopped at last night, called and asked if she could come over and talk to him."

"I see," Neil said distractedly, jiggling the cutlery his mother had set in front of him.

Dolores stopped her preparations and turned and looked at him. "When you start fiddling like that, it means you're worried," she said.

"I am. If I had called Maggie as I intended last Friday, I

would have had her phone number, I would have called, and I would have found out what happened. And I would have been here to help her." He paused. "Mom, you just don't know how *hungry* she was to spend this time with her stepmother. You'd never guess if you met her, but Maggie's had a pretty bad time of it."

Over waffles and bacon, he told her all he knew about Maggie. What he didn't tell her was how angry he was at himself for not knowing more.

"She really does sound lovely," Dolores Stephens said. "I'm anxious to meet her. But listen, you've got to stop driving yourself crazy. She is staying in Newport, and you've left her a note, and you have the phone number. You'll *surely* reach her or hear from her today. So just relax."

"I know. It's just that I have this rotten feeling that there have been times when she needed me and I wasn't there for her."

"Afraid of getting involved, right?"

Neil put his fork down. "That's not fair."

"Isn't it? You know, Neil, a lot of the smart, successful young men of your generation who didn't marry in their twenties decided they could play the field indefinitely. And some of them will—they really *don't* want to get involved. But some of them also never seem to know when to *grow up*. I just wonder if this concern on your part doesn't reflect a sudden realization that you care a lot about Maggie Holloway, something you wouldn't admit to yourself earlier because you didn't want to get involved."

Neil stared at his mother for a long moment. "And I thought Dad was tough."

Dolores Stephens folded her arms and smiled. "My grandmother had a saying: 'The husband is the head of the family; the wife is the neck.' " She paused. " 'And the neck turns the head.' "

Seeing Neil's startled expression, she laughed. "Trust me, I don't agree with that particular piece of down-home wisdom. I think of a husband and wife as equals, not game players. But sometimes, as in our case, what *seems* to be is not necessarily what *is*. Your father's fussing and complaining is his way of showing concern. I've known that since our first date."

"Speak of the devil," Neil said, as, through the window, he spotted his father walking down the path from his office.

His mother glanced out. "Uh-oh, he's bringing Cora in. She looks upset."

In a very few minutes after his father and Cora Gebhart joined them at the kitchen table, Neil understood why she was upset. On Wednesday she had sold her bonds through the broker who had been so persistent in trying to get her to invest in a venture stock he had recommended, and she had given the transaction a go-ahead.

"I couldn't sleep last night," she said. "I mean, after what Robert said at the club about not wanting another one of his ladies to lose her shirt . . . I had the awful feeling he was talking about me, and I sensed suddenly that I'd made a terrible mistake."

"Did you call this broker and cancel the buy?" Neil asked.

"Yes. That may be the one intelligent thing I did. Or *tried* to do—he said it was too late." Her voice trailed off and her lip trembled. "And he hasn't been in his office since then."

"What *is* this stock?" Neil asked.

"I've got the information," his father said.

Neil read the prospectus and the fact sheet. It was even worse than he expected. He phoned his office and directed

Trish to put him through to one of the senior traders. "Yesterday you bought fifty thousand shares at nine," he told Mrs. Gebhart. "We'll find out what's happening to it today."

Tersely he appraised his trading associate of the situation. Then he turned again to Mrs. Gebhart. "It's at seven now. I'm putting in a sell order."

She nodded her assent.

Neil stayed on the line. "Keep me posted," he ordered. When he hung up, he said, "There was a rumor a few days ago that the company whose stock you purchased was being bought by Johnson & Johnson. But unfortunately, I'm positive it's just that—a rumor intended to inflate the value of the stock artificially. I'm terribly sorry, Mrs. Gebhart; at least we should be able to save *most* of your capital. My associate will call us back as soon as he makes a trade."

"What makes me furious," Robert Stephens growled, "is that this is the same broker who got Laura Arlington to invest in a fly-by-night company and caused her to lose her savings."

"He seemed so nice," Cora Gebhart said. "And he was so knowledgeable about my bonds, explaining how even though they were tax-free, the return didn't justify all that money being tied up in them. And some were even losing buying power because of inflation."

The statement caught Neil's attention. "You must have told him about your bonds, if he was so knowledgeable," he said sharply.

"But I didn't. When he phoned to ask me to lunch, I explained I had no interest in discussing investments, but then he talked about the kind of clients he had—like Mrs. Downing. He told me that she had had bonds similar to the ones many older people hold and that he made a fortune for her. Then he talked about exactly the bonds I hold."

"Who is this Mrs. Downing?" Neil asked.

"Oh, everybody knows her. She's a pillar of the Providence old guard. I did call her, and she simply raved about Douglas Hansen."

"I see. Even so, I'd like to run a check on him," Neil said. "He sounds to me like just the kind of guy our business doesn't need."

The phone rang.

Maggie, Neil thought. Let it be Maggie.

Instead, it was his associate at the investment house. Neil listened, then turned to Cora Gebhart. "He got you out at seven. Count yourself lucky. There's a rumor just starting to circulate that Johnson & Johnson is going to issue a statement saying it has absolutely no interest in taking over that company. Whether the rumor is true or not, it's enough to send the company's stock into a tailspin."

When Cora Gebhart left, Robert Stephens looked at his son affectionately. "Thank God you were here, Neil. Cora has a good head and a big heart, but she's too trusting. It would have been a damn shame to have her wiped out by one mistake. As it is, this may mean that she'll have to give up the idea of moving into Latham Manor. She had her eye on a particular apartment there, but maybe she'll still be able to take a smaller one."

"Latham Manor," Neil said. "I'm glad you mentioned it. I need to ask you about that place."

"What on earth do you want to know about Latham Manor?" his mother asked.

Neil told them about the Van Hillearys, his clients who were looking for a retirement base. "I told them I'd investigate that place for them. I'd almost forgotten. I should have made an appointment to see it."

"We're not teeing up until one," Robert Stephens said, "and Latham isn't that far from the club. Why don't you call over and see if you can make an appointment now, or at least pick up some literature about it for your clients."

"Never put off till tomorrow what you can do today," Neil said with a grin. "Unless, of course, I can get hold of Maggie first. She must be home by now."

After six unanswered rings, he replaced the receiver. "She's still out," he said glumly. "Okay, where's the phone book? I'll call Latham Manor; let's get it out of the way."

Dr. William Lane could not have been more pleasant. "You're calling at a very good time," he said. "We have one of our best suites available—a two-bedroom unit with a terrace. It's one of four such apartments, and the other three are occupied by charming couples. Come right over."

) *44*

DR. LARA HORGAN, THE NEW MEDICAL EXAMINER FOR THE state of Rhode Island, had not been able to figure out what was making her uneasy. But then, it had been a busy week for her department: extraordinary deaths had included two suicides, three drownings, and a felony murder.

The death of the woman at the Latham Manor residence, on the other hand, was to all appearances purely routine. Still, something about it was bothering her. The medical history of the deceased woman, Greta Shipley, had been perfectly straightforward. Her longtime doctor had retired, but his associate verified that Mrs. Shipley had a ten-year history of hypertension and had suffered at least one silent heart attack.

Dr. William Lane, the director and attending physician at Latham Manor, seemed competent. The staff had experience, and the facilities were first-rate.

The fact that Mrs. Shipley had had a weak spell at the funeral Mass of her friend, the murder victim, Nuala Moore, and a second spell only verified the tension she must have been under.

Dr. Horgan had seen a number of instances where an elderly spouse expired hours or even minutes after the death of the husband or wife. Someone horrified by the circumstances of a dear friend's death might easily experience that same fatal stress.

As state medical examiner, Dr. Horgan was familiar as well with the circumstances surrounding the death of Nuala Moore, and she was aware how upsetting they might be to someone as close to the victim as Mrs. Shipley had been. Multiple vicious blows to the back of Mrs. Moore's head had proven fatal. Grains of sand mixed in with blood and hair suggested that the perpetrator had found the weapon, probably a rock, somewhere on the beach and had entered the house carrying it. It also suggested that the perpetrator had known the resident of the house was small and frail, perhaps even actually knew Mrs. Moore. That's what it is, she told herself. The niggling feeling that Nuala Moore's death is somehow tied in with the one at Latham Manor is what's sending alarm signals to me. She decided to call the Newport police and ask if they had turned up any leads as yet.

The newspapers from earlier in the week were stacked on her desk. She found a brief item on the obituary page detailing Mrs. Shipley's background, her community activities, her membership in the DAR, her late husband's position as board chairman of a successful company. It listed her survivors as three cousins, residing in New York City, Washington, D.C., and Denver.

No one nearby watching out for her, Dr. Horgan thought, as she put the paper down and turned to the mountain of work on her desk.

Then a final thought teased her: Nurse Markey. She was the one who had found Mrs. Shipley's body at Latham Manor. There was something about that woman she didn't like, a kind of sly, know-it-all quality. Maybe Chief Brower should talk to her again.

) *45*

AS PART OF HIS RESEARCH FOR HIS LECTURE SERIES, EARL Bateman had begun to take rubbings from old tombstones. He had made them the subject of one of his talks.

"Today, minimal information is recorded on gravestones," he would explain, "only birth and death dates, really. But in other centuries, wonderful histories could be read from headstones. Some are poignant, while some are rather remarkable, as in the case of the sea captain buried with his five wives—none of whom, I might add, lived more than seven years once married."

At that point, he was usually rewarded by a ripple of laughter.

"Other markers," he would explain, "are awesome in the majesty and history they convey."

He would then cite the chapel in Westminster Abbey, where Queen Elizabeth I was entombed only a few feet from the cousin she had ordered beheaded, Mary, Queen of Scots.

"One interesting note," he would add, "in Ketchakan, Alaska, in the nineteenth century, Tombstone Cemetery, the burial ground there, reserved a special section for the 'Soiled Doves,' as they called the young women who resided in bordellos."

On this Friday morning, Earl was preparing a synopsis of the lectures he proposed to deliver in the potential cable television series. When he came to the subject of tombstone rubbings, he was reminded that he had intended to look for other interesting ones; then, realizing it was a beautiful day, perfect for such an activity, he decided to visit the oldest sections of St. Mary's and Trinity cemeteries.

He was driving down the road that led to the cemeteries when he saw a black Volvo station wagon come out through the open gates and turn the other way. Maggie Holloway had the same make and color car, he thought. Could she possibly have been here visiting Nuala's grave?

Instead of going to the old section, he drove to the left and circled up the hill. Pete Brown, a cemetery worker he had come to know from his various meanderings among the old tombstones, was weeding a gravel path in the vicinity of Nuala's grave.

Earl stopped the car and opened the window. "Pretty quiet around here, Pete," he offered. It was an old joke they shared.

"Sure is, Professor."

"I thought I saw Mrs. Moore's stepdaughter's car. Was she visiting the grave?" He was sure that everyone knew the details of Nuala's death. There weren't *that* many murders in Newport.

"Nice looking lady, skinny, dark hair, young?"

"That would be Maggie."

"Yep. And she must know half of our guests," Pete said, then laughed. "One of the fellows was saying that he saw her go from one plot to another and drop off flowers. All the guys noticed her. She's a doll."

Now isn't that interesting? Earl thought. "Take care, Pete," he said, then waved as he drove off slowly. Knowing that the all-seeing eyes of Pete Brown were on him, he continued on to the oldest section of Trinity and began wandering among the seventeenth-century headstones there.

) *46*

LETITIA BAINBRIDGE'S STUDIO APARTMENT AT LATHAM Manor was a large corner room with a magnificent ocean view. Proudly she pointed out the oversized dressing room and bath. "Being a charter member here has its perks," she said briskly. "I remember how Greta and I decided to sign up right away, at that presentation reception. Trudy Nichols hemmed and hawed, and then never forgave me for picking off this unit. She ended up paying another hundred and fifty thousand for one of the largest apartments, and the poor darling only lived two years. The Crenshaws have it now. They were at our table the other night."

"I remember them. They're very nice." *Nichols*, Maggie thought. *Gertrude Nichols.* Hers was one of the graves that has the bell.

Mrs. Bainbridge sighed, "It's always hard when one of us goes, but especially hard when it's someone from our table. And I just *know* that Eleanor Chandler will get Greta's place. When my daughter Sarah took me to my family doctor yesterday, she told me the word is out that Eleanor is moving in here.''

''Aren't you feeling well?'' Maggie asked.

''Oh, I'm fine. But at my age anything can happen. I told Sarah that Dr. Lane could check my blood pressure just fine, but Sarah wanted me to be seen by Dr. Evans.''

They sat down opposite each other on slipper chairs that were placed by the windows. Mrs. Bainbridge reached over and plucked a framed snapshot from among the many on a nearby table. She showed it to Maggie. ''My crowd,'' she said proudly. ''Three sons, three daughters, seventeen grandchildren, four great-grandchildren and three on the way.'' She smiled with great satisfaction. ''And the nice part is that so many of them are still in New England. Never a week goes by that somebody in the family isn't around.''

Maggie consciously stored that piece of information; something to consider later, she thought. Then she noticed a picture that had been taken in the grand salon here at Latham Manor. Mrs. Bainbridge was in the center of a group of eight. She picked it up. ''Special occasion?'' she asked.

''My ninetieth birthday, four years ago.'' Letitia Bainbridge leaned forward and indicated the women at either end of the group. ''That's Constance Rhinelander on the left. She just died a couple of weeks ago, and of course you knew Greta. She's on the right.''

''Mrs. Shipley didn't have close family, did she?'' Maggie asked.

''No. Neither did Constance, but we were family for each other.''

It was time to ask about the bells, Maggie decided. She looked around for inspiration as to how to bring up the subject. The room had obviously been furnished with Mrs. Bainbridge's personal belongings. The ornately carved four-poster bed, the antique English pie-crust table, the Bombay chest, the delicately toned Persian carpet, all spoke of generational history.

Then she saw it: a silver bell on the fireplace mantel. She got up and crossed over to it. ''Oh, isn't this lovely?'' She picked it up.

Letitia Bainbridge smiled. ''My mother used it to summon her maid. Mother was a late sleeper, and Hattie patiently sat in attendance outside the door each morning until the bell summoned her. My granddaughters find that 'a hoot,' as they put it, but the bell gives me many warm memories. A lot of us old girls grew up in that milieu.''

It was the opening Maggie wanted. She sat down again and reached into her purse. ''Mrs. Bainbridge, I found *this* bell on Nuala's grave. I was curious as to who left it there. Is there a custom here of putting a bell on the grave of a friend?''

Letitia Bainbridge looked astonished. ''I never heard of such a thing. You mean someone deliberately left that object there?''

''Apparently, yes.''

''But how bizarre.'' She turned away.

With a sinking heart, Maggie realized that for some reason the bell had upset Mrs. Bainbridge. She decided not to say anything about the fact that she had found bells on other graves as well. Clearly this did not represent a tribute that old friends gave to each other.

She dropped the bell back in her shoulder bag. ''I'll bet I know what happened,'' she improvised. ''There was a little girl in the cemetery the other day. She came over to talk to me while I arranged flowers around Nuala's headstone. It was after she left that I found the bell.''

Happily, Letitia Bainbridge reached the conclusion Maggie wanted. ''Oh, I think that must be it,'' she said. ''I mean, surely no adult would think of leaving a bell on a grave.'' Then she frowned. ''What is it I'm trying to remember? Oh, dear, something just came into my mind and now it's gone. That's old age, I guess.''

There was a knock at the door, and Mrs. Bainbridge commented, ''That will be the lunch tray.'' She raised her voice, ''Come in, please.''

It was Angela, the young maid whom Maggie had met on her earlier visits. She greeted her, then got up. ''I really must run along,'' Maggie said.

Mrs. Bainbridge rose. ''I'm so glad you stopped in, Maggie. Will I see you tomorrow?''

Maggie knew what she meant. ''Yes, of course. I'll be at the funeral parlor, and at Mrs. Shipley's Requiem.''

When she went downstairs, she was glad to see that the foyer was empty. Everyone must be in the dining room, she thought as she opened the front door. She reached in her pocketbook for her car keys and inadvertently hit the bell. A muffled ringing sound made her grab the clapper to silence it.

Ask not for whom the bell tolls, Maggie thought as she walked down the steps of Latham Manor.

) 47

DR. LANE, NEIL STEPHENS, AND HIS FATHER CONCLUDED their tour of Latham Manor at the entrance to the dining room. Neil took in the hum of conversation, the animated faces of the well-dressed seniors, the overall ambiance of the beautiful room. White-gloved waiters were serving, and the aroma of freshly baked bread was enticing.

Lane picked up a menu and handed it to Neil. "Today the main course is a choice of Dover sole with white asparagus, or chicken salad," he explained. "The dessert choices are frozen yogurt or sorbet, with home-baked cookies." He smiled. "I might add that this is a typical menu. Our chef is not only cordon bleu, but also a dietary specialist."

"Very impressive," Neil said, nodding appreciatively.

"Neil, we tee up in thirty minutes," Robert Stephens reminded his son. "Don't you think you've seen enough?"

"More important," Dr. Lane said gently, "do you feel that you might recommend the available suite to your clients? Without meaning to pressure them, I can tell you that it won't last long. Couples especially are attracted to the large units."

"I'm going to speak to my clients on Monday when I get back to New York," Neil said. "The place is most impressive. I'll certainly send them the prospectus and recommend that they come up and look over everything for themselves."

"Wonderful," Dr. Lane said heartily, as Robert Stephens pointedly held up his watch, turned and began to walk down the corridor to the front door. Neil and Dr. Lane followed. "We like having couples here," Dr. Lane continued. "Many of the guests are widows, but that doesn't mean they don't enjoy having men around. In fact, we've had several romances develop between single guests."

Robert Stephens slowed and fell into step with them. "If you don't settle down soon, Neil, maybe you should put in your application. This place may be your best chance."

Neil grinned. "Just don't ever let my father move in," he told the doctor.

"Don't worry about me. This place is too rich for my blood," Robert Stephens declared. "But that reminds me.

Doctor, do you remember receiving an application from a Mrs. Cora Gebhart?"

Dr. Lane frowned. "That name is familiar. Oh yes, she's in what we call the 'pending file.' She visited here about a year ago, filled out an application but did not want it activated. It's our practice to phone someone like that once or twice a year to see whether they're nearer to a decision. The last time I spoke to Mrs. Gebhart, I had the impression that she was seriously considering joining us."

"She was," the elder Stephens said shortly. "All right, Neil, let's be on our way."

Neil tried calling Maggie once more from the car phone, but he still got no answer.

Even though it was a beautiful day and he played excellent golf, Neil found the afternoon unconscionably long. He could not shake the ominous feeling that something was wrong.

) 48

ON HER WAY HOME, MAGGIE DECIDED TO PICK UP GROCERIES. She drove to a small market she had noticed near the wharf. There she gathered the makings of green salad and pasta pomodoro. I've had my fill of scrambled eggs and chicken soup, she thought. Then she saw a sign for freshly prepared New England clam chowder.

The clerk was a weathered-faced man in his sixties. "New here?" he asked affably, when she gave him her order.

Maggie smiled. "How can you tell?"

"Easy. When the missus makes her clam chowder, everyone buys at least a quart."

"In that case, you'd better give me a second pint."

"Got a head on your shoulders. I like that in young people," he said.

As she drove away, Maggie smiled to herself. And another reason for keeping the house in Newport, she thought, was that with so many senior citizens around, she would be considered a youngster for quite a while to come.

And besides, I can't just sort out Nuala's things, take the best offer for the house, and walk away, she told herself. Even if Nuala *was* killed by a stranger, there are too many unanswered questions.

The bells, for instance. Who would put them on those graves? Maybe one of the old-guard friends does it on her own and never dreamt anyone would notice them, she acknowledged. For all I know, she thought, there may be bells on half the graves in Newport. On the other hand, one of them is missing. Did whoever it was change his or her mind about leaving it?

Pulling into the driveway at Nuala's house, she carried the groceries around to the kitchen door and let herself in. Dropping the packages on the table, she turned and quickly locked the door. That's something else, she thought. I meant to call in a locksmith. Liam would ask about that tonight. He had been so concerned about Earl showing up unexpectedly.

One of Nuala's favorite expressions ran through Maggie's head as she searched for a phone book: *Better late than never.* Maggie remembered how Nuala had said it one Sunday morning when she came running out to the car where Maggie and her father were already waiting.

Maggie hated to think about her father's response, so typical of him: "And better still, never late, particularly when the rest of the congregation manages to show up on time."

She found the phone book in a deep kitchen drawer, and smiled at the sight of the clutter beneath it: Xeroxed recipes, half-burned candles, rusty scissors, paper clips, small change.

I'd hate to try to find anything in this house, Maggie thought. There's such a jumble. Then she felt her throat close. *Whoever ransacked this house was looking for something, and chances are he didn't find it,* an interior voice whispered to her.

After she left a message on the machine of the first locksmith she called, she finished putting away the groceries and fixed herself a cup of the clam chowder, which at first taste made her glad she had bought more than she'd intended. Then she went up to the studio. Restlessly her fingers reached into the pot of wet clay. She wanted to go back to the bust she had started of Nuala but knew she could not. It was Greta Shipley whose face demanded to be captured— not really so much the face as the eyes, knowing, candid, and watchful. She was glad she had brought several armatures with her.

Maggie stayed at the worktable for an hour until the clay had taken on an approach to the likeness of the woman she had known so briefly. Finally the surging disquietude had passed, and she could wash her hands and start the job she knew she would find hardest: the task of sorting out Nuala's paintings. She had to decide which to keep and which to offer to a dealer, knowing that a majority of them probably would end up in a scrap heap, cut out from their frames— frames some people would value more than the art they had once enhanced.

* * *

At three o'clock she started going through the works that had not yet been framed. In the storage closet off the studio, she found dozens of Nuala's sketches, watercolors, and oils, a dizzying array that Maggie soon realized she could not hope to analyze without professional assistance.

The sketches for the most part were only fair, and only a few of the oils were interesting—but some of the watercolors were extraordinary. Like Nuala, she thought, they were warm and joyous, and filled with unexpected depths. She especially loved a winter scene in which a tree, its branches laden and bent with snow, was sheltering an incongruous ring of flowering plants, including snapdragons and roses, violets and lilies, orchids and chrysanthemums.

Maggie became so engrossed in the task that it was after five-thirty when she hurried downstairs just in time to catch the phone that she thought she heard ringing.

It was Liam. "Hey, this is my third attempt to get you. I was afraid I was being stood up," he said, relief in his voice. "Do you realize that my only other offer tonight was my cousin, Earl?"

Maggie laughed. "I'm sorry. I didn't hear the phone. I was in the studio. I guess Nuala didn't believe in extension telephones."

"I'll buy you one for Christmas. Pick you up in about an hour?"

"Fine."

That should give me just enough time for a soak in the tub, Maggie thought as she hung up. It was obvious the evening air was turning cool. The house felt drafty, and in an odd and uncomfortable way it seemed to her she could still feel the chill of the damp earth she had touched at the graves.

When the water was rushing into the tub, she thought she heard the phone again and quickly turned off the taps. No sound of ringing came from Nuala's room, however. Either I didn't hear anything, or I missed another call, she decided.

Feeling relaxed after her bath, she dressed carefully in the new white evening sweater and calf-length black skirt she had purchased earlier in the week, then decided that a little care with her makeup was in order.

It's fun to dress up for Liam, she thought. He makes me feel good about myself.

At quarter of seven she was waiting in the living room when the bell rang. Liam stood on the doorstep, a dozen long-stemmed red roses in one hand, a folded sheet of paper in the other. The warmth in his eyes and the light kiss that for a moment lingered on her lips gave Maggie a sudden lift of the heart.

"You look spectacular," he told her. "I'll have to change the plans for the evening. Obviously McDonald's won't do."

Maggie laughed. "Oh dear! And I was so looking forward to a Big Mac." She quickly read the note he had brought in. "Where was this?" she asked.

"On your front door, madame."

"Oh, of course. I came in through the kitchen earlier." She refolded the piece of paper. So Neil is in Portsmouth, she thought, and wants to get together. Isn't that nice? She hated to admit to herself how disappointed she had been when he hadn't called last week before she left. And then she reminded herself of how she had chalked it up as another indication of his indifference toward her.

"Anything important?" Liam asked casually.

"No. A friend who's up for the weekend wants me to call. Maybe I'll give him a ring tomorrow." And maybe I won't, she thought. I wonder how he found me.

She went back upstairs for her handbag, and as she picked

it up she felt the extra weight of the bell. Should she show it to Liam? she wondered.

No, not tonight, she decided. I don't want to talk about death and graves, not now. She took the bell out of her purse. Even though it had been there for hours, it still felt cold and clammy to her touch, causing her to shiver.

I don't want this to be the first thing I see when I get in later, she thought as she opened the closet door and put it on the shelf, pushing it back until it was completely out of sight.

Liam had made a reservation in the Commodore's Room of The Black Pearl, a toney restaurant with a sweeping view of Narragansett Bay. "My condo isn't far from here," he explained, "but I miss the big house I was raised in. One of these days I'm going to bite the bullet and buy one of the old places and renovate it." His voice became serious. "By then I'll have settled down and, with any luck, will have a beautiful wife who's an award-winning photographer."

"Stop it, Liam," Maggie protested. "As Nuala would have said, you sound half daft."

"But I'm not," he said quietly. "Maggie, please start looking at me with different eyes, won't you? Ever since last week, you haven't been out of my mind for a minute. All I've been able to think about is that if you had walked in on whatever hophead attacked Nuala, the same thing could have happened to you. I'm a big, strong guy, and I want to take *care* of you. I know that such sentiments are out of fashion, but I can't help it. It's who I am, and it's how I feel." He paused. "And now that's entirely enough of that. Is the wine okay?"

Maggie stared at him and smiled, glad that he had not asked for a further response from her. "It's fine, but Liam, I have to ask you something. Do you *really* think a stranger on drugs attacked Nuala?"

Liam appeared astonished at her question. "If not, who else?" he asked.

"But whoever did it must have seen that guests were expected and yet still took time to ransack the house."

"Maggie, whoever did it was probably desperate to get a fix and searched the place for money or jewelry. The newspaper account said Nuala's wedding ring was taken off her finger, so robbery *must* have been the motive."

"Yes, the ring was taken," Maggie acknowledged.

"I happen to know she had very little jewelry," Liam said. "She wouldn't let Uncle Tim give her an engagement ring. She said that two of them in one lifetime was enough, and besides, both of them had been stolen when she lived in New York. I remember her telling my mother after that happened that she never wanted to own anything except costume jewelry."

"You know more than I do," Maggie said.

"So except for whatever cash was around, her killer didn't get much, did he? At least that gives me some satisfaction," Liam said, his voice grim. He smiled, breaking the dark mood that had settled over them. "Now, tell me about your week. I hope Newport is beginning to get under your skin? Or better yet, let me continue to give you my life history."

He told her how, as a child, he had counted the weeks in boarding school until it was time to go to Newport for the summer, about his decision to become a stockbroker like his father, about leaving his position at Randolph and Marshall and starting his own investment firm. "It's pretty flattering that some gilt-edged clients elected to come with me," he said. "It's always scary to go out on your own, but their vote of trust led me to believe I'd made the right decision. And I had."

By the time the crème brûlée had arrived, Maggie was fully relaxed. "I've learned more about you tonight than I knew from a dozen other dinners," she told him.

"Maybe I'm a little different on my home territory," he said. "And maybe I just want you to see what a terrific guy I am." He raised an eyebrow. "I'm also trying to let you know what a substantial guy I am. Just so you know, in *these* parts, I'm considered quite a catch."

"Stop that kind of talk right now," Maggie said, trying to sound firm, but unable to suppress a slight smile.

"Okay. Your turn. *Now* tell me about your week."

Maggie was reluctant to really go into things. She did not want to destroy the almost festive mood of the evening. It was impossible to talk about the week and not to speak of Greta Shipley, but she put the emphasis on how much she had enjoyed her in the time she had spent with her, and then she told him about her blossoming friendship with Letitia Bainbridge.

"I knew Mrs. Shipley, and she was a very special lady," Liam said. "And, as for Mrs. Bainbridge, well, she's great," he enthused. "A real legend around here. Has she filled you in on all the goings-on in Newport's heyday?"

"A little."

"Get her going sometime on her mother's stories about Mamie Fish. She really knew how to shake up the old crew. There's a great story about a dinner party she threw, when one of her guests asked to bring Prince del Drago from Corsica with him. Of course Mamie was delighted to give permission, so you can imagine her horror when 'the prince' turned out to be a monkey, in full evening dress."

They laughed together. "Mrs. Bainbridge is probably one

of the very few left whose parents took part in the famous 1890s parties," Liam said.

"What's nice is that Mrs. Bainbridge has so many protective family members nearby," Maggie said. "Just yesterday, after she heard that Mrs. Shipley died, her daughter came over to take her to the doctor for a checkup, because she knew she'd be upset."

"That daughter would be Sarah," Liam said. Then he smiled. "Did Mrs. Bainbridge happen to tell you about the stunt my idiot cousin Earl pulled that sent Sarah into orbit?"

"No."

"It's priceless. Earl lectures about funeral customs. You've heard that, haven't you? I swear the guy is batty. When everybody else is off playing golf or sailing, his idea of a good time is to spend hours in cemeteries, taking tombstone rubbings."

"In cemeteries!" Maggie exclaimed.

"Yes, but that's only a small part of it. What I'm getting to is the time he lectured on funeral practices to a group at Latham Manor, of all places. Mrs. Bainbridge wasn't feeling well, but Sarah had been visiting her and attended the lecture.

"Earl included in his little talk the story about the Victorian bell ringers. It seems that wealthy Victorians were so afraid of being buried alive that they had a hole built into the top of their caskets, for an air vent reaching up to the surface of the ground. A string was tied to the finger of the presumed deceased, run through the air vent, and attached to a bell on top of the grave. Then someone was paid to keep watch for a week in case the person in the casket did, in fact, regain consciousness and try ringing the bell."

"Dear God," Maggie gasped.

"No, but here's the best part now, the part about Earl. Believe it or not, he has a sort of museum up here near the funeral home that's filled with all kinds of funeral symbols and paraphernalia, and he got the brainstorm to have a dozen replicas of a Victorian cemetery bell cast to use to illustrate the lecture. Without telling them what they were, the jerk passed them out to twelve of these ladies, all in their sixties and seventies and eighties, and tied the string attached to them onto their ring fingers. Then he told them to hold the bell in their other hand, wiggle their fingers, and pretend they were in a casket and trying to communicate with the grave watcher."

"How appalling!" Maggie said.

"One of the old girls actually fainted. Mrs. Bainbridge's daughter collected Earl's bells and was so irate she practically threw him and his bells off the premises."

Liam paused, then in a more somber voice added, "The worrisome part is that I think Earl relishes telling that story himself."

) 49

NEIL HAD TRIED TO PHONE MAGGIE SEVERAL TIMES, FIRST from the locker room of the club, and again as soon as he got home. Either she's been out all day, or she's in and out, or she's not answering the phone, he thought. But even if she was in and out, she surely would have seen his note.

Neil accompanied his parents to a neighbor's home for cocktails, where he tried Maggie again at seven. He then elected to take his own car to dinner so that if he did reach her later, it might be possible to stop by her house for a drink.

There were six people at the table in the dinner party at Canfield House. But even though the lobster Newburg was superb, and his dinner companion, Vicky, the daughter of his parents' friends, was a very attractive banking executive from Boston, Neil was wildly restless.

Knowing it would be rude to skip the after-dinner drink in the bar, he agonized through the chitchat, and when everyone finally stood up to go at ten-thirty, Neil managed to refuse gracefully Vicky's invitation to join her and her friends for tennis on Sunday morning. Finally, with a sigh of relief, he was in his own car.

He checked the time; it was quarter of eleven. If Maggie was home and had gone to bed early, he didn't want to disturb her. He justified his decision to drive by her house by telling himself that he simply wanted to see if her car was in the driveway—just to be sure she was still in Newport.

His initial excitement at seeing that her car was indeed there was tempered when he realized that another car was parked in front of her place, a Jaguar with Massachusetts plates. Neil drove by at a snail's pace and was rewarded by seeing the front door open. He caught a glimpse of a tall man standing next to Maggie, then, feeling like a *voyeur,* he accelerated and turned the corner at Ocean Drive, heading back to Portsmouth, his stomach churning with regret and jealousy.

) *50*

THE REQUIEM FOR GRETA SHIPLEY AT TRINITY CHURCH was well-attended. As she sat and listened to the familiar prayers, Maggie realized that all the people who had been invited to Nuala's dinner party were in attendance.

Dr. Lane and his wife, Odile, sat with a number of the guests from the residence, including everyone who had been at Mrs. Shipley's table on Wednesday evening, with the exception of Mrs. Bainbridge.

Malcolm Norton and his wife, Janice, were there. He had a hangdog look, Maggie thought. When he passed her on the way in, he stopped to say he had been trying to reach her and would like to meet with her after the funeral.

Earl Bateman had come over to speak to her before the service began. "After all this, when you think about Newport, I'm very much afraid that your memories of the place will be of funerals and cemeteries," he said, his eyes owlish behind lightly tinted round-frame sunglasses.

He hadn't waited for an answer but had walked past her to take an empty place in the first pew.

Liam arrived halfway through the service and sat down next to her. "Sorry," he murmured in her ear. "Damn alarm didn't go off." He took her hand, but after an instant she withdrew it. She knew that she was the object of many sidelong glances and did not want to have rumors swirling about her and Liam. But, she admitted to herself, her sense of isolation was relieved when his firm shoulder brushed against hers.

When she had filed past the casket at the funeral home, Maggie had studied for an instant the tranquil, lovely face of the woman she had known so briefly yet liked so much. The thought had crossed her mind that Greta Shipley and Nuala and all their other good friends were probably having a joyous reunion.

That thought had brought with it the nagging question of the Victorian bells.

When she passed the three people who had been introduced as Mrs. Shipley's cousins, their faces were fixed in appropriately serious expressions, but she detected there none of the honest, raw pain that she saw in the eyes and countenances of Mrs. Shipley's close friends from Latham Manor.

I've got to find out when and how each of those women whose graves I visited died, and how many of them had close relatives, Maggie thought, information that she had recognized as pertinent during her visit to Mrs. Bainbridge.

For the next two hours, she felt as if she were operating on some kind of remote control—observing, recording, but not *feeling*. "I am a camera" was her own reaction to herself as, Liam at her side, she walked away from Greta Shipley's grave after the interment.

She felt a hand on her arm. A handsome woman with

silver hair and remarkably straight carriage stopped her. "Ms. Holloway," she said, "I'm Sarah Bainbridge Cushing. I want to thank you for visiting Mother yesterday. She so appreciated it."

Sarah. This was the daughter who had tangled with Earl about his lecture on Victorian bells, Maggie reflected. She wanted to have a chance to talk privately to her.

In the next breath, Sarah Cushing provided the opportunity: "I don't know how long you're staying in Newport, but tomorrow morning I'm taking Mother out for brunch, and I'd be delighted if you could join us."

Maggie agreed readily.

"You're staying at Nuala's house, aren't you? I'll pick you up at eleven o'clock, if that's all right." With a nod, Sarah Cushing turned and dropped back to rejoin the group she had been with.

"Let's have a quiet lunch," Liam suggested. "I'm sure you're not up to any more post-funeral get-togethers."

"No, I'm not. But I really *do* want to get back to the house. I simply have to go through Nuala's clothes and sort them out."

"Dinner tonight, then?"

Maggie shook her head. "Thanks, but I'm going to stay at the sort-and-pack job till I drop."

"Well, I have to see you before I go back to Boston tomorrow night," Liam protested.

Maggie knew he wasn't going to allow her to say no. "Okay, call me," she said. "We'll figure something out."

He left her at her car. She was turning the key in the ignition when a rap at the window startled her. It was Malcolm Norton. "We need to talk," he said urgently.

Maggie decided to bite the bullet and not waste his time or hers. "Mr. Norton, if it's about buying Nuala's house, I can only tell you this: I have absolutely *no* plans of selling it at this time, and I'm afraid that, absolutely unsolicited, I have already received a substantially higher offer than yours."

Murmuring, "I'm sorry," she slid the selector into DRIVE. She found it almost painful to see the horrified shock in the man's expression.

☽ *51*

NEIL STEPHENS AND HIS FATHER TEED UP AT SEVEN o'clock and were back in the clubhouse by noon. This time, Neil heard the phone being picked up after the second ring. When he recognized Maggie's voice, he let out a sigh of relief.

Sounding disjointed, even to himself, he told her how he had phoned her after she left on Friday, how he had gone to Jimmy Neary to try to get Nuala's name so he could contact her here, how he had learned of Nuala's death, and was so terribly sorry . . . "Maggie, I have to see you, today," he finished.

He sensed her hesitation, then listened as she told him she had to stay in and finish clearing out her stepmother's personal effects.

"No matter how busy you are, you still have to eat dinner," he pleaded. "Maggie, if you won't let me take you out, I'm going to arrive on your doorstep with meals-on-wheels." Then he thought about the man with the Jaguar. "Unless somebody else is already doing that," he added.

At her response, a smile broke out on his face. "Seven o'clock? Terrific. I found a great place for lobster."

"I gather you reached this Maggie of yours," Robert Stephens said dryly when Neil joined him at the door of the clubhouse.

"Yes, I did. We're going out to dinner tonight."

"Well, then, we'll be happy for you to bring her along with us. You know we're having your mother's birthday dinner at the club tonight."

"Her birthday isn't until tomorrow," Neil protested.

"Thanks for telling me! *You're* the one who asked that we have the celebration this evening. You said you wanted to get started home by midafternoon tomorrow."

Neil stood with his hand to his mouth, as though in deep thought. Then he silently shook his head. Robert Stephens smiled. "A lot of people consider your mother and me good company."

"You *are* good company," Neil protested feebly. "I'm sure Maggie will enjoy being with you."

"Of course she will. Now let's get home. Another client of mine, Laura Arlington, is coming over at two. I want you to go over what's left of her stock portfolio and see if you can recommend any way to upgrade her income. Thanks to that sleazy broker, she's really in bad shape."

I don't want to risk telling Maggie over the phone about the change in plans, Neil thought. She'd probably bow out. I'll show up at her doorstep and plead my case.

Two hours later, Neil sat with Mrs. Arlington in his father's office. She *is* in bad shape, he thought. She had once owned blue-chip stocks that paid good dividends but had sold them all to buy into another of those crazy venture offerings. Ten days ago, Mrs. Arlington had been persuaded to buy one hundred thousand shares of some piece of trash at five dollars a share. The next morning the stock went to five and a quarter, but by that afternoon it had begun to plunge. Now it was valued below a dollar.

So five hundred thousand dollars in stock is reduced to about eighty thousand, assuming there's even a buyer, Neil thought, glancing with pity across the desk at the ashen-faced woman whose entwined hands and slumping shoulders betrayed her agitation. She's only Mother's age, he thought, sixty-six, yet right now she looks twenty years older.

"It's pretty awful, isn't it?" Mrs. Arlington asked.

"I'm afraid so," Neil said.

"You see, that was the money I was going to use when one of the larger apartments in Latham Manor became available. But I've always felt guilty about the idea of using so much money selfishly. I have three children, and when Douglas Hansen was so persuasive, and Mrs. Downing told me how much money she had made in less than a week with his help, I thought, well, if I double that money, I'll have an inheritance for the children as well as being able to live in Latham Manor."

She tried to blink back tears. "Then not only did I lose my money last week, but the very next day I got a call that one of the big apartments was available, the one that Nuala Moore had been scheduled to take."

"Nuala Moore?" Neil said quickly.

"Yes, the woman who was murdered last week." Mrs. Arlington held a handkerchief to the tears that she could no longer hold back. "Now I don't have the apartment, and the children not only don't get an inheritance but one of them may be stuck with having to take me in."

She shook her head. "I've known this for over a week, but seeing the confirmation of the stock purchase in writing this morning just about did me in." She dabbed at her eyes. "Oh, well."

Laura Arlington stood up and attempted a smile. "You're just as nice a young man as your father keeps telling all of us you are. So you think I should just leave what's left of my portfolio alone?"

"Absolutely," Neil said. "I'm sorry this happened, Mrs. Arlington."

"Well, think of all the people in this world who don't have half a million dollars 'to piss away,' as my grandson would put it." Her eyes widened. "I cannot *believe* I said that! Forgive me." Then a hint of a smile appeared on her lips. "But you know something? I feel a lot better for saying it. Your mother and father wanted me to stop in and visit. But I think I'd better run along. Do thank them for me, please."

When she left, Neil went back to the house. His parents were in the sunroom. "Where's Laura?" his mother asked anxiously.

"I knew she wouldn't want to visit now," Robert Stephens commented. "Everything that has changed for her is just beginning to sink in."

"She's a classy lady," Neil said heatedly. "I'd like to strangle that jerk, Douglas Hansen. But I swear that first thing Monday morning I'm going to dig up every last little bit of dirt I can get to pin on him, and if there's any way I can file a complaint with the SEC, trust me, I'll do it."

"Good!" Robert Stephens said enthusiastically.

"You sound more and more like your father every day," Dolores Stephens said dryly.

Later, as Neil watched the rest of the Yankees–Red Sox game, he found himself annoyed by the feeling that he had missed something in Laura Arlington's portfolio. There was something wrong there other than a misguided investment. But what? he wondered.

) 52

DETECTIVE JIM HAGGERTY HAD KNOWN AND LIKED GRETA Shipley nearly all his life. From the time he was a little boy delivering newspapers to her door, he could never remember a single time when she hadn't been gracious and friendly to him. She also paid promptly and tipped generously when he collected on Saturday mornings.

She wasn't like some of the tightwads in the other swanky houses, he thought, who ran up bills, then paid for six weeks of papers and added on a ten-cent tip. He particularly remembered one snowy day when Mrs. Shipley had insisted he come in and get warm and had dried his gloves and knit cap on the radiator while he drank the cocoa she made for him.

Earlier that morning, when he had attended the service at Trinity Church, he was sure that many in the congregation shared the thought that he couldn't get out of his mind: Greta Shipley's death had been hastened by the shocking murder of her close friend Nuala Moore.

If someone has a heart attack when a crime is taking place, the perpetrator can sometimes be tried for murder, Haggerty thought—but how about when a friend dies in her sleep a few days later?

At the service for Mrs. Shipley, he was surprised to see Nuala Moore's stepdaughter, Maggie Holloway, sitting with Liam Payne. Liam always had an eye for pretty women, Haggerty mused, and Lord knows enough of them had had an eye for him over the years. He was one of Newport's "most eligible" bachelors.

He had also spotted Earl Bateman in church. Now *there* is a guy who may be educated enough to be a professor, but who still isn't playing with a full deck of cards, Haggerty had thought. That museum of his is like something out of the Addams Family—it gave Haggerty the shivers. Earl should have stayed in the family business, he thought. Every shirt on his back had been paid for by someone's next of kin.

Haggerty had slipped away before the recessional, but not before he deduced that Maggie Holloway must have gotten very close to Mrs. Shipley to have taken the time to come to her funeral service. The thought occurred to him that maybe if she had visited Mrs. Shipley at Latham Manor, she might have learned something from her that could be helpful in understanding why Nuala Moore had canceled the sale of her house to Malcolm Norton.

Norton was the guy Jim Haggerty believed knew something he wasn't telling. And it was that thinking that brought him unannounced to 1 Garrison Avenue at three o'clock that afternoon.

When the bell rang, Maggie was in Nuala's bedroom, where she was separating carefully folded clothing into piles: good, usable clothing for Goodwill; older, well-worn outfits for the ragbag; fairly expensive, dressy outfits for the hospital thrift shop.

She was keeping for herself the blue outfit Nuala had worn that night at the Four Seasons, as well as one of her painting smocks. Memory Lane, she thought.

In the crammed closets she had come across several

cardigans and tweed jackets—Tim Moore's clothing, she was sure, sentimentally kept by Nuala.

Nuala and I were always on the same wavelength, she mused, thinking of the box in her walk-in closet in the apartment. It held the dress she had worn the night she met Paul, as well as one of his flight suits and their matching jogging outfits.

As she sorted, Maggie's mind worked ceaselessly on an explanation for the presence of the bells at the graves. It *had* to be Earl who had placed them there, she reasoned. Was it his idea of a sly joke on women from the residence, because of the uproar that had followed his handing out the bells during his lecture at Latham Manor?

It was an explanation that made sense. He probably knew all of these women. After all, most of the residents of Latham Manor were originally from Newport, or at least had spent the spring and summer months there.

Maggie held up a robe, decided it had seen its day, and put it in the ragbag. But Nuala didn't live in Latham, she reminded herself. Did he put a bell on her grave as a tribute of friendship? He seemed to have honestly liked her.

One of the graves did not have a bell, though. Why? she wondered. I have the names of all those women, Maggie thought. Tomorrow I'm going to go back to the cemetery and copy the date they died from their tombstones. There must have been an obituary in the newspaper for each of them. I want to see what those say.

The sound of the doorbell was an unwelcome interruption. Who would just drop in? she wondered as she headed downstairs. Then she found herself praying it was not another unexpected visit from Earl Bateman; she didn't know if she could handle that this afternoon.

It took a moment to realize that the man at the door was one of the Newport police officers who had responded originally to her 911 call the night of Nuala's murder. He introduced himself as Detective Jim Haggerty. Once inside the house, he settled in the club chair with the air of a man who had nothing to do except exchange pleasantries for the day.

Maggie sat facing him, balanced on the edge of the couch. If he had any appreciation of body language, he would see that she hoped to keep this interview as brief as possible.

He began by answering a question she had not asked. "I'm afraid we're still in the dark as far as having a real suspect in mind. But this crime isn't going to go unpunished. I can promise you that," he said.

Maggie waited.

Haggerty tugged on his glasses till they rested on the end of his nose. He crossed his legs and massaged his ankle. "Old skiing injury," he explained. "Now it lets me know if the wind is shifting. It'll be raining by tomorrow night."

You didn't come to talk about the weather, Maggie thought.

"Ms. Holloway, you've been here a little over a week, and I'm glad most of our visitors don't experience the kind of shock that greeted you. And then today, I saw you in church, at the funeral for Mrs. Shipley. I guess you got friendly with her since coming here."

"Yes, I did. Actually it was a request Nuala made in her will, but it was something I did with pleasure."

"Wonderful woman, Mrs. Shipley. Knew her all my life. A shame she didn't have a family. She liked kids. Do you think she was happy at Latham Manor?"

"Yes, I do. I had dinner there with her the night she died, and she clearly enjoyed her friends."

"Did she tell you why her best friend, your stepmother, changed her mind at the last minute about moving there?"

"I don't think anyone knows that," Maggie said. "Dr.

Lane was confident that Nuala would change it yet again and decide to take the apartment. No one can be sure of her state of mind."

"I guess I was hoping that Mrs. Moore might have explained to Mrs. Shipley her reason for canceling her reservation. From what I understand, Mrs. Shipley was real pleased that her old friend was going to be under the same roof."

Maggie thought of the caricature Nuala had sketched on the poster, showing Nurse Markey eavesdropping. Was that still in Greta Shipley's apartment? she wondered.

"I don't know if this had any bearing," she said carefully, "but I believe that both Nuala and Mrs. Shipley were very careful of what they said when one of the nurses was around. She had a way of barging in without notice."

Haggerty stopped kneading his ankle. "Which nurse?" he asked, his tone a shade quicker.

"Nurse Markey."

Haggerty got up to go. "Any decisions made about the house, Ms. Holloway?"

"Well, of course the will still has to be probated, but I'm absolutely not putting it on the market at this time. In fact I may very well never put it up for sale. Newport is lovely, and it would make a nice retreat from Manhattan."

"Does Malcolm Norton know that?"

"As of this morning, he does. In fact, I told him not only do I *not* want to sell, but I have received a substantially better offer for the property."

Haggerty's eyebrows raised. "Now, this is a lovely old house, so I hope you understand I'm not being denigrating when I say that this place must have buried treasure hidden in it. I hope you find it."

"If there's anything to be found here, I intend to unearth it," Maggie said. "I'm not going to have any peace until someone pays for what happened to a woman I loved very much."

As Haggerty got up to go, Maggie impulsively asked, "Do you know if it's possible to look up some information at the newspaper office this afternoon, or is it closed on Saturday?"

"I think you'll have to wait till Monday. I happen to know that because we always have visitors wanting to look through the old society pages. They get a kick out of reading about the fancy parties."

Maggie smiled without comment.

As Haggerty drove away he made a mental note to chat with the clerk in the newspaper office on Monday and find out exactly what information Ms. Holloway was searching for in their morgue.

Maggie went back up to Nuala's room. She was determined to get through the contents of the closets and dressers before she quit today. This is the room I should use for sorting, she thought as she dragged cartons full of things into the small third bedroom.

Nuala had always enjoyed having things scattered around that reminded her of special moments. As Maggie discarded seashells from the dresser tops, stuffed animals from the window seat, a stack of restaurant menus from the nightstand, and inexpensive souvenirs from everywhere, the inherent beauty of the rock maple furniture became apparent. I'd move the bed to that wall. It's a better place for it, she decided, and get rid of that old chaise . . . And I'd keep all of Nuala's paintings that she had framed and hung. They're the part of her that I'll never lose or give up.

At six o'clock she was going through the final item of clothing in the larger closet, a pale gold raincoat that had fallen to the floor. She remembered that when she had rehung Nuala's blue cocktail suit the other day, the raincoat had been hanging precariously behind it.

As with the other garments, she ran her hand into the pockets to be sure nothing was in them.

The left-side pocket of the raincoat was empty. But when her fingertips explored the right pocket, they touched grit.

Maggie closed her fingers over the substance and removed her hand. Long shadows filled the room as she walked over to the dresser and turned on the light. A wad of dry dirt crumbled beneath her fingers. Surely Nuala didn't put dirt in her pocket, Maggie thought. Surely she didn't garden in this coat. It's practically new.

As a matter of fact, Maggie told herself, I think they had this same coat in the boutique where I shopped the other day.

Uncertainly, she laid the coat across the bed. Instinct made her decide that she wouldn't brush the rest of the dirt from the pocket now.

There was just one task left before this room would be cleared out completely. The shoes and boots and slippers that covered the floor of the larger closet had to be sorted through and categorized. Most would no doubt be discarded, but some might be worth giving to Goodwill.

No more for tonight, though, she decided. That's tomorrow's job.

It was time for the hot soak she had come to look forward to at this time of the day. And then she would get dressed for her dinner with Neil, something she hadn't thought about much during the day but which she now realized she was looking forward to.

❱ 53

JANICE AND MALCOLM NORTON HAD DRIVEN TOGETHER TO the funeral service and interment of Greta Shipley. Both of them had known Shipley all their lives, although they had never been more than acquaintances. When Janice had looked around the congregation during the eulogy, she was made freshly and bitterly aware of the financial gap that existed between her and so many of the people there.

She saw Regina Carr's mother off to one side. Regina was now Regina Carr Wayne. She had been Janice's roommate at Dana Hall, and they both had gone to Vassar. Now Wes Wayne was the chief stockholder and CEO of Cratus Pharmaceuticals, and you could be sure that Regina was not an accountant in an old-folks home.

Arlene Randel Greene's mother was weeping softly. Arlene was another Dana Hall girl from Newport. Bob Greene, an unknown screenwriter when Arlene married him, was now a powerful Hollywood producer. She was probably off on a cruise somewhere at this very moment, Janice thought, a frown of envy creasing her face.

And there were others: mothers of her friends and acquaintances. They had all come to say good-bye to their dear friend Greta Shipley. Later, as Janice accompanied them as they walked from the grave site, she listened with sour envy as they outdid each other, chronicling the busy social lives of "the girls" and their grandchildren.

She felt an emotion somewhat akin to loathing as she

watched Malcolm rush ahead to catch up with Maggie Holloway. My handsome husband, she thought bitterly. If only I hadn't wasted all that time trying to turn him into something he never could be.

And he had seemed to have it all: the good looks, the impeccable background, the excellent schools—Roxbury Latin, Williams, Columbia Law—even a membership in Mensa, where a genius IQ was the admittance requirement. But in the end, none of it had mattered; for all his credentials, Malcolm Norton was a loser.

Then to top it all, she thought, he was planning to leave me for another woman, and he had no intention of sharing with me any of the killing he expected to make off the sale of that house. Her angry ruminations were interrupted when she realized that Regina's mother was talking about Nuala Moore's death.

"Newport isn't what it used to be," she said. "And to think the house was *ransacked.* I wonder what whoever it was could have been looking for?"

Arlene Greene's mother said, "I hear that Nuala Moore changed her will the day before she died. Maybe someone who was being cut out of the old will was searching for the new one."

Janice Norton's hand flew to her mouth to stifle a gasp. Had someone suspected Nuala might be planning to write a new will, then killed her to prevent it? If Nuala had died before she actually *wrote* the new will, the sale of her house to Malcolm would have been completed, she thought. There was a signed agreement in place, and Malcolm, as executor of her estate, would have managed to complete the purchase. Besides, Janice reasoned, no one who didn't know about the impending change in the Wetlands Act would have been interested in the property.

Was Malcolm desperate enough to kill Nuala, just to get

his hands on that house? she asked herself, wondering suddenly if her husband had still more secrets he was trying to keep from her.

At the end of the walkway, good-byes were exchanged and people scattered. Ahead of her, Janice saw Malcolm walking slowly to their car. As she neared him, she saw the anguish on his face and knew Maggie Holloway must have told him she would not sell him the house.

They did not speak as they got in the car. Malcolm stared ahead for a few moments, then he turned toward her. "I'll pay off the mortgage on our house," he said quietly, his voice a monotone. "Holloway won't sell now, and she says she has a substantially higher offer anyway, which means if she does change her mind, it won't do me any good."

"*Us* any good," Janice corrected automatically, then bit her lip. She did not want to antagonize him, not now.

If he ever found out that she had had a hand in the counteroffer that was made on Nuala's house, he might well be angry enough to kill *her,* she thought with rising uneasiness. Her nephew Doug had made the offer, of course, but if Malcolm found that out, he would surely know that she had put him up to it. Had Maggie Holloway told him anything that might implicate her? she wondered.

As though reading her mind, her husband turned toward her. "Surely you haven't talked to anyone, have you, Janice?" he asked quietly.

"A bit of a headache," he had said when they reached home, his tone remote but cordial. Then he had gone upstairs to his room. It had been years since they had shared a bedroom.

He did not come downstairs again until nearly seven o'clock. Janice had been watching the evening news and looked up as he stopped at the door of the family room. "I'm going out," he said. "Good night, Janice."

She stared unseeingly at the television screen, listening carefully for the sound of the front door closing behind him. He's up to something, she thought, but what is it? She allowed him plenty of time to leave, then turned off the TV and collected her purse and car keys. She had told Malcolm earlier that she was going out to dinner. They had grown so distant of late that he didn't ask her whom she was meeting any more than she bothered to inquire about his plans.

Not that she would have told him if he had asked, Janice thought grimly as she headed for Providence. There, at a small out-of-the-way restaurant, her nephew would be waiting. And there, over steaks and scotch, he would pass her an envelope containing cash, her share for supplying him with a detailed account of Cora Gebhart's financial situation. As Doug had happily told her, "This one was a real bonanza, Aunt Janice. Keep 'em coming!"

) 54

AS MAGGIE WAS DRESSING FOR HER DATE WITH NEIL STEphens, she realized there was a stronger-than-usual hint of dampness in the sea-scented breeze that came in through the bedroom window. Ringlets and waves, she thought with resignation. She would just fluff her hair with her fingers after she had brushed it, she decided. On a night like this, it was inevitable that the natural curl would assert itself.

She thought about Neil as she continued getting ready.

Over these past months she had found herself more and more looking forward to his calls and too disappointed when they didn't come.

But it was very obvious that, to Neil, she was an occasional date and nothing more. He'd certainly made that clear. Even so, she really had expected him to call before she left for Newport, and now she was determined to place no special significance on this evening. She knew that grown children—and especially single men—when visiting their parents, frequently looked for excuses to get away.

And then there was Liam, Maggie thought briefly. She didn't quite know what to make of his sudden show of interest. "Oh well," she shrugged.

All tarted up, she thought wryly after she applied eye shadow and mascara and blush, then carefully made up her lips in a soft coral shade.

Looking through the outfits she had to choose from, she picked the one she had intended to wear to Nuala's dinner party, a vivid blue silk print blouse and matching long skirt. A narrow gold chain and earrings were her only jewelry, except for the oval-shaped sapphire ring that had belonged to her mother.

When she passed Nuala's bedroom on the way downstairs, Maggie entered for a moment and turned on the lamp on the nightstand. As she looked around, she decided definitely to make this her room. She would move into it tomorrow, after she returned from the brunch with Mrs. Bainbridge and her daughter. I can shove the furniture around by myself, she decided, and the only things I haven't cleaned out are the shoes and whatever is on the closet floor, and it won't take long to finish with that.

Walking through the living room, she noticed that the roses Liam had brought needed a change of water. She refilled the vase at the kitchen sink, reached into the clutter drawer for scissors, cut the stems, and rearranged the roses before taking them back to the living room. Then she walked around the room, "fussing" with little things, like straightening the ottoman in front of the club chair, removing some of the profusion of small framed pictures on the mantel and tabletops, leaving only a few of the most flattering ones of Nuala and her husband, plumping the pillows on the couch.

In a few minutes the room took on a more tranquil, less busy feeling. Maggie studied the space and mentally rearranged the furniture, knowing that the love seat behind which Nuala's body had been hunched would have to go. The very sight of it haunted her.

I'm nesting, she told herself, more than I've ever done anyplace since that silly little apartment Paul and I had in Texas. She was at once surprised and pleased with herself.

The front doorbell rang at ten of seven. Neil was early. Realizing how ambivalent she felt about the evening ahead of her, she waited a long minute before answering the ring. When she opened the door, she was careful to keep her voice and smile friendly but impersonal.

"Neil, how nice to see you."

Neil did not answer but stood looking down at her, studying her face, unsmiling, his eyes troubled.

Maggie opened the door wider. "As my father used to ask, 'Cat got your tongue?' Come in, for heaven's sake."

He stepped inside and waited as she closed the door; then he followed her into the living room.

"You look lovely, Maggie," he said finally, as they stood facing each other.

She raised her eyebrows. "Surprised?"

"No, of course not. But I was sick when I heard what happened to your stepmother. I know how much you were looking forward to being with her."

"Yes, I was," Maggie agreed. "Now, where are we going for dinner?"

Fumbling with his words, he asked if she'd mind having dinner with his parents to celebrate his mother's birthday.

"Why don't we just try doing this some other time?" Maggie asked curtly. "I'm sure your folks don't need a perfect stranger horning in on a family party."

"They're looking forward to meeting you, Maggie. Don't back out," Neil pleaded. "They'll know it's because of them that you didn't come."

Maggie sighed. "I guess I have to eat."

She let Neil do the talking as they drove to the restaurant, answering his questions as directly and succinctly as possible. She noted with some amusement, however, that he was being especially attentive and charming, and it took all of her determination to maintain her aloofness.

She had intended to continue treating Neil with distinct reserve throughout the evening, but the warmth of his parents' greeting and their obviously sincere distress over what had happened to Nuala made it impossible not to loosen up.

"My dear, you didn't know a soul up here," Dolores Stephens said. "How awful for you to go through all that alone."

"Actually I do know one person fairly well—the man who took me to the party at the Four Seasons where I met Nuala again." Maggie looked over at Neil. "Maybe you know him, Neil. Liam Payne. He's in the investment business, too. He has his own firm in Boston but comes to New York regularly."

"Liam Payne," Neil said thoughtfully. "Yes, I do know him slightly. He's a good investment guy. Too good for his former bosses at Randolph and Marshall, if I remember correctly. He took some of their best clients with him when he went out on his own."

Maggie could not resist a feeling of satisfaction at seeing the frown on Neil's face. Let him wonder if Liam is important to me, she thought. He's already made it plain how unimportant I am to him.

Nevertheless over a relaxing meal that included lobster and chardonnay, she found herself thoroughly enjoying Neil's parents and was flattered to learn that Dolores Stephens was familiar with her fashion photography.

"When I read the newspaper about your stepmother's death," Mrs. Stephens said, "and then when Neil spoke about Maggie, I didn't connect you with your work. Then this afternoon when I was reading *Vogue,* I saw your name under the Armani spread. A thousand years ago—before I was married—I worked in a small advertising agency, and we had the Givenchy account. That was before Givenchy became famous. I used to have to go to all the shoots."

"Then you know all about . . ." Maggie began, and soon found herself telling war stories about temperamental designers and difficult models, ending with the last job that she had done before coming to Newport. They agreed there was nothing worse for a photographer than a nervous and indecisive art director.

As she opened up more, Maggie found herself telling them about her inclination to keep the house. "It's too soon to be sure, so the best thing is to do nothing for a while, I guess. But in a way, living in the house this week makes me understand why Nuala was so reluctant to give it up."

At Neil's inquiry, she told them about Nuala canceling her reservation at Latham Manor. "It was even for the large unit she had particularly wanted," she explained. "And I understand that they go quickly."

"Neil and I were over there today," Robert Stephens said. "He's scouting it for one of his clients."

"It sounds to me as though the apartment your stepmother

didn't take is the one that's being offered right now," Neil commented.

"And it's the same one that Laura Arlington wanted," his father noted. "Seems to me there is a real scramble for those places."

"Someone else wanted it?" Maggie asked quickly. "Did she change her mind?"

"No. She got talked into investing the bulk of her money in a fly-by-night stock and, unfortunately, lost it all," Neil said.

The conversation drifted to many other subjects, with Neil's mother gradually drawing her out about her childhood. While Neil and his father got into a discussion about how Neil might follow through in looking into the bad investment Mrs. Arlington had made, Maggie found herself telling Dolores Stephens that her birth mother had died in an accident when she was an infant and how happy she had been the five years Nuala and she had lived together.

Finally, realizing that tears were close, she said, "No more nostalgia and no more wine. I'm getting mushy."

When Neil drove Maggie home, he walked her to the door and took the key from her hand. "I'll only stay a minute," he said, opening the door. "I just want to see something. Which way is the kitchen?"

"Back through the dining room." Bewildered, Maggie followed him.

He went immediately to the door and examined the lock. "From what I read, the police think that the intruder either found this door unlocked, or your stepmother opened it for someone she knew."

"That's right."

"I offer a third possibility: That lock is so loose anyone

could open it with a credit card," he said, and then proceeded to demonstrate the fact.

"I have a call in to a locksmith," Maggie said. "I guess I'll hear from him Monday."

"Not good enough. My dad is a wunderkind around the house, and I grew up as his unwilling little helper. I, or maybe both of us, will be back tomorrow to install a dead bolt and check all the windows."

No "if you'd like" or "is that okay?" Maggie thought, feeling a surge of irritation. Just "this is the way it is."

"I'm going out to brunch," she told him.

"Brunch is usually over by two," Neil said. "Let's figure on that time, or if you want, you can tell me where you'll hide a key."

"No, I'll be here."

Neil picked up one of the kitchen chairs and wedged it under the doorknob. "At least this would make noise if anyone tried to get in," he said. Then he looked around the room before turning to her. "Maggie, I don't want to alarm you, but from everything I've heard, the consensus of opinion is that whoever murdered your stepmother was looking for something, and no one knows what it was, or if he got it."

"Assuming it was a 'he,' " Maggie said. "But you're right. That's exactly what the police think."

"I don't like the idea of you being here alone," he said as they walked to the front door.

"I'm honestly not nervous, Neil. I've been taking care of myself for a long time."

"And if you were nervous, you'd never admit it to me. Right?"

She looked up at him, taking in his grave, questioning face. "That's right," she said simply.

He sighed as he turned and opened the door. "I enjoyed tonight very much, Maggie. See you tomorrow."

Later, as Maggie tossed about in bed, she found she could take no satisfaction in having wounded Neil, and it was obvious she had. Tit for tat, she tried to tell herself, but knowing she had evened the score didn't make her feel any better. Game playing in relationships was not one of her favorite pastimes.

Her last thoughts as she finally began to doze off were disjointed, seemingly irrelevant, emerging totally from her subconscious.

Nuala had applied for an apartment at Latham Manor, then died shortly after withdrawing the application.

The Stephenses' friend, Laura Arlington, had applied for the same apartment, then lost all her money.

Was that apartment jinxed, and if so, *why?*

) **55**

AT HIS WIFE'S URGING, DR. WILLIAM LANE HAD BEGUN the practice of joining the residents and their guests at Latham Manor's Sunday brunch.

As Odile had pointed out, the residence functioned as a kind of family, and visitors invited to partake of the brunch were potential future residents who might thus come to view Latham in a very favorable light.

"I don't mean we have to spend *hours* there, darling," she fluttered, "but you're such a caring person, and if people know that their mothers or aunts or whoever are in such good hands, then when the time comes for them to make a change they might want to join us as well."

Lane had thought a thousand times that if Odile were not so empty-headed, he might suspect that she was being sarcastic. But the truth was, since they had started the formal Sunday brunches, which also had been her suggestion, and then begun attending them, the number of people filling out forms indicating "possible future interest" had increased sharply.

But when he and Odile entered the grand salon that Sunday morning, Dr. Lane was anything but pleased to see Maggie Holloway with Mrs. Bainbridge's daughter, Sarah Cushing.

Odile had spotted them as well. "Maggie Holloway *does* seem to make friends quickly," she murmured to him.

Together they made their way across the room, pausing to chat with residents, to greet familiar visitors, and to be introduced to others.

Maggie had not seen them approaching. When they spoke to her, she smiled apologetically. "You must think I'm like *The Man Who Came to Dinner*," she said. "Mrs. Cushing asked me to join her and Mrs. Bainbridge for brunch, but Mrs. Bainbridge was feeling a little tired this morning, so she thought it best if we didn't go out."

"You are always welcome," Dr. Lane said gallantly, and then turned to Sarah. "Should I look in on your mother?"

"No," Sarah said decisively. "She'll be along in a moment. Doctor, is it true that Eleanor Chandler has decided to become a resident here?"

"As a matter of fact, it is," he said. "When she heard of Mrs. Shipley's demise, she phoned to request that apartment. She wants her decorator to redo it, so she probably won't actually move in for several months."

"And I think that's better," Odile Lane volunteered earnestly. "This way, Mrs. Shipley's friends will have a period of adjustment, don't you think?"

Sarah Cushing ignored the question. "The only reason I asked about Mrs. Chandler is that I want to make it absolutely clear that she is not to be put at my mother's table. She is an *impossible* woman. I suggest you seat her with any hard-of-hearing guests you may have. They, mercifully, would miss some of her overbearing opinions."

Dr. Lane smiled nervously. "I will make a special note of the seating arrangements, Mrs. Cushing," he said. "As a matter of fact, an inquiry was made yesterday about the large two-bedroom apartment, on behalf of the Van Hillearys from Connecticut. The gentleman is going to recommend that they come to see it. Perhaps if it works out, your mother would want to consider having them at the table."

The gentleman . . . He's talking about Neil, Maggie thought.

Mrs. Cushing raised an eyebrow. "Of course I'd want to meet them first, but Mother does enjoy having men around."

"Mother certainly does," Mrs. Bainbridge said dryly. They all turned as she joined them. "Sorry to be late, Maggie. Seems as though it takes longer and longer to do less and less these days. Do I understand that Greta Shipley's apartment is already sold?"

"Yes, it is," Dr. Lane said smoothly. "Mrs. Shipley's relatives will be here this afternoon to remove her personal effects and arrange for her furniture to be shipped out. Now if you'll excuse us, Odile and I should visit with some of the other guests."

When they were out of earshot, Letitia Bainbridge said, "Sarah, when *I* close my eyes, make sure that nobody goes near my apartment until the first of the next month. The maintenance fee is supposed to guarantee that much. Seems to me that around here you're not allowed to get cold before they've replaced you."

Soft chimes signaled that brunch was being served. As soon as they were seated, Maggie noticed that everybody at their table had shifted places, and wondered if that was customary after a death.

Sarah Cushing was the right person for this group today,

she thought. Like her mother, she was a good storyteller. As Maggie nibbled on eggs Benedict, and sipped her coffee, she listened appreciatively to Sarah Cushing's skillful management of the conversation, directing it so that everyone was involved and cheerful.

During the second round of coffee, however, the talk turned to Greta Shipley. Rachel Crenshaw, who with her husband was sitting opposite Maggie, said, "I still can't get used to it. We know we're all going to die, and when someone moves to the long-term care area, you know it's usually only a matter of time. But Greta and Constance—it was just so sudden!"

"And last year Alice and Jeanette went the same way," Mrs. Bainbridge said, and then sighed.

Alice and Jeanette, Maggie thought. Those names were on two of the graves I visited with Mrs. Shipley. They both had bells embedded next to the tombstones. The woman whose grave didn't have a bell was named Winifred Pierson. Trying to sound casual, Maggie said, "Mrs. Shipley had a close friend, Winifred Pierson. Was she a guest here as well?"

"No, Winifred lived in her own home. Greta used to visit her regularly," Mrs. Crenshaw said.

Maggie felt her mouth go dry. She knew immediately what she had to do, and the full realization came with such force that she almost stood up from the table with the shock of it. She had to visit Greta Shipley's grave and see if a bell had been placed there.

When good-byes were said, most of the Latham residents began drifting into the library, where a violinist was scheduled to perform for the Sunday afternoon entertainment.

Sarah Cushing stayed to visit with her mother, and Maggie headed for the front door. Then, on sudden impulse, she turned and went up the stairs to Greta Shipley's apartment. Let the cousins be there, she prayed fervently.

The door of the apartment was open, and she saw the familiar signs of packing and sorting, which was being done by the three relatives she had seen at the funeral.

Knowing there was no simple way to make the request, she offered brief condolences and plunged in to tell them what she wanted. "When I was visiting Mrs. Shipley on Wednesday, she showed me a sketch my stepmother and she had made. It's right in that drawer." Maggie pointed to the table by the couch. "It was one of the last things Nuala did, and if you're thinking of discarding it, it would mean a lot to me to have it."

"Absolutely." "Go right ahead." "Take it," they chorused amiably.

"We haven't gotten to anything except the bureau so far," one of them added.

Maggie opened the drawer expectantly. It was empty. The sketch to which Nuala had added her own face, Greta Shipley's face, and the image of Nurse Markey eavesdropping, was gone. "It isn't here," she said.

"Then perhaps Greta either moved it or disposed of it," said a cousin who bore a striking resemblance to Mrs. Shipley. "Dr. Lane told us that after anyone passes away, the apartment is immediately locked until the family comes in and removes personal items. But do tell us what the sketch looks like in case we come across it."

Maggie described it, gave them her phone number, thanked them, and left. Somebody *took* that sketch, she thought as she left the room. But why?

Stepping into the hall, she almost ran into Nurse Markey.

"Oh, excuse me," the nurse said. "I just want to see if I can give Mrs. Shipley's relatives a hand. Have a nice day, Miss Holloway."

) 56

IT WAS NOON WHEN EARL BATEMAN ARRIVED AT ST. Mary's cemetery. He circled the winding roads slowly, ever anxious to get a look at the kinds of people who were spending a part of their Sunday visiting a loved one.

Not too many out so far today, he noted: a few oldsters, a middle-aged couple, a large family, probably showing up for an anniversary, after which they would have brunch at the restaurant down the road. The typical Sunday crew.

He then drove through to the old section of Trinity cemetery, where he parked and got out. After a quick glance around, he began to scrutinize the tombstones for interesting inscriptions. It had been several years since he took rubbings here, and he knew he might well have missed some.

He prided himself that his awareness of subtleties had heightened considerably since then. Yes, he thought, tombstones definitely would be a subject to outline for the cable series. He would start with a reference from *Gone With the Wind,* which said that three infant boys, all named Gerald O'Hara, Jr., were buried in the family plot on Tara. *Oh, the hopes, and dreams, we see sculpted on stone, fading, ignored, no longer read, but still leaving a message of lasting love. Think of it—three little sons!* That's the way he would begin that lecture.

Of course, he would move quickly from tragic to upbeat by telling about one of the stones he had seen in a Cape Cod cemetery, actually advertising the fact that the business operation that had been run by the deceased was being carried on by his son. It even gave the new address.

Earl frowned as he looked about him. Even though it was a warm and pleasant October day, and even though he thoroughly enjoyed his profitable hobby, he was upset and angry.

As they had arranged, last night Liam had come to his house for drinks and then they had gone out to dinner together. Even though he had left his three-thousand-dollar check right next to the vodka bottle on the bar where it couldn't possibly be missed, Liam had pointedly ignored it. Instead, he had emphasized yet again that Earl ought to go golfing instead of haunting cemeteries.

"Haunting" indeed, Earl thought, his face darkening. I could show him what haunting is all about, he said to himself.

And he was damned if he would let Liam warn him away from Maggie Holloway again. It simply was none of his business. Liam had asked if he had seen her, and when he told Liam that since Monday night he had seen Maggie only at the cemetery and, of course, at Mrs. Shipley's funeral, Liam had said, "Earl, you and your cemeteries. I'm getting worried about you. You're becoming obsessive."

"He didn't *believe* me when I tried to explain my premonitions," Earl muttered aloud. "He never takes me seriously." He stopped suddenly and looked about. There was no one. Don't think about it anymore, he warned himself, at least not now.

He walked along the paths of the oldest section of the cemetery, where some of the barely discernible carvings on the small headstones bore dates from the 1600s. He squatted by one that had almost fallen over, squinting to read the faint lettering. His eyes brightened as he made out the inscription: "Betrothed to Roger Samuels but gathered to the Lord . . ." and the dates.

Earl opened his kit to take a rubbing of the stone. Another angle to discuss in one of his lectures on tombstones would be the tender age at which so many young people were struck down in the old days. *There had been no penicillin to treat the pneumonia that resulted when winter cold made its insidious way into chests and lungs . . .*

He knelt down, enjoying the feel of the soft earth that sent its cool dampness through his old trousers to his skin. As he began his careful effort to transfer the stone's poignant sentiment onto thin, almost translucent parchment, he found himself thinking of the young girl who lay beneath him, her body sheltered by the ageless ground.

She had just passed her sixteenth birthday, he calculated.

Had she been pretty? Yes, very pretty, he decided. She had had a cloud of dark curls, and sapphire blue eyes. And she had been small boned.

Maggie Holloway's face floated before him.

At one-thirty, as he was driving back toward the entrance of the cemetery, Earl passed a vehicle with New York plates parked at the curb. It looks familiar, he thought, then realized that it was Maggie Holloway's Volvo wagon. What was she doing here again today? he wondered. Greta Shipley's grave was nearby, but certainly Maggie wasn't so close to Greta that she would feel the need to visit the grave again, only a day after the funeral.

Slowing his car, he looked about. When he spotted Maggie in the distance, walking toward him, he put his foot on the accelerator. He didn't want her to see him. Clearly something was going on. He had to think about this.

He did make one decision. Since he did not have classes tomorrow, he would stay an extra day in Newport. And whether Liam liked it or not, tomorrow he was going to visit Maggie Holloway.

) 57

MAGGIE WALKED QUICKLY AWAY FROM GRETA SHIPLEY'S grave, her hands jammed in the pockets of her jacket, her eyes not seeing the path she was following.

In every fiber of her being, she felt chilled and shaken. She had found it, buried so deeply that, had she not run her hand over every inch of the area at the base of the tombstone, she might have missed it.

A bell! *Exactly* like the one she had taken from Nuala's grave. Like the bells on the other women's graves. Like the bells that well-to-do Victorians had placed on their graves in case they were buried while still alive.

Who had come back here since the funeral and put that object on Mrs. Shipley's grave? she wondered. And *why?*

Liam had told her that his cousin Earl had had twelve of these bells cast to use to illustrate his lectures. He had also indicated that Earl apparently relished the fact that he had frightened the women at Latham Manor by handing the bells out during his talk there.

Was this Earl's idea of a bizarre joke, Maggie wondered,

putting these bells on the graves of Latham Manor residents?

It's possible, she decided as she reached her car. It could be his warped and demented way of taking some small revenge for having been criticized publicly by Mrs. Bainbridge's daughter. According to Liam, Sarah had gathered the bells, thrust them at Earl, and then had practically ordered him out of the residence.

Revenge was a logical, if appalling, explanation. I'm glad I took the one from Nuala's grave, Maggie thought. I feel like going back and collecting the others too—especially the one from Mrs. Shipley's plot.

But she decided against it, at least for the time being. She wanted to be certain that they were, in fact, nothing more than Earl's childish and sickening act of revenge. I will come back later, she decided. Besides, I've got to get home. Neil said he would be there at two.

As she drove down her street, she noticed that two cars were parked in front of her house. Pulling into the driveway, she saw that Neil and his father were sitting on the porch steps, a tool kit between them.

Mr. Stephens waved aside her apologies. "You're not late. It's only one minute of two. Unless my son is mistaken, which is a distinct possibility, he said we'd be here at two."

"Apparently I make a lot of mistakes," Neil said, looking directly at Maggie.

She ignored the remark, refusing to rise to the bait. "It's awfully nice of both of you to come," she said sincerely. Unlocking the door, she led them in.

Robert Stephens examined the front door as he closed it. "Needs weather stripping," he observed. "Pretty soon that sea air will get mighty cold, with a stiff wind behind it. Now I'd like to start at that back door Neil told me about, and then we'll check all the window locks and see which ones need replacing. I have some spares with me, and I'll come back if you need more."

Neil stood beside Maggie. Keenly aware of his nearness, she stepped away as he said, "Humor him, Maggie. My grandfather built an atomic-bomb shelter after World War II. When I was growing up, my friends and I used it as a hangout. By then people realized those shelters would be as useless in a nuclear attack as a parasol in a tornado. *My* father has something of *his* father's 'anticipate the worst' mentality. He always anticipates the unthinkable."

"Absolutely true," Robert Stephens agreed. "And in this house I would say the unthinkable took place ten days ago."

Maggie saw Neil wince and said hastily, "I'm very grateful you're here."

"If you want to do anything, we won't be in your way," Robert Stephens told her as they went into the kitchen and he opened his tool kit, spreading it out on the table.

"I think you should stay with us," Neil urged. "We might want to ask you about something." He added, "Don't disappear, Maggie."

Looking at him, dressed as he was in a tan shirt, chinos, and sneakers, Maggie found herself wishing she were holding her camera. She realized there was an aspect to Neil she had never seen in the city. He doesn't have that "Don't invade my territory" air about him today, she thought. He looks as though he actually might care about other people's feelings. Even *my* feelings.

His forehead was creased with a look of worried concern, and his dark brown eyes had the same questioning look Maggie had observed last night.

Then, as his father began working at the old door lock, Neil said in a low voice, "Maggie, I can tell something is bothering you. I wish to God you'd let me in on it."

"Neil, give me the big screwdriver," his father ordered.

Maggie settled in an old bentwood chair. "I'll watch. Maybe I can learn something useful."

For nearly an hour, father and son worked, going from room to room, examining windows, tightening some locks, noting others for replacement. In the studio, Robert Stephens asked to examine the clay sculptures on the refectory table. When Maggie showed him the one she was beginning of Greta Shipley, he said, "I hear she wasn't well at the end. Last time I saw her, she was pretty sprightly, even feisty."

"Is this Nuala?" Neil asked, pointing to the other bust.

"There's a lot of work to do on it, but yes, that was Nuala. I guess my fingers saw something I didn't realize. She always had such a merry look, but it isn't there for me now."

When they were on the way downstairs, Robert Stephens pointed to Nuala's room. "I hope you're planning to move in there," he said. "It's twice the size of the guest rooms."

"As a matter of fact, I am," Maggie admitted.

Mr. Stephens stood at the door. "That bed should be opposite the windows, not where it is now."

Maggie felt helpless. "I'm planning to put it there."

"Who was going to help you?"

"I thought I'd just start yanking. I'm stronger than I look."

"You're kidding! You don't mean you were going to try to shove this rock maple around yourself? Come on, Neil, we'll start with the bed. Where do you want the dresser moved, Maggie?"

Neil paused only long enough to say, "Don't take it personally. He's like this with everyone."

"Everyone I *care* about," his father corrected.

In less than ten minutes the furniture had been rearranged. As she watched, Maggie planned the way she would redecorate the room. The old wallpaper needed replacing, she decided. And then the floor would have to be refinished, and then she would get area rugs to replace the faded green carpet.

Nesting again, she thought.

"Okay, that's it," Robert Stephens announced.

Maggie and Neil followed him down the stairs as he said, "I'm on my way. Some folks coming over for a drink later. Neil, you'll be up next weekend?"

"Absolutely," Neil said. "I'm taking Friday off again."

"Maggie, I'll be back with the other locks, but I'll call you first," Robert Stephens said as he headed out the door. He was in his car before Maggie could even thank him.

"He's wonderful," she said as she watched his car disappear.

"Incredible as it may seem, I think so too," Neil said, smiling. "Some people, of course, find him overwhelming." He paused for a moment. "Were you at your stepmother's grave this morning, Maggie?"

"No, I wasn't. What makes you think that?"

"Because the knees of your slacks are stained with dirt. I'm sure you weren't gardening in that outfit."

Maggie realized that, with Neil and his father here, she had shaken off or at least suspended the profound uneasiness caused by finding the bell on Greta Shipley's grave. Neil's question quickly brought back the old concern.

But she couldn't talk about it now, not to Neil, not to anyone, really, she decided. Not until she had found some way to determine whether Earl Bateman was responsible for the placement of the bells.

Seeing the change in her face, Neil confronted her. "Maggie, what the hell is the matter?" he asked, his voice low and intense. "You're mad at me and I don't know why, except that I didn't phone you in time to get this number before you left. I'll kick myself for that for the rest of my life. If I had known what had happened, I'd have been here for you."

"Would you?" Maggie shook her head, looking away. "Neil, I'm trying to work a lot of things through, things that don't make sense and may be the product of my overactive imagination. But they're things I've got to work through myself. Can we leave it at that for now?"

"I assume I have no choice," Neil said. "Look, I've got to be on my way. I have to get ready for a board meeting in the morning. But I'll call you tomorrow, and I'll be here Thursday afternoon. You're staying until next Sunday?"

"Yes," Maggie replied, adding to herself, And maybe by then I'll have some answers to my questions about Earl Bateman and about these bells and . . .

Her thoughts were interrupted as, unbidden, Latham Manor Residence jumped into her mind. "Neil, last night you said that you and your father were at Latham Manor yesterday. You were looking at a two-bedroom suite for your clients, weren't you?"

"Yes. Why?"

"Nuala almost took that suite. And didn't you say that another woman would have taken it but couldn't because she lost her money in a bad investment?"

"That's right. And he stung another client of Dad's who was on Latham's waiting list—Cora Gebhart. And that's something else I intend to take care of this week. I'm going to investigate the snake who roped both of them into making those investments, and if I can find anything at all to hang on Doug Hansen, I'll turn him in to the SEC. Maggie, what are you driving at?"

"Doug Hansen!" Maggie exclaimed.

"Yes. Why? Do you know him?"

"Not really, but let me know what you find out about him," she said, remembering that she had told Hansen she would not discuss his offer. "It's just that I've heard of him."

"Well, don't invest money with him," Neil said grimly. "Okay, I've got to go." He bent down and kissed her cheek. "Lock the door behind me."

She didn't hear his footsteps on the porch stairs until the decisive click of the dead-bolt lock signaled that the house was secure.

She watched him drive away. The front windows faced east, and late afternoon shadows were already filtering through the leaf-filled branches of the trees.

The house felt suddenly quiet and empty. Maggie looked down at her cream-colored slacks and pondered the streaks of dirt Neil had questioned.

I'll change and go up to the studio for a while, she decided. Then tomorrow morning I'll clean out the closet floor and move my things into Nuala's room. There were so many questions Maggie wished she could ask Nuala. Refining her features in the clay would be a way of communicating with her. And maybe I'll be able to think through my fingers what we can't talk about together, she thought.

And she could ask questions that needed to be answered, like, "Nuala, was there some reason you were *afraid* to live in Latham Manor?"

) 58

MALCOLM NORTON OPENED HIS OFFICE ON MONDAY MORN-
ing at the usual time, nine-thirty. He passed through the
reception area where Barbara Hoffman's desk faced the
door. The desk, however, was now cleared of all Barbara's
personal belongings. The framed pictures of her three children and their families, the narrow vase in which she had
kept seasonal flowers or a sprig of leaves, the orderly pile
of current work—all of these were missing.

Norton shivered slightly. The reception area was clinical
and cold once more. Janice's idea of interior decorating, he
thought grimly. Cold. Sterile. Like her.

And like me, he added bitterly as he crossed into his
office. No clients. No appointments—the day loomed long
and quiet before him. The thought occurred to him that he
had two hundred thousand dollars in the bank. Why not just
withdraw it and disappear? he asked himself.

If Barbara would join him, he would do just that, in

an instant. Let Janice have the mortgaged house. In a good market, it was worth nearly twice the amount of the mortgage. Equitable distribution, he thought, remembering the bank statement he had found in his wife's briefcase.

But Barbara was gone. The reality of it was just beginning to sink in. He had known the minute Chief Brower left the other day that she would leave. Brower's questioning of both of them had terrified her. She had felt his hostility, and it had been the deciding thing for her—she had to leave.

How much did Brower know? Norton wondered. He sat at his desk, his hands folded. Everything had been so well planned. If the buy agreement with Nuala had gone into effect, he would have given her the twenty thousand he had gotten by cashing in his retirement money. They wouldn't have closed on the sale for ninety days, which would have given him time to sign a settlement with Janice, then float a demand loan to cover the purchase.

If only Maggie Holloway hadn't come into the picture, he thought bitterly.

If only Nuala hadn't made a new will.

If only he hadn't had to let Janice in on the change in the wetlands preservation laws.

If only . . .

Malcolm had driven past Barbara's house this morning. It had the closed look that houses get when the summer residents lock up for the winter. Shades were drawn on every window; a smattering of unswept leaves had blown onto the porch and the walk. Barbara must have left for Colorado on Saturday. She had not called him. She just left.

Malcolm Norton sat in his dark, still office, contemplating his next move. He knew what he was going to do, the only question now was when to do it.

) 59

ON MONDAY MORNING, LARA HORGAN ASKED AN ASSIStant in the coroner's office to run a check on Zelda Markey, the nurse employed at the Latham Manor Residence in Newport who had found Mrs. Greta Shipley's body.

The initial report was in by late morning. It showed she had a good work record. No professional complaints ever had been filed against her. She was a lifelong resident of Rhode Island. During her twenty years of practice, she had worked at three hospitals and four nursing homes, all within the state. She had been at Latham Manor since it opened.

Except for Latham, she'd done a lot of moving around, Dr. Horgan thought. "Follow up with the personnel people at the places where she's worked," she instructed the assistant. "There's something about that lady that bothers me."

She then phoned the Newport police and asked to speak to Chief Brower. In the short time since she was appointed coroner, they had come to like and respect each other.

She asked Brower about the investigation of the Nuala Moore murder. He told her they had no specific leads but were following up on a couple of things and trying to approach the crime from all the logical angles. As they were speaking, Detective Jim Haggerty stuck his head in the chief's office.

"Hold on, Lara," Brower said. "Haggerty was doing a little follow-up on Nuala Moore's stepdaughter. He has an expression on his face that tells me he's onto something."

"Maybe," Haggerty said. "Maybe not." He took out his notebook. "At 10:45 this morning, Nuala Moore's stepdaughter, Maggie Holloway, went into the morgue at the *Newport Sentinel* and requested to see the obituaries of five women. Since all five were longtime Newport residents, extensive features had been written on each of them. Ms. Holloway took the computer printouts and left. I have a copy of them here."

Brower repeated Haggerty's report to Lara Horgan, then added, "Ms. Holloway arrived here ten days ago for the first time. It's pretty certain she couldn't have known any of these women except Greta Shipley. We'll study those obits to see if we can figure out what might have made them so interesting to her. I'll get back to you."

"Chief, do me a favor," Dr. Horgan asked. "Fax copies of them to me too, okay?"

) 60

JANICE NORTON OBSERVED WITH A NOTE OF CYNICISM THAT life in Latham Manor did manage to survive the momentary upheaval caused by a recent death. Spurred on by her nephew's lavish praise for the assist she had provided in relieving Cora Gebhart of her financial assets, Janice was anxious to dip once more into Dr. Lane's applicant file, which he kept in his desk.

She had to be careful never to be caught going through

his desk. To avoid being found out, she scheduled her furtive visits at times when she was sure he was out of the residence.

Late Monday afternoon was one of those times. The Lanes were driving to Boston for some sort of medical affair, a cocktail party and dinner. Janice knew that the rest of the office staff would take advantage of his absence and would be scurrying out at five o'clock on the dot.

That would be the ideal time to take the entire file to her own office and to study it carefully.

Lane's in a really sunny mood, she thought as he popped his head into her office at three-thirty to announce he was leaving. Soon she understood the reason for his upbeat manner as he told her that someone had been by over the weekend to look at the big apartment for some clients and then had recommended it to them. The Van Hillearys had called to say they would be coming up next Sunday.

"From what I understand, they're very substantial people who would use the residence as their base in the northeast," Dr. Lane said with obvious satisfaction. "We could wish for more guests like that."

Meaning much less service for all that money, Janice thought. It sounds unlikely that they'll be much good to Doug and me. If they like this place, then they already have an apartment available to them. But even if they were just going on the waiting list, there is too much risk in ripping off a couple with major assets, she reasoned. Inevitably they were surrounded by financial advisers who kept a hawk-eye watch on investments. Even her charming nephew would have a tough time softening them up.

"Well, I hope you and Odile enjoy the evening, Doctor," Janice said as she turned briskly back to the computer. He would have been suspicious if she had stepped out of character by making small talk.

The rest of the afternoon crawled by for her. She knew it wasn't just the anticipation of getting at the files that made the day drag. It was also the faint, nagging suspicion that someone had gone through her briefcase.

Ridiculous, she told herself. Who could have done it? Malcolm doesn't come near my room, never mind his turning into a snooper. Then a thought came that brought a smile to her face. I'm getting paranoid because that's exactly what I'm doing to Dr. Lane, she reasoned. Besides, Malcolm doesn't have enough brains to spy on me.

On the other hand, she *did* have a hunch he was up to something. From now on she resolved to keep her personal bank statements and her copies of the files away from any place where he would have a chance to happen on them.

) *61*

NEIL'S TWO EARLY MEETINGS ON MONDAY MORNING KEPT him out of his office until eleven o'clock. When he finally arrived there, he immediately called Maggie, but got no answer.

He then called the Van Hillearys and briefly gave them his impression of Latham Manor, concluding with a recommendation that they visit there so they could judge the place for themselves.

His next call was to the private investigator who worked on confidential assignments for Carson & Parker, requesting a dossier on Douglas Hansen. "Dig deep," he instructed,

"I know there's got to be something there. This guy is a world-class sleaze."

He then called Maggie again and was relieved when she picked up. She sounded breathless when she answered. "I just got in," she told him.

Neil was sure he could hear agitation and anxiety in her voice. "Maggie, is anything wrong?" he asked.

"No, not at all."

Her denial was almost a whisper, as though she were afraid of being overheard.

"Is someone with you?" he asked, his concern growing.

"No, I'm alone. I just got here."

It wasn't like Maggie to repeat herself, but Neil realized that, once again, she was not going to let him in on whatever was bothering her. He wanted to bombard her with questions, like "Where have you been?" and "Have you come up with any answers to the things you said were bothering you?" and "Can I help?" but he didn't. He knew better.

Instead, he said simply, "Maggie, I'm here. Just remember that if you want to talk to someone."

"I'll remember."

And you'll do nothing about it, he thought. "Okay, I'll call you tomorrow."

He replaced the receiver and sat for long minutes before punching in the number of his parents' home. His father answered. Neil got straight to the point. "Dad, have you got those locks for Maggie's windows?"

"Just picked them up."

"Good. Do me a favor and phone over there and tell her you want to put them in this afternoon. I think something has come up that is making her nervous."

"I'll take care of it."

It was a mixed comfort, Neil thought wryly, that Maggie might be more willing to confide in his father than in himself. But at least his father would be on the alert to pick up any hint of problems.

Trish came into his office the moment he was off the phone. In her hand she held a stack of messages. As she placed them on his desk, she pointed to the one on top. "I see your new client asked you to sell stock she doesn't own," she said severely.

"What are you talking about?" Neil demanded.

"Nothing much. Just the clearinghouse has notified us that they have no record of Cora Gebhart owning the fifty thousand shares of stock you sold for her on Friday."

☽ 62

MAGGIE HUNG UP AT THE END OF HER CALL FROM NEIL and went to the stove. Automatically she filled the kettle. She wanted the feeling of hot tea warming her. She needed something that would help her separate the jarring reality of the obituaries from the disturbing, even crazy, thoughts that were shooting through her head.

She did a quick mental review of what she had learned so far.

Last week when she had taken Greta Shipley to the cemetery, they had left flowers at Nuala's grave and the graves of five other women.

Someone had placed a bell on three of those graves as well as on Nuala's. She had found them there herself.

There was an impression, as if a bell had been sunk into

the earth, near Mrs. Rhinelander's tombstone, but for some reason *that* bell was missing.

Greta Shipley had died in her sleep two days later, and barely twenty-four hours after she was buried a bell had been placed on her grave as well.

Maggie laid the printouts of the obituaries on the table and read quickly through them again. They confirmed what had occurred to her yesterday: Winifred Pierson, the one woman in that group whose grave showed no evidence of a bell, had a large, caring family. She had died with her personal physician in attendance.

With the exception of Nuala, who had been murdered in her own home, the other women had died in their sleep.

Meaning, Maggie thought, that no one was in attendance at the time of death.

They had all been under the ongoing care of Dr. William Lane, director of Latham Manor.

Dr. Lane. Maggie thought of how quickly Sarah Cushing had rushed her mother to an outside doctor. Was it because she knew, or maybe subconsciously suspected, that Dr. Lane was not a skillful practitioner?

Or perhaps *too* skillful a practitioner? a nagging inner voice queried. Remember, Nuala was murdered.

Don't think that way, she warned herself. But no matter how one looked at it, she thought, Latham Manor had been a jinx for a lot of people. Two of Mr. Stephens' clients had lost their money while they were waiting to get into the place, and five women, all Latham residents—who weren't that elderly, or that sick—had died in their sleep there.

What had made Nuala change her mind about selling her house and going to live there? she wondered again. And what made Douglas Hansen, who had sold stocks to the women who lost their money, show up here wanting to buy this house? Maggie shook her head. There has to be a connection, she told herself, but what is it?

The kettle was whistling. As Maggie got up to make the tea, the phone rang. It was Neil's father. He said, "Maggie, I've got those locks. I'm on my way over. If you have to go out, tell me where I can find a key."

"No, I'll be here."

Twenty minutes later he was at the door. After a "Good to see you, Maggie," he said, "I'll start upstairs."

While he changed the locks, she worked in the kitchen, straightening drawers, tossing out the odds and ends she found in most of them. The sound of his footsteps overhead was reassuring; she used the time while she worked to once more think through all that she knew. Putting together all the pieces of the puzzle she had so far, she came to a decision: she had absolutely no right to voice any suspicions about Dr. Lane as yet, but there was no reason not to talk about Douglas Hansen, she decided.

Robert Stephens came back to the kitchen. "Okay, you're all set. No charge, but can you spare a cup of coffee? Instant is fine. I'm easy to please."

He settled in a chair, and Maggie knew he was studying her. Neil sent him, she thought. He could tell I was upset.

"Mr. Stephens," she began, "you don't know very much about Douglas Hansen, do you?"

"Enough to know that he's wrecked the lives of some very nice women, Maggie. But have I ever met him? No. Why do you ask?"

"Because both the ladies you know who lost their money thanks to him had been planning to go into Latham Manor, which meant they could afford a sizable outlay of money. My stepmother also had planned to live there, but she changed her mind at the last minute. Last week, Hansen showed up here and offered me fifty thousand dollars more for this house than Nuala almost sold it for, and from what I've learned, that's much more than it's worth.

"My point is, I wonder how he happened to contact the women you know who invested with him, and I wonder what made him show up on this doorstep. There's got to be more than just coincidence at play here."

) 63

EARL BATEMAN DROVE PAST MAGGIE'S HOUSE TWICE. ON the third trip, he saw that the car with the Rhode Island plates was gone; Maggie's station wagon, however, was still in the driveway. He slowed to a halt and reached for the framed picture he had brought with him.

He was fairly sure that if he had phoned and said he would like to see her, Maggie would have turned him down. But now she wouldn't have a choice. She would *have to* invite him in.

He rang the doorbell twice before she opened the door. It was obvious that she was surprised to see him. Surprised and nervous, he thought.

He quickly held up the package. "A present for you," he said enthusiastically. "A marvelous picture of Nuala that was taken at the Four Seasons party. I framed it for you."

"How nice of you," Maggie said, trying to smile, a look of uncertainty on her face. Then she reached out her hand.

Earl pulled the package back, withholding it. "Aren't you going to ask me in?" he asked, his tone light and joking.

"Of course."

She stood aside and let him pass, but to his annoyance, she swung the door wide open and left it that way.

"I'd close that if I were you," he said. "I don't know if you've been out today, but there's a stiff breeze." He again saw her uncertainty and smiled grimly. "And no matter what my dear cousin has told you, I don't bite," he said, finally handing her the package.

He walked ahead of her into the living room and sat in the big club chair. "I can see Tim ensconced here with his books and newspapers and Nuala fussing around him. What a pair of lovebirds they were! They invited me over to dinner occasionally, and I was always glad to come. Nuala wasn't much of a housekeeper, but she was an excellent cook. And Tim told me that, often, when they were alone and watching TV late at night, she'd curl up in this chair with him. She was such a petite lady."

He looked around. "I can see you're already putting your stamp on this place," he said. "I approve. There's a much calmer feeling. Does that love seat spook you?"

"I'll do some refurnishing," Maggie said, her tone still wary.

Bateman watched her as she opened the package and congratulated himself on thinking of the photograph. Just seeing the way her face lit up confirmed how smart he had been to think of it.

"Oh, it's a *wonderful* picture of Nuala!" Maggie said enthusiastically. "She looked so pretty that evening. Thank you. I really am glad to have this." Her smile was now genuine.

"I'm sorry Liam and I are in it as well," Bateman said. "Maybe you can have us airbrushed out."

"I wouldn't do that," Maggie answered quickly. "And thank you for taking the time to bring it yourself."

"You're most welcome," he said as he leaned further back into the deep chair.

He's not going to go, she thought in dismay. His scrutiny made her uncomfortable. She felt as though she were under a spotlight. Bateman's eyes, too large behind his round-framed glasses, were fixed on her with an unwavering stare. Despite his apparent effort at nonchalance, he seemed almost to be at attention, his body rigid. I couldn't imagine him curling up anywhere, or even being comfortable in his own skin, she reflected.

He's like a wire, stretched too far, ready to snap, she thought.

Nuala was such a petite lady . . .

Wasn't much of a housekeeper . . . excellent cook . . .

How often had Earl Bateman been here? Maggie wondered. How well did he know this house? Maybe he knew the reason Nuala had decided not to become a resident of Latham Manor, she decided, about to voice the question until another thought hit her.

Or maybe he suspected the reason—and killed her!

She jumped involuntarily when the telephone rang. Excusing herself, she went to the kitchen to answer it. Police Chief Brower was calling. "Ms. Holloway, I was wondering if I could stop in and see you late this afternoon," he said.

"Of course. Has something come up? I mean about Nuala?"

"Oh, nothing special. I just wanted to talk with you. And I may bring someone with me. Is that all right? I'll phone before I come."

"Of course," she said. Then, suspecting that Earl Bateman might be trying to overhear what she was saying, she raised her voice slightly. "Chief, I'm just visiting with Earl Bateman. He brought over a wonderful picture of Nuala. I'll see you in a while."

When she went back into the living room, she saw that the ottoman in front of Earl's chair had been pushed aside, indicating that he had stood up. He *did* eavesdrop, she thought. Good. With a smile, she said, "That was Chief Brower." Something you already know, she added silently. "He's coming over this afternoon. I told him you were visiting."

Bateman's nod was solemn. "A good police chief. Respects people. Not like security police in some cultures. You know what happens when a king dies? During the mourning period, the police seize control of the government. Sometimes they even murder the king's family. In fact, in some societies that was a regular occurrence. I could give you so many examples. You know I lecture on funeral customs?"

Maggie sat down, oddly fascinated by the man. She sensed something different about Earl Bateman's expression, which had become one of almost religious absorption. From a living example of the awkward, absentminded professor, he was transformed entirely into a silver-voiced, messianic other. Even the way he was sitting was different. The rigid schoolboy posture had been replaced by the comfortable stance of a man who was secure and at ease. He was leaning slightly toward her, his left elbow on the arm of the chair, his head slightly tilted. He was no longer staring at *her;* his eyes were fixed instead somewhere just to her left.

Maggie felt her mouth go dry. Unconsciously she had sat on the love seat, and now she realized he was looking just beyond her, focused on the place where Nuala's body had been hunched.

"Did you know I lecture on funeral customs?" he asked again, and she realized with a start that she had not answered his question.

"Oh, yes," she said quickly. "Remember? You told me that the first night we met."

"I'd really like to talk to you about it," Bateman said earnestly. "You see, a cable company is very interested in having me do a television series, provided I am able to offer a range of subjects for at least thirteen thirty-minute programs. That's not a problem. I've got more than enough material for the programs, but I'd like to include some visuals."

Maggie waited.

Earl clasped his hands. Now his voice became coaxing. "The response to this kind of offer shouldn't be delayed. I need to act on it soon. You're a very successful photographer. Visuals are what you understand. It would be such a favor if you'd let me take you to see my museum today. It's downtown, right next to the funeral parlor my family used to own. You know where that is, of course. Would you just spend an hour with me? I'll show you the exhibits, and explain them, and maybe you could help me decide which ones to suggest to the producers."

He paused. "Please, Maggie."

He has to have overheard me, Maggie thought. He knows Chief Brower is coming here, and he knows I told him who was visiting me. Liam had told her about Earl's Victorian bell replicas. He's supposed to have twelve of them. Suppose they're on exhibit, she thought. And suppose there are only six of them now. If so, then it would be reasonable to believe that he put the others on the graves.

"I'd be glad to go," she said after a moment, "but Chief Brower is coming to see me this afternoon. Just in case he gets here early, I'll leave a note on the door saying that I'm with you at the museum, and that I'll be back by four."

Earl smiled. "That's very wise, Maggie. That should give us plenty of time."

❯ *64*

AT TWO O'CLOCK, CHIEF CHET BROWER SUMMONED DEtective Jim Haggerty to his office but learned that Haggerty had left just a few minutes earlier, saying that he would be back shortly. When he came in, he was carrying papers identical to the ones Brower had been hunched over at his desk—copies of the obituaries Maggie Holloway had looked up at the *Newport Sentinel*. Haggerty knew that, as requested, another set had been faxed to Lara Horgan at the coroner's office in Providence.

"What did you see, Jim?" Brower demanded.

Haggerty slumped into a seat. "Probably the same thing you did, Chief. Five of the six deceased women lived at that fancy retirement home."

"Right."

"None of those five had close relatives."

Brower looked at him benignly. "Very good."

"They all died in their sleep."

"Uh-huh."

"And Dr. William Lane, the director of Latham Manor, was in attendance in each instance. Meaning he signed the death certificates."

Brower smiled approvingly. "You catch on real fast."

"Also," Haggerty continued, "what the articles don't say is that when you die at Latham Manor, the studio or apartment you had purchased to live in reverts to the management, which means it can be sold again, pronto."

Brower frowned. "I didn't think of that angle," he admitted. "I just spoke to the coroner. Lara picked up on all of this too. She's running a check on Dr. William Lane. She already was investigating the background of a nurse there, Zelda Markey. She wants to come with me to talk to Maggie Holloway this afternoon."

Haggerty looked pensive. "I knew Mrs. Shipley, the woman who died at Latham last week. I liked her a lot. It occurred to me that her next of kin were still in town. I asked around, and they've been staying at the Harborside Inn, so I just popped over there."

Brower waited. Haggerty wore his most noncommittal expression, which Brower knew meant he had stumbled onto something.

"I extended my sympathy and talked to them a bit. Turned out that yesterday, who should be at Latham Manor but Maggie Holloway."

"Why was she there?" Brower snapped.

"She was a guest at brunch of old Mrs. Bainbridge and her daughter. But afterward she did go up and speak to Mrs. Shipley's relatives when they were packing up her effects." He sighed. "Ms. Holloway had an odd request. She said her stepmother, Nuala Moore, who taught an art class at Latham, had helped Mrs. Shipley make a sketch, and she asked if they minded if she took it. Funny thing, though, it wasn't there."

"Maybe Mrs. Shipley tore it up."

"Not likely. Anyhow, later a couple of the residents stopped in to talk to Mrs. Shipley's relatives while they were doing the packing, and they asked them about the sketch. One of the old girls said she had seen it. It was supposed to be a World War II poster that showed a spy eavesdropping on two defense workers."

"Why would Ms. Holloway want that?"

"Because Nuala Moore had put her own face and Greta Shipley's face over those of the defense workers, and in place of the spy, guess who she'd sketched?"

Brower looked at Haggerty, his eyes narrowed.

"Nurse Markey," the detective said with satisfaction. "And one more thing, Chief. The rule at Latham Manor is that when a death occurs, as soon as the body is removed, the room or apartment is locked until the family has had a chance to come to take possession of valuables. In other words, nobody had any business being in there and taking that sketch." He paused. "Kind of makes you wonder, doesn't it?"

) 65

NEIL CANCELED A LUNCH DATE HE HAD MADE AND INSTEAD had a sandwich and coffee at his desk. He had instructed Trish to fend off all but the most urgent calls as he worked feverishly to clear his calendar for the next few days.

At three o'clock, just as Trish came back with a fresh batch of papers, he phoned his father. "Dad, I'm coming up tonight," he said. "I've been trying to get that Hansen guy on the phone, but they keep telling me he's out. So I'm going to come up there and track him down myself. There's a lot more going on with that guy than just giving lousy advice to old women."

"That's what Maggie said, and I'm sure she's onto something."

"Maggie!"

"She seems to think there's some kind of connection between Hansen and the women who put in applications to Latham Manor. I've been talking to Laura Arlington and Cora Gebhart. It turns out Hansen called them out of the blue."

"Why didn't they just hang up on him? Most people don't get involved over the phone with stock peddlers they don't know."

"Apparently using Alberta Downing's name gave him credibility. He urged them to call her for a reference. But then—and this is where it gets interesting—he talked about how some people have investments that are losing buying power because of inflation, and he just *happened* to give as examples the very stocks and bonds that Cora Gebhart and Laura Arlington owned."

"Yes," Neil said. "I remember Mrs. Gebhart saying something of the sort. I need to talk to this Mrs. Downing. Something's definitely not right here. And, by the way, I expected you'd call me as soon as you saw Maggie," he added, knowing that now he sounded annoyed. "I've been worried about her. Was she okay?"

"I planned to call you as soon as I finished checking out her take on Hansen," Robert Stephens answered. "I thought perhaps *that* was more important than filing a report with you," he added acerbically.

Neil rolled his eyes. "Sorry," he said. "And thanks for going over to see her."

"You must know I went immediately. I happen to like that young lady very much. One more thing: Hansen dropped in on Maggie last week and made an offer on her house. I've been talking to real estate agents to get their opinions of its value. Maggie had speculated that his offer was too high, given the condition of the house, and she's right. So while you're at it, try to figure out what game he's playing with her."

Neil remembered Maggie's startled reaction when he mentioned Hansen's name, and how when he had asked if she knew him, her answer had been evasive.

But I was right about one thing: She *did* open up to Dad, he thought. When I get to Newport, I'm going straight to her house, and I'm not leaving until she tells me just what it is I've done wrong.

When he got off the phone, he looked over at Trish and the papers in her hand. "You'll have to take care of those. I'm out of here."

"Oh my, my," Trish said, her tone teasing but affectionate. "So her name is Maggie and you're worried sick about her. What a learning experience for *you*." Then she frowned. "Wait a minute, Neil. You really *are* worried, aren't you?"

"You bet I am."

"Then what are you waiting for? Get moving."

) 66

"I'M VERY PROUD OF MY MUSEUM," EARL EXPLAINED AS he held the door for Maggie to get out of her car. She had declined his offer to drive with him and was aware that he had been annoyed at the refusal.

As she had followed his gray Oldsmobile into town and past the Bateman Funeral Home, she realized why she hadn't noticed the museum. It fronted on a side street to the rear of the large property and had its own parking lot behind it. The lot was empty now except for one other vehicle, parked in the corner—a shiny black hearse.

Earl pointed to it as they walked toward the museum. "That's thirty years old," he said proudly. "My father was going to trade it in when I was starting college, but I talked him into letting me have it. I keep it in the garage here and only pull it out in the summer. That's when I invite visitors to the museum, although just for a couple of hours on weekends. It kind of sets the tone for the place, don't you think?"

"I guess so," Maggie said uncertainly. In these last ten days I've seen enough hearses for a lifetime, she thought. She turned to study the three-story Victorian house with its wide porch and gingerbread trim. Like the Bateman Funeral Home, it was painted glistening white with black shutters. Black crepe streamers draped around the front door fluttered in the breeze.

"The house was built in 1850 by my great-great-grandfather," Earl explained. "It was our first funeral parlor, and back then the family lived on the top floor. My grandfather built the present establishment, and my father expanded it. This house was used by a caretaker for a while. When we sold the business ten years ago, we separated the house and an acre of the property, and I took it over completely. I opened the museum shortly after that, although I'd been putting it together for years."

Earl put his hand on Maggie's elbow. "You're in for a treat. Now remember, I want you to look at everything with an eye toward what I should suggest for visuals. I don't mean just for the individual lectures, but maybe something as well for an opening and closing signature for the series."

They were on the porch. Located on the broad railing, and helping to offset somewhat the overall funerary gloom, were several planters filled with violets and mountain pinks. Bateman lifted the edge of the nearest planter and withdrew a key. "See how I trust you, Maggie? I'm showing you my secret hiding place. This is an old-fashioned lock, and the key is much too heavy to bother carrying around."

Pausing at the door, he pointed to the crepe. "In our society it used to be the custom to drape the door like this to signify that this was a house of mourning."

My God, how he enjoys this! Maggie thought, shivering slightly. She realized her hands were damp and shoved them in the pockets of her jeans. The irrational thought went through her head that she had no business entering a house of grief dressed in a plaid shirt and jeans.

The key turned with a grating sound, and Earl Bateman pushed the door open and then stood back. "Now what do you think of that?" he asked proudly, as Maggie moved slowly past him.

A life-sized figure of a man in black livery stood at attention in the foyer, as though ready to receive guests.

"In Emily Post's first etiquette book, published in 1922, she wrote that when a death occurred, the butler in his day clothes should be on duty at the door until a footman in black livery could replace him."

Earl flicked something Maggie could not see from the sleeve of the mannequin.

"You see," he said earnestly, "the downstairs rooms show our grief culture in *this* century; I thought the liveried figure would be interesting to people as they came in. How many people today, even wealthy people, would have a footman in black livery stationed at the door when someone in the family dies?"

Maggie's thoughts abruptly leaped back to that painful day when she was ten years old and Nuala told her she was going away. "You see, Maggie," she had explained, "for a long time after my first husband died, I carried dark glasses with me. I cried so easily that I was embarrassed. When I felt it coming on, I'd reach in my pocket and grab the glasses, and I'd think 'Time to put on the grief equipment again.' I hoped your father and I could love each other that way. I've tried hard, but it just can't be. And for the rest of my life, whenever I think of the years I'm going to miss with you, I'll have to reach for my grief equipment."

Remembering that day always brought tears to Maggie's eyes. I wish I had some grief equipment right now, she thought as she brushed the moisture off her cheek.

"Oh, Maggie, you're touched," Earl said, his tone reverent. "How understanding of you. Now on this floor, as I told you, I have rooms that exhibit twentieth-century death rituals."

He pushed aside a heavy curtain. "In this room, I've staged Emily Post's version of a very small funeral. See?"

Maggie looked in. The figure of a young woman, dressed in a pale green silk robe, was laid out on a brocaded sofa. Long auburn ringlets spilled around a narrow satin pillow. Her hands were folded over silk replicas of lilies of the valley.

"Isn't that charming? Doesn't she look just like she's sleeping?" Earl whispered. "And look." He pointed to a discreet silver lectern near the entrance. "Today, this would be where visitors sign the guest book. What I did instead was to copy a page from the original Emily Post book about the care of the bereaved. Let me read it to you. It's really quite fascinating."

His voice echoed through the too-quiet room:

" 'The ones in sorrow should be urged if possible to sit in a sunny room and where there is an open fire. If they feel unequal to going to the table, a very little food should be taken to them on a tray. A cup of tea or coffee or bouillon, a little thin toast, a poached egg, milk if they like it hot, or milk toast. Cold milk is bad for one who is already over-chilled. The cook may suggest something that appeals usually to their taste . . .' "

He stopped. "Isn't that something? How many people today, no matter how much money they have, have a cook who is worried about what appeals to their taste? Right? But I think this would make a wonderful individual visual, don't you? The signatures for the opening and closing, though, have to have a broader scope."

He took her arm. "I know you don't have a lot of time, but please come on upstairs with me. I've got some great replicas of archaic separation rites from ancient times. Banquet tables, for example. It would seem that diverse people inherently understood that death must include a banquet or feast at the end of the ceremony, because extended grief is debilitating to the individual and to the community. I've got typical examples set up.

"Then there's my burial section," he continued enthusiastically as they ascended the stairs. "Have I mentioned a custom of the Sudan people who suffocated their leader when he was becoming old or feeble? You see, the principle was that the leader embodied the vitality of the nation and must never die or the nation would die with him. So when the leader was clearly losing his power, he was secretly put to death, then walled up in a mud hut. The custom then was to believe that he had not died but, rather, had vanished." He laughed.

They were on the second floor. "In this first room, I've created a replica of a mud hut. Now just between us, I've already gotten started on an outdoor museum where the burial area can be even more realistic. It's about ten miles from here. So far I've had some excavation done, basically just some bulldozing. I'm designing the entire project myself. But when it's completed, it really will be quite wonderful. In one area I'll have a miniature replica of a pyramid, with a section of it transparent so that people can see how the ancient Egyptians entombed their pharaohs with their gold and priceless jewels to accompany them into the hereafter . . ."

He's babbling, Maggie thought, a leaden sense of unease settling over her. He's *crazy!* Her mind was racing as he propelled her from room to room, each of them containing what resembled an elaborately structured stage setting. Earl was holding her hand now, pulling her along as he darted about to show everything, explain everything.

They were almost at the end of the long hallway, and Maggie realized that she still had not seen anything resembling the bells she had found on the graves.

"What do you have on the third floor?" she asked.

"That's not ready for exhibits yet," he replied absently. "I use it for storage."

Then he stopped abruptly and turned to her, his eyes intense. They were at the end of the hallway, in front of a heavy door. "Oh, Maggie, this is one of my best exhibits!"

Earl turned the handle and with a dramatic flourish threw open the door. "I combined two rooms to get the effect I wanted here. This depicts an aristocrat's funeral in ancient Rome." He pulled her inside. "Let me explain. First they built a bier, then they put the couch on it. On top of that were placed two mattresses. Maybe this would make a good opening shot for the series. Of course, right now the torches just have red light bulbs, but we *could* really have them flaming. The old man who made this bier for me was a real craftsman. He copied it exactly from the picture I gave him. Look at the fruit and flowers he carved into the wood. Feel it."

He grasped her hand and ran it along the bier. "And this mannequin is a treasure. He's dressed just like a dead aristocrat would be dressed. I found that fancy raiment in a costume shop. What a show these funerals must have been! Think of it. Heralds, musicians, flaming torches . . ."

Abruptly he stopped and frowned. "I do get carried away on this subject, Maggie. Forgive me."

"No, I'm fascinated," she said, trying to sound calm, hoping he would not notice the dampness of the hand he was at last relinquishing.

"Oh, good. Well, there's just one more room. Right here. My coffin room." He opened the last door. "Quite a spread here too, wouldn't you say?"

Maggie stood back. She did not want to go in that room. Only ten days ago she had been the one to choose a casket for Nuala. "Actually, Earl, I should be heading back," she said.

"Oh. I'd like to have explained these. Maybe you'll come back. By the end of the week, I'll have the newest one in. It's shaped like a loaf of bread. It was designed for the corpse of a baker. The custom in some African cultures is to bury the deceased in a coffin that symbolizes the way that person's life has been spent. I included that story in one of the lectures I gave to a women's club right here in Newport."

Maggie realized that he might have given her the opening she had been seeking. "Do you lecture in Newport very often?"

"Not anymore." Earl closed the door of the coffin room slowly, as though he were reluctant to leave it. "You've heard it said that a prophet is without honor in his own country, no doubt? First they expect to get you without even an honorarium, then they insult you."

Was he talking about the reaction to his lecture at Latham Manor? Maggie wondered. The closed doors of the rooms shut out most of the light, and the hall was filled with shadows, but even so she could see that his face was turning crimson. "Surely, no one insulted you?" she asked, her voice controlled, caring.

"Once," he said darkly. "It upset me terribly."

She didn't dare tell him that Liam had been the one to tell her about the incident with the bells. "Oh, wait a minute," she said slowly. "When I visited Mrs. Shipley at Latham Manor, didn't I hear that something unpleasant had happened to you when you were kind enough to speak there? Something involving Mrs. Bainbridge's daughter?"

"That's exactly what I mean," Earl replied sharply. "She upset me so much that I stopped giving one of my most effective lectures."

As they walked down the stairs to the first floor, past the mannequin of the liveried footman and out onto the porch, where, Maggie realized, the daylight felt unexpectedly strong after the dim interior of the museum, Bateman told of that evening at Latham Manor and described handing out the replicas of the Victorian bells.

"I had them *cast* specially," he said, his voice ominous with anger. "Twelve of them. Maybe it *wasn't* smart to have let those people hold them, but that was no reason for treating me the way that woman did."

Maggie spoke carefully. "I'm sure other people don't react that way."

"It was very upsetting to all of us. Zelda was furious."

"Zelda?" Maggie asked.

"Nurse Markey. She knows my research and had heard me speak a number of times. I was there because of her. She had told the activities chairperson at Latham how well I lecture."

Nurse Markey, Maggie thought.

His eyes narrowed, became cautious. She could see he was studying her. "I don't like to talk about this. It upsets me."

"But I would think that would be a fascinating lecture," Maggie persisted. "And maybe those bells would be a good visual for an opening or closing shot."

"No. Forget it. They're all in a box up in the storeroom, and that's where they'll stay."

He replaced the key under the planter. "Now don't tell anyone it's here, Maggie."

"No, I won't."

"But if you'd like to come back yourself and maybe take some pictures of the exhibits that you think I should submit to the cable people, that would be fine. You know where to find the key."

He walked her to her car. "I have to get back to Providence," he said. "Will you think about the visuals and see if you can come up with some suggestions? Can I call you in a day or so?"

"Of course," she replied as, with relief, she slid into the driver's seat. "And thank you," she added, knowing that she had absolutely no intention of using the key, or of ever coming back to this place if she could help it.

"See you soon, I hope. Say hello to Chief Brower for me."

She turned the key in the ignition. "Good-bye, Earl. It was very interesting."

"My cemetery exhibit will be interesting too. Oh, that reminds me. I better put the hearse back in the garage. Cemetery. Hearse. Funny how the mind works, isn't it?" he said as he walked away.

As Maggie drove out onto the street, she could see in the rearview mirror that Earl was sitting in the hearse, holding a phone. His head was turned in her direction.

She could feel his eyes, wide and luminous, watching her intently until at last she was beyond his range of vision.

) 67

SHORTLY BEFORE FIVE, DR. WILLIAM LANE ARRIVED AT the Ritz-Carlton Hotel in Boston, where a cocktail party and dinner for a retiring surgeon were being held. His wife, Odile, had driven up earlier to go shopping and to keep an appointment with her favorite hairdresser. As usual when they had that kind of schedule, she had taken a room for the afternoon at the hotel.

As he drove through Providence, Lane's earlier good mood gradually dissipated. The satisfaction he had felt after hearing from the Van Hillearys had dissolved, and in its place there resounded in his mind a warning, not unlike the beeping caused by a failing battery in a smoke detector. Something was wrong, but he wasn't clear as yet just what it was.

The mental alarm had started just as he was leaving the residence, when Sarah Bainbridge Cushing called to say she was on her way in to visit her mother again. She had informed him that Letitia Bainbridge had phoned shortly after lunch to say that she wasn't feeling well, and that she had become terribly nervous because Nurse Markey was darting in and out of her room without knocking.

He had warned Markey about that very thing after Greta Shipley complained last week. What was she up to? Dr. Lane fumed. Well, he wouldn't warn her again; no, he would call Prestige and tell them to get rid of her.

By the time he arrived at the Ritz, Lane was thoroughly

on edge. When he got up to his wife's room, the sight of Odile in a frilly robe, just beginning to put on her makeup, annoyed him intensely. Surely she can't have been shopping all this time, he thought with growing irritation.

"Hi, darling," she said with a smile, looking up girlishly as he closed the door and crossed to her. "How do you like my hair? I let Magda try something a little different. Not too many trailing tendrils, I hope?" She shook her head playfully.

True, Odile had beautiful frosted blond hair, but Lane was tired of being trapped into admiring it. "It looks all right," he said, irritation apparent in his voice.

"Only all right?" she asked, her eyes wide, her eyelids fluttering.

"Look, Odile, I have a headache. I shouldn't have to remind you that I've had a rough few weeks at the residence."

"I know you have, dear. Look, why don't you lie down for a while while I finish painting the lily?"

That was another coy trick of Odile's that drove him wild, the use of "paint the lily," when most people said "gild the lily" instead. She loved it when someone tried to correct her. When they did, she was only too happy to point out that the line was often misquoted, that Shakespeare actually had written "To gild refined gold, to paint the lily."

The would-be intellectual, Lane thought, his teeth on edge. He glanced at his watch. "Look, Odile, that party starts in ten minutes. Don't you think you'd better get a move on?"

"Oh, William, *nobody* gets to a cocktail party the minute it starts," she said, again using her little-girl voice. "Why are you so cross with me? I know you're terribly worried about something, but please share it with me. I'll try to help. I've helped you before, haven't I?"

She looked to be on the verge of tears.

"Of course you have," Dr. Lane said, relenting now, his voice softer. Then he paid her the compliment he knew would appease her: "You're a beautiful woman, Odile." He tried to sound affectionate. "Even before you paint the lily, you're beautiful. You could walk into that party right now and outshine every woman there."

Then, as she began to smile, he added, "But you're right. I *am* worried. Mrs. Bainbridge wasn't feeling well this afternoon, and I'd be a lot more comfortable if I were around, just in case there were to be an emergency. So . . ."

"Oh." She sighed, knowing what was coming. "But how disappointing! I was looking forward to seeing everybody here tonight, and to spending time with them. I love our guests, but we do seem to give our whole lives to them."

It was the reaction he had hoped to receive. "I'm not going to let you be disappointed," he said firmly. "You stay and enjoy yourself. In fact, keep the room overnight and come back tomorrow. I don't want you driving home at night unless I'm following you."

"If you're sure."

"I'm sure. I'll just make an appearance at the party now and head back. You can say hello for me to anyone who asks." The warning beep in his head had become a keening siren. He wanted to bolt, but he paused to kiss her good-bye.

She took his face between her hands. "Oh, darling, I hope nothing happens to Mrs. Bainbridge, at least not for a long while. She is very old, of course, and can't be expected to live forever, but she's such a dear. If you suspect anything is seriously wrong, please call her own doctor in immediately. I wouldn't want you to have to sign yet another death certificate for one of our ladies so soon after the last one. Remember all the trouble at the last residence."

He took her hands from his face and held them. He wanted to strangle her.

255

☽ 68

WHEN MAGGIE GOT BACK TO THE HOUSE, SHE STOOD FOR long minutes on the porch, breathing in deeply, inhaling the fresh, clean, salt scent of the ocean. It seemed to her that after the museum visit the smell of death was in her nostrils.

Earl Bateman *enjoyed* death, she thought, feeling a shiver of repulsion run up her spine. He enjoyed talking about it, re-creating it.

Liam had told her that Earl had relished describing how frightened the Latham residents had been when he had made them handle the bells. She could certainly understand their fright, although Earl's version of the incident was that it had upset *him* so much, he had packed away the bells in the third-floor storeroom.

Maybe it was a little bit of both, she thought. He might have enjoyed terrifying them, but he certainly had been furious when he was sent packing, she thought.

He had seemed so anxious to show her everything in that strange museum. So why hadn't he offered to show the bells to her as well? she wondered. Surely it couldn't have been just because of painful memories over what had happened to him at Latham Manor.

So was it because he had hidden them on the graves of women from the residence—women who might have been in the audience the night of that lecture? Another thought struck her. Had Nuala attended that lecture?

Maggie realized that she was hugging her arms tight

against her body and practically shivering. As she turned to go in the house, she took the note she had left for Chief Brower off the door. Once inside, the first thing she saw was the framed picture Earl had brought her.

She picked it up.

"Oh, Nuala," she said aloud, "Finn-u-ala." She studied the photo for a minute. It would be possible to crop it to show Nuala alone, and she could have it enlarged.

When she had started the sculpture of Nuala, she had collected the most recent pictures she could find of her around the house. None were as recent as this, though; it would be a wonderful help in the final stages of creating the bust. She would take it upstairs now, she decided.

Chief Brower had said he would stop by this afternoon, but it was already a little after five. She decided to go ahead and do a little work on the sculpture. But on the way up to the studio, Maggie remembered that Chief Brower had said he would phone before he came. She wouldn't hear the phone in the studio.

I know, Maggie thought, as she passed the bedroom, this would be a good time to clean out the rest of Nuala's things from the closet floor. I'll just take the picture to the studio and come back.

In the studio, she took the photograph out of the frame and carefully tacked it to the bulletin board by the refectory table. Then she switched on the spotlight and examined the picture closely.

The photographer must have told them to smile, she thought. Smiling had come naturally to Nuala. If there's anything wrong with this picture, it's that it isn't enough of a close-up to show what I saw in her eyes that night at dinner.

Standing next to Nuala, Earl Bateman looked uncomfortable, ill at ease, his smile definitely forced. Still, she thought, there was nothing about him that suggested the frightening obsessiveness she had witnessed this afternoon.

She remembered Liam saying once that a crazy streak ran in the family. She had taken his remark as a joke at the time, but now she wasn't so sure.

Liam probably never took a bad photograph in his life, she thought, as she continued to study the picture. There's a strong family resemblance between the cousins, mostly the facial structure. But what looks peculiar on Earl, looks good on Liam.

I was so lucky Liam brought me to that party, and so lucky I spotted Nuala, she mused as she turned away and started down the stairs. She remembered how it almost hadn't happened, how she had decided to go home because Liam was so preoccupied, racing from one group of cousins to the next. She had definitely felt neglected that evening.

He's certainly changed his tune since I arrived up here, though, she thought.

How much should I tell Chief Brower when he comes? she asked herself. Even if Earl Bateman put those bells on the graves, there's nothing inherently illegal about that. But why would he lie about the bells being in the storeroom?

She went into the bedroom and opened the closet door. The only two items that remained hanging there were the blue cocktail suit Nuala had worn that night at the Four Seasons, and the pale gold raincoat that she had rehung in the closet when Neil and his father moved the bed.

Every inch of the closet floor, however, was covered with shoes and slippers and boots, mostly in disarray.

Maggie sat on the floor and began the job of sorting them out. Some of the shoes were quite worn, and those she tossed behind her to discard. But others, like the pair she thought she remembered Nuala wearing at the party, were both new and fairly expensive.

True, Nuala wasn't a neatnik, but surely she never would have tossed new shoes around like that, Maggie decided. Then she caught her breath. She knew the bureau drawers had been ransacked by the intruder who killed Nuala, but had he even taken the time to rummage through her *shoes?*

The telephone rang and she jumped. Chief Brower, she thought, and realized she would not be at all sorry to see him.

Instead of Brower, however, it was Detective Jim Haggerty, calling to say that the chief would like to postpone the meeting until first thing in the morning. "Lara Horgan, the state medical examiner, wants to come with him, and they both are out on emergencies right now."

"That's all right," Maggie said. "I'll be here in the morning." Then, remembering that she had felt comfortable with Detective Haggerty when he had stopped by to see her, she decided to ask him about Earl Bateman.

"Detective Haggerty," she said, "this afternoon Earl Bateman invited me to see his museum." She chose her words carefully. "It's such an *unusual* hobby."

"I've been there," Haggerty said. "Quite a place. I guess it's not really an unusual hobby for Earl, though, when you consider he's from a fourth-generation funeral family. His father was mighty disappointed he didn't go into the business. But you could say that in his own way he has." He chuckled.

"I guess so." Again Maggie spoke slowly, measuring what she was about to say. "I know his lectures are very successful, but I gather that there was one unfortunate incident at Latham Manor. Do you know about that?"

"Can't say as I do, but if I were the age of those folks, I wouldn't want to hear about funerals, would you?"

"No, I wouldn't."

"I've never gone to one of his lectures myself," Haggerty

continued, then lowered his voice. "I'm not one to gossip, but folks around here thought that museum idea was crazy. But heck, the Batemans could buy and sell most of the Moores. Earl may not look it or sound it, but he's got serious money in his own right. Came to him from his father's side."

"I see."

"The Moore clan call him Cousin Weirdo, but I say most of it's because they're jealous."

Maggie thought of Earl as she had seen him today: staring past her at the spot where Nuala's body had been lying; frenetically charged as he dragged her from exhibit to exhibit; sitting in the hearse, his eyes staring intently after her.

"Or maybe it's because they know him too well," she said. "Thanks for calling, Detective Haggerty."

She hung up, grateful that she had made the decision not to talk about the bells. She was sure Haggerty would have laughingly ascribed their ghoulish appearance on the graves to another eccentricity of a rich man.

Maggie went back to the job of sorting out the shoes. This time she decided that the simplest thing to do was to bundle most of them in garbage bags. Worn shoes in a small, narrow size certainly wouldn't be much use to anyone else.

The fur-lined boots, however, were worth saving. The left one was lying on its side, the right one standing. She picked up the left one and put it beside her, then reached for the other.

As Maggie lifted it, she heard a single muffled clang coming from the interior of the boot.

"Oh, God, no!"

Even before she forced herself to put her hand down into the furry interior, she knew what she would find. Her fingers closed over cool metal, and as she withdrew the object, she was certain that she had found the thing Nuala's killer had been seeking—the missing bell.

Nuala took this from Mrs. Rhinelander's grave, she thought, her mind working with a steadiness independent of her shaking hands. She stared at it; it was the exact twin of the bell she had taken from Nuala's grave.

Streaks of dry dirt clung to the rim. Other tiny particles of soft earth crumbled loose on her fingers.

Maggie remembered that there had been dirt in the pocket of the gold raincoat, and she recalled that when she rehung the cocktail suit the other day she had had the impression of something falling.

Nuala was wearing her raincoat when she took this bell off Mrs. Rhinelander's grave, she thought. It must have frightened her. She left it in her pocket for a reason. Did she find it the day she changed her will, Maggie wondered, the day before she died?

Did it in some way validate suspicions Nuala was beginning to have about the residence?

Earl claimed that the bells he had cast were in the storeroom of the museum. If the twelve he had were still there, someone else might have been placing others on the graves, she reasoned.

Maggie knew that Earl had gone back to Providence. And that the key to the museum was under the planter on the porch. Even if she told the police about the bells, they would have no legal right to go into the museum and look for the twelve Earl said were there, assuming they took her seriously, which they probably wouldn't.

But he *did* invite me to let myself into the museum at any time, to try to come up with visuals for his cable programs, Maggie thought. I'll take my camera with me. That will give me an excuse for being there if anyone happens to see me.

But I don't want anyone to see me, she told herself. I'll wait until it's dark, then I'll drive over there. There's only one way to find out for sure. I'll look in the storeroom for the box with the bells. I'm sure I won't find more than six of them.

And if that's all I find, I'll know he's a liar. I'll take pictures so I can compare them with the bells on the graves and the two I have. Then tomorrow, when Chief Brower comes, I'll give him the roll of film, she decided, and I'll tell him that I think Earl Bateman has found a way to take revenge on the residents of Latham Manor. And he's doing it with the help of Nurse Zelda Markey.

Revenge? Maggie froze with the realization of what she was considering. Yes, placing the bells on the graves of women who had been party to his humiliation would be a form of revenge. But would that have been enough for Earl? Or could he possibly, somehow, have been involved with their deaths as well? And that nurse, Zelda Markey—clearly she was tied to Earl somehow. Could she be his accomplice?

) 69

ALTHOUGH IT WAS WELL PAST HIS NORMAL DINNERTIME, Chief Brower was still at the station. It had been a hectic and senselessly tragic afternoon, involving two terrible incidents. A carful of teenagers out for a joyride had plowed into an elderly couple, and they were now in critical condition. Then an angry husband had violated a restraining order and shot his wife, from whom he was separated.

"At least we know the wife will make it," Brower told Haggerty. "And thank God; she's got three kids."

Haggerty nodded.

"Where've you been?" Brower asked sourly. "Lara Horgan's waiting to hear what time Maggie Holloway can see us tomorrow morning."

"She told me she'll be home all morning," Haggerty said. "But wait a minute before you call Dr. Horgan. I want to tell you first about a little visit I paid to Sarah Cushing. Her mother, Mrs. Bainbridge, lives at Latham Manor. When I was a kid I was in a Boy Scout troop with Sarah Cushing's son. Got to know her real well. Nice lady. Very impressive. Very smart."

Brower knew there was no use rushing Haggerty when he got into one of these accounts. Besides, he looked especially pleased with himself. To speed things along, the chief asked the expected question: "So what made you go see her?"

"Something Maggie Holloway said when I phoned her for you. She mentioned Earl Bateman. I tell you, Chief, that young lady has a real nose for trouble. Anyhow, we nattered a little."

Like you're doing right now, Brower thought.

"And I got the distinct impression that Ms. Holloway is very nervous about Bateman, maybe even afraid of him."

"Of Bateman? He's *harmless*," Brower snapped.

"Now that's exactly what I would have thought, but maybe Maggie Holloway has a sharp eye when it comes to detecting what makes people tick. She *is* a photographer, you know. Anyhow, she mentioned a little problem that Bateman had at Latham Manor, a little 'incident' that took place not all that long ago, and I called one of my friends whose cousin is a maid there, and one thing led to the other, and she finally told me about a lecture Bateman gave there one afternoon that even caused one of the old girls to pass out, and she told me also how Sarah Cushing happened to be there, and that she gave Bateman hell."

Haggerty saw the chief's mouth tighten, his signal that it was time to come to the point. "So that's why I went to see Mrs. Cushing, and she told me that the reason she hustled Bateman out was for upsetting the guests with his lecture about people worrying about being buried alive, and then handing out replicas of the bells they used to put on graves in Victorian times. Seems there would be a string or wire attached to the bell, and the other end was then tied to the finger of the deceased. The string ran through an air vent from the casket to the surface of the ground. That way if you woke up in the coffin, you could wiggle your finger, the bell would ring on top of the grave, and the guy who was paid to listen for it would start digging.

"Bateman told the ladies to slip their ring finger into the loop at the end of the string, to pretend they'd been buried alive, and then to start ringing the bells."

"You're kidding!"

"No, I'm not, Chief. That's when all hell broke loose apparently. One eighty-year-old who's claustrophobic started screaming and fainted. Mrs. Cushing said she grabbed the bells, broke up the lecture, and all but threw Bateman out the door. Then she made it her business to find out who had suggested he lecture there."

Haggerty paused just an instant for effect. "That person was Nurse Zelda Markey, the lady who apparently has a habit of sneaking in and out of rooms. Sarah Cushing heard through the grapevine that Markey took care of Bateman's aunt in a nursing home years ago, and got real close to the family. She heard also that the Batemans were mighty generous in rewarding her for taking special care of old Auntie."

He shook his head. "Women do have a way of finding

out things, don't they, Chief? You know how there's a question now that there just might be a little problem about all those ladies dying in their sleep over at the home? Mrs. Cushing remembers that at least some of them were at that lecture, and she's not sure, but she thinks all of them who have died recently might have been there."

Before Haggerty even finished, Brower was on the phone to Coroner Lara Horgan. At the conclusion of his conversation with her, he turned to the detective. "Lara is going to initiate proceedings to have the bodies of both Mrs. Shipley and Mrs. Rhinelander, the two people who died most recently at Latham Manor, exhumed. And that's just for starters."

) *70*

NEIL CHECKED HIS WATCH AT EIGHT O'CLOCK. HE WAS PASSing the Mystic Seaport exit on Route 95. Another hour and he would be in Newport, he thought. He had considered calling Maggie again, but decided against it, not wanting to give her a chance to tell him she didn't want to see him tonight. If she's not there, I'll just park in front of her house until she comes back, he told himself.

He was angry that he hadn't gotten away earlier. And as if it wasn't bad enough to hit all the commuter traffic along the way, then he had been stymied by that damned jack-knifed semitrailer that brought 95 North to a standstill for over an hour.

It hadn't been all wasted time, though. He had finally had

an opportunity to think through what it was that had nagged at him about his conversation with Mrs. Arlington, his father's client who had lost just about all her money investing with Hansen. The confirmation of the purchase: something about that had just not seemed right.

Finally it had registered, when he remembered that Laura Arlington said that she had *just* received the confirmation of her stock purchase. Those documents are mailed out right after the transaction, so she should have received it days earlier, Neil said to himself.

Then, this morning, he had learned that there was no record that Mrs. Gebhart had owned the stock Hansen claimed he bought for her at nine bucks a share. Today that stock was down to two dollars. Was Hansen's game to let people think they had bought a stock at one price—a stock he happened to know was on the skids—and then to wait to put the transaction through once it had reached a very low point? That way, Hansen could pocket the difference.

Accomplishing that would involve faking a confirmation of the order from the clearing house. It wasn't simple, but it wasn't impossible, Neil reflected.

So I actually may be onto what Hansen is doing, he thought as he finally passed the WELCOME TO RHODE ISLAND sign. But what in hell made that crook bid on Maggie's house? How does that relate to stealing money from gullible older ladies? There must be something else in play there.

Be home when I get there, Maggie, Neil implored silently. You're setting too much in motion, and I won't let you do it alone any longer.

☽ 71

AT EIGHT-THIRTY, MAGGIE DROVE TO EARL BATEMAN'S FU-
neral museum. Before leaving, she had taken the bell she
found in Nuala's closet and compared it with the bell she
had dug out of Nuala's grave. Both were now placed side
by side on the refectory table in the studio, an overhead
spotlight shining on them.

Almost as an afterthought she had pulled out the Polaroid
camera she used when she was setting up a shoot, and had
snapped a picture of the two bells lying together. She hadn't
waited to see the picture, however, but had pulled the print
from the camera and tossed it on the table to study when
she returned.

Then with her equipment bag in hand, heavy with two
cameras and all the film and lenses, she had headed out. She
hated the thought of going back into that place, but there
seemed to be no other way to get the answers she needed.

Get it over with, she told herself, as she double locked
the front door and got into the station wagon.

Fifteen minutes later, she was passing the Bateman Funeral Home. Obviously the establishment had experienced a
busy evening. A stream of cars were pulling out of the
driveway.

Another funeral tomorrow . . . Well, at least it isn't someone connected with Latham Manor, Maggie thought grimly.
As of yesterday, at least, all the residents were present and
accounted for.

She turned right, onto the quiet street where the funeral museum was located. She drove into the parking lot, grateful to see that the hearse was gone, remembering that Earl had said he was going to garage it.

As she approached the old house, she was surprised to see faint light emerging from behind a curtained ground-floor window. It's probably on a timer and will go off later, she thought, but at least it will help me get my bearings. She had brought a flashlight to use when inside, however; even though Earl Bateman had suggested she come back later on her own, she didn't want to announce her presence by turning on more lights.

The key was under the planter where Earl had left it. As before, it made a loud, grating sound when she turned it in the old-fashioned lock. And as in the earlier visit, the first thing her eye encountered was the liveried-footman mannequin, although now his gaze seemed less attentive than hostile.

I really don't want to be here, Maggie thought as she darted for the stairs, intent on avoiding even a glimpse of the room where the mannequin of a young woman was lying on the couch.

Likewise, she tried not to *think* about the exhibits on the second floor, as she switched on the flashlight at the top of the first staircase. Keeping the beam pointed down, she continued up the next flight. Still, the memory of what she had seen there earlier haunted her—those two large end rooms, one depicting an ancient Roman aristocrat's funeral, the other, the coffin room. Both were grisly, but she found the sight of all those coffins in one room to be the most disturbing.

She had hoped the third floor here would be like Nuala's third level—a studio, surrounded by large closets and shelves. Unfortunately, what she found instead was clearly another floor of rooms. With dismay, Maggie remembered Earl saying that originally the house had been his great-great-grandparents' living quarters.

Trying not to allow herself to be nervous, Maggie opened the first door. In the cautiously low beam of the flashlight, she could see that this was an exhibit in the making; a wooden hutlike structure set atop two poles was off to one side. God knows what it means, she thought, shuddering, or what it's for, but at least the room was empty enough to tell that there was nothing else there she needed to look at.

The next two rooms were similar; both seemed to contain partially completed death-ritual scenes.

The last door proved to be the one she had been seeking. It opened into a large storage room, its walls covered with shelves that were crammed with boxes. Two racks of clothing, ranging from ornate robes to virtual rags, were blocking the windows. Heavy wooden crates, all apparently sealed, were piled randomly on top of each other.

Where can I begin? Maggie thought, a sense of helplessness overtaking her. It would take her *hours* to go through everything, and though she had been there only minutes, already she was anxious to leave.

With a deep sigh, she fought back the urge to bolt, slipped the equipment bag from her shoulder, and set it on the floor. Reluctantly she closed the door of the storeroom, hoping to prevent any spill of light out into the hall and thus through the uncurtained window at the end of the passage.

All that clothing should be enough to make sure that nothing would show through the windows in the room, she told herself. Still, she felt herself shaking as she moved tentatively into the large room. Her mouth was dry. Every nerve in her body seemed to be quivering, urging her to get out of this place.

There was a stepladder to her left. Obviously it was used

to get at the top shelves, she reasoned. It looked old and heavy, and it would mean taking even more time if she had to drag it around every few feet. She decided to start her search in the shelves right behind the ladder and work her way around the room from there. When she climbed up and looked down, she found that there were neat labels pasted on the tops of all the boxes. At least Earl had identified everything, she realized, and for the first time she felt a glimmer of hope that this would not be as difficult a process as she had feared.

Even so, the cartons seemed to be arranged in no particular order. Some that were labeled DEATH MASKS filled a whole section of shelves; others were marked MOURNING RAIMENT, HOUSEHOLD LIVERY, TORCHÈRE REPLICAS, DRUMS, BRASS CYMBALS, RITUAL PAINTS, and so forth—but no bells.

It's hopeless, Maggie thought. I'll never find them. She had only moved the ladder twice, and her watch told her that already she had been there more than half an hour.

She moved the ladder again, hating the rasping screech it made on the floor. Once again she started to climb up it, but as she put her foot on the third rung, her glance fell on a deep cardboard box wedged between two others, almost hidden behind them.

It was labeled BELLS/BURIED ALIVE!

She grasped the box and tugged, finally wrestling it loose. Almost losing her balance when it came free, she got down from the ladder and placed the carton on the floor. With frantic haste, she squatted beside it and yanked off the lid.

Brushing aside the loose popcorn packing, she uncovered the first of the metal bells, wrapped and sealed in plastic, a covering that gave it a deceptively shiny appearance. Eagerly, her fingers fished through the popcorn, until she was sure that she had found everything in the box.

Everything was six bells, identical to the others she had found.

The packing slip was still inside the box: "12 Victorian bells, cast to the order of Mr. Earl Bateman," it read.

Twelve—and now only six.

I'll take shots of them and the packing slip, and then I can get out of here, Maggie thought. Suddenly she was almost desperate to be safely away from this place, outside with her proof that Earl Bateman was certainly a liar, possibly even a murderer.

She wasn't sure what first made her realize that she was no longer alone.

Had she actually heard the faint sound of the door opening, or was it the narrow beam of light from another flashlight that had alerted her?

She spun around as he raised the flashlight, heard him speaking as it crashed down on her head.

And then there was nothing but impressions of voices and movement, and finally dreamless oblivion, until she awoke to the terrible silent darkness of the grave.

⟩ 72

NEIL ARRIVED AT MAGGIE'S HOUSE WELL AFTER NINE o'clock, much later than he had wished. Intensely disappointed to see that her station wagon wasn't in the driveway, he had a moment of hope when he noticed that one of the bright studio lights was on.

Maybe her car was being serviced, he told himself. But

when there was no answer to his insistent ringing of the doorbell, he went back to his car to wait. At midnight he finally gave up and drove to his parents' house in Portsmouth.

Neil found his mother in the kitchen, making hot cocoa. "For some reason I couldn't sleep," she said.

Neil knew that she had expected him to arrive hours earlier, and he felt guilty for worrying her. "I should have called," he said. "But then why didn't you try me on the car phone?"

Dolores Stephens smiled. "Because no thirty-seven-year-old man wants his mother checking up on him just because he's late. It occurred to me that you probably had stopped at Maggie's, so I really wasn't that worried."

Neil shook his head glumly. "I did stop at Maggie's. She wasn't home. I waited around till now."

Dolores Stephens studied her son. "Did you eat any dinner?" she asked gently.

"No, but don't bother."

Ignoring him, she got up and opened the refrigerator. "She may have had a date," she said, her tone thoughtful.

"She was in her *own* car. It's *Monday* night," Neil said, then paused. "Mom, I'm worried about her. I'm going to phone every half hour until I know she's home."

Despite protesting that he really wasn't hungry, he ate the thick club sandwich his mother made for him. At one o'clock, he tried Maggie's number.

His mother sat with him as he tried again at one-thirty, then at two, at two-thirty, and again at three.

At three-thirty his father joined them. "What's going on?" he asked, his eyes heavy with sleep. When he was told, he snapped, "For goodness sake, call the police and ask if any accidents have been reported."

The officer who answered assured Neil that it had been a quiet night. "No accidents, sir."

"Give him Maggie's description. Tell him what kind of car she drives. Leave your name and this phone number," Robert Stephens said. "Dolores, you've been up all this time. You get some sleep. I'll stay with Neil."

"Well—" she began.

"There may be a perfectly simple explanation," her husband said gently. When his wife was out of earshot, he said, "Your mother is very fond of Maggie." He looked at his son. "I know that you haven't been seeing Maggie for all that long a time, but why does she seem indifferent to you, sometimes even downright chilly? Why is that?"

"I don't know," Neil confessed. "She's always held back, and I guess I have too, but I'm positive there's something special going on between us." He shook his head. "I've gone over and over it in my mind. It certainly isn't just that I didn't call her in time to get her number before she came up here. Maggie isn't that *trivial*. But I thought about it a lot driving up, and I've come up with one thing that I can maybe pin it on."

He told his father about the time he saw Maggie weeping in the theater during a film. "I didn't think I should intrude," he said. "At the time I thought I should just give her space. But now I wonder if maybe she knew I was there and perhaps resented the fact I didn't at least say something. What would you have done?"

"I'll tell you what I'd have done," his father said immediately. "If I'd seen your mother in that situation, I'd have been right beside her, and I'd have put my arm around her. Maybe I wouldn't have *said* anything, but I'd have let her know I was there."

He looked at Neil severely. "I'd have done *that* whether or not I was in love with her. On the other hand, if I was trying to deny to myself that I loved her, or if I was afraid of getting involved, then maybe I'd have run away. There's a famous biblical incident about washing the hands."

"Come on, Dad," Neil muttered.

"And if I were Maggie, and I had sensed you were there, and maybe had even wanted to be able to turn to you, I'd have written you off if you walked out on me," Robert Stephens concluded.

The telephone rang. Neil beat his father to grabbing the receiver.

It was a police officer. "Sir, we found the vehicle you described parked on Marley Road. It's an isolated area, and there are no houses nearby, so we don't have any witnesses as to when it was left there, or by whom, whether it was Ms. Holloway or another person."

Tuesday, October 8th

) **73**

AT EIGHT O'CLOCK ON TUESDAY MORNING, MALCOLM NORton walked downstairs from his bedroom and looked into the kitchen. Janice was already there, seated at the table, reading the paper and drinking coffee.

She made the unprecedented offer to pour him a cup, then asked, "Toast?"

He hesitated, then said, "Why not?" and sat opposite her.

"You're leaving pretty early, aren't you?" she asked.

He could see she was nervous. No doubt she knew he was up to something.

"You must have had a late dinner last night," she continued, as she placed the steaming cup in front of him.

"Ummmm," he responded, enjoying her unease. He had known she was awake when he came in at midnight.

He took a few sips of the coffee, then pushed his chair back. "On second thought, I'll skip the toast. Good-bye, Janice."

* * *

When he reached the office, Malcolm Norton sat for a few minutes at Barbara's desk. He wished he could write a few lines to her, something to remind her of what she had meant to him, but it would be unfair. He didn't want to drag her name into this.

He went into his own office and looked again at the copies he had made of the papers he had found in Janice's briefcase, as well as the copy of her bank statement.

He could pretty much figure what she must have been up to. He had guessed it the other night when he saw that crooked nephew of hers hand her an envelope in the restaurant he had followed her to. Seeing her financial records only confirmed what he had suspected.

She was giving Doug Hansen privileged financial information about applicants to Latham Manor so that he could try to cheat rich old women. Maybe "attempt to defraud" charges wouldn't stick against her, but they certainly wouldn't help her in this town. And, of course, she would lose her job.

Good, he thought.

Hansen was the one who made a higher offer to Maggie Holloway. He was *sure* of it. And Janice had tipped him off about the upcoming change in the law. They probably planned to raise the ante until Holloway sold.

If only Maggie Holloway hadn't come on the scene and spoiled it all, he thought bitterly. Knowing he could make a killing on the house, he would have found a way to keep Barbara.

Make a killing. He smiled grimly. That was rich!

Of course, none of that mattered anymore. He would never buy the house. He would never have Barbara in his life. He really *had* no more life. It was over now. But at least he had gotten even. They would know that he wasn't the empty suit Janice had sneered at for years.

He moved the manila envelope addressed to Chief Brower to the far corner of the desk. He didn't want it to get stained.

He reached for the pistol he kept in the deep bottom drawer. He took it out and held it for a moment, studying it thoughtfully. Then he punched in the number of the police station and asked for Chief Brower.

"It's Malcolm Norton," he said pleasantly, as he picked up the gun in his right hand and held it to his head. "I think you'd better get over here. I'm about to kill myself."

As he pulled the trigger, he heard the final, single word: *"Don't!"*

) 74

MAGGIE COULD FEEL THE BLOOD THAT MATTED THE HAIR on the side of her head, which was sensitive to the touch and still ached. "Be calm," she kept whispering to herself. "I've got to be calm."

Where am I buried? she wondered. Probably in some isolated spot in the woods where no one can possibly find me. When she tugged the string on her ring finger, she could feel a heavy pressure on the other end.

He must have attached the string to one of the Victorian bells, she reasoned. She ran her index finger up inside the tube that the string was threaded through. It felt like solid metal and seemed to be about an inch in diameter. She should be able to get enough air through it for breathing, she decided, unless it became clogged.

But why had he bothered with all this? she wondered. She was sure there was no clapper in the bell, because she would be able to hear at least some faint sound if there had been one. That meant no one could hear her.

Was she in a real cemetery? If so, was there a chance that people might visit or attend a funeral? Would she be able to hear even faintly the sound of cars?

Plan! Maggie told herself. You've got to plan. She would keep tugging the string until her finger felt raw, until her strength gave out. If she was buried where someone might pass by, then there was always the hope that the moving bell might attract attention.

She also would try to shout for help at what she calculated to be ten-minute intervals. There was no way of knowing, of course, if her voice actually carried up the tube, but she had to try. She mustn't wear out her voice too soon, though, and not be able to attract attention if she did hear sounds of someone nearby.

But would he come back? she wondered. He was insane, she was sure of that. If he heard her shouting, he might cover the air vent and let her suffocate. She had to be careful.

Of course, it might all be for naught, she realized. There was a strong likelihood that she was buried in a completely remote spot, and that he was visualizing her clawing at the lid of the casket and yanking on the string the way some Victorians reportedly had done when they realized they were buried alive. Only those people had someone waiting to hear their alarm. Wherever she was, she was certain that she was completely alone.

) 75

AT TEN O'CLOCK, NEIL AND HIS FATHER SAT TENSELY IN Chief Brower's office and listened as he soberly revealed the contents of Malcolm Norton's suicide note. "Norton was a bitter and disappointed man," he said. "According to what he's written, because of a change in environmental laws, Ms. Holloway's property is going to be worth a lot of money. When he made the offer to Nuala Moore to buy her house, he obviously was prepared to cheat her by not telling her of its true value, so it's very possible that he got wind that she was changing her mind about making the sale to him and killed her. He might well have been searching the house, trying to find her revised will."

He paused to reread a paragraph of the lengthy note. "It's very obvious that he blamed Maggie Holloway for everything having gone wrong, and although he doesn't say it, he may have taken revenge on her. He's certainly managed to get his wife in serious trouble."

This can't be happening, Neil thought. He felt his father's hand on his shoulder and wanted to shake it off. He was afraid that sympathy would undermine his resolve, and he would not let that happen. He wasn't going to give up. *Maggie wasn't dead.* He was sure of that. She *couldn't* be dead.

"I've talked to Mrs. Norton," Brower continued. "Her husband came home at the usual time yesterday, then left and didn't return until midnight. This morning when she tried to find out where he'd been, he wouldn't answer."

"How well did Maggie know this guy Norton?" Robert Stephens asked. "What would make her agree to meet him? Do you think he might have forced her into her own car, then driven to where you found it? But then, what did he do with Maggie, and since he left her car there, how did he get home?"

Brower was shaking his head as Stephens spoke. "It's a very unlikely scenario, I agree, but it's an angle we have to pursue. We're bringing in dogs to try to follow Ms. Holloway's scent, so if she is in that area, we'll find her. But it's a long way from Norton's home. He'd have to have acted in tandem with someone else, or he'd need to have gotten a ride home from a passerby, and frankly both of those options seem unlikely. This woman he was crazy about, Barbara Hoffman, is in Colorado visiting her daughter. We checked on her already. She's been there since the weekend."

The intercom rang, and Brower picked up his phone. "Put him on," he said after a moment.

Neil buried his face in his hands. Don't let them have found Maggie's body, he silently pleaded.

Brower's conversation lasted only a minute. When he got off, he said, "In a way, I think we have good news. Malcolm Norton had dinner last night at the Log Cabin, a small restaurant near where Barbara Hoffman lived. Apparently she and Norton ate there together frequently. The owner tells us that Norton was there until well after eleven, so he must have gone directly home."

Which means, Neil thought, he almost certainly had nothing to do with Maggie's disappearance.

"Where do you go from here?" Robert Stephens asked.

"To interrogate the people Ms. Holloway pointed us to," Brower said, "Earl Bateman and Nurse Zelda Markey."

His intercom sounded again. After listening without comment, Brower hung up his phone and stood. "I don't know what kind of game Bateman is up to, but he just phoned to report that last night a coffin was stolen from his funeral museum."

) 76

Dr. William Lane realized that there was very little he could say to his wife this Tuesday morning. Her stony silence indicated to him that even *she* could be driven too far.

If only she hadn't come home last night and found him like that, he thought. He hadn't had a drink in what seemed like ages, not since the incident at the last place he worked. Lane knew that he owed this job to Odile. She had met the owners of Prestige Residence Corporation at a cocktail party and had touted him for the director's job at Latham, which was then being renovated.

Latham Manor was to be one of Prestige's franchised residences, as opposed to fully owned and operated; but they had agreed to meet with him, and then later had submitted his résumé to the franchiser. Remarkably, he got the job.

All thanks to Odile, as she constantly reminded him, he thought bitterly.

He knew that the slipup last night was a sign the pressure was getting to him. The orders to keep those apartments filled; don't let them pass a month unsold. Always the implied threat of being let go if he didn't perform. *Let go,* he thought. Go where?

After the last incident, Odile had told him that if she saw him drunk even once, she was leaving.

As enticing as the prospect was, he couldn't let that happen. The truth was he needed her.

Why hadn't she stayed in Boston last night? he thought.

Because she suspected that he was panicking, he reasoned.

She was right, of course. He had been in a state of terror ever since he learned that Maggie Holloway had been looking for a sketch Nuala Moore had made that showed Nurse Markey eavesdropping.

He should have found a way to get rid of that woman long ago, but Prestige had sent her, and in most respects she was a good nurse. Certainly many of the residents valued her. In fact, he sometimes wondered if she wasn't *too* good a nurse. She seemed to know more than he did about some things.

Well, whatever was going on between him and Odile, Dr. Lane knew he had to go over to the residence and make his morning rounds.

He found his wife drinking coffee in the kitchen. Uncharacteristically she hadn't bothered to put on even a minimum of makeup this morning. She looked drawn and tired.

"Zelda Markey just phoned," she told him, an angry glint in her eye. "The police have asked her to be available for questioning. She doesn't know why."

"For *questioning?*" Lane felt the tension run through his body, gripping every muscle. It's all over, he thought.

"She also told me that Sarah Cushing gave strict orders that neither she nor you was to enter her mother's room. It seems that Mrs. Bainbridge isn't well, and Mrs. Cushing is making arrangements to transfer her immediately to the hospital."

Odile looked at him accusingly. "You were supposed to be rushing home to see Mrs. Bainbridge last night. Not that you'd have been allowed anywhere near her, but I hear you didn't show up at the residence till nearly eleven. What were you *doing* until then?"

☽ 77

NEIL AND ROBERT STEPHENS DROVE TO THE REMOTE ROAD where Maggie's station wagon was still parked. Now it was surrounded with police tape, and as they got out of their car they could hear the yapping of search dogs in the nearby woods.

Neither man had spoken since they left the police station. Neil used the time to think through all he knew so far. It amounted to very little, he realized, and the longer he felt in the dark, the more frustrated he became.

It was good, even essential, to have the understanding presence of his father, he realized. Something I didn't give to Maggie, he told himself bitterly.

Through the heavy woods and thick foliage, he could make out the figures of at least a dozen people. Policemen or volunteers? he wondered. He knew they had found nothing so far, so the search had spread out over a wider area. In despair, he realized that they were expecting to find Maggie's body.

He shoved his hands into his pockets and bowed his head.

Finally he broke the silence. "She can't be dead," he said. "I'd know it if she were dead."

"Neil, let's go," his father said quietly. "I don't even know why we came out here. Standing around here isn't helping Maggie."

"What do you suggest I do?" Neil asked, anger and frustration showing in his voice.

"From what Chief Brower said, the police haven't spoken to this guy Hansen yet, but they found out he's expected at his office in Providence around noon. At this point they consider him small potatoes. They'll turn over the fraud information Norton left with his note to the district attorney. But it wouldn't hurt for us to be at Hansen's office when he comes in."

"Dad, you can't expect me to worry about stock deals now," Neil said angrily.

"No, and at this moment I'm not worried about them either. But you did authorize the sale of fifty thousand shares of stock that Cora Gebhart didn't own. You certainly have a right to go to Hansen's office and demand some answers," Robert Stephens urged.

He looked into his son's face. "Don't you see what I'm driving at? Something made Maggie mighty uneasy about Hansen. I don't think it's just a coincidence that he's the guy who fronted an offer on her house. You can get him on the defensive about the stocks. But the real reason I want to see him right away is to try and find out if he knows anything at all about Maggie's disappearance."

When Neil continued to shake his head, Robert Stephens pointed to the woods. "If you believe Maggie's body is lying out there somewhere, then go join the search. I happen to hope—to believe—that she's still alive, and if she is, I bet her abductor didn't leave her in the vicinity of the car."

He turned to leave. "Get a ride from someone else. I'm going to Providence to see Hansen."

He got into the car and slammed the door. As he was turning the ignition key, Neil jumped in on the passenger side.

"You're right," he admitted. "I don't know where we'll find her, but it won't be here."

❫ 78

AT 11:30, EARL BATEMAN WAS WAITING FOR CHIEF Brower and Detective Haggerty on the porch of his funeral museum.

"The casket was here yesterday afternoon," Bateman said heatedly. "I know, because I gave a tour of the place, and I remember pointing it out. I can't believe anyone would have the insolence to desecrate an important collection like this just as a prank. Every single object in my museum was purchased only after meticulous research.

"Halloween is coming," he continued, as he nervously thumped his right hand on his left palm. "I'm positive a bunch of kids pulled this stunt. And I can tell you right now that if that's what happened, I *will* press charges. No 'boyish prank' excuses, do you understand?"

"Professor Bateman, why don't we go inside and talk about it?" Brower said.

"Of course. Actually I may have a picture of the casket in my office. It's an item of particular interest, and, in fact, I've been planning to make it the focal point of a new exhibit when I expand the museum. Come this way."

The two policemen followed him through the foyer, past the life-sized figure dressed in black, to what obviously had been the kitchen. A sink, refrigerator, and stove still lined the far wall. Legal-size files were under the back windows. An immense old-fashioned desk stood in the center of the room, its surface covered with blueprints and sketches.

"I'm planning an outdoor exhibit," Bateman told them. "I have some property nearby that will make a wonderful site. Go ahead, sit down. I'll try to find that picture."

He's awfully worked up, Jim Haggerty thought. I wonder if he was this agitated when they threw him out of Latham Manor that time? Maybe he *isn't* the harmless weirdo I pegged him for.

"Why don't we just ask you a few questions before you look for the picture," Brower suggested.

"Oh, all right." Bateman yanked out the desk chair and sat down.

Haggerty took out his notebook.

"Was anything else taken, Professor Bateman?" Brower asked.

"No. Nothing else seems to have been disturbed. Thank God the place wasn't vandalized. You should realize that this could have been done by someone working alone, because the catafalque is missing too, and it would have been no trouble to wheel the casket out."

"Where was the casket located?"

"On the second floor, but I have an elevator for moving heavy objects up and down." The telephone rang. "Oh, excuse me. That will probably be my cousin Liam. He was in a meeting when I called to tell him what happened. I thought he'd be interested."

Bateman picked up the receiver. "Hello," he said, then

listened, nodding to indicate that it was the call he had been expecting.

Brower and Haggerty listened to the one-sided conversation as Bateman informed his cousin of the theft.

"A very valuable antique," he said excitedly. "A Victorian coffin. I paid ten thousand dollars for it, and that was a bargain. This one has the original breathing tube with it and was—"

He stopped suddenly, as though interrupted. Then in a shocked voice, he cried, "What do you mean Maggie Holloway is missing? That's impossible!"

When he hung up, he seemed dazed. "This is *terrible!* How could something happen to Maggie? Oh, I just *knew* it, I *knew* she wasn't safe. I had a premonition. Liam is *very* upset. They are very close, you know. He called from his car phone. He said he just heard about Maggie on the news, and he's on his way down from Boston." Then Bateman frowned. "You knew Maggie was missing?" he asked Brower accusingly.

"Yes," Brower said shortly. "And we also know she was here with you yesterday afternoon."

"Well, yes. I'd brought her a picture of Nuala Moore taken at a recent family reunion, and she was very appreciative. Because she's such a successful photographer, I asked her to help me by suggesting visuals for the television series I'm going to do about funeral customs. That's why she came to see the exhibits," he explained earnestly.

"She looked over just about everything," he went on. "I was disappointed that she hadn't brought her camera, so when she left I told her to come back on her own at any time. I showed her where I hide the key."

"That was yesterday afternoon," Brower said. "Did she come back here last night?"

"I don't think so. Why would she come here at night?

Most women wouldn't." He looked upset. "I hope nothing bad has happened to Maggie. She's a nice woman, and very attractive. I've been quite drawn to her, in fact."

He shook his head, then added, "No, I think it's a safe bet that *she* didn't steal the casket. Why, when I showed her the place yesterday, she wouldn't even set foot in the coffin room."

Is that supposed to be a joke? Haggerty wondered. This guy had that explanation right on tap, he noted. Ten to one he'd already heard about Maggie Holloway's disappearance.

Bateman got up. "I'll go look for the picture."

"Not yet," Brower said. "First I'd like to talk to you about a little problem you had when you gave a lecture at Latham Manor. I heard something about Victorian cemetery bells and your being asked to leave."

Bateman angrily slammed his fist on the desk. *"I don't want to talk about that!* What's the matter with all of you? Only yesterday I had to tell Maggie Holloway the same thing. Those bells are locked in my storeroom, and there they'll stay. *I won't talk about it.* Got it?" His face was white with anger.

) 79

THE WEATHER WAS CHANGING, BECOMING SHARPLY cooler. The morning sun had given way to clouds, and by eleven the sky was bleak and gray.

Neil and his father sat on the two upright wooden chairs that, along with a secretary's desk and chair, were the sole furnishings in the reception area of Douglas Hansen's office.

The one employee was a laconic young woman of about twenty who disinterestedly informed them that Mr. Hansen had been out of the office since Thursday afternoon, and that all she knew was that he had said he would be in by about ten today.

The door leading to the inside office was open, and they could see that that room appeared to be as sparsely furnished as the reception area. A desk, chair, filing cabinet, and small computer were all they could see in it.

"Doesn't exactly look like a thriving brokerage firm," Robert Stephens said. "In fact, I'd say it looks like more of a setting for a floating crap game—set up so you can get out of town fast if someone blows the whistle."

Neil found it agonizing to have to simply sit there, doing nothing. *Where is Maggie?* he kept asking himself.

She's alive, she's alive, he repeated with determination. And I'm going to find her. He tried to concentrate on what his father was saying, then replied, "I doubt he shows this place to his potential clients."

"He doesn't," Robert Stephens answered. "He takes them to fancy lunches and dinners. From what Cora Gebhart and Laura Arlington told me, he can put on the charm, although they both said he sounded very knowledgeable about investments."

"Then he's taken a crash course somewhere. Our security guy who ran the check on him told me that Hansen's been fired from two brokerage houses for just plain ineptitude."

Both men spun their heads sharply as the outer door opened. They were just in time to catch the startled expression on Douglas Hansen's face when he saw them.

He thinks we're cops, Neil realized. He must already have heard about his uncle's suicide.

They stood up. Robert Stephens spoke first. "I represent Mrs. Cora Gebhart and Mrs. Laura Arlington," he said formally. "As their accountant, I'm here to discuss the recent investments you *purport* to have made for them."

"And I'm here to represent Maggie Holloway," Neil said angrily. "Where were you last night, and what do you know about her disappearance?"

) 80

MAGGIE BEGAN TO SHIVER UNCONTROLLABLY. HOW LONG had she been here? she wondered. Had she drifted off to sleep, or lost consciousness? Her head hurt so much. Her mouth was dry with thirst.

How long was it since she last called for help? Was anyone looking for her? Did anyone even *know* that she was *missing?*

Neil. He said he would call tonight. No, *last* night, she thought, trying to make sense of time. I was in the museum at nine o'clock, she reminded herself. I know I've been here for hours. Is it morning now, or even later than that?

Neil would call her.

Or would he?

She had rejected his expressions of concern. Maybe he wouldn't call. She *had* been cold to him. Maybe he had washed his hands of her.

No, no, she prayed. Neil wouldn't do that. Neil would look for her. *"Find* me, Neil, *please* find me," she whispered, then blinked back tears.

His face loomed in her mind. Troubled. Concerned. Worried about her. If only she had told him about the bells on the graves. If only she had asked him to go with her to the museum.

The museum, she thought suddenly. The voice behind her.

Mentally she replayed what had happened in the attack. She turned and saw the look on his face before he crashed the flashlight down on her head. Evil. Murderous.

As he must have looked when he murdered Nuala.

Wheels. She hadn't been totally unconscious when she felt herself being wheeled.

A woman's voice. She had heard a familiar woman's voice talking to him. Maggie moaned as she remembered whose voice it was.

I've *got* to get out of here, she thought. I can't die; knowing this, I *mustn't* die. She'll do it again for him. I know she will.

"Help," she shrieked. "Help me."

Over and over she called until she finally was able to force herself to stop. Don't panic, she warned herself. Above all, don't panic.

I'll count to five hundred very slowly and then call out three times, she decided. I'll keep doing that.

She heard a steady, muffled sound from above, then felt a cold trickle on her hand. It was raining, she realized, and the rain was dripping down through the air vent.

❭ *81*

AT ELEVEN-THIRTY, CHIEF BROWER AND DETECTIVE HAG-gerty entered Latham Manor. It was obvious that the residents knew that something was wrong. They were standing in small groups in the entrance hall and library.

The officers were aware of the curious gazes that followed them when the maid led them to the office wing.

Dr. Lane greeted them courteously. "Come right in. I'm at your service." He indicated they should be seated.

He looks like hell, Haggerty thought, taking in the bloodshot eyes, the gray lines around the doctor's mouth, and the beads of perspiration on his forehead.

"Dr. Lane, at this point we're simply asking some questions, nothing more," Brower began.

"Nothing more than what?" Lane asked, attempting a smile.

"Doctor, before you took this position, you'd been unemployed for several years. Why was that?"

Lane was silent for a moment, then said quietly, "I suspect you already know the answer to that."

"We'd prefer to hear your version," Haggerty told him.

"My version, as you put it, is that we'd had an outbreak of flu in the Colony Nursing Home where I was in charge. Four of the women had to be transferred to the hospital. Therefore, when others came down with flu-like symptoms, I naturally assumed that they'd caught the same virus."

"But they hadn't," Brower said quietly. "In fact, in their

section of the nursing home there was a faulty heater. They were suffering the effects of carbon monoxide poisoning. Three of them died. Isn't that true?"

Lane kept his eyes averted and did not answer.

"And isn't it true that the son of one of those women had told you that his mother's disorientation did not seem consistent with flu symptoms, and even *asked* you to check for the possible presence of carbon monoxide?"

Again Lane did not answer.

"Your license was suspended for gross negligence, and yet you were able to secure this position. How did that happen?" Brower asked.

Lane's mouth became a straight line. "Because the people at Prestige Residence Corporation were fair enough to recognize that I had been the director of an overly crowded, low-budget facility, that I was working fifteen hours a day, that a number of the guests were suffering from flu, and the misdiagnosis therefore was understandable, and that the man who complained was constantly finding fault with everything from the hot water temperature, to doors that squeaked, to drafty windows."

He stood up. "I find these questions insulting. I suggest that you leave these premises immediately. As it is, you have thoroughly upset our guests. Someone apparently felt the need to inform everyone that you were coming here."

"That would be Nurse Markey," Brower said. "Please tell me where I can find her."

Zelda Markey was openly defiant as she sat across from Brower and Haggerty in the small second-floor room that served as her office. Her sharp-featured face was an angry red, her eyes cold with rage.

"My patients need me," she said tartly. "They're aware that Janice Norton's husband committed suicide, and they've heard a rumor that she's been doing something illegal here. They're even more distressed to learn that Miss Holloway is missing. Everyone who met her was very fond of her."

"Were you fond of her, Ms. Markey?" Brower asked.

"I did not know her well enough to become fond of her. The few times I spoke with her, I found her very pleasant."

"Ms. Markey, you're a friend of Earl Bateman's, aren't you?" Brower asked.

"To me, friendship implies familiarity. I know and admire Professor Bateman. He, like all the family, were very solicitous of his aunt, Alicia Bateman, who was a guest at the Seaside Nursing Home, where I was formerly employed."

"In fact, the Batemans were quite generous to you, weren't they?"

"They felt that I was taking excellent care of Alicia and were kind enough to insist on rewarding me."

"I see. I'd like to know why you thought a lecture on death might be of interest to the residents of Latham Manor. Don't you think they'll all be facing it soon enough?"

"Chief Brower, I am aware that this society has a horror of the word 'death.' But the older generation has a much greater sense of reality. At least half of our residents have left specific instructions for their own final arrangements, and, indeed, frequently even joke about it."

She hesitated. "However, I will say that it was my understanding that Professor Bateman was planning to give his talk on royal funerals through the ages, which, of course, is quite an interesting subject. If he had stuck to that . . ." She paused for a moment, then continued, "And I will admit also that the use of the bells upset some people, but the way Mrs. Sarah Cushing treated Professor Bateman was unpardonable. He meant no harm, yet she treated him inhumanly."

"Do you think *he* was very angry?" Brower asked mildly.

"I think he was humiliated, *then* perhaps angry, yes. When he's not lecturing, he's actually very shy."

Haggerty looked up from his notes. An unmistakable softness had come into the nurse's tone and expression. Interesting, he thought. He was sure Brower had noticed as well. *Friendship implies familiarity.* Methinks the lady doth protest too much, he decided.

"Nurse Markey, what do you know about a sketch that Mrs. Nuala Moore made with the late Mrs. Greta Shipley?"

"Absolutely nothing," she snapped.

"It was in Mrs. Shipley's apartment. It seems to have vanished after her death."

"That is absolutely impossible. The room or apartment is locked immediately. Everyone knows that."

"Uh-huh." Brower's tone became confidential. "Nurse Markey, just between us, what do you think about Dr. Lane?"

She looked at him sharply, then paused before speaking. "I'm at the point where even if it means hurting someone I'm very fond of, I'm willing to lose another job by speaking my mind. I wouldn't let Dr. Lane treat my cat. He's probably the stupidest physician I have ever dealt with, and, believe me, I've dealt with my share of them."

She stood up. "I also have had the honor of working with magnificent doctors. Which is why I cannot understand how the Prestige people chose Dr. Lane to run this establishment. And before you ask, *that* is the reason I check so frequently on residents about whom I am concerned. I don't think he is capable of giving them the care they need. I'm aware that sometimes they may resent it, but I am only doing it for their own good."

) *82*

NEIL AND ROBERT STEPHENS DROVE DIRECTLY TO NEW-
port police headquarters. "Damn good thing you got that
restraining order in yesterday," Robert said to his son. "That
guy was ready to skip. At least this way with his bank
account tied up, we stand a chance at getting Cora's money
back, or some of it, anyhow."

"But he doesn't know what happened to Maggie," Neil
said bitterly.

"No, I guess he doesn't. You can't be an usher at a five
o'clock wedding in New York, offer dozens of names of
people who will state that you stayed for the entire reception, and be up here at the same time."

"He had a lot more to say about his alibi than he did
about his stock dealings," Neil said. "Dad, that guy has
nothing in that office to indicate that he's dealing in securities. Did you see *one* financial statement, *one* prospectus, or
anything like what you see in my office?"

"No, I did not."

"Trust me, he's not really working out of that dump.
Those transactions are coming out of another place. And
one that's probably pulling this same sort of swindle." Neil
paused, looking grimly out the car window. "God, this
weather is lousy."

It's getting cold and it's pouring. Where is Maggie? he
thought. Is she out in this somewhere? Is she scared?

Is she *dead?*

Once again, Neil rejected the thought. She *couldn't* be dead. It was as if he could hear her calling to him to help her.

They arrived at the police station to find that Chief Brower was out, but Detective Haggerty saw them. "There's nothing helpful to report," he said candidly to their urgent queries about Maggie. "No one remembers seeing that Volvo station wagon in town last night. We've gotten in touch with Ms. Holloway's neighbors here. When they passed her house on the way to dinner at seven o'clock, her car was in her driveway. It was gone when they returned at nine-thirty, so we have to assume that she left somewhere in that two-and-a-half-hour time frame."

"That's all you can tell us?" Neil asked, his tone incredulous. "My God, there's got to be something more than *that*."

"I wish there were. We know that she went over to that funeral museum Monday afternoon. We spoke to her before she left and after she returned."

"Funeral museum?" Neil said. "That doesn't sound like Maggie. What was she doing there?"

"According to Professor Bateman, she was helping him select visuals for some television series he'll be doing," Haggerty responded.

"You said 'According to Professor Bateman,'" Robert Stephens said sharply.

"Did I? Well, I mean, we have no reason to doubt the professor. He may be a bit eccentric, but he grew up here, people know him, and he's got no record of any trouble." He hesitated. "I'll be totally honest with you. Ms. Holloway seemed to indicate that there was something about him that bothered her. And when we checked, we did learn that, while nothing involving the police was in his history, he was responsible for a stir one afternoon among a number of the residents at the Latham Manor retirement home. Seems like they ended up throwing him out of the place."

Latham Manor again! Neil thought.

"Bateman also volunteered that Maggie knew where the key to the museum was hidden, and that he had invited her to come back with her camera at any time."

"Do you think she actually went there last night? *Alone?*" Neil asked incredulously.

"I wouldn't think so. No, the fact is, there seems to have been a robbery at the museum last night—if you can believe it, a coffin is missing. What we are doing is interrogating some teenage kids from the general neighborhood who have given us trouble before. We think they're probably responsible. We think they may also be able to give us some information about Ms. Holloway. If she had gone into the museum, and they saw her car parked there, I've gotta believe they would have made sure she was gone before they went in themselves."

Neil stood to leave. He *had* to get out of there; he *had* to be doing something. Besides, he knew that there was nothing more he could learn here. But he *could* go back to Latham Manor and maybe find out something. His excuse would be that he wanted to talk to the director about the Van Hillearys' possible application.

"I'll check in with you later," he told Haggerty. "I'm going over to Latham Manor and try to talk to some of the people there. You never know who might have some bit of information that could be of help. And I have a good excuse for visiting. I was by there on Friday to inquire about the facilities on behalf of a couple who are my investment clients, and I've just come up with a few more questions."

Haggerty raised his eyebrows. "You'll probably find out that we were there a little while ago."

"Why?" Robert Stephens asked quickly.

"We spoke to the director and to one of the nurses there, a Zelda Markey, who it seems is a close friend of Professor Bateman's. I can't say more than that."

"Dad, what's your car-phone number?" Neil asked.

Robert Stephens took out a business card and scribbled the number on the back. "Here."

Neil handed the card to Haggerty. "If there are any developments, try us at this number. And we'll be calling in to you every hour or so."

"That's fine. Ms. Holloway's a close friend, isn't she?"

"She's more than that," Robert Stephens said brusquely. "Consider us her family."

"As you wish," Haggerty said simply. "I *do* understand." He looked at Neil. "If my wife were missing, I'd be going through the same kind of hell. I've met Ms. Holloway. She's real smart and, I believe, very resourceful. If there's any way she can help herself, trust her to do it."

The look of genuine sympathy on Haggerty's face brought Neil to an acute awareness of just how close he might be to losing someone who, surprisingly, he now couldn't imagine living without. He swallowed over the sudden lump in his throat. Not trusting himself to speak, he nodded, and left.

In the car, he said, "Dad, why do I feel that Latham Manor is at the center of all this?"

) 83

"MAGGIE, YOU'RE NOT CALLING FOR HELP, ARE YOU? THAT isn't wise."

Oh God, *no! He was back!* His voice, hollow and echoing, was barely discernible through the rain beating on the earth above her.

"You must be getting wet down there," he called. "I'm glad. I want you to be cold and wet and scared. I'll bet you're hungry, too. Or maybe just thirsty?"

Don't answer, she told herself. Don't plead with him. It's what he wants.

"You ruined everything for me, Maggie, you and Nuala. She had begun to suspect something, so she had to die. And it was all going so well, too. Latham Manor—I own it, you know. Only the outfit that manages it doesn't know who I am. I have a holding company. And you were right about the bells. Those women weren't buried alive, maybe just a little bit sooner than God intended. They should have had more time. That's why I put the bells on the graves. It's my little joke. *You're* the only one who really is buried alive.

"When they exhume those women, they'll blame Dr. Lane for their deaths. They'll think it was his fault that the medicines got mixed. He's a lousy doctor anyway, with a terrible record. And a drinking problem. That's why I had them hire him. But your stupid interference does mean I won't be able to call on my little angel of death to help the little ladies along to an early grave. And that's too bad; I want the money. Do you know how much profit there is in turning over those rooms? Lots. *Lots.*"

Maggie shut her eyes, struggling to blot out his face from her mind. It was almost as though she could see him. He was crazy.

"I guess you figured out that the bell on your grave has no clapper, haven't you? Now figure this out: How long will you last when the air vent is clogged?"

She felt a rush of dirt on her hand. Frantically she tried to poke open the vent with her finger. More dirt tumbled down.

"Oh, one more thing, Maggie," he said, his voice suddenly more muffled. "I took the bells from the other graves. I thought that was a good idea. I'll put them back when they bury the bodies again. Sweet dreams."

She heard the thump of something hitting the air vent; then she heard nothing. He was gone. She was sure of it. The vent was packed. She did the only thing she could think of to help herself. She flexed and unflexed her left hand so that the string on her ring finger would keep the mud from hardening around it. Please God, she prayed, let someone see that the bell is moving.

How long would it be before she used up all the oxygen? she wondered. Hours? A day?

"Neil, help me, help me," she whispered. "I need you. I love you. *I don't want to die.*"

☽ 84

LETITIA BAINBRIDGE HAD ABSOLUTELY REFUSED TO GO TO the hospital. "You can cancel that ambulance or ride in it yourself," she tartly informed her daughter, "but I'm not going anywhere."

"But Mother, you're not well," Sarah Cushing protested, knowing full well that to argue with her was useless. When her mother got a certain mulelike look, there was no point in further discussion.

"Who's well at ninety-four?" Mrs. Bainbridge asked. "Sarah, I appreciate your concern, but there's a lot going on around here, and I don't intend to miss it."

"Will you at least take your meals on a tray?"

"Not dinner. You do realize Dr. Evans checked me out just a few days ago. There's nothing wrong with me that being fifty wouldn't cure."

Sarah Cushing gave up the argument reluctantly. "Very well, but you've got to promise me one thing. If you don't feel well, you'll let me take you to Dr. Evans again. I don't want Dr. Lane treating you."

"Neither do I. Sneak that she is, Nurse Markey did see a change in Greta Shipley last week and tried to get Lane to do something about it. He, of course, couldn't find anything; he was wrong and she was right. Does anyone know why the police were talking to her?"

"I'm not sure."

"Well, find out!" she snapped. Then in a quieter tone, she

added, "I'm so worried about that wonderful girl, Maggie Holloway. So many young people today are so indifferent or impatient with old fossils like me. Not her. We're all praying that she'll be found."

"I know, and so am I," Sarah Cushing agreed.

"All right, go downstairs and find out the latest. Start with Angela. She doesn't miss a thing."

Neil had called on the car phone to tell Dr. Lane he would like to stop by to discuss the Van Hillearys' interest in residing at Latham Manor. He found Lane's voice curiously indifferent when he agreed to a meeting.

They were admitted to Latham Manor by the same attractive young maid they had seen before. Neil remembered that her name was Angela. When they arrived she was talking to a handsome woman who appeared to be in her mid-sixties.

"I'll let Dr. Lane know you're here," Angela said softly. As she crossed the entrance hall to the intercom, the older woman came over to them.

"I don't want to seem inquisitive, but are you from the police?" she asked.

"No, we're not," Robert Stephens said quickly. "Why do you ask? Is there a problem?"

"No. Or at least I certainly hope not. Let me explain. I am Sarah Cushing. My mother, Letitia Bainbridge, is a resident here. She has become very fond of a young woman named Maggie Holloway, who seems to have gone missing, and she is terribly anxious for any news about her."

"We're very fond of Maggie, too," Neil said, once again experiencing the lump in his throat that now was threatening to undermine his composure. "I wonder if it would be possible to speak to your mother after we see Dr. Lane?"

Noting a look of uncertainty in Sarah Cushing's eyes, he felt he had to explain. "We're groping at straws to see if

303

Maggie may have said anything to anyone, even casually, that might help us to find her."

He bit his lip, unable to go on.

Sarah Cushing studied him, sensing his distress. Her frosty blue eyes softened. "Absolutely. You can see Mother," she said briskly. "I'll wait in the library for you and take you up when you're ready."

The maid had returned. "Dr. Lane is ready to see you," she said.

For the second time, Neil and Robert Stephens followed her to Lane's office. Neil reminded himself that as far as the doctor was concerned, he was here to discuss the Van Hillearys. He forced himself to remember the questions that he had intended to ask, on their behalf. Was the residence owned and operated by Prestige, or was it franchised by them? He would need proof of sufficient reserve capital.

Was there any allowance for the Van Hillearys if they opted to decorate and refurbish the suite themselves?

Both men were shocked when they reached Dr. Lane's office. The man seated at the desk was so radically changed that it was like seeing and talking to a different human being. The suave, smiling, courteous director they had met last week was gone.

Lane looked ill and defeated. His skin was gray, his eyes sunken. Listlessly he invited them to sit down, then said, "I understand you have some questions. I'll be happy to answer them. However, a new director will be meeting your clients when they come up on the weekend."

He's been fired, Neil thought. Why? he wondered. He decided to plunge ahead. "Look, I don't know what's been going on here, obviously, and I'm not asking you to explain the reasons behind your departure." He paused. "But I am aware that your bookkeeper had been giving out privileged financial information. That was one of my concerns."

"Yes, that's something that has just been brought to our attention. I'm very sure it won't happen again in this establishment," Lane said.

"I can sympathize," Neil continued. "In the investment business, we unfortunately always seem to face the problem of insider trading." He knew his father was looking at him curiously, but he had to try to learn if that was the reason Lane was being fired. Secretly he doubted it and suspected that it had something to do with the sudden deaths of some of the residents.

"I'm aware of the problem," Lane said. "My wife worked in a securities firm in Boston—Randolph and Marshall—before I took this position. It would seem that dishonest people crop up everywhere. Ah, well, let me try to answer whatever questions you have. Latham Manor is a wonderful residence, and I can assure you that our guests are very happy here."

When they left fifteen minutes later, Robert Stephens said, "Neil, that guy is scared stiff."

"I know. And it's not just because of his job." I'm wasting time, he thought. He had brought up Maggie's name, and Lane's only response was an expression of polite concern for her welfare.

"Dad, maybe we should skip meeting with anyone here," he said as they reached the entrance hall. "I'm going to break into Maggie's house to search it. Maybe there's something there that will give us some idea of where she was going last night."

Sarah Cushing was waiting for them, however. "I phoned up to Mother. She wants very much to meet you."

Neil was about to protest but saw his father's warning glance. Robert Stephens said, "Neil, why don't you pay a visit for a few minutes? I'll make some calls from the car. I was about to tell you that I happened to keep an extra key to the new lock on Maggie's door, in case she ever forgot hers. I told her about it. I'll call your mother and have her meet us there with it. And I'll call Detective Haggerty, too.''

It would take his mother half an hour to get to Maggie's house, Neil calculated. He nodded. "I'd like to meet your mother, Mrs. Cushing."

On the way up to Letitia Bainbridge's room he decided to ask her about the lecture that Earl Bateman gave at Latham Manor, the one that got him banished from the place. *Bateman was the last person to admit seeing Maggie yesterday,* he reasoned. *She had spoken to Detective Haggerty later, but no one had reported seeing her.*

Had anyone thought about that? Neil wondered. Had anyone checked to confirm Earl Bateman's story that he had gone directly to Providence after he left the museum yesterday afternoon?

"This is Mother's apartment," Sarah Cushing said. She tapped, waited for the invitation to enter, then opened the door.

Now fully dressed, Mrs. Letitia Bainbridge was seated in a wing chair. She waved Neil in and pointed to the chair nearest her. "From what Sarah tells me, you seem to be Maggie's young man. You must be so worried. We all are. How can we help?"

Having deduced that Sarah Cushing had to be nearly seventy, Neil realized that this bright-eyed, clear-voiced woman had to be around ninety or more. She looked as if she missed nothing. Let her tell me something that will help, he prayed.

"Mrs. Bainbridge, I hope I won't upset you by being absolutely frank with you. For reasons I don't understand as yet, Maggie had begun to be very suspicious about some of the recent deaths in this residence. We know that only yesterday morning she looked up the obituaries of six different women, five of whom had resided here, and who died recently. Those five women died in their sleep, unattended, and none of them had close relatives."

"Dear God!" Sarah Cushing's voice was shocked.

Letitia Bainbridge did not flinch. "Are you talking about neglect or murder?" she asked.

"I don't know," Neil said. "I just know that Maggie started an investigation that's already leading to an order for the exhumation of at least two of the dead women, and now she's disappeared. And I've just learned that Dr. Lane has been fired."

"I just found out that too, Mother," Sarah Cushing said. "But everyone thinks it's because of the bookkeeper."

"What about Nurse Markey?" Mrs. Bainbridge asked her daughter. "Is that why the police questioned her? I mean because of the deaths?"

"Nobody is sure, but she's mighty upset. And, of course, so is Mrs. Lane. I hear that the two of them are closeted in Markey's office."

"Oh, those two are always whispering together," Letitia Bainbridge said dismissively. "I can't imagine what they have to say to each other. Markey may be terribly annoying, but at least she has a brain. The other one is as empty-headed as they get."

This isn't getting me anywhere, Neil thought. "Mrs. Bainbridge," he said, "I can only stay a minute longer. There's one other thing I'd like to ask you. Were you at the lecture Professor Bateman gave here? The one that apparently caused such an uproar?"

"No." Mrs. Bainbridge shot a look at her daughter. "That was another day when Sarah insisted I rest, so I missed all the excitement. But Sarah was there."

"I can assure you, Mother, that you wouldn't have enjoyed being handed one of those bells and being told to pretend you were buried alive," Sarah Cushing said spiritedly. "Let me tell you exactly what happened, Mr. Ste-phens."

Bateman has to be crazy, Neil thought as he listened to her version of the events.

"I was so upset that I gave that man a real tongue-lashing and nearly threw the box with those appalling bells after him," Sarah Cushing continued. "At first he seemed embar-rassed and contrite, but then a look came over his face that almost frightened me. I think he must have a fearful temper. And, of course, Nurse Markey had the gall to *defend* him! I spoke to her about it later, and she was quite impudent. She told me that Professor Bateman had been so upset that he said he now feared he wouldn't be able to stand the sight of the bells, which apparently had cost him quite a bit of money."

"I'm still sorry I wasn't there," Mrs. Bainbridge said. "And as far as Nurse Markey goes," she continued reflec-tively, "in perfect fairness, many of the residents here con-sider her an excellent nurse. I just find her to be nosy and pushy and intrusive, and I want her kept away from me whenever possible." She paused, then said, "Mr. Stephens, this may sound ridiculous, but I think that whatever his faults and shortcomings, Dr. Lane is a very kind man, and I'm a pretty good judge of character."

A half-hour later, Neil and his father drove to Maggie's house. Dolores Stephens was already there. She looked at her son and reached up and took his face between her hands. "We're going to find her," she said firmly.

Unable to speak, Neil nodded.

"Where's the key, Dolores?" Robert Stephens demanded.

"Right here."

The key fit the new lock on the back door, and as they

walked into the kitchen, Neil thought, It all started right here, when Maggie's stepmother was murdered.

The kitchen was neat. There were no dishes in the sink. He opened the dishwasher; inside were a few cups and saucers, along with three or four small plates. "I wonder if she had dinner out last night," he said.

"Or made a sandwich," his mother suggested. She had opened the refrigerator and seen a supply of cold cuts. She pointed to several knives in the utensils basket of the dishwasher.

"There's no message pad near the phone," Robert Stephens said. "We knew she was worried about something," he snapped. "I'm so damn mad at myself. I wish to God that when I came back here yesterday, I had bullied her into staying with us."

The dining room and living room both were orderly. Neil studied the vase of roses on the coffee table, wondering who had sent them. Probably Liam Payne, he thought. She mentioned him at dinner. Neil had only met Payne a few times, but he could have been the guy Neil had glimpsed leaving Maggie's Friday night.

Upstairs, the smallest bedroom contained the evidence of Maggie's packing up her stepmother's personal effects: Neatly tagged bags of clothing, purses, lingerie, and shoes were piled there. The bedroom she had used initially was the same as when they had fixed the window locks.

They went into the master bedroom. "Looks to me as though Maggie planned to stay in here last night," Robert Stephens observed, pointing to the freshly made bed.

Without answering, Neil started upstairs to the studio. The light that he had noticed last night, when he parked outside waiting for Maggie to come home, was still on, pointed toward a picture tacked to the bulletin board. Neil remembered that the picture had not been there Sunday afternoon.

He started across the room, then stopped. A chill ran through his body.

On the refectory table, in the glare of the spotlight, he saw two metal bells.

As surely as he knew that night followed day, he knew that these were two of the bells that Earl Bateman had used in his infamous lecture at Latham Manor— the bells that had been whisked away, never to be seen again.

) 85

HER HAND ACHED AND WAS COVERED WITH DIRT. SHE HAD continued to move the string steadily back and forth, hoping to keep the tube open, but now no more dirt seemed to be falling through the air vent. The water had stopped trickling down, too.

She couldn't hear the beating of the rain anymore either. Was it getting colder, or was it just that the dampness inside the coffin was so chilling? she wondered.

But she was actually starting to feel warm, even too warm.

I'm getting a fever, Maggie thought drowsily.

She was so lightheaded. The vent is sealed, she thought. There can't be much oxygen left.

"One . . . two . . . three . . . four . . ."

Now she was whispering the numbers aloud, trying to

force herself to stay awake, to start calling out again when she reached five hundred.

What difference would it make if he came back and heard her? What more could he do than he already had done?

Her hand was still flexing and unflexing.

"Make a fist," she said aloud. "All right, relax." That's what the nurses had told her to do when she was little and they were taking a blood sample. "This is so you'll get all better, Maggie," they had said.

After Nuala came to live with them, she had stopped being afraid of needles. Nuala had made a game of it. "We'll get that out of the way first and then we'll go to a movie," she would say.

Maggie thought of her equipment bag. What had he done with it? Her cameras. They were her friends. There were so many pictures she had planned to take with them. She had so many ideas she wanted to try out, so many things she wanted to shoot.

"One hundred fifty . . . one hundred fifty-one . . ."

She had known Neil was sitting behind her that day in the theater. He had coughed a couple of times, a peculiar little dry cough that she had recognized. She knew he *had* to have seen her, to have seen her unhappiness.

I made it a test, she thought. *If you love me, you will understand that I need you*—that was the thought she had willed him to hear and to act on.

But when the film ended and the lights went on, he was gone.

"I'll give you a second chance, Neil," she said aloud now. "If you love me, you'll know that I need you, and you'll find me."

"Four hundred ninety-nine, five hundred!"

She began to cry out for help again. This time she

screamed until her throat was raw. There was no use trying to save her voice, she decided. Time was running out.

Still, resolutely she began to count again. *"One . . . two . . . three . . ."*

Her hand moved in cadence with the count: *flex . . . unflex . . .*

With every fiber of her being, she fought the urge to sleep. She knew that if she slept, she would not wake up again.

) 86

WHILE HIS FATHER STARTED DOWNSTAIRS TO PHONE POLICE headquarters, Neil hesitated for a moment, studying the picture he had found pinned to the bulletin board.

The inscription on the back read, "Squire Moore Birthday Anniversary. September 20th. Earl Moore Bateman—Nuala Moore—Liam Moore Payne."

Neil studied Bateman's face. The face of a liar, he thought bitterly. The last man to see Maggie alive.

Aghast at what he feared his subconscious was telling him, he dropped the picture next to the bells and hurried to join his father.

"I have Chief Brower on the phone," Robert Stephens said. "He wants to talk to you. I told him about the bells."

Brower came immediately to the point. "If these are two of the same bells Bateman claims are locked in the storeroom of his museum, we can bring him in for interrogation. The problem is that he'll know enough to refuse to answer questions, and he'll call a lawyer, and everything will get delayed. Our best bet is to confront him with the bells and hope that he'll say something to give himself away. When we talked to him about them this morning, he went berserk."

"I intend to be there when you confront him," Neil said.

"I have a squad car watching the museum from the funeral parlor parking lot. If Bateman leaves the premises, he'll be followed."

"We're on our way," Neil said, then added, "Wait a minute, Chief, I know you've been questioning some teenagers. Did you find out anything from them?"

He heard the hesitation in Chief Brower's voice before he answered. "Something that I'm not sure I believe. We'll talk about it when I see you."

"I want to hear about it now," Neil snapped.

"Then please understand we don't necessarily credit the story. But one of the kids admitted that they were in the vicinity of the museum last night, or more specifically that they were across the street from it. At about ten o'clock that kid claims he saw two vehicles—a hearse, followed by a station wagon—drive out of the museum's parking lot."

"What kind of station wagon?" Neil asked urgently.

"The kid isn't sure of the make, but he swears it was black."

) 87

"TAKE IT EASY, EARL," LIAM MOORE PAYNE SAID FOR THE tenth time in an hour.

"No, I won't take it easy. I know how much this family has ridiculed the Batemans, and me especially."

"No one's ridiculed you, Earl," Liam said soothingly.

They were sitting in the office of the museum. It was nearly five o'clock, and the old-fashioned globed chandelier spread a murky glow over the room.

"Look," Liam said, "you need a drink."

"You mean *you* need a drink."

Without answering, Liam got up, went to the cupboard over the sink, got out the scotch bottle and glasses, then the ice tray and a lemon from the refrigerator.

"Double scotch on the rocks, with a twist, coming up, for both of us," he said.

Mollified, Earl waited until the drink was set in front of him, then said, "I'm glad you stopped by, Liam."

"When you called, I could tell how upset you were. And, of course, I'm more than *upset* about Maggie's disappearance." He paused. "Earl, I've dated her casually over the last year or so. You know, I'd call and we'd go out for dinner when I was in New York. But that night at the Four Seasons, when I realized she'd left without saying a word to me, something happened."

"What happened was that you ignored her because you were glad-handing everyone at the party."

"No, what happened was that I realized what a jerk I'd been, and that if she told me to go to hell, I'd have crawled there on my hands and knees, trying to make it up to her. But besides making me realize how important Maggie has become to me, that night gives me hope that maybe she's okay."

"What's that supposed to mean?"

"The fact that she walked out without saying a word when she was upset. God knows she's had plenty of reason to be upset since the minute she arrived in Newport. Maybe she just needed to get away."

"You seem to have forgotten that her car was found abandoned."

"For all we know she got on a plane or train and left her car parked somewhere and someone stole it. Maybe even kids joyriding."

"Don't talk to me about joyriding kids," Earl said. "My theory is those same kind of juvenile delinquents committed the theft here last night."

The shrill sound of the doorbell startled both men. Earl Bateman answered his cousin's unasked question: "I'm not expecting anyone," he said, and then smiled brightly. "But then, maybe it's the police telling me they found the casket."

Neil and his father joined Chief Brower in the funeral museum parking lot, and the chief cautioned Neil to control his tongue and to leave the questioning to the police. The bells from Maggie's house had been placed in a shoe box, which Detective Haggerty now carried unobtrusively under his arm.

When Earl took them to the museum office, Neil was startled to see Liam Payne sitting there. Suddenly uncomfortable in the presence of his rival, he greeted him with minimum courtesy, although he took some comfort in knowing that neither Earl nor Liam knew of his relationship with Maggie. He and his father were introduced simply as two of her concerned friends from New York.

Bateman and Payne went to get chairs for the men, taking them from the funeral scene in the front room. The irritation was clear on Bateman's face when they returned. He snapped at his cousin. "Liam, your shoes are muddy, and that's a very expensive carpet. Now I'm going to have to vacuum that whole viewing room before I leave."

Then, in an abrupt shift, he turned to the detectives. "Have you any news about the casket?" he asked.

"No, we don't, Professor Bateman," Brower said, "but we do have news about some other artifacts we think you own."

"That's ridiculous. Nothing else is missing except the catafalque," he said. "I checked. The casket is what I want to know about. You have no idea the plans I had for it. The outdoor display I told you about. That casket was going to be part of the most important exhibit there. I've even ordered mannequins of horses with black plumes, and I'm having a replica built of the kind of funeral carriage the Victorians used. It will be a stunning display."

"Earl, take it easy," Liam Payne said soothingly. He turned to Brower. "Chief, is there any new information about Maggie Holloway?"

"No, unfortunately there isn't," Brower told him.

"Have you considered my suggestion that Maggie simply wanted to escape the terrible pressures of the last week and a half?"

Neil looked at Liam scornfully. "You don't know Maggie at all," he said. "She doesn't try to escape problems. She faces them head on."

Brower ignored both men and spoke to Bateman. "Professor, at this point we're simply trying to clarify a few matters. You're not required to answer our questions. You do understand that?"

"Why wouldn't I answer your questions? I have nothing to hide."

"All right. From what we understand, the bells that you had cast for your lecture on Victorians who feared being buried alive are all packed away. Is that true?"

The anger was clear on Earl Bateman's face. "I simply will not go into that Latham Manor incident again," he said sharply. "I've told you that."

"I understand. But will you answer the question, please?"

"Yes. I packed the bells away. Yes."

Brower nodded to Haggerty who opened the shoe box. "Professor, Mr. Stephens found these bells in Maggie Holloway's home. Are they similar to the ones you have?"

Bateman paled. He picked up one of the bells and examined it minutely. "That woman is a thief!" he exploded. "She must have come back here and stolen these last night."

He jumped up and ran down the hall and up the stairs, the others following him. On the third floor, he threw open the door of the storeroom and hurried to a shelf on the right-hand wall. Reaching up, he yanked at a box that was wedged between two others and pulled it out.

"It's too light. I can tell already," he muttered, "some of them are missing." He rifled through the protective plastic popcorn until he had satisfied himself as to the carton's contents.

Turning to the five men standing behind him, his face a deep crimson, his eyes blazing, he said, "There are only *five* of them here. Seven are missing! That woman must have stolen them. No *wonder* she kept harping on them yesterday.''

Neil shook his head in dismay. This guy is crazy, he said to himself. He really believes what he's saying.

''Professor Bateman, I must ask you to accompany me to police headquarters,'' Brower said, his tone formal. ''I have to inform you that you are now a suspect in the disappearance of Maggie Holloway. You have a right to remain silent—''

''You can forget your damned Miranda warning,'' Earl shouted. ''Maggie Holloway sneaked back in here, stole my bells—and maybe even my casket—and you blame *me? Ridiculous!* I think you should be looking for the person who helped her. She never did this alone.''

Neil grabbed the lapels of Bateman's coat. ''Shut up,'' he shouted. ''You know damn well Maggie never took that stuff. Wherever she found the two bells she had, they meant something mighty significant to her. And you answer me something. Some kids saw a hearse and Maggie's station wagon leave here around ten o'clock last night. Which one were you driving?''

''You shut up, Neil,'' Brower ordered.

Neil saw the anger on the police chief's face as Robert Stephens yanked him away from Earl Bateman.

I don't give a damn, he thought. This is no time to tiptoe around this liar.

''You mean *my* hearse?'' Bateman asked. ''That's impossible. It's in the garage.''

More rapidly than he had ascended the stairs, Bateman rushed down them and directly outside to the garage. He yanked up the door and ran inside, closely followed by the other men.

''Someone *did* use it,'' he exclaimed, peering through the vehicle's window. ''Look at it. There's dirt on the carpet!''

Neil wanted to throttle the man, to beat the truth from him. How had he gotten Maggie to follow him in that hearse? Or was someone else driving her car?

Liam Payne took his cousin's arm. "Earl, it's going to be all right. I'll go with you to headquarters. I'll call a lawyer."

Neil and his father refused to go home. They sat in a waiting area at the police station. From time to time, Detective Haggerty joined them. "The guy has refused a lawyer; he's answering everything. He insists that he was in Providence last night and can prove it with phone calls he made from his apartment during the evening. At this point, we simply can't hold him."

"But we know he's done something to Maggie," Neil protested. "He's got to help us find her!"

Haggerty shook his head. "He's more worried about his casket and the dirt in that old hearse than he is about Ms. Holloway. His scenario is that she brought someone with her to steal the casket and bells, someone who drove the casket away in the hearse. The ignition key was in clear sight on a hook in the office. In a few minutes, his cousin is going to take him back to the museum to pick up his car."

"You *can't* let him go," Neil protested.

"We can't *not* let him go," Haggerty said.

The detective hesitated, then said, "This will come out anyhow, and it's something you'd be interested in knowing. You know we also are looking into accusations of improprieties at Latham Manor, thanks to the suicide note of that lawyer who killed himself. While we were out, the chief got a message. He'd made it top priority to find out who really owns Latham Manor. Guess who does? None other than Bateman's cousin, Mr. Liam Moore Payne."

Haggerty looked around cautiously as though afraid Payne would appear behind him. "I guess he's still inside.

He insisted on staying with his cousin during the questioning. We asked him about owning Latham. Readily admitted it. Says it's a sound investment. But apparently he doesn't want it known that he owns the place. Says that if people knew, he'd have the residents calling him with complaints or requests for favors. That kind of makes sense, doesn't it?''

It was nearly eight o'clock when Robert Stephens turned to his son. "Come on, Neil, we'd better get home," he urged.

Their car was parked across the street from police headquarters. As soon as Stephens turned the ignition key, the phone rang. Neil answered it.

It was Dolores Stephens. She had gone home when they left for the museum. "Any word about Maggie?" she asked anxiously.

"No, Mom. We'll be home soon, I guess."

"Neil, I just received a phone call from a Mrs. Sarah Cushing. She said that her mother, Mrs. Bainbridge, is a resident at Latham Manor, and that you were talking to her today."

"That's right." Neil felt his interest quicken.

"Mrs. Cushing's mother remembered something that she thought might be important and called her daughter, who looked up our number trying to track you down. Mrs. Bainbridge said that Maggie mentioned something about a bell she had found on her stepmother's grave. She asked if placing a bell like that was some sort of custom. Mrs. Bainbridge said it just occurred to her that Maggie might have been talking about one of Professor Bateman's Victorian bells. I'm not sure what any of this means, but I wanted you to know right away," she said. "I'll see you in a while."

Neil gave his father the details of the message Dolores

Stephens had passed along. "What do you make of it?" Robert Stephens asked his son as he started to put the car into drive.

"Hold it a minute, Dad. Don't pull out," Neil said urgently. "What do I make of it? Plenty. The bells we found in Maggie's studio must have been taken from her stepmother's grave and from someone else's, probably one of the women from the residence. Otherwise why would she have asked that question? If she *did* go back to the museum last night, which I still have trouble believing, it was to see if any of the bells Bateman claimed were in that box were missing."

"Here they come," Robert Stephens murmured as Bateman and Payne emerged from the police station. They watched as the men got into Payne's Jaguar and, for a few minutes, sat in the car, talking animatedly.

The rain had ended and a full moon brightened the already well-lighted area around the station.

"Payne must have taken dirt roads when he came down from Boston today," Robert Stephens observed. "Look at those wheels and tires. His shoes were pretty messy, too. You heard Bateman yell at him about that. It's also a surprise that he owns that retirement place. There's something about that guy I don't like. Was Maggie dating him seriously?"

"I don't think so," Neil said tonelessly. "I don't like him either, but he obviously is successful. That residence cost a fortune. And I checked on his investments operation. He has his own firm now, and clearly he was smart enough to take with him some of Randolph and Marshall's best clients."

"Randolph and Marshall," his father repeated. "Isn't that where Dr. Lane said his wife used to work?"

"What did you say?" Neil demanded.

"You heard me. I said that Lane's wife used to work at Randolph and Marshall."

"That's what's been bugging me!" Neil exclaimed. "Don't you see? Liam Payne is connected to everything. He owns the residence. He must have had the final say in hiring Dr. Lane. Doug Hansen also worked for Randolph and Marshall, although for only a brief time. He has an arrangement now whereby his transactions go through their clearing house. I said today that Hansen had to be operating out of another office, and I also said that he's clearly too stupid to have worked out that scheme for defrauding those women. He was just the front man. Someone had to be programming him. Well, maybe that someone was Liam Moore Payne."

"But it doesn't all quite fit together," Robert Stephens protested. "If Payne owns the residence, he could have gotten the financial information he needed without involving either Hansen or Hansen's aunt, Janice Norton."

"But it's much safer to stay a step removed," Neil pointed out. "That way, Hansen becomes the scapegoat if anything goes wrong. Don't you see, Dad? Laura Arlington and Cora Gebhart had applications *pending*. He wasn't just turning over the apartments of residents. He was cheating applicants when there were no apartments.

"It's obvious that Bateman uses Payne as a sounding board for his problems," Neil continued. "If Bateman had been upset because Maggie inquired about the Latham Manor incident, wouldn't he be likely to tell Payne about it?"

"Maybe. But what are you saying?"

"I'm saying that this Payne guy is the key to all this. *He* secretly owns Latham Manor. Women there are dying under what seem to be *un*exceptional circumstances, yet when you consider *how many* have died recently, and factor in the similarities—all of them pretty much alone, no close family to check on them—it all starts to look suspicious. And who stands to gain from their deaths? Latham Manor does, through reselling those now-empty apartments to the next name on the list."

"Do you mean to say that Liam Payne killed all those women?" Robert Stephens asked, his tone incredulous.

"I don't know that yet," his son replied. "The police suspect that Dr. Lane and/or Nurse Markey may have had a hand in the deaths, but when I talked to Mrs. Bainbridge, she made a point of saying that Dr. Lane was 'kind,' and that Markey was a good nurse. My hunch is, she knows what she's talking about. She's sharp. No, I don't know who killed those women, but I think Maggie had come to the same conclusion about their deaths, and she must have been getting too close for comfort for the actual killer."

"But where do the bells come in? And Bateman? I don't get it," Robert Stephens protested.

"The bells? Who knows? Maybe it's the killer's way of keeping score. Chances are, though, that if Maggie found those bells on graves and looked up those women's obituaries, she had started to figure out what really happened. The bells might signify that those women were murdered." Neil paused. "As for Bateman, he seems almost too weird to be able to take part in anything as calculating as this. No, I think Mr. Liam Moore Payne is our connection here. You heard him make that idiotic suggestion to explain Maggie's disappearance." Neil snorted derisively. "I bet he knows what has happened to Maggie and he's just trying to ease the pressure of the search."

Noting that Payne had started his car, Robert Stephens turned to his son. "I take it we're following him," he said.

"Absolutely. I want to see where Payne is going," Neil said, then added his own silent prayer: *Please, please let him lead me to Maggie.*

) 88

DR. WILLIAM LANE DINED AT LATHAM MANOR WITH SOME of the charter members of the residence. He explained Odile's absence by saying that she was devastated to be leaving her dear friends. As for himself, while he regretted having to give up something that had been so pleasant an experience, it was his firm belief that, as the axiom goes, "the buck stops here."

"I want to reassure everyone that this sort of outrageous indiscretion will never happen again," he promised, referring to Janice Norton's violation of privileged information.

Letitia Bainbridge had accepted the invitation to dine at the doctor's table. "Do I understand that Nurse Markey is filing an ethics complaint against you, stating that, in effect, you stand by and let people die?" she asked.

"So I gather. It isn't true, of course."

"What does your wife think about that?" Mrs. Bainbridge persisted.

"Again, she's truly saddened. She considered Nurse Markey a close friend." And more the fool for it, Odile, he added to himself.

His farewell was gracious and to the point. "Sometimes it is appropriate to let other hands take the reins. I've always tried to do my best. If I am guilty of anything, it is of trusting a thief, but not of gross negligence."

On the short walk between the manor and the carriage

house, Dr. Lane thought, I don't know what will happen now, but I do know whatever job I get will be on my own.

Whatever happened, he had decided he wasn't going to spend another single day with Odile.

When he went upstairs to the second floor, the bedroom door was open and Odile was on the phone, apparently screaming at an answering machine. "You can't do this to me! You can't just *drop* me like this! *Call me!* You've got to take care of me. You promised!" She hung up with a crash.

"And to whom were you speaking, my dear?" Lane asked from the doorway. "Perhaps the mysterious benefactor who against all odds hired me for this position? Don't trouble him or her or whoever it is any longer on my account. Whatever I do, I won't be needing *your* assistance."

Odile raised tear-swollen eyes to him. "William, you can't mean that."

"Oh, but I *do.*" He studied her face. "You really *are* frightened, aren't you? I wonder why. I've always suspected that under that empty-headed veneer, something else was going on.

"Not that I'm interested," he continued, as he opened his closet and reached for a suitcase. "Just a bit curious. After my little relapse last night, I was somewhat foggy. But when my head cleared, I got to thinking and made a few calls of my own."

He turned to look at his wife. "You didn't stay for the dinner in Boston last night, Odile. And wherever you went, those shoes of yours got terribly muddy, didn't they?"

☽ 89

SHE COULDN'T KEEP TRACK OF THE NUMBERS ANYMORE. IT was no use.

Don't give up, Maggie urged herself, trying to force her mind to stay alert, to remain connected. It would be so easy to drift away, so easy just to close her eyes and retreat from what was happening to her.

The picture Earl had given her—there had been something about Liam's expression—the superficial smile, the calculated sincerity, the practiced warmth.

She should have guessed that there was something dishonest about his sudden attentiveness. He had been more in character when he abandoned her at the cocktail party.

She thought back to last night, to the voice. Odile Lane had been arguing with Liam. She had heard them.

Odile had been frightened. "I can't do it anymore," she had wailed. "You're insane! You promised you'd sell the place and we'd go away. I warned you that Maggie Holloway was asking too many questions."

So clear. For the moment so clear.

She could barely flex her hand any longer. It was time to scream for help again.

But now her voice was only a whisper. No one would hear her.

Flex . . . unflex . . . take short breaths, she reminded herself.

But her mind kept coming back to just one thing, the first
childhood prayer she had ever learned: "Now I lay me down
to sleep . . ."

) 90

"YOU COULD AT LEAST HAVE TOLD ME THAT YOU OWNED
Latham Manor," Earl Bateman said accusingly to his
cousin. "I tell you everything. Why are you so secretive?"

"It's just an investment, Earl," Liam said soothingly.
"Nothing more. I am completely removed from the day-to-
day operation of the residence."

He drove into the parking lot of the funeral museum,
stopping next to Earl's car. "Go home and get a good night's
sleep. You need it."

"Where are you going?"

"Back to Boston. Why?"

"Did you come rushing down today just to see me?" Earl
asked, still annoyed.

"I came because you were upset, and I came because I
was concerned about Maggie Holloway. Now, as I've explained, I'm not as concerned about her. My guess is that
she'll show up soon."

Earl started to get out of the car, then paused. "Liam, you
knew where I kept the key to the museum, *and* the ignition
key to the hearse, didn't you?" he asked.

"What are you driving at?"

"Nothing, except to ask if you told anyone about where I keep them?"

"No, I didn't. Come on, Earl. You're tired. Go on home so I can get on my way."

Earl got out and slammed the door.

Liam Moore Payne drove immediately out of the parking lot to the end of the side street. He didn't notice a car pull out from the curb and follow at a discreet distance when he turned right.

It was all unraveling, he thought glumly. They knew he owned the residence. Earl had already started to suspect that he had been the one in the museum last night. The bodies were going to be exhumed, and they'd find that the women had been given improper medications. If he was lucky, Dr. Lane would be blamed, but Odile was ready to crack. They would get a confession out of her in no time. And Hansen? He would do *anything* to save his own skin.

So that leaves *me,* Liam thought. All that work for nothing! The dream of being the second Squire Moore, powerful and rich, was gone. After all the risks he had taken—borrowing from his clients' securities; buying the residence on a shoestring and pouring money into it; figuring out Squire-like ways to get other people's money—he was, after all that, just another failed Moore. Everything was slipping through his fingers.

And Earl, that obsessed fool, was rich, really rich.

But fool though he was, Earl wasn't stupid. Soon he would start to put two and two together, and then he would know where to look for his casket.

Well, even if he figured it all out, Liam thought, he wouldn't find Maggie Holloway alive.

Her time had run out, of that he was certain.

⟩ 91

CHIEF BROWER AND DETECTIVE HAGGERTY WERE ABOUT to leave for the day when the call came in from Earl Bateman.

"They all hate me," he began. "They like to ridicule the Bateman family business, ridicule me for my lectures—but the bottom line is they're all jealous because we're rich. We've been rich for generations, long before Squire Moore ever saw his first crooked dollar!"

"Could you get to the point, Professor?" Brower asked. "What do you want?"

"I want you to meet me at the site of my planned outdoor exhibit. I have a feeling that my cousin Liam and Maggie Holloway together have played their version of a practical joke on me. I'll bet anything they took my casket to one of the open graves at the exhibit and dumped it there. I want you to be present when I find it. I'm leaving now."

The chief grabbed a pen. "Where exactly *is* your exhibit site, Professor?"

When he hung up, Brower said to Haggerty, "I think he's cracking up, but I also think we may be about to find Maggie Holloway's body."

) 92

"Neil, look at that!"

They were driving along a narrow dirt road, following the Jaguar. When they left the main road, Neil had turned off the headlights, hoping that Liam Payne wouldn't realize they were there. Now the Jaguar was turning left, its headlights briefly illuminating a sign Robert Stephens strained to make out.

"Future site of the Bateman Outdoor Funeral Museum," he read. "That must have been what Bateman was talking about when he said the stolen casket was going to be part of an important exhibit. Do you think it's here?"

Neil did not answer. A fear so terrible that his mind could not tolerate it was exploding within him. *Casket. Hearse. Cemetery.*

If Liam Payne had been ordering residents of Latham Manor to be murdered, and then placed symbolic bells on their graves, what would he be likely to do to someone who had put him in danger?

Suppose he had been in the museum last night and found Maggie there?

He and someone else, Neil thought. It must have taken two of them to drive Maggie's car and the hearse.

Had they killed her and taken her out in that coffin?

Oh, God, no, no, please!

"Neil, he may have spotted us. He's turning around and coming back."

Neil made an instant decision. "Dad, you follow him. Call the police. I'm staying here."

Before his father could protest, Neil had jumped out of the car.

The Jaguar raced past them. "Go," Neil shouted. "Go!"

Robert Stephens executed a precarious U-turn and pressed down on the accelerator.

Neil began to run. A sense of urgency so profound that it permeated every nerve ending in his body made him race onto the construction site.

The moonlight illumined the muddy, bulldozed acreage. He could see that trees had been felled, undergrowth cleared, paths staked out. And graves dug. Scattered, the holes yawned all around the area, seemingly at random, next to some of them, great piles of clay.

The cleared area seemed huge, extending almost as far as he could see. Was Maggie here somewhere? Had Payne been insane enough to dump the casket with her inside it in one of those open graves and then cover it with earth?

Yes, clearly he *was* that insane.

Neil began to crisscross the site, shouting Maggie's name. At one open grave, he slipped, tumbled into it, and wasted precious minutes trying to get a toehold to scramble out. But even then he kept shouting, "Maggie . . . Maggie . . . Maggie . . ."

Was she dreaming? Maggie forced her eyes open. She was so tired. It was too much effort. She just wanted to sleep.

She couldn't move her hand anymore. It was so stiff and swollen. She couldn't scream anymore, but that didn't matter. There was no one to hear her.

Maggie . . . Maggie . . . Maggie . . .

She thought she heard her name. It sounded like Neil's voice. But it was too late.

She tried to call out, but no sound came from her throat. There was only one thing she could try. With painful effort she grasped her left hand with the fingers of her right hand and forced it up and down, up and down . . .

Vaguely she sensed from the tugging of the string that the bell must be moving.

Maggie . . . Maggie . . . Maggie . . .

Again she thought she heard her name being called, only it seemed fainter, and so very far away . . .

Neil was sobbing now. *She was here.* Maggie was here! He was *sure* of it! He could feel her presence. But *where?* Where was she? Was it too late? He had gone over almost all of the bulldozed area. She might be buried under any one of those mounds of dirt. It would take machines to dig through them, to move them. There were so many.

He was running out of time. And so was she. He could sense it.

"Maggie . . . Maggie . . ."

He stopped and looked around despairingly. Suddenly he noticed something.

The night was still. There wasn't even enough breeze to stir a leaf. But over in the far corner of the lot, almost hidden by one of the giant piles of soil, something was glistening in the moonlight. And it was moving.

A bell. *Moving back and forth.* Someone was trying to signal from the grave. *Maggie!*

Running, stumbling around open pits, Neil reached the bell and saw that it was attached to a pipe, its opening almost packed with mud.

With his hands he began to claw at the dirt around it, claw and dig and sob.

As he watched, the bell stopped moving.

Chief Brower and Detective Haggerty were in the police car when the call from Robert Stephens was relayed to them. "Two of our guys have picked up the chase on the Jaguar," the dispatcher said. "But Stephens thinks that the missing woman may have been buried on that outdoor museum site."

"We're almost there," Brower said. "Dispatch an ambulance and emergency equipment out here now. With luck we'll need both." He leaned forward. "Turn on the siren," he ordered.

When they arrived, they found Neil, using his hands like shovels, digging and clawing at the wet clay. An instant later, Brower and Haggerty were beside him, their powerful hands joining in the effort, digging, digging, digging.

Under the surface the soil became looser, less packed. Finally they reached the satiny wood. Neil jumped down into the hole, scraping dirt off the surface of the casket and hurling it away. Finally he yanked out the clogged air vent and brushed the entry site clear.

Sliding to the side of the wide grave, he got his fingers under the casket lid and with a superhuman effort yanked it partially open. He held it that way with his left shoulder as he reached in, grabbed Maggie's limp body, and lifted it up to the eager hands reaching down from above.

As her face brushed his, he saw that her lips were moving and then heard her faint whisper, "Neil . . . Neil . . ."

"I'm here, love," he said, "and I'll never let you go."

⟩ 93

FIVE DAYS LATER, MAGGIE AND NEIL WENT TO LATHAM Manor to say good-bye to Mrs. Bainbridge.

"We'll be up for Thanksgiving weekend with Neil's parents," Maggie said, "but I couldn't leave without seeing you now."

Letitia Bainbridge's eyes were sparkling. "Oh, Maggie, you don't know how we prayed that you'd be all right."

"I think I do," Maggie assured her. "And your caring enough to let Neil know about the bell I'd found on Nuala's grave may have saved my life."

"That was the clincher," Neil agreed. "It led to my being sure that Liam Payne was involved. If I hadn't followed him, it would have been too late."

He and Maggie were sitting side by side in Mrs. Bainbridge's apartment. He put his hand over Maggie's, unwilling yet to have her beyond his reach, still living the nightmare of searching for her.

"Has everybody pretty well settled down here?" Maggie asked.

"Oh, I think so. We're more resilient than you'd think. I understand the Prestige people have arranged to buy the residence."

"Liam Payne will need a lot of the money he killed for to pay his lawyers, and I hope they don't do him any good," Neil said forcefully. "His girlfriend too, although she's going to end up with a public defender. Realistically, I don't think either one of them stands a chance of escaping conviction on multiple murder charges. I understand that Odile has confessed to deliberately switching medicines on orders from Liam."

Maggie thought of Nuala and Greta Shipley, and of the women whom she had not known, all of whose lives Liam and Odile had cut short. At least I helped to stop them from killing again, she consoled herself.

"And they shouldn't get off, either," Mrs. Bainbridge said severely. "Were Janice Norton and her nephew Douglas involved in these deaths?"

"No," Neil said. "Chief Brower told us that he believes that Hansen and Mrs. Norton were just involved with Liam's scheme to swindle applicants to the residence. Even Odile didn't know what they were up to. And Janice Norton had no idea that her nephew was working through Liam Payne. They're up on fraud charges, not murder."

"According to Chief Brower, Odile can't talk fast enough, trying to get some sort of clemency," Maggie said soberly. "She and Liam became involved when she worked in his former brokerage firm, just when he was buying this place. She had told Liam about what happened to Dr. Lane at the last nursing home, and when Liam proposed this scheme to her, she jumped at it. Dr. Lane simply isn't a good doctor, so he was the perfect person to put in charge.

Zelda Markey is a pretty lonely person. Odile made a friend of her and was able to remove herself from ever being connected to the deaths."

"She was always chatting with Nurse Markey," Letitia Bainbridge said, nodding.

"And pumping her for information. Odile dropped out of nursing school, but it wasn't because she failed her courses. She knew exactly what drugs to combine to cause heart failure. Apparently several women whom Liam had targeted escaped only because Nurse Markey was so solicitous. Odile claims she begged Liam not to make her tamper with Mrs. Rhinelander's medication, but he was too greedy. By then Nuala had decided to go into the manor provided she could have a two-bedroom unit."

"Was it Connie Rhinelander's death that made Nuala suspicious?" Mrs. Bainbridge asked sadly.

"Yes, and then when she found that bell on Mrs. Rhinelander's grave, she apparently began to be sure that something terrible was going on at the residence. She must have asked some very pointed questions of Nurse Markey, who innocently reported them to Odile."

"And Odile warned Liam," Maggie said. Oh, Finnuala, she thought.

Bainbridge's lips tightened. "Squire Moore's god was money. I remember my father saying Moore actually bragged that it was more interesting to cheat someone out of it than make it honestly. Obviously Liam Payne is cut from the same evil cloth."

"I would say so," Neil agreed. "Liam was an excellent investment broker for the clients he didn't cheat. Fortunately both Mrs. Gebhart and Mrs. Arlington should be able to reclaim the money they entrusted to him from Payne's personal assets."

"One last thing," Maggie said. "Odile took that sketch

Nuala and Mrs. Shipley had made. One of the maids had seen it and joked about it. Odile knew it could get people thinking."

"I'm glad Dr. Lane wasn't involved in all this." Letitia Bainbridge sighed. "Oh, I must tell you. Our new director arrived yesterday. He seems very pleasant and comes highly recommended. He doesn't have Dr. Lane's charm, but we can't have everything, can we? His wife is a refreshing change from Odile, although she has a rather braying laugh."

It was time to leave. They would drive in tandem back to New York.

"We'll visit you when we get back up here in November," Maggie promised as she bent to kiss Letitia Bainbridge's cheek.

"I'm already looking forward to it," Mrs. Bainbridge said briskly, then sighed. "You are so pretty, Maggie, and so nice and so smart. You're everything a grandmother would want for her grandson." She looked at Neil. "You take good care of her."

"He did save my life." Maggie smiled. "He has to get some points for that."

Fifteen minutes later they were ready to leave for New York. Her station wagon was already packed in her driveway. The house was locked up. For a moment, Maggie stood looking at it, remembering that night only two weeks ago, when she had arrived.

"It'll be fun to come up here on vacations and weekends, won't it?" she said.

Neil put his arm around her. "You're sure it won't hold too many bad memories?"

"No." She inhaled deeply. "Not as long as you're around to dig me up when I need help."

Then she laughed. "Don't look so shocked. Gallows humor has gotten me through some pretty bad times."

"From now on, that will be my job," Neil said as he opened the door of the station wagon for her. "Now remember, don't speed," he cautioned. "I'll be right behind you."

"You sound like your father," Maggie said. Then she added, "And I like that just fine."

POCKET
BOOKS

Two Little Girls in Blue
Mary Higgins Clark

Returning home from a black-tie dinner in New York, Margaret and Steve Frawley find the police in their house and their twin daughters gone. The kidnapper, who calls himself the 'Pied Piper', soon makes his terms known: on delivery of a ransom, a phone call will reveal the girls' whereabouts. The ransom is delivered but, when the call comes, only Kelly is in the car parked behind a deserted restaurant. The driver is dead from a gunshot wound and has left a suicide note, confessing to killing Kathy and dumping her body in the ocean.

When strange occurrences begin to suggest that Kathy may still be alive, and communicating with Kelly, Margaret finds herself alone in wanting to continue the search for her daughter. But as Kelly's warnings become increasingly specific and alarming, the FBI agents set out to search for Kathy. As they close in on the Pied Piper and his accomplices, Kathy's life hangs by a thread . . .

ISBN-13: 978-1-4165-0260-9
ISBN-10: 1-4165-0260-2
PRICE £6.99

**POCKET
BOOKS**

This book and other **Pocket** titles are available from
your local bookshop or can be ordered
direct from the publisher.

1416502602	Two Little Girls in Blue	Mary Higgins Clark	£6.99